a timeless series novel

Daylight

book three

For Sam—
The best life editor
ever! Lisa
Wiedmeier

Lisa L Wiedmeier

COPYRIGHT

Copyright © 2013 by Lisa L. Wiedmeier
Editor: Sam Dogra
Copy Editor: Jodi Tahsler
Front cover art by: Phatpuppy Art
Cover design by: Timeless Productions
For more information on the Timeless Series visit:
http://www.lisawiedmeier.com/ timelessseriesnovels.com /
www.facebook.com/TimelessSeriesNovels /
http://lisawiedmeier.blogspot.com/
Edition-I
ISBN: 978-0-9839052-7-1

For Andre. Fat tans better.

Acknowledgements

Special thanks to Glenn, Coley & Cody, who without their patience and support, I wouldn't be where I am today.

For Laura and Jessie, you bring me laughter.

For my Mom and Dad, thanks for believing in me.

To Sam, who as always, is my life editor.

Death leaves a heartache no one can heal, love heals a memory no one can steal.

~From a headstone in Ireland

CHAPTER 1

Memories linger, misty like the shadows, tingling the senses. Ever close, yet far away. Craving to come near, only to brush past for a fleeting moment, before they disappear into the deep recesses once again.

"Is this seat taken?" an unfamiliar voice asked.

I jumped, knocking the pencil off my desk. I hadn't heard anyone approach.

"No," I replied as I looked up. A tall blond boy I'd never seen before was hovering over me. His smile reached all the way to his icy blue eyes.

I glanced around the classroom. Was he talking to me?

"I'm Colt O'Shea, and you are?" He stuck his hand out, and I hesitated.

I wasn't keen on making friends, not when I moved so much. Besides, I'd done a good job avoiding other students in the past and for the first three weeks of this school year. I planned on keeping it that way.

"I won't bite." He winked.

Knowing I wouldn't get rid of him so easily, I extended my hand and watched it get swallowed up in his.

"I'm Cheyenne, Cheyenne Wilson."

He pulled up a chair beside me. He ran his fingers through his hair, taking a sudden interest in the textbook on my desk. "Whatcha reading?"

"Calculus." Why was he being so persistent? My body language and short answers should make it obvious I didn't want to carry on a conversation. I really wasn't in the mood, and it wasn't like we'd be living here much longer. Making friends made the loneliness harder when we left.

"Sounds like fun."

I raised a brow. "Should be, since we're *in* Calculus."

"Oh." Colt chuckled and began arranging his books. "I thought this was my English Literature class. Um..." He looked up sheepishly. "Do you mind sharing? It seems I've gotten my schedule mixed up." He flashed another brilliant smile. "I'd run back to my locker, but I don't want to get a tardy my first day in a new school."

"Sure." I slid the book closer. As much as I didn't want to talk to him, I definitely knew what it was like to get lost in a new place. "You know, you should probably have someone help you..."

"You offering?" His eyes brightened.

"Uh..." Great, I had to open my mouth. I was inviting him in even though I didn't want to.

"Don't tell me you're as disorganized as I am."

I rolled my eyes and held out my hand. "Let's take a look at your schedule."

He pulled it from his pack and handed it over. I scanned it and quickly realized it was oddly familiar. "Hey, you have the same schedule as me."

His smile grew.

"Wow, what are the chances? Guess you're stuck with me, huh?"

I sucked in a deep breath, and my eyes shot open. I couldn't decide which was worse: the pain of the memory, or the fact that it was already fading.

"It's okay, Cheyenne," Callon said as he stroked my arm. "It's just a bit of turbulence."

My head was resting on his shoulder, and I quickly remembered we were on a plane. I turned away, staring at the seat in front of me. I didn't need to see the sorrow in his hazel eyes. I wanted sleep to claim me again and bring my sunshine to me, my Colt. My few happy moments...my reason for living.

I'd never imagined our meeting that day would lead to all this. At first it had hurt, knowing he'd been sent to watch over me, to protect me. A friendship built on lies. I'd been angry, devastated by his betrayal, until I slowly realized how much he meant to me. What he'd done and the circumstances around us couldn't change; they could only be accepted. But even after our shared words of forgiveness and love, fate—the same fate that brought us together—ripped him from my arms. *Forever.*

How was I supposed to go on without him? He'd been my rock when my adoptive parents were murdered. He'd been the strong shoulder to cry upon when the world crashed down around me. I'd fought to push both him and Callon away after I learned of the betrothals, but Colt was relentless. He'd promised never to give up on me.

When my transformation into a Timeless began, almost killing me, he'd never left my side. When my first powers surfaced, he believed in me. When I ran away, he followed, and yet he had eventually understood my feelings and given me space. When I was stolen away by Marcus, Colt came for me. He defied Callon's orders...he'd said we'd always be together...

Until Marcus killed him.

*Marcus...*the name burned in my mind. The man who murdered my birth parents, my adoptive parents, and now Colt. The man whose sole purpose in life was revenge for all the wrongs against him. He wanted not only to rule over all the Timeless, but the world as well. He was tired of hiding from humans. The only thing he needed was my power; then he'd be unstoppable in his conquest.

Colt and the others had come to my rescue, almost getting me clear of Marcus's army, but then Marcus struck. Making the biggest mistake of his life. That day, as Colt fell before my eyes, I'd nearly killed everything in the valley. I could think of nothing else but to destroy Marcus, not caring for anyone else's life. Until Callon had crawled to me and begged me to stop. He had stopped me from becoming as cruel and twisted as the man who murdered my love.

I tilted my head slightly so I could stare at Maes. His head hung low, his black hair drifting over his rugged features, his eyes closed. Maes, a Tresez, a shape shifter cursed to serve Marcus, was now bound to me. He had sworn to protect me, because I was the only one who could break his curse; a curse my grandfather had put upon them for serving the Sarac. A curse I knew nothing about, let alone how to break it.

Maes had been difficult from the start. Rude, sarcastic, mean...and yet somehow he'd changed. He wasn't the same man anymore. He'd help free me from Marcus, even though he knew it could cost him his life. But was it because he wanted freedom from his curse, or was his loyalty genuine?

Daniel leaned forward, and our gaze met. He looked awful, with bags under his eyes and his hair sticking up in every direction. He'd lost his brother, and was fearful he'd lose me as well. Even seeing his heart breaking, I wasn't sure I could hold on. Life held nothing for me anymore. I had no reason to stay. A dark vortex swirled around me, drowning me in a bottomless pit of shadows. I was inches from the edge, an edge I didn't know if I could return from. It would trap me in its suffocating grip, and snuff out the last light within me.

A shiver raked me. I just wanted the pain to stop.

Callon adjusted the blanket, pulling it over my shoulders, and I closed my eyes once more. My heart begged for my sunshine, to push the darkness away. Restlessly I waited for the small spark that wouldn't come.

Callon stilled, and I looked up, studying his slumbering features. He was my future now. I'd been promised to him from the start, even before I'd ever known I was a Timeless, as I was the last surviving heir of the Kvech clan. He seemed peaceful as he slept, but I knew deep down he was suffering as much as I was. He'd lost his brother, his best friend...his heart was crushed as well.

He seemed to hover over me protectively, even in his sleep. His gaunt expression, his unshaven whiskers. We were all barely surviving Colt's death. We were all holding on by a thread. And mine was fraying...

Maes elbow nudged my leg. He was sitting beside me, and watching me. He had seen me stir. His lips parted as if he wanted to speak, but he said nothing. What could he say? What could I say? My last stinging words were to Callon, telling him he'd gotten what he'd wished for. That with Colt gone, I was all his, as he'd wanted from the start. It had been too many days since I'd said it. And I could never take it back.

4

Yet I hadn't spoken completely out of grief and anger. Callon had known the truth, but refused to reveal it to me until it was too late. His refusal to give me information had triggered everything that had led to Colt's death. Running from the Trackers, meeting Maes, escaping from my guardians, and finally getting captured by Marcus. If he'd told me the whole story when I'd asked, I wouldn't have acted so rashly.

But then again, he knew me too well. He knew I was stubborn, that I wouldn't have listened. I'd still have tried to take on destiny by myself, fighting for a way for Colt and me to be together...

The cabin's light dimmed, and I looked away from Maes's gaze. I was waiting, waiting for the darkness to overtake my soul and finish me off, but that would be too easy. This was going to be long, slow and painful. Why should destiny be kind to me? She'd ripped everything else away. She had no reason to be merciful.

The seat in front of me moved, and I exhaled. Why couldn't I sleep? Being Timeless, I didn't require much, but after the hard traveling and draining journey, I needed rest.

After what seemed like years, a voice broke through the cabin, announcing our arrival to Ireland. The lights flickered on, and Callon touched my shoulder. I lay still, content to stay put, but Callon pulled me up so my seat could be "returned to its upright position." I sighed.

He drew his arm around me. His mouth pressed near my ear.

"It's going to be okay, Cheyenne." A gentle kiss followed. "Another day and we'll be home at the estate. You'll have time to rest and heal."

I stared at my hands, folding them in my lap. It was never going to be okay. Colt had been taken away, and nothing else mattered. Rest would never find me; my heart would never feel the light again. Besides, what good was a home when not all the family members could be there? It would always have a missing piece...

The plane began to descend, and I felt the vibrations through the floor. The captain announced that the local time was eleven thirty at night. My jaw tightened. More blackness to feed my distressed heart. Why couldn't there have been sunlight? Where was the source of strength I needed?

The landing was smooth, and soon we disembarked. I followed behind Callon as he led us through the terminal, his fingers intertwined with mine. If he hadn't been pulling me along, I would have remained on the plane. I was only vaguely aware of Daniel and Maes beside us, dragging our bags. I kept my head down, watching the ground. Only part of me registered what was happening as I was escorted to a taxi. Callon moved in beside me and I stared at the picture of the driver hanging on the back of his seat.

Colt should have been here with us. It had been the plan all along, at least initially, before Callon had decided to banish Colt. Why had everyone been so against us? What was wrong with wanting to be with the one you loved?

"Cheyenne," Callon said. "Come on, we're here."

I hadn't even noticed the time pass. He tugged on my arm and helped me out of the cab. I looked up to see a hotel. I shivered as a chilly breeze brushed over us. It was as cold and lifeless as I was inside.

It wasn't long before we were in our room. We were on the fifth floor; the only reason I knew was the annoying chime of the elevator. We stopped just inside and I kept my gaze averted, studying the drab carpeting beneath my feet. Footsteps echoed in different directions as I stood, waiting.

"Cheyenne." Callon was waiting near a doorway. "Come on, you need to rest."

His tone left no room to argue. I lowered my head once again and walked towards him. He grasped my arm and pulled me towards the bathroom. He closed the door behind me, and I slumped against it. I didn't want to be here, didn't want to do anything. I couldn't.

My gaze fell to the sink top, where a nightie lay folded. Tears welled in my eyes, and I choked back a sob. It had been a gift from Colt. I turned away and quickly turned on the shower, desperate to wash away the gloom inside.

When I came out again, only a dim light in the corner of the bedroom was on. Callon sat waiting on the bed, his shoulders sagging, no longer strong and confident. He pulled down the covers for me, and I crawled in.

"Sleep, Cheyenne." A tender kiss touched my head.

The door only made the slightest creak as he closed it, but it was as if my heart understood. It was the final closure for it as well. I was alone now; completely and utterly alone. I had no living relatives, no best friend, and no sunshine.

I curled my legs into my chest and held tight, waiting for sleep to come.

"Cheyenne," Colt's whispery voice called out. *"Why'd you have to run away? Why'd you have to leave me?"*

"Colt!" I cried. "I'm here! I'm here!"

"Cheyenne..."

"No!" My body shook, as the memory of that day flashed before me. Marcus's face was twisted with malice as he raised his hands towards Colt.

"No!" I bellowed. "No, Marcus, no!"

The blinding light blazed around me, and I was thrown to the ground. The air grew frigid as I looked up to see Colt's lifeless body. Cold, hardened rage took over, and a surge of energy burst through my veins. The darkness I'd been fighting to contain was rising, consuming everything. My anguish, sorrow, pain and anger were expanding, mixing together and feeding me with power.

"Why'd you leave me?" Colt whispered. *"Why'd you leave me..."*

My hate-filled eyes met Marcus. I didn't see a man; only a demon. One who'd stolen everything from me. I raised my hands, ready to reduce him to dust, when Marcus spoke:

"This is all your doing, Cheyenne. This is all because of your selfish actions. You killed Colt!"

I stopped breathing, tremors taking over my body. I'd brought this upon myself. I'd bottled up all my doom and despair, and now it was unleashed, a wild beast that couldn't be tamed.

My vision blurred with tears, and I began sobbing uncontrollably. My light, my sunshine, was gone, and it was my fault! I could never bring Colt back. I could never bring my parents or adoptive parents back. They'd all died because of me!

"Take me!" I screamed, wishing for the darkness to run through me. I wanted it to suffocate me, drown me, numb the agonizing misery.

Just make it all go away...

"Cheyenne!" Callon's voice broke through my nightmare, and strong arms pinned me to the bed.

The shadows in my mind were stronger, and I pushed him away.

"Cheyenne!" Callon bellowed. "Wake up!"

Let it take me. Let it take me and let this miserable life be done with. *Leave me be, and let the blackness take my pain away forever.*

"Cheyenne!" Daniel screeched. "We're here! We're right here! Come back!"

A stinging sensation radiated against my cheek, but it only lasted for a moment.

"Do it again!" Maes screamed.

My head rolled to the side, but my eyes fluttered open. Firm hands suddenly grasped my face and forced it upright. I blinked. Callon was straddling me, while Maes and Daniel hovered at my bedside. They were staring, horrified.

"Breathe, Cheyenne, breathe," Maes said. My mouth opened, and I gasped as air filled my lungs. Tears were streaming down my cheeks. Why hadn't they let me go?

"Where are you?" Callon whispered as he stroked my cheek, still hot from where he'd slapped me. "Come back. I need you."

I pulled away from his grasp and rolled to my side. He moved to sit beside me, cradling my head in his arms.

"It was just a dream, sweetheart," he spoke quietly. "It was nothing more than a dream."

I knew it was more than just a dream. It was my wish to get away. I was withdrawing, seeking refuge from this horrible reality I'd created.

My breathing slowed and my racing heart calmed, but nothing could remove the ache in my chest. Not Callon, not Daniel, not Maes. Colt was the only one who could save me, and he was gone.

"I need you to get dressed," Callon said quietly. "We're going to be leaving soon."

I pushed him away and rolled out of bed. Once in the bathroom, I leaned on the closed door, staring at the mirror. An unrecognizable woman stared back, and my hand flew to my mouth. The others didn't need my explanation to work out what was going on; the answer was clear for all to see.

My blue eyes had faded to a drab gray. My once bright blond hair was dull and lifeless. There was no color in my cheeks, only a sickly pallor. A cloak of something dark and wild lurked just under the surface, draining me from the inside. It was a violent storm cloud waiting to erupt.

A knock at the door jarred me back into the present, and I opened it. Callon gently pushed his way in. His hands grasped my shoulders, but I refused to meet his eyes. He didn't need to see any further within me. He sighed, then hesitated, unsure what to say next.

"You have to fight this, Cheyenne," he said. "But you can't do this alone. I want to help you. You have to let me in."

I stared at the floor, my mind growing foggier by the moment. I had to push everything down deep, push it all away and hibernate in my safe place.

"Cheyenne." He took my chin and forced my head up. "Listen to me." His hazel eyes—always so calm and controlled—were now full of uncertainty. "I can't...I won't lose you to this. We're all hurting, but you have to fight through this. Do you hear me?"

I snapped my eyes shut. I didn't want to fight anymore.

He drew me into his chest, his warm lips pressing against my cheek.

"I can't lose you...I can't." He softly rubbed my back. "If I could bring Colt back for you, I would, but he's gone." His voice faltered. "I want him back as much as you do. I feel as if a part of me has been ripped away. We have to fight through this together."

I heard his worthless words, and frowned. He said he'd bring him back if he could, yet he was the one who'd banished Colt to begin with.

Callon pulled away, his shoulders firming with determination.

"I've ordered you a meal. You'll eat and drink before we leave this morning. You won't run off to spit it out."

I said nothing, remembering my behavior at the airport. I had no need for food now. It was all tasteless. Meaningless.

His eyes narrowed slightly, waiting for me to acknowledge him. I responded by looking away.

"Get dressed," he ordered. "I'll be back in five minutes."

By the time I was done, Callon was waiting near the door. He pointed towards the main room, and I followed behind him. Daniel and Maes stood in the corner, and a small table with covered plates lay before them. Daniel pulled the chair out and I sat.

I glanced towards the windows; the pre-dawn light was arriving. I'd have my sunlight soon, and maybe that would keep the dark demons at bay for a while.

"Eat, Cheyenne," Callon said as he uncovered the dishes. The sight alone of breakfast made me nauseated.

Maes pushed the fork closer. I picked it up and began moving the eggs around on the plate. Taking one small bite, the tasteless mixture settled to the side of my mouth. I couldn't bring myself to swallow.

"Another," Maes said. I took a second bite, once again pushing it to the side.

I reached for my napkin only to have it taken away.

Maes shook his head. "Swallow it."

I closed my eyes and forced myself to swallow the now mushy mixture, gagging slightly before it settled in my stomach.

"All of it," Callon added as I was about to put my fork down.

Reluctantly, I finished the meal as best I could; spreading the items around to make it appear I'd eaten more.

Maes pushed a glass of orange juice before me. "You need to drink too, Cheyenne," Maes said.

I stared at it, unmoving.

"If you'd just say a few words, *mon espoir*, you won't have to drink it."

*If I'd just say something...*I had no words to say. Nothing I said would bring back my Colt. Nothing would change all the mistakes I'd made. Nothing would bring me out of the pits of despair. Nothing would turn back time.

My fingers grasped the cold glass, and I closed my eyes as the liquid touched my lips. The sour taste was somehow fitting, given how bitter my life had become.

I placed the glass on the table, and Maes turned away, but not before I caught a glimpse of his own sorrow. I was his hope, his only hope, and now I was fading away.

Callon grasped my arm, and we headed for the door. I kept my head bowed to avoid further eye contact. I didn't need to be reminded of yet another task I'd failed at.

By the time we made it to the front entrance, I felt a bit off, as if my body was moving half a beat behind. My foot missed a step, but Callon was quick to catch me and help me inside the car.

Maes turned around in the front seat.

"You'll fight through this, *mon espoir*. You're stronger than the darkness." His accent thickened. "You'll find your courage again someday, and your light will return."

Daniel pulled out of the parking lot. Each leg of this journey numbed my heart further. My eyes wanted to water, but it was as if everything inside had dried up. I instead focused on the shadows retreating from the dark alleyways. The sun was finally emerging from the night. Streaming rays poked through the clouds, and I blinked, trying to clear the blurred spots from my vision.

What was wrong with me now? Wasn't it enough already? I was suffering, dying on the inside, and now my eyes were throwing me a curve ball as well. The objects outside began spinning, and I had to close my eyes.

"It's okay, Cheyenne. Rest now," Callon said softly.

What had he done?

My head suddenly became too heavy to hold up and rocked to Callon's shoulder. I felt the hefty weight of emptiness ready to push me under.

"Sleep now, love." A warm caress touched my forehead. "You're going to be just fine. I'll take care of you."

Without any strength left, I inhaled deeply and allowed the darkness to win.

CHAPTER 2

Alone...alone...alone...

The word filtered through my mind and I gasped for air. Covers tangled around me like a snake snaring its prey, and I fought to dislodge myself. I tumbled to the floor, trembling.

I was no longer in the car.

A flickering to the right caught my eye. The last remnants of sunshine were streaming through a window. The deep shadows were looming again, and panic set in. I raced to the panes and watched as the light drifted down over the horizon.

No! My fist hit the window in protest, rattling the old frame.

I stepped back, and pressed my shaking hands to my face. What was I to do now? I tried not to hyperventilate as I studied my surroundings. This must be the house in Ireland Callon had talked about. The home we all were supposed to find safety in, but there was no safety for Colt.

I clawed at my face as the words ran through me again. *Alone...alone...alone...* I was once again alone. There was no sunshine, there was no Colt, no Mom and Dad. It was just me in this prison of misery with no escape.

I'd brought this all upon myself. This was my fault.

I couldn't stay in the room that was starting to feel like a cage, so I threw open the door. The hall was dark, and a shiver rushed through me. I couldn't face the shadows. Inhaling a shaky breath, I retreated back into the room. My arms hugged my torso, trying to hold off the inevitable.

I had to stop this.

Creeping back towards the bed, my foot hit something. Callon's medical bag was resting by the door. I ripped it open, breaking the lock in the process. Frantically I dumped the contents on the floor and began shoving the small bottles around.

He'd given me something before we left the hotel, he must have. I wouldn't have slept otherwise. I twisted a small bottle towards the dim lighting, but couldn't make out the name. I dropped it and grabbed another. They were all medicines, all meant to take pain away. What did it matter which one I chose?

My fingers scrambled for a needle and I shoved it in the bottle, draining it completely. Whatever he'd given me before worked. It would numb the misery and force me to forget.

My shaking hands plunged the needle into my arm and I dispensed the drug. I leaned back against the bed waiting for the effects to take place. Minutes passed, and nothing happened. Of course, I was Timeless now—I'd need to increase the dose. I ripped open another bottle and filled it again, stabbing it into my arm for a second time.

My right hand fell limp before I could remove the needle, and my head slumped. The blackness crept over me, and I began to sink into its depths.

Loud noises broke through as I began to drift to *that* place of nowhere and nothing...my sanctuary.

"Cheyenne!" Callon shouted and caught me as I tumbled to the floor. "What have you done?!"

He yanked the needle from my arm and searched for the bottle. Daniel's blurry form hovered above me, and the dark shadow I'd come to know was cursing in French.

"Chey..." Daniel choked. Tears brimmed in his eyes and he drew me closer. "Why? Why are you trying to hurt yourself?"

He didn't understand. None of them did. My mind was a constant whirlwind of tragic events. I couldn't take them anymore. Couldn't face the mistakes I'd made, the lives I'd sacrificed, the loved ones I'd hurt. I couldn't face knowing I was the reason Colt was dead. And all the while this uncontrollable power raged inside, waiting for an excuse to take over. It promised to take the pain away, to leave my broken heart in peace. I had no use for dreams anymore. I should let it win.

"She's not going anywhere!" Callon roared as he jabbed another shot into my arm.

The mind-numbing heaviness swamped over me, and I closed my eyes. Fingers touched my neck as all my thoughts drifted to gray. The smoky emptiness gave me a temporary peace.

My heavy lids struggled to open. Light filled the space.

"Cheyenne." The warmth in Daniel's voice brought little comfort. "Cheyenne, don't go away. I need you." He sat by the side of the bed, his eyes full of gloom. "I lost my brother. I can't bear the thought of losing you too. Please!"

I turned away, only to be confronted by Maes's shadow.

"What the hell were you thinking?" Rage dripped from his voice. "You think you're the only one to have ever suffered a loss? Do you honestly think you can just give up and run away?" He seized my arm to drag me out of bed when Callon's hand clamped over his.

"Don't," Callon growled. "Leave her be."

"Are you growing weak as well, Callon?" Maes snapped.

"No, I'm finally growing wiser."

Maes snarled. "So it's wise for her to think it's okay to run away whenever things get tough?"

"She's not running away."

"Then what do you call what just happened? An accidental overdose?"

Callon didn't reply.

Maes let go of me and stepped back, shaking his head. "You're a fool, Callon."

"Fools never admit to their mistakes," Callon shot back. "I've pushed her too far. I left her with few choices, and denied her the one thing that gave her happiness. This was bound to happen."

"So then what?" Maes asked.

"We wait." Callon looked down at me with an expression I couldn't read.

"Chey," Daniel said again softly. "You can do this. I believe in you."

Tears I couldn't control rose to the surface. Colt's last words had been the same...

14

I buried my face in my hands and curled into a tight ball. How could anyone believe in me? I was an utter failure. Everyone who came in contact with me suffered in some way. And the ones I'd opened my heart to, all were dead and gone. Was my love that tainted? Destined to hurt those it touched?

If that was the case, I truly deserved to be swallowed up in misery.

I sat in the chair and stared at the wall. Rain pelted the window, falling from the grizzled sky. The sunlight and warmth were further away than ever, and slowly I felt the darkness slide closer.

"Is she ever coming back?" Daniel whispered.

Callon replied with a deep sigh.

"I feel so lost, Callon," Daniel said. "I wish..."

"So do I," Callon said. "So do I."

Time must have passed, but I wasn't following. I spent them in a chair by the fireplace or in bed, wherever I was led. Food came and went, and I ate only what was needed. Why I still wanted to stay alive I didn't understand, but something inside wouldn't allow me to give up yet. Was it my rage, unwilling to forgive being dealt this awful hand, or was it something more? A nagging feeling haunted me that maybe this was just a dream, that I'd suddenly wake up and realize Colt hadn't died. Or was it that deep down I knew Colt would have wanted me to live? My parents would've told me to fight for what I believed in... but what *I* believed in was gone.

I'd never had a choice from the beginning. I'd been fooled into believing I could be with Colt, could choose the one I wanted to be with. Could choose the one I loved.

They'd all played a part in this: destiny, Callon, and Colt. They'd each given me false hope. *It was supposed to be this way*, Callon had said. *We were always meant to be together.* But if we were always meant to be, then why did Colt have to work his way into my heart as well?

Callon had the rings, and he hadn't hesitated to use them to his advantage just like Marcus. But Colt, he'd had my friendship. From the start he'd worked on me to make me fall in love with him. It had felt natural, regardless of the fact that he was my protector. With

Callon I'd been forced into the situation. Yet while it had been awkward to begin with, I'd grown to love him, too.

Really, when it all came down to it, I had no choice of my own. Everything had been set out, and I was forced to confront destiny. No matter how I'd tried, it had won in the end.

I had to follow its plan.

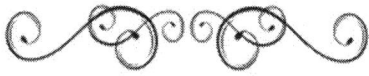

"Happy Birthday, Cheyenne."

Daniel's soft voice caused me to look up. I'd been lying on the bed, as I often did since coming to Ireland. Everything had lumped together in a haze, and I hadn't realized what day it was. I glanced towards him, and spotted a small pink cupcake on a crisp white plate set before me, a single candle burning.

My light.

"I'm here, Cheyenne," Colt whispered. *"I said I'd always be your light. I promised never to leave you. Remember?"* His fingers brushed the stray hairs from my eyes, and I grasped for his hand, pulling it to my chest.

A carefree smile broke over his lips. *"You remember when I took you for a hike?"*

I nodded.

"I led you to a mountain meadow."

"I remember," I whispered as my mind drifted towards that memory.

It was warm, the perspiration running down my brow as I climbed the hill. Colt stood waiting, his playful eyes meeting mine.

"Hurry up," he called out.

"What's the rush?" I asked, knowing he was anxious to show me his surprise. I suddenly stopped and plopped down on a tree stump just to be stubborn. "I'm exhausted."

He stalked towards me, and I giggled.

"Seriously, Cheyenne, you can do better than that." He rolled his eyes and grasped my hand.

"You're so pushy," I laughed.

We paused at the top of the ridge between the trees, and I became still. He'd brought me to a field, where thousands of bright yellow wildflowers with patches of red poppies danced in the breeze. Colt pulled me forward and wrapped his arms around.

"Look, your own personal patch of sunshine." He grew silent, more thoughtful. *"I didn't think I'd ever find anything as close to heaven as this."* He looked at me, and I knew he wasn't talking about the flowers.

"You made me a crown out of flowers," I said.

"I did. I told you you'd always be my princess."

I blinked away the tears.

"Cheyenne."

"Yes?"

"You'll always be my princess."

"I love you, Colt," I whispered.

"I love you too. I'll always be with you..."

Tears streamed down my cheeks as Colt's image faded from my vision.

"Cheyenne?"

My eyes cleared enough to see the remnants of the candle burning and Callon holding my hand. Daniel must have called for backup.

"I miss him so much." Callon was speaking differently, in a tone of voice I'd never heard before. It cut through my despair, reaching far enough to touch my place of retreat. "I was breaking our family apart. I was the one who was so determined to push you in the right direction. I'm the one to blame for all of this, not you. It's because of you that I realized how much my family meant to me. It's because of you my heart aches...because of what *I* put you through. I'm so sorry..." He bowed his head as the candlelight faded away.

The thin wisp of smoke trailed upwards. My light was gone, but Callon was here. Callon was here baring his soul, and I couldn't reject him anymore.

I moved closer, tossing the cupcake and plate to the floor.

"I'm here, Callon," I murmured, my silence finally broken. "I'm here."

His arms came around me, and he buried his head in my hair as we both held on. Holding on for all our losses and for all our pain.

A sudden peace began to cover me like a warm blanket. Daniel had wrapped himself around both of us. His salty tears ran down my arm.

"You're back," Daniel whispered. "You came back."

Eventually Daniel let go, but Callon held on until my limbs became heavy and sleep overwhelmed me.

I woke to the softest caress on my cheek.

"Cheyenne," Callon murmured. "Cheyenne?"

I inhaled and looked up into weary eyes.

"I'm here," I whispered.

A weak smile broke through. "I want you to stay."

I grasped his hand.

"I'll try." I knew I couldn't say anymore than that. My heart was still heavy, broken, shattered, but I knew I needed to move on. I could deal with this heartache the way I'd dealt with the others...I'd bury it deep in my heart. It would all blend into the darkness at some point, it had to.

"I want you to leave this room." He hesitated. "I want you to come with me."

I pressed my eyes closed for a moment. This room had been my sanctuary. Leaving it would open me up. I was safe here.

"It'll be okay." He encouraged. "Daniel, Maes and I are here. It's going to be all right. I want you to live here, to see and explore my home. We're going to help you move on."

My hands began to shake at the thought of the unknown. *Move on.* I knew I needed to, but Callon vocalizing it caused me to panic. I didn't want to move on from Colt. I wanted him to be alive and with me always.

"Cheyenne." Callon said softly, convincing. "He'd want you to see it."

Callon helped me to sit up and pulled me to the side of the bed. I stood and suddenly my legs felt like jelly.

"It's okay. I've got you." His arm quickly snaked around my waist. "You've been in bed a long time. It will take time to get your strength back. But I'll be here every step of the way."

He led me to the bathroom, and for the first time I actually took in my surroundings. The room was decorated with white marble and ornate fixtures. Callon didn't live in any ordinary home. This was plush and elegant, luxury at its finest.

After cleaning up and opening the door, I was astonished at what

I'd chosen to ignore. An expansive four-poster bed adorned the center of the room, the bed I'd slept in with its silken fabrics. Large oil paintings hung throughout and a sitting area with antique furnishings was nestled in a private corner. I glanced to my left and saw the sunlight peeking through the curtains.

"Do you like it?" Callon's hand covered mine.

"Yes," I whispered. "It's just that I..."

"I know," he replied. "But you're here now, and you can take it all in."

His hazel eyes glowed with warmth. These were eyes that I'd come to adore and the man I needed to make things right with.

"I'm sorry." Once again, I was crying, but these tears were for a different reason.

"I know." He drew my hand up and kissed my knuckles. "Let me distract you for a while, okay?"

I nodded and allowed him to lead the way.

My bedroom door opened and I hesitated as Callon stepped out into the hall. I looked back. This was my safe place. I couldn't leave.

"It's going to be okay." He tugged on my hand.

I lowered my head and stepped into the unknown.

The shadows seemed to follow me as we headed down the long hall. My feet padded quietly over the carpet, and we headed down the cascading stairs. I couldn't bring myself to look up, not yet. My heart began to race as Callon took me through another larger living space. The gloom from the darkened room seemed to close in around me.

Light, I needed light!

"Here," Callon said as he opened a door and led me out onto a terrace.

I inhaled, not realizing I'd been holding my breath.

"Let's just sit in the sunshine for awhile first, okay?" His fingers squeezed mine, and I nodded.

He took us to a double chaise and we sat, looking out into the lush forest surrounding us. A lake lay in the distance, dark and mysterious.

My mind wandered to the light of the candle. It was the light that brought me out, as well as the memory of Colt and my realization that I'd pressed Callon's hand to my chest. He'd been staring into my eyes, and I'd finally seen him. He'd brought me back.

19

"Callon, I need to tell you something..." I had to let him know about this feeling, this unknown darkness before it got out of control.

"You haven't been well, Cheyenne."

"It's more than that, it's..."

"You feel something different."

I inhaled a shaky breath. He knew.

"I didn't know how to handle it. I didn't know what to do except hide." I pushed my shaking hand to my forehead. "I—I didn't try to kill myself with the medicine, either."

"Oblivion was your only safe place," he said, expressing my thoughts for me.

I nodded, lowering my head in shame. "Colt was my light, and with him gone, I didn't know where to turn." I swallowed. "I didn't know how to tell you. It was like the words wouldn't form on my lips to speak. I'm sorry."

He drew me closer, his arms coming around me. "I'm going to help you. *We're* going to help you."

"I'm scared, Callon," I whispered. "I'm scared of falling back."

"Then let me help you." He rubbed my back tenderly.

"I need you. I don't want to go back there. I'm so sorry for all that I've put you through. You deserve so much more."

His fingers brushed the hair from my eyes.

"I'm the one to blame here," he said. "I contributed to your sorrow, and put you through so much. I'm the one who doesn't deserve you. Let me be your light, Cheyenne. Let me be your strength. Let me love you the way you were meant to be loved."

"I don't know if I have anything left."

Callon rested his hand on my chest, and my heartbeat quickened.

"It's right here," he said. "Not gone, only hidden. You've been through so much. Of course you'd try and protect yourself."

"We have to find the rest of me before it's swallowed up by the..." I couldn't even say the words, as if that would confirm it.

"Then let's search together."

He leaned closer and placed a tender kiss on my forehead. I snuggled in close as we quietly took in the moment. Callon would help me. He wouldn't allow me to lose to the gloom and despair, but I needed more. My eyes drifted to his right hand, where he wore his Consilador ring. His clan ring that bound us together.

I couldn't stop myself as I reached for it. I just needed that deeper connection, that tingling sensation running under my skin to let me know I was alive and he was here with me. My breath caught as I locked my ring over his, and I heard his gasp as well. The electricity flowed through me as he further sealed his fingers with mine. I held on, allowing the pulsing rhythm to warm my cold heart. I took in every ounce and let it roam freely. I didn't need to hold back anymore.

"Callon?"

Daniel's voice broke the moment, and Callon unlocked our fingers.

"Yes?" he replied.

"Is everything..."

"It's fine."

I curled my legs to my chest as I watched the sun disappear over the horizon. A shiver rolled over me. Nightfall, shadows were coming...shadows I knew were something more.

A warm hand touched my shoulder.

"Cheyenne?" Daniel's brows pinched together, his expression grim. "We want to help."

"I know," I whispered.

"You want to come inside? Are you hungry?"

I nodded, pulling my legs to the edge of the chaise.

It was time to start moving on.

I followed Daniel up the terrace stairs and into the main sitting area. Callon ambled behind, unrushed. As I entered, a surge of unease hit me as the dimly lit room cast shadows in every direction.

"We call this the sitting room," Daniel smirked. "Cuz all we end up doing in here is sitting." He disappeared for a moment as he clicked all the lights on. "That's better," he said.

I took in the sitting room. Floor to ceiling windows flanked the walls, which would give an excellent view of the terrace and scenery during the day. Directly in front of the windows was a semi-formal sitting area anchored with a large rug. Beyond that lay a grand piano with chairs and what looked like a music area. Black instrument cases were arranged nearby.

Daniel waved me further into the room towards a smaller sitting area. As I glanced about, I noticed large oil paintings were placed at intervals along the walls between the windows. Some were landscapes and others were portraits. Were they of the O'Shea family?

"If you're cold, we can make a fire later," Daniel added as he pointed to the massive fireplace.

"I'd like that," I replied. The light and warmth would hopefully fill the empty feeling inside.

"There's also a lot of pictures and stuff to look at when you're ready," Daniel said. He pointed to the gallery hallway and I nodded.

"There's no rush," Callon said. "Take your time."

He led us back towards a dining area that housed an enormous table. It must've seated at least twenty or more. Everything was built to such scale, it was making my head spin.

"How about some dinner?" Callon asked as he pushed us through a double swinging door leading to a chef's kitchen. He pulled out a stool for me as he disappeared into a large pantry and returned with various items.

Daniel moved closer, his shoulder brushing mine. His face was full of anxiety. Despite his cheerful words, I could tell he was lost on what to do to help me. Even his touch was different. In the past it had always brought comfort, even as it did the other day, but right now I felt nothing.

"So you finally decided to come out of your hole, huh, Cheyenne?" Maes's growl caused me to jump. I turned, frowning.

"Maybe," I replied and turned away. I really didn't need his coldness right now.

"Congratulations on a fine job as the lost Kvech heir," Maes went on. "Running from your responsibilities. You are certainly your mother's daughter."

"Leave her be, Maes," Daniel said with icy coolness.

"I don't think so, Daniel. She's hidden herself long enough. Heck, she even tried to end her miserable life, coward that she is."

My eyes flared, and I spun around, my hands shaking.

"You know *nothing*, Maes." My teeth began to grind together.

"I know that you're afraid."

"I—I was...I *am* broken hearted." Why was he doing this? "Can't you let me grieve Colt's death?"

"You don't have time to grieve, you—"

"Stop!" Callon bellowed.

He stepped forward, glaring at Maes. His knuckles were white

22

from gripping a kitchen knife. Daniel moved closer to me.

Maes stood immobile, the veins in his neck bulging. Suddenly he began spouting words in French, his hands flailing around, before he stormed off, slamming the door behind him.

Callon's eyes met mine for the briefest moment, before he turned and continued cooking as if nothing had happened.

"It's okay, Chey," Daniel whispered. "Maes has been going on like this since we got here."

I folded my shaking hands together in my lap. An unsettling feeling bubbled in my stomach, and suddenly I leapt up, running from the room. Maes's words had hurt, but every one had been true. I wasn't a leader who could stand up to Marcus. I was a coward who couldn't face reality. The darkness stirred again, and I held a hand to my chest. How much more till I was pushed too far over that edge?

Daniel appeared, and I stopped mid-stride. He blocked my way to the exit, his blue eyes unsure.

My body trembled. I was once again hurting those around me. I turned away from him as other footsteps neared.

Callon moved closer. His usual confident step staggered as he drew me into his hold. "I'm sorry. I should have stopped Maes."

I collapsed into his chest, my fingers gripping his shirt. "I'm tired of failing," I murmured.

"You're not a failure. I am."

Now Callon was taking the blame for me. No, this wasn't his fault. It fell solely on my shoulders. I'd allowed the shadows to creep in. I'd allowed myself to believe that I could be with Colt. I was the one who ran away... This wasn't because of Callon's doings. This was because I was being stubborn and didn't want to listen.

Callon pulled me into the sitting room near the fireplace. I looked up to see that Daniel had already started a fire.

"I know the darkness is frightening, Cheyenne," Callon said softly as he grasped my chin and forced me to look into his eyes. "But you can't have shadows without light. You just have to find it."

My vision grew hazy for a moment, and a slight smile emerged from my lips as Colt's image began to form before my eyes.

CHAPTER 3

That familiar feeling rustled within me and I sat up, gasping. A fierce chill ran over me. I pulled my legs to my chest, wrapping my arms around them.

"Hey, it's all right, Cheyenne," Daniel croaked as he appeared at my side, looking like he just woke up himself. "You fell asleep on the couch."

I was still in the sitting room. Footsteps approached from the hall, and I turned. Callon paused, glancing at Daniel. Callon gave a slow nod and moved closer.

"Did you have a bad dream?" he asked.

I looked away. What had happened? Last I remembered, I was sitting with Callon and Daniel and then began having memories of Colt...somehow I fell asleep with no dreams till now. But wait, it wasn't a dream. It was a *feeling.* It was that unknown something inside me wanting to wake again.

"Sweetheart, you have to tell me so I can help," Callon cooed softly. His hand rested on my forearm.

Tell him what? I didn't know how to explain it. This wild presence inside me wanted its release again like on the mountainside.

"Cheyenne, look at me." He lifted my chin and forced my eyes to meet his. "It's okay. But I can't help unless you speak."

Daniel shifted uncomfortably.

"I'm fine," I whispered.

"You're shaking, Cheyenne," Daniel said, his voice quivering. "I—I just want to help."

24

"I know."

"Time will heal all wounds, Cheyenne. You just need time," Callon said.

I shook my head. Time would never heal this wound; I could only hope it would make it bearable.

I looked beyond Callon's shoulder and watched the morning light stream through the terrace doors. Sunlight was what I needed. "I want to go outside."

"Let's go." Callon stood, extending his arm.

I followed him and quickly walked out to the terrace. The morning air was crisp and clean, and I inhaled deeply.

"Over here," Daniel chirped with false cheer, and I went to the chaise he'd moved closer.

As the red and coppery lights began to glow on the horizon, I stared out at the lake, watching the mist retreat from the dark surface, dancing its way back into the forest. It would stay in the background waiting for night again, not unlike what was inside me. Always lurking, waiting...

The sun lingered across the treetops, and the streaks of light now glistened off the water. Warmth finally touched my cheeks, and I closed my eyes. A peace began to flow over me, and I realized Daniel had moved closer as well.

I was back—here if only for the moment—if only for the day.

"I'm going to be all right," I murmured.

Callon squeezed my hand as I continued to soak in the light.

"Do you want to tour the place?" Daniel piped up. "You only saw a small bit yesterday." There was still that uncertainty as he brushed the hair from his eyes.

"I don't want to overwhelm you." He pushed his hands into his pockets.

I smiled. "I'd love to."

The playful grin that I loved about Daniel emerged, if only for a moment, allowing me to glimpse a small bit of happiness. Quickly he pushed it back down and replaced it with worry.

"How about we start from the front?" Callon asked.

I nodded and headed after them into the house. We passed through the main sitting room, connecting to the long gallery, and then out the enormous entry doors. I didn't bother to look back as we strolled down the large stone porch with a fountain circling it. We stopped, but the long gravel drive continued, disappearing into the lush trees.

"Turn around," Daniel said.

I did as he asked and was shocked at the sheer size of the home.

"Welcome to the O'Shea Estate," Callon said.

"It's a bit overwhelming," I muttered. I couldn't remove my gaze from the gray stone. It wasn't anything I could have imagined. Acres of green fields flanked both sides, before they disappeared into the forest beyond. "So it belongs to all of you?"

"It belongs to me," Callon replied. "To you and me now."

I looked down at the gravel beneath my feet...*you and me*. Not Colt, Daniel and himself, but he and I. I swallowed, and pushed back the tears that wanted to flow. There would never be anything belonging to Colt again.

"Cheyenne?" Daniel jumped closer.

I faintly smiled, trying to give them some optimism. I should focus on the estate. I needed a distraction, and this would serve well.

The stone terrace we'd passed over earlier ran around the entire front of the house. It was dotted with small seating areas and stone benches. To the left were the large windows that opened up to the main sitting area inside; to my right lay a second wing.

As we moved down the gravel drive, I took into account the details of the landscape. Every bush had been hand-trimmed, and the grass was manicured with the most precise detail. Even the flowerbeds were spectacular. How many workers oversaw these?

"I'm very particular," Callon commented, as if he knew what I was thinking.

I lifted a brow. "I'd never have known."

A small smile emerged as he reached for my hand.

"You have no idea," Daniel said, the first time he teased in a while.

"Come on," Callon said.

We headed back to the main entrance, and I couldn't help but wonder where the black entry doors came from and how they got them here. I felt so slight and small standing before them. They had to be at least ten feet tall.

I followed Callon inside, and my gaze fell upon the hallway. It was filled with beautiful tiles that I hadn't noticed earlier.

"They're from a local quarry," Callon explained. "It's called

Connemara marble."

"It's stunning." I said. The lighter and darker shades of brown blended together seamlessly. If was as if an artist had meticulously perfected each one with a fine brush.

My eyes took in the stairs. The handrails, spindles, and stairs were made of the same material with a red oriental carpet runner trailing down the center.

Daniel suddenly appeared to my right, and I caught sight of another room with glass doors and bookcases. A library.

He pointed to the top of the stairs, and I followed Callon up. A small bench sat below a scenic oil painting. I paused, studying it. Somehow it was oddly familiar.

"It's the lake you can see off the terrace," Callon explained. "We used to swim in it in our younger days." He remained still, as if lost in some far off memory. I watched as his jaw tightened and brow furrowed before he looked away from the scene and faintly smiled. "It was always cold, but we didn't seem to mind."

Guilty I'd brought up a painful memory, I pointed down the hall. It was my turn to distract him. "How many rooms?"

"Fifteen bedrooms."

My eyes widened. I'd never been in a home with fifteen bedrooms; never been in one with more than *four*. But this was a manor, not a home. And it was ours now.

"How big was your family again?" He'd told me at one time, but I just couldn't remember clearly.

"Big." Another smile perched on his lips, but it didn't quite reach his eyes.

"And how many wives did your father have?"

"Too many," Daniel chimed in.

I hesitated for a moment. "He wasn't married to them all at once, was he?"

"No," Callon replied.

"So what happened to them?"

"Some died by accident, childbirth or acts of war."

"Childbirth and accidents?" I was about to add more, but thought better as the too-fresh memory of Colt's death rose to the surface. It was a fact, Timeless could die.

Sympathy crossed over Callon's face, and he squeezed my hand.

I sighed, dreading my next question.

27

"How many wives do you have, Callon?"

Daniel fidgeted and looked down the hall. Callon was staring at the painting when he finally answered.

"None."

I swallowed, knowing it may be true, but not the whole truth. Once again, he was hiding the truth from me, but why? If I was to marry him, why did he continue to keep secrets? Didn't he know this built a barrier between us?

"Do you know which room you're staying in?" Daniel jumped to my side, acting as a mediator.

I glanced back down the hall and realized I hadn't a clue. I could get lost in this place. "No."

"This way." Daniel pointed, and I followed.

I counted the doors so I'd know in the future. They all looked the same to me. We stopped, and Daniel slipped a pink tassel on the crystal handle. He smiled.

"There. This way you won't forget."

My chest tightened. This was my Daniel, always looking out for me. I leaned forward and drew him into a hug.

"Thanks," I whispered.

"I'd do anything for you, Chey. All you need do is ask."

"Hmph, how pathetic." A low French accent growled in the hall. *Maes.*

"What's it to you?" I stared down the jade-eyed monster before me.

Moments passed with no reply, but I noted that Callon exchanged a dark glance with Maes.

"So you've seen the estate," Maes stated. "It's about time you came out of that room."

My entire body began to tighten. My irritation was flaring, and that *thing* splayed too near the surface. It was as if I was ready to do battle, my anger suddenly growing at the hand that I'd been dealt. My fingers balled into fists, but before I could act, the hall vanished, and I was back downstairs.

"You don't need to deal with him right now," Daniel said softly. He whisked me into the kitchen and pulled out a stool for me. "Here, have a seat and I'll make you a sandwich since you didn't eat last night."

He opened the fridge door and began gathering his supplies. I

28

watched, taking deep breaths and letting the rage fade. As much as Daniel sympathized, he couldn't understand what I was dealing with. None of them could.

I was adrift in a dark stormy sea with nothing to cling to. My light, my hope, had all been crushed. Everything I'd ever loved had been dragged away from me and pushed below the raging waters, never to be seen again.

"Ham and cheese?"

Briefly broken from my thoughts, I nodded.

The only resolution in sight was Marcus's death. That would mean this dark force inside me would have to be freed, but how could I even think of such a thing? I'd almost killed everyone by allowing it out the first time. I pressed my shaking hand to my forehead, brushing my hair aside.

A plate slid before me. My hands curled in my lap as I stared at it.

"I promise I didn't poison it," Daniel forced out a chuckle.

"I know." I picked up the sandwich and ate half before I couldn't stomach anymore.

He packed up the sandwich and placed it in the fridge. "I'll save it for you in case you get hungry later." Hopeful eyes met mine. "I know I sound like Callon, but you've really lost too much weight, Chey."

I stared down at my hands. I knew I'd lost weight, but I really didn't care. Food had no taste anymore. Nothing had flavor.

"I'll try and eat more," I promised.

Daniel remained quiet for a few moments.

"We have a surprise for you." He waved me towards the door. "Come on, you'll like this."

I remained still. What was he up to?

He turned back, waiting for me.

I sighed and followed him out of the kitchen and onto the terrace. Irritated voices instantly drifted toward me, one French and another familiar tone that I hadn't heard for a long time.

"Cheyenne!" Lilly cried out. She hurried up the terrace stairs and wrapped me in her arms. "Sweetheart, we're here. It's all going to be better now."

My heart pounded against my chest. Dex and Lilly were here! But what had Callon told them?

Lilly's black hair pressed against my cheek. "We're so sorry."

I began to shake, trembling from head to toe. The feelings I'd pushed away all came flooding back at once. Memories of Colt flashed before my eyes. Our last day together in the cave where he showed me the magical glowing stones, before I found out I was betrothed to Callon.

I fought to inhale, but the air wouldn't fill my lungs.

"Shh," Dex whispered as his arms encased us further. "We're here to help, Cheyenne."

"He's gone," I muttered. "Colt's gone."

"We know," Dex replied.

"We're here now," Lilly repeated, her tears mingling with mine. "I wish I could change things for you. I wish you didn't have to suffer as much as you have." Her voice shook. "It's going to be okay. You're not alone, Cheyenne. You've never been alone."

We remained in a silent embrace for what seemed like an eternity before Dex and Lilly drew back. I kept my head lowered as Callon came to my side, his hand rubbing my back.

"It's been a bit rough around here," Callon said softly. "But Cheyenne's strong. She'll pull through."

"Strong?" Maes muttered under his breath, "She knows nothing of suffering."

"Maes!" Callon jerked away from me. "Enough!"

Jade-rimmed eyes met mine—cold, dark and unemotional. The dog had no heart after all.

"Come on." Lilly locked her arm around me and pulled me towards the field. "Let's go for a walk."

Lilly led us down a grass path, leaving the rumbling voices behind. The sound of horses whinnying in the distance caught my attention.

"I've missed you greatly, Cheyenne," Lilly said. "I—I wish Dex and I could have been the ones to raise you..."

My throat grew tight, and I kept my eyes forward. "If you'd been my guardians, then chances are you wouldn't be here right now," I replied.

She sighed. "It's just that you would have known us. We would have told you the truth, and you wouldn't have closed yourself off so much."

I didn't reply. Chances are they would've hidden things from me as well, especially if that had been my parent's wish. There was also

30

a reason why I'd closed myself off. No connection meant no pain when they departed. Colt had been the only one to break down that barrier, and now he was gone too. Proving I'd been right all along.

Lilly stopped and turned towards me.

"Don't lock us out, Cheyenne. Callon told us what's been going on." Her shaking hand brushed her black locks behind her ear, and our eyes met. "I wanted to come the moment we found out, but Callon held us back. He didn't want to push you farther over the edge than you already were." Her blue eyes softened. "I want to help. I want to be the one you confide in. I want to love and nurture you..."

"You want to take the place of my mother," I finished her sentence.

"I want to love you as your mother, Sahara, would have wanted me to." Her shoulders sagged forward as her gaze moved to the grass. "Your mother and I became close in her final years, and yet she never told me about you. I know why now." Tears began to stream down her cheeks. "It's because she wanted me to be here for you now. She knew her life was coming to a close, and she was ensuring you were taken care of."

I stared at the fragile woman before me. She was baring her heart to me, opening it up if I'd just accept it. Was this truly what my mother would have wanted? I just couldn't accept any more misery in my life if something were to happen to Lilly or anyone else.

"I know," I whispered. I reached out and touched her hand, squeezing it.

A tear-stained smile rose on her lips.

The fenced pasture ahead caught my eye. Two black stallions caught my attention. We stopped at the fence and watched them run and prance until they neared. I stood up on the rail.

They were tall, at least eighteen hands each. Their black coats shimmered in the sunlight, giving off a bluish tint. I studied them as they gave wild snorts. They were almost identical. The only distinguishing difference between them was that one had a notch missing in his ear.

I reached out to them with my mind, cooing and calming them until they became still. I stretched my hand out, and the notched-eared beauty moved closer, nudging my hand across his snout. His black eyes met mine in understanding. The other moved closer, his

31

head hovering near my cheek. A gentle nod caused his snout to brush my cheek and then he moved away. Both, however, remained immobile just a few steps away from me.

"I knew you had this gift, Cheyenne," Lilly said softly. "I could see it even before your transformation."

I stepped down and looked around at the vast estate around us.

"You can talk with them, right?" she asked.

I nodded.

"Can they communicate with you?"

"No, it's just one-sided."

"I used to be able to talk with animals..." Lilly trailed off.

I stopped in my tracks. "Used to?"

She smiled. "Yes."

"What happened?"

Before she could answer, a voice spoke.

"Enjoying your walk, ladies?" Callon asked. I jumped, releasing a small squeak. Where'd he come from?

Lilly smiled. "Yes, I thought it would be nice for the two of us to have some *girl* time."

Callon's smile brightened, and for the first time in a long time it seemed to reach his eyes. "I think that would be the best thing for Cheyenne right now," he replied.

I turned my attention back to the matter at hand. "Lilly, you said used to."

She smiled and then glanced at Callon, but no reply came.

I was so over this non-disclosure. I turned on Callon, brows puckering, shoulders tensing when suddenly it all faded away. I stared at the man whose face had softened and weary eyes pleaded. He reached out and took my hands in his as Lilly departed.

"I promise not to hold back on you, Cheyenne, but I've just barely gotten you back. I won't allow anything or anyone to push you to those dark depths."

"But I just want to know..."

"And you will, but I need you whole again before the weight of all that you bear comes crashing down on you. I was wrong in holding back earlier, but you have to believe me that it was always for your protection." He moved closer, lifting his hand to tilt my chin up. "First, I want to see those bright blue eyes of yours once more. Not the gray clouded haziness that's been there. I want the Cheyenne that I came to love and adore before all of this started. I want to see you smile. I want to hear your laughter. I want to feel the love I know you still have inside of you."

Soft, warm, supple lips touched mine. A swarm of butterflies erupted in my stomach, and my lids lowered.

"I want you to be surrounded with love and support, the love of your family, of those that care about you more than caring about what you will become." His words were full of passion. "You told me that you wanted to start over, love. Well, I'm asking the same for me. I want to start over; I want to hold nothing back. I want to love you with my whole heart, and I want to protect yours from ever being broken again."

A tender caress brushed the corner of my mouth, and my breathing hitched.

"I love you, Cheyenne, and I intend to love you for the rest of my life," he whispered.

A cool wind swirled around us, and I shivered from the chill.

He pulled me into a hug, his strong arms surrounding me. Strength was what I needed right now. I was weak. Too many failures that I could never take back encircled me.

"Come on." He kissed my forehead. "Let's get back before your goosebumps get any bigger."

I nodded and fell into step beside him.

"You see the lake?" he asked.

My eyes followed the shoreline as it disappeared into the tree-lined hills.

"It looks pretty big."

He smiled. "It is." He turned us and pointed out towards the estate. "You see all this land to the left and right of the estate?"

"Yes."

"That's all ours."

"Looks like a lot of work."

He chuckled. "It is."

"Who takes care of it?" I asked. "Since obviously you don't live here all the time."

"It's been in my family for many generations. We have an arrangement with the Campbell family, who maintain it for us."

"So they're human?"

"Yes."

"But wouldn't they know you and your family are different?"

"Yes, but they took an oath."

"An oath?"

"Yes, an oath to serve us and preserve our lands and protect our names."

I stopped. "What do they get in return?"

"Protection."

Okay, but still.

"They've never once let out that you were different?" I asked.

He faintly smiled. "No. It's different over here. Families serve for generations upon generations. They knew the oath they were taking, and knew the consequences if it were ever broken."

I raised a brow. "What would be the consequences?"

Callon looked away. "Death."

"Seriously?"

"Yes."

I hesitated. "So—so you'd follow through on this if the oath was broken?"

"Of course."

Here was another side of Callon I hadn't seen before. Somehow I knew it was there, but maybe I'd chosen to ignore it. It made sense. Callon was a leader. He was one to follow all the rules—always.

"Come on." He pulled me along.

We continued meandering through the field, stopping to pick wildflowers before we made it back to the terrace.

"Here, let me put those in water for you," Callon said. "I'll be right back."

He disappeared through the doors and I sat on a chaise, staring out into the horizon, watching a lone crow fly overhead.

I'd made it another day.

"Cheyenne," Maes rumbled.

My breath caught, and I scrambled back onto the chaise.

"Quit sneaking up on me!" I snapped, glaring at him.

A small smirk rose on his lips. Before I could retort again, the crow cawed. I turned, watching small sparrows chase it away.

"Did you know," Maes said, "that in Irish mythology, crows are associated with Morrigan, the goddess of war and death."

I stared at him blankly for a few moments. "What's that supposed to mean?"

He sat in a chair across from me.

"Morrigan was the goddess of battle. She'd sometimes appear in the form of a crow and fly above the warriors. Her purpose was not to attack, but to render the warriors helpless at the right moment."

My eyes narrowed.

"Are you trying to scare or warn me?"

"That is entirely up to you, *mon espoir.*"

Great, now he was back to calling me his hope.

"Don't call me that, Maes."

"More are coming."

"What?" I grew rigid. "Who's coming?"

"Koda, Nakari, Clayton and Skylar."

My stomach began to roll with nausea. Dex and Lilly were here— that was all I needed. Why bring others I didn't know?

And why Koda...

"Maes!" Callon snapped. "Get in here!"

Maes smirked to himself, before he departed through the terrace doors. But my anger was now directed at a new target.

What did Callon think he was doing to me?

CHAPTER 4

I couldn't believe this. They were all coming; the ones who rescued me from Marcus. I knew I should be relieved—they'd all risked their lives to get me out—but the thought of seeing Koda again was too much. He was identical to Colt in just about every way. His blond hair and blue eyes, his massive arms and tall frame, the way he'd produce a crooked smile, making me see the man I loved all over again.

The man I'd lost...

Tears stung my eyes. Why was Callon doing this? How could he think I was ready for all those horrible memories to be unearthed again? I'd barely escaped from the depths of my despair, and now he was cutting my lifeline and throwing me right back!

A chill breeze crept over the terrace, and the last of the sunlight streamed over the manor. Yet even when the wind stopped, I was still shivering. It wouldn't be long now before the familiar darkness reached out, calling me to join with it. To let go and let the shadows take over. Then all my light would be extinguished, and I'd be perched on the edge of the black abyss. An endless pit of shadows where a pair of crimson eyes lurked, waiting for me to take that final step.

I closed my eyes. No, I couldn't let that happen. I had to keep fighting for the little brightness I still had.

I turned back towards the house. It was completely black; no lights were on. Swallowing, I gazed towards the sky, but even the stars wouldn't give me any hope.

The shadows began to draw closer, crossing the lake, field, and forest until they surrounded me. I held myself tighter. My fingers traced the outline where Colt's bracelet should have been. I wished I still had them so I could lock them together and make the light come forth. How could I ever go on without him? He was still here with me, wedged deep into my heart and soul. But I needed his touch, his smile, his arms around me...

My body ached for him, my need so great to reach out and feel his warmth beneath my fingers, but it would never be. My heart raced, and I suddenly stood up, unable to bear it any longer. My throat was tight, longing to release a cry, to let out the tears once more. I needed to get away—I needed to move before it overwhelmed me and I fell off the edge.

I leapt from the terrace, and landed hard on the gravel. The impact probably hurt, but I didn't notice as my legs took over and I bolted into the field. Faster and faster I ran, desperate to leave the abyss behind, and yet still it remained, looming over my shoulder; as close to me as my own shadow. It would never let me be.

I reached the lake and halted, my breathing ragged. The water lapped at the bank as it must have done for years, eroding into the earth. It was almost funny, how such a gentle trickle could carve through entire mountains eventually. Was this what would happen to me in the end? The darkness would eat away at me, little by little, day by day, until it consumed me completely. It didn't matter if I tried to resist—it would win through in the end. Perhaps not today, or tomorrow, but someday.

No!

Biting my lip, I sprinted along the bank, towards the forest. I didn't stop, entering the trees and chasing the broken trails. The moon fought to peer down between the branches, brooding. I tried to follow its light, but it always disappeared before I could reach it.

At last, my body couldn't keep up anymore. My chest ached, my heart drummed against my ribs, and finally my legs gave way.

I hit the ground, and the last of my strength fell with me. The spicy scent of wet earth was rich in my nostrils, and the cold dampness began to seep into my skin. It was finding its home, slithering over my broken defenses, uniting with the darkness and wrapping tight around me. Another piece of my light snatched away, never to return. I couldn't go on like this. Please, just take the pain away...

The wind rustled through the forest, the mournful creaks and groans of the trees echoing the laments in my heart. I didn't want to close my eyes, but I was so tired. The darkness was too powerful. I couldn't fight it alone. Oh Colt, come back, come back to me! I need you...

"Cheyenne."

I froze. That soft voice mingled with the breeze. It couldn't be...

"Cheyenne, you promised me you'd live."

"I can't!" I cried. "I can't go on without you."

"I'm still here. I've never left you."

"But I need your touch, your warmth, your smile," I whispered.

"Cheyenne, you have Callon now. You need to live for Callon."

Callon.

The darkness stirred within, and I frowned. Callon, who'd invited everyone here without regard to my feelings. Callon, who didn't understand what was going on inside me, who couldn't accept that my heart belonged to Colt and had fought to break us apart. Who had kept my real life and heritage from me, had deceived and lied to me! I was nothing but a tool to him, a weapon against Marcus. How could I live for someone so...

I shot upright, my forehead suddenly slick with sweat. No, that wasn't right. He had done those things, but only to protect me. And he had never wished for Colt to die. He was doing everything he could to help me, and yet all I'd done in return was run away. Pushed him aside, refused to let him heal my wounded heart.

What was I doing? Who was I becoming?

I pushed myself upright and leaned against a tree, wiping the moisture from my cheeks. Colt was right. I needed to live for Callon. I had to. I had to go on before the line between the darkness and myself blurred further. It was becoming difficult to see where I ended and where it began.

Slowly, I began to walk back the way I'd come. Soon, though, I started to realize my mistake. I hadn't kept track of landmarks; I was completely lost. The moon, too, had disappeared behind the clouds. I had nothing to guide me. Panic set in, and I broke into a run.

My foot caught on a loose branch, and I fell to my knees. I didn't bother to stand again. Instead I stared into the forest, into the unknown. Inside and outside, I was surrounded by blackness. It pressed in closer, and my chest tightened. I couldn't breathe.

"Help me!"

My plea echoed across the trees, before it was snatched away by the wind. My head slumped. This was it. I was on my own. I lay listening to the night's sounds, waiting for it to take me away.

A branch behind me cracked, and I stiffened. Suddenly footsteps reached my ear, heavy and full of purpose.

Maes.

I closed my eyes and waited for his berating, but it didn't come. Instead there was only silence.

He stopped a few paces away, watching me. I didn't look at him, but glanced to the horizon. The pre-dawn light was beginning to emerge. At last it broke through the clouds, and a stream of sunlight danced before me. The sight brought back memories of my mother, Alexis. *"Sunshine smiles, Cheyenne. Look!"* I could still hear her words so clearly, and felt my tears renew. When would it ever stop?

"Cheyenne," Maes said, his French accent breaking through. "I've come to bring you back."

I didn't reply.

"Cheyenne." A heavy hand touched my shoulder. "You shouldn't be alone."

"What does it matter to you, Maes?" I hissed, pushing down my sadness. "You're only here for yourself. I'm your hope, remember?" My hands flew out before I was able to stop them and I sent a blast of air into the forest, causing a small tree to crack. I clasped my fingers together. What was wrong with me? It was as if I couldn't control my emotions any longer...

"Cheyenne."

I shrugged off his hand and rose on shaky legs. His jade-rimmed eyes met mine and I paused, unsure of his expression. Was he actually showing remorse? Was he allowing me to see past all those barriers he'd set in place to protect himself?

"I loved once," he rumbled. His subdued tone made me gasp. He'd never spoken like this before. It was somewhat frightening. "I've begged for the cold grip of death to come and take me away rather than living out the nightmare every day. I watched the one I loved perish right before my eyes and was helpless to prevent it. I replay that image over and over, feeling the guilt and shame for my failure, almost every day." He paused, and looked me straight in the eye. "I know the darkness you're fighting, because I've been there myself."

I swallowed.

"You've seen the crimson eyes staring back at you, haven't you?" he said.

My eyes widened. How did he know what I'd seen? It was what I imagined it to look like, and I'd told no one.

He stepped closer, his voice lowering.

"Don't fall into the abyss like I did. Fight it, conquer it, and live on. Because once you fall in, the climb out will be worse than hell itself."

"But you came out."

"Because of you, Cheyenne. You gave me hope again; hope enough to claw myself back into the light." His jaw tensed. "I won't allow you to disappear."

"Stop saying that!" I snapped. "I've had enough of the lies. I don't need yours on top of them!"

"What are you—"

"Don't pretend you're innocent!" I cut him off. "I know you only want me to free you from your stupid curse. I'm just a tool to be used when the moment calls for it." I balled my hands into fists. "Why do you all do this? You push so many expectations onto me, and you don't even give a single thought to my feelings!"

"And how can we, when you close yourself off all the time?" Maes shot back; the barriers were up again. "You don't speak to us. Instead you hide away like a whimpering pup, feeling sorry for yourself and blaming others for the isolation you've brought upon yourself!"

His words struck home, and moisture tingled behind my eyes.

"I can't be the person you want me to be," I said, my voice trembling. "I can't. I couldn't protect the ones I love, and if it wasn't for Callon, I'd have killed you all that day."

Maes sighed. "Perhaps I have been too harsh on you. You are stronger than this, *mon espoir*. That is not an expectation I place on you; that is a fact I have seen. You must not burden yourself with things you cannot change. The darkness will always be there, but you shouldn't cower from it. You must learn to master it." He looked away, as if afraid I'd see into his heart again. "Or it will consume you."

Stunned, I could only nod. Maes had to be desperate if he was apologizing for shouting at me.

"You need to find a way to distract yourself. Focus on building your strength. Your aim is to beat me in a fight. Let's see if you can do it."

"You want me to fight you?"

"I want you to become stronger, so when the time comes you'll be ready for battle." He stood motionless for a few moments as we both pondered his words. "Come," Maes said. He strode into the forest. I trailed behind, fixing my gaze on his broad shoulders. Last time I'd done this was when he'd fished me out of a river, and I'd struggled to keep up. Now that I was Timeless, it wasn't so hard, though I did notice he wasn't taking such big strides as before.

My mind wandered back to Callon, and my shoulders sagged. How many more second chances was he going to give me before he decided this *fresh start* was over? I'd told him I needed help, and yet once again I'd run away. Maes was right; I was a whimpering pup.

"I said I didn't mean that, Cheyenne," Maes said.

I stopped. "What?"

"You're not a whimpering pup."

"Why would you say that?" How did he know what I was thinking?

"Because I know you well enough to see you're wallowing, and you need to stop. What's done is done. Move on."

I was quiet for a moment. "But you told Callon I ran away at the first sign of trouble."

He didn't reply.

"Well, I think you're bipolar," I huffed. "One moment you're supportive and then next you're…"

"I won't coddle you. You're stronger than that." He picked up his stride, forcing me to jog.

We spent the remainder of the way back in silence. The beast inside had finally calmed; however, I knew it would return again. It was far from over.

I hadn't realized how far I'd run into the forest, but the sun was high by the time we finally reached the meadow. Callon, Daniel, Dex and Lilly were on the terrace, looking tense. I hesitated, unsure of how they'd react. I was sure it would only be with disappointment.

Rustling in the grass caught my attention, and I looked across to the lake. Callon and Daniel stood just a few feet away. Both were worn out with worry. I clenched my hands, my nails digging into my palms. I couldn't face him, not after what I'd put him through.

Callon took a step forward, then paused.

"Cheyenne?" He wasn't sure what else to say.

The dull ache in my chest grew more intense. I'd let him down, *again*. I'd run instead of seeking him out. Practically telling him he wasn't good enough to comfort me.

"I'm sorry," I murmured. "I'm so sorry."

Warmth engulfed me, and I clung to him. I wanted to cry, but there weren't any tears left to shed. He pressed me close, crooning softly in my ear.

"Why?" he whispered, "Why didn't you come and find me?"

I could've given a dozen excuses, but in reality it came down to one: fear. Fear of all the failures and all the letdowns yet to come. Fear of that unknown *thing* inside of me, feeding off all my hurt and anger. Fear that one day I'd allow myself to be overrun and I wouldn't care anymore, destroying everything I held dear. "I'm sorry."

Callon's soft lips pressed against my ear.

"I'm here for you. I'll always be here for you, love."

I moved in closer, wanting to wash away the memories of letting him down once again.

"What am I going to do with you?" He stroked my back.

"I'm more trouble than I'm worth, Callon." I knew the truth in my words. He'd warned me so many times, and yet I hadn't listened, and had paid the price for my recklessness. How could he have so much patience with me?

"No." He kissed my ear lobe and drew back, gripping my cheeks. "You're more than worth it. I'm just lost on what to do." He sighed. "Come on, you look miserable. You need to rest."

I nodded and followed, my hand held in his. I kept my gaze averted as we passed the terrace. I didn't need to see any more discerning stares.

Callon escorted me to my room and waited while I changed and cleaned up. He was waiting beside the bed with the covers down. I crawled in.

"Will you be okay if I leave for a while? I can send Lilly up," he offered.

I nodded my head.

He brushed the stray hairs from my eyes. "I'll be back in a few hours to check on you. We have more guests arriving."

I looked away. The guests Maes had purposely mentioned last night. *Koda.* My stomach began to churn again.

"Sweetheart, you can handle this," he assured me.

"I'm not ready for Koda." I curled onto my side, pulling away from him.

He leaned over me. "You have to face it sooner or later."

"Callon," my voice shook.

"There will be more," he warned me.

"Why?"

"Because we need them. We can't fight this alone." He placed a tender kiss on my forehead. "Rest, I'll be back soon." He rose, but hesitated. "I love you, Cheyenne."

I gave no reply as he headed for the door. I couldn't say the words yet, not when saying them made me feel like I was betraying Colt, and not knowing if my love were truly toxic. I couldn't face another painful loss.

"Cheyenne, Colt's here!" I heard Dad calling.

"Give me a minute!" I yelled back; I was in the kitchen, taking a sheet of cookies from the oven.

"Hey, Colt, hope the drive up wasn't too rough?" Dad was talking with Colt in the hall. "What are you two up to tonight?"

"Movies," Colt replied cheerfully. "The new one that everyone's talking about, *The Gate.*"

I smiled. We'd been waiting weeks to go see it, and tonight was opening night. Colt had pre-purchased the tickets, in celebration of finishing finals and Christmas break, and I was really looking forward to it.

"Mom," I said. "The cookies are done. I'm gonna leave them—"

"Did someone say cookies?" Colt rushed beside me, staring hungrily at the baking sheet.

"They're hot!" I slapped his hands as he tried to pull one off. "You can have them when we get back."

He pouted.

"Oh, stop it, you know the cute routine doesn't work on me. Let's go."

With a playful grin, he trailed behind me as I grabbed my gray coat.

"Have fun," Dad smiled.

"We will," Colt grinned, opening the door.

"Be safe, Cheyenne," Mom added. "I love you."

The door closed and I sighed, the taste of snowflakes rich on my tongue. The snow had been falling all day, and I could barely find the driveway. As I stepped towards Colt's truck, it crunched deliciously.

"Here, let me." Colt opened the truck door and helped me in.

"I can't believe you got us tickets," I said as he climbed into the driver's seat.

"It wasn't easy," he replied, pulling out onto the highway.

"Yeah right, it wasn't easy," I teased. "All you ever have to do is bat an eyelash, and the girls would fall over to do anything for you."

"Hey, that's not true. I have to smile too, you know."

I laughed, and he winked.

We continued down the icy roads until we reached the movie theatre. The parking lot was packed, but we managed to squeeze into a space. Colt hopped out quickly and caught me before I slipped on the ice.

"You just can't do anything right, can you?" he snickered.

"Oh whatever!" I pushed his hand away only to latch onto his arm again as I lost my footing once more.

"Told you so."

I rolled my eyes. "You parked there on purpose to make me hold onto your arm."

"Oh yeah, nothing to do with the fact this was the only space."

Once we were on the sidewalk, I let go of him. Ahead, a long line had already formed. We secured our spot and then waited. I began to shake and blew on my hands.

"Cold?" Colt asked.

"I'm fine."

He shifted a little closer.

"I'll be glad to have a huge bag of popcorn though." I grinned. "I can warm my hands in it."

He chuckled and the line moved. Now I could see the posters, and I rubbed my hands together. The movie was based off a novel that

Colt had given me as an early Christmas present. He'd laughed because I'd read it so fast he said it made his head spin. Even the movie trailers I'd seen looked awesome. I couldn't wait.

"This is going to be so great, Colt. Do you know how long we've been waiting for this?"

"Forever." He smiled down on me. "Hope it's as good as they say it is."

"I sure hope the male actor lives up to my imagination."

"Well, don't get your hopes up. He looks nothing like me."

I hit Colt's arm playfully and he laughed.

"Here's to hoping," he chuckled.

The line began to move quicker. We were next to be admitted, when Colt reached into his coat pocket. Suddenly his eyes widened.

"You're kidding me..." He trailed off.

"What?" I looked up.

Colt swallowed.

"Cheyenne, um, you're so gonna kill me."

I frowned.

"Nice try, Colt, but you're going to have to do better than that to pretend you forgot the tickets." I continued moving with the crowd.

"I'm not pretending!"

I stopped in my tracks.

"You're serious?"

He burrowed into every pocket, removing his keys, his wallet, his cell phone, but the tickets never appeared. Then he snapped his fingers. "I know. I changed jackets before heading out, and I left them in my other coat."

My heart sank.

"Aw, that's a bummer."

The line began to grow anxious since Colt and I hadn't moved. He took my arm and pulled us aside, muttering apologies.

"I'm really sorry, Cheyenne."

I blew out a breath. I'd been waiting to see this movie for ages, but there was no point getting angry. It was just a mistake.

"Should we go back?" Colt asked.

I shook my head. "You know, on the way here we passed the botanical garden, and it was all lit up with Christmas lights. How about we go there for a walk?" I suggested.

Colt grabbed both my hands. "I'm sorry. I know you really wanted to see the movie."

"It's okay," I told him. "We can see it later. Besides, it'll be more fun hanging with you and the lights."

He nodded, and we headed back towards his truck. The drive to the gardens wasn't long. Even before we stopped, I was spellbound. Every tree, shrub and trellis was covered with colored lights, and it was the most beautiful thing I'd ever seen.

"Wow," I whistled. "Check it out!" I dashed out of the truck, eager to see more.

"Hey, slow down!" Colt laughed, stumbling after me.

"But there's so much to see!" My feet took over again, and we walked briskly through the whole garden. At last we came to a bench that offered a perfect view, and we sat down.

"I'm glad you forgot the tickets, Colt," I smiled. "This is amazing."

"Yes, you are," he said quietly. "Thanks for sharing it with me."

He leaned down and placed a warm kiss on my cheek. A shiver escaped me, but it wasn't because of the cold. I looked up into his icy blue eyes.

He'd never kissed me before...

"Cheyenne," Callon's voice broke through my oblivion. "Sweetheart, I need you to wake up."

The hazy room came into focus, and I rubbed my eyes. The afternoon had waned, and the cool hush of the evening shadows blanketed the furniture. Goosebumps rose on my arms. I'd been dreaming of Colt again.

"Hey." He moved closer, rolling me to my back. "I let you sleep as long as I could." A faint smile rose. "But the guests are getting restless. They want to meet you."

Guests?

My body tensed, and my heart began to pound.

"Cheyenne." Callon gripped my shoulders firmly. "Calm down. They're here to help."

"But I can't..."

"Stop!" he growled. "Enough of this." His voice lowered, "Do you think that for one moment I don't think of that day? That I don't have my own regrets for allowing what happened?"

"But you weren't the one who ran away."

"I was the one who pushed you away. I was the one who caused to you run in the first place. I've made mistakes too, mistakes that can't ever be taken back."

He pulled my chin up. "Look at me, Cheyenne. Do you think I won't feel pain when I see Koda, knowing full well it's not Colt?"

I lifted my heavy lids and stared into his hazel eyes. Usually so bright and intense, now they were replaced with the same misery I heard in his voice.

"I think about Colt every day. Koda's presence will bring back memories, loads of them, but we have to move on. Colt would have wanted us to."

I inhaled a shaky breath and nodded my understanding.

"Go wash up. I'll be waiting."

My bare feet touched the cold floor, and a shiver ran up my spine. I headed to the bathroom, knowing what I was about to face head on.

Callon was waiting near the terrace doors, staring out into the darkening sky. I'd never noticed before, but he didn't stand tall like he used to. My heart ached. I was being selfish. Callon was trying to push me forward, push *us* forward, and move towards recovery, while all I wanted was to stay in my misery and mourn my Colt. Yet it was worse for me, because it was my fault he was gone. If I hadn't run away, if I hadn't insisted I knew better, hadn't been so hungry for answers I never found anyway, he'd be here, waiting for me downstairs.

"Callon," I said quietly.

He turned, and for a brief moment I witnessed grief pass through his hazel eyes. He moved closer, his gray T-shirt tight over his chest as he crossed his arms. He sighed heavily. I frowned slightly, unsure of what he was planning. Was he purposely delaying our appearance?

We stood in silence, each searching, for what I didn't know. Maybe it was for a way to end this misery; maybe it was to find out who we now were. Or maybe it was to see what was to become of us.

He'd told me he loved me, and I didn't say the words back. That had to have been playing on his mind. I'd never actually verbalized those simple words. I'd given the collective *I love you* to the group when I ran away, but never said them to him alone.

"Shall we?" He pointed towards the door.

I placed my hand on his arm and forced myself towards the stairs. Soft voices echoed off the walls and into the hall. I instantly recognized Koda's and stiffened. Callon's hand clasped over mine, and he pulled us along.

We rounded the corner to the sitting room, and suddenly everything became still. A movement in the shadows caught my eyes. Maes was hovering near the music area, away from the others, insurance that I didn't disappear.

I focused on the marble and carpets as we neared the group. I didn't need to look up to know they were all staring at me. Lilly's shoulder brushed mine as she moved closer. They were all afraid I'd bolt again.

I swallowed, my jaw tightening, and tears misted in my eyes. Koda was just a few steps away, looking concerned. No, please, don't, don't remind me...

"Cheyenne," Callon said. "This is Clayton, Skylar and Nakari of the Silloquize Clan." He squeezed my arm and an olive-skinned hand rose, forcing me to shake it.

"I'm Clayton," a man with scruffy brown hair said. "I—I'm glad to finally meet you, Cheyenne." I managed a nod, and his dark brown eyes warmed. He didn't continue the conversation, though, probably afraid he'd provoke something he shouldn't.

What had Callon told everyone?

Daniel came forward, accompanied by a gangly man with wild blond hair.

"I'm Skylar." He pushed his hands into his pockets and looked around nervously. "I'm so sorry for your, um..." He fumbled for words. "Colt was a good man. He's going to be missed greatly."

I choked back a sob. Couldn't they just say hello and be done with it?

"Cheyenne," a soft whispery voice broke the tension. "I'm Nakari."

Dex stepped closer, his hand coming to rest on my shoulder as Callon drew me near and Lilly clasped my hand. I forced myself to meet her eyes.

"I know this is the last thing you want right now, but we're here to help in any way we can." Nakari's gaze drifted towards Callon, and he nodded.

Was she searching for his approval?

She bowed her auburn head, but hesitated in stepping back. Her dark skirt swept over my sandaled feet and she looked up. Eyes as deep as the green forest met mine before she glanced at Callon again, eyes filled with sympathy and grief of her own.

A tall slender woman pushed her way in, her long black hair cascading over her shoulders. Her eyes were a shimmering blue, and she smiled politely.

"I'm Andre of the Silloquize Clan." She glared to my right. "Apparently I almost missed the big moment of meeting you."

"I told you…" Koda began.

"You told me nothing!" Andre snapped. She turned back, forcing her smile to return. "Anyway, it's nice to meet you." She headed to her seat again, but not before glaring at Koda with a look that could have melted stone.

Koda…

I knew he was close, but I couldn't look up. I couldn't bear the sight of seeing him and knowing it wasn't Colt.

"Cheyenne," Koda said softly. "I—I'm sorry. I know this is hard on you…" He cleared his throat, nervous. "Well, if there's anything I can do to make this easier, you just have to say the word."

Leave.

I shifted uncomfortably. I knew what my body wanted to do—run. Run fast, run hard, run to my safe place.

Without consent, my eyes met his. That same icy blue, the same blond locks of hair, the same wide berth of his chest, the pleading eyes wanting to make things right.

Daniel moved to stand beside Koda, and my throat began to burn. It was just like seeing the brothers together again. Koda pushed his hand through his hair nervously, and that did it. I snapped my head down, staring at the floor, but the memory was already playing out in my mind.

Callon guided me to a chair and began talking, but his words were lost on me. I was back in the forest, the roaring fires in my ears and the scent of smoke in my lungs. We were almost there, almost to freedom, when Marcus appeared. His hand rose, crackling with electricity, and then the lightning bolt shot out. My fingers tore into Colt's shirt, screaming at him to move, and yet he remained, shielding me, and taking the full brunt of the blast. Then we were on the ground, and he wasn't moving. Marcus was laughing, and the darkness ignited within—he was going to pay for this, pay dearly!

"Cheyenne?"

Lilly held onto my arm, and I blinked, broken from the scene. My hand was in the air, my fingers poised as if I was going to summon a hurricane. Just like that day...

I clasped my hands together, feeling that familiar presence awaken within. It was back, waiting at the edge of my conscience. Testing, stretching, goading. Fueled with my fresh rage and sorrow, it stalked beneath the surface, waiting to seize control.

Light laughter broke out, and I narrowed my eyes. Koda, Daniel and Skylar were smiling. My nostrils flared. How dare they! How dare they laugh and joke around as if nothing had happened! Colt was dead—*dead*! Didn't they care? Didn't they care that I was suffocating under a blanket of guilt, grief and anger? Why should I have to suffer alone?!

"Cheyenne, is something wrong?" Lilly asked, her face wrought with concern.

A hiss escaped me.

"Am I the only one mourning Colt's death?" I growled.

All attention focused on me, their previous conversations forgotten.

"Cheyenne," Callon said, easing a hand on my shoulder. "It's okay to laugh and smile at memories."

I pulled away from Callon, snarling.

"Like what? Memories of him dying on that ravine? Memories of you driving him away? Memories of all we had to endure? And you're laughing and telling jokes at a time like this?" My voice rose to a shriek. "Don't you even care about your own brother?!"

"Chey—" Daniel sputtered.

"Shut up!" I barked. "I've had enough!"

I bolted from the room, meaning to go to the front door, but Maes was in my way. Knowing I wouldn't get far, I stormed up the stairs to my room. Heartless monsters, every one of them! Why should they be allowed to share their happiness when all of mine had been stolen away?

Thundering steps chased after me, but I didn't look back, slamming my door behind me. Seconds later it opened again. Callon was there, staring at me in confusion. A few tears escaped, and I clenched my fists at my side. I couldn't tolerate Koda's laughter, identical to my Colt's. A sound I'd never hear again.

"Cheyenne." Callon stood beside me as I choked back a sob. "Cheyenne, please. You need to calm down."

"Why?" I spat. "So you can pretend nothing happened, that Colt's still here and we're all fine?"

Callon sighed.

"You're not the only one suffering, Cheyenne. I miss Colt more than you can imagine..."

"Like hell you do!"

"Stop it!" Callon gripped my shoulders. "You might not think I do, but I remember that day as clearly as if it happened yesterday. And it hurts just as much. But I'm not letting it rule me. I can't afford to." His hold relaxed. "Why can't you just let me help you?"

I didn't reply, as suddenly the answer came. I knew what I had to do. I had to close myself off. But this wouldn't be like before. Now I wouldn't let *anyone* inside. Nobody would be allowed to play with my heart again. And I wouldn't let them get away with all the hurt and lies they'd dealt me. No, I'd let it out, let loose that dark *thing* inside me and let it have its revenge. I'd let it have the power it thirsted for. I'd let it have *me*.

"Cheyenne, answer me."

I looked up at him.

"It's done," I whispered.

"What? What's done? I don't understand..."

"I do," Maes snarled. He shoved past Callon and grabbed my wrist, forcing me to face him. His muscles were taut, consumed by hot rage, and he glared deep into my eyes. "What have you done, Cheyenne?"

"Leave her be!" Lilly screamed. She hurriedly placed herself between us, fighting Maes's hold. "Hasn't she been through enough without you manhandling her like this? Haven't your words cut enough, Maes!" She pushed us back, away from Callon and Maes. Dex joined her, his arms coming around us.

"Maes, I think you need to leave now," Dex commanded.

"She will never be worth anything if you all continue to baby her!" Maes roared. He stormed out of the room.

"You need to rest, sweetheart," Lilly said softly as she gently rubbed my back.

Callon stood in the doorway, completely torn. Now I finally saw the pain he'd been fighting, holding back for my sake.

"I've been a fool," he said softly. "You weren't ready for this. Forgive me."

He turned and headed for the stairs. The sight of him walking away, leaving me again, frightened me, and set off a dull ache. The darkness, however, remained, delving deeper as my lips parted, wanting to call him back. No, I didn't need him and his false comfort. I'd keep everything to myself and bury it. I wouldn't cry, I wouldn't love, and I'd become the weapon they all wanted.

I pulled myself free from Dex and Lilly.

"I'm tired. I'm going to bed." I headed for the bathroom, closing the door behind me and pressing my hands to my face. No more fighting—I'd given the beast what it wanted—regardless of my own feelings.

And they would have to reap the consequences of what they'd sown.

CHAPTER 5

Sunlight peeked through the sheer windows, bringing with it the cool morning air. I shivered, but it wasn't from the cold. Last night's events kept replaying in my head, and each memory burned deep inside. I'd felt the *beast* wrap around me last night, and I didn't struggle. I'd just waited for it to take what it wanted—*me*.

I rolled over. The room was empty. It wouldn't take the group downstairs long to figure out what was going on, that I'd allowed this beast its freedom. Callon had probably already informed them. There was no point in hiding it any longer. I'd do what they asked of me and leave love out of the equation. How I was going to do this, I didn't know. I only knew love hurt, and I was tired of hurting.

I forced myself up and into the bathroom, stopping before the mirror. My reflection told me what I already knew. I was no longer *me* anymore. The Cheyenne that had been so naïve was gone, replaced with another. One who would be stronger, and wiser—no longer feeble. They wanted me to move on...I would.

As I exited the bathroom, I found the terrace doors open and Callon standing near the rail. He'd left me last night when he could have turned the tide, could have talked me out if it, prevented this hostile takeover. All I'd gotten was *please forgive me*. Why should I pay the price for his mistakes?

I'd tossed and turned all night. The crimson eyes were no longer looking up at me, but staring right through me. It scared me, but I'd reached out and taken the beast's hand, inviting it in. I had no other choice. There was no turning back now. It had taken my emotions and buried them in the fires, along with any dreams of happiness I might have had.

I straightened and moved towards Callon. He turned and again we stood in silence. He was searching for the right words to say, words I couldn't give him.

He moved closer and brushed a stray hair behind my ear before his hand came to rest on my shoulder.

"Where are you, Cheyenne?" he whispered. "Why are you leaving me again when all I want to do is help?"

I looked away. "I haven't gone anywhere."

"You keep running."

I met his hazel eyes. "I'm right here."

"No, it's your body, but it's not you." His free hand came to rest on my waist and he gently tugged me closer. "I want *you*, love, the you that you're hiding from everyone else, but I don't know how to bring you back."

Bring me back? The only way to bring me back would be to turn back time or erase my memory. Make me forget all the awful moments that constantly flashed before my eyes. Make me forget the guilt for all my mistakes. Force me to forget what my heart felt for Colt.

"I want to forget..." I whispered, and the beast moved inside.

Callon hesitated, but I didn't. My mouth was suddenly hovering above his. I pressed closer, and my eyes shut.

I could feel my breath hitch as I neared the corner of his mouth. Slowly and deliberately, my lips touched the corner of his mouth and glided across his. It was like the softest of whispers. His warm tongue jolted my senses as it ran over my lower lip, and soon my mouth was covered in his gentle caress.

My hands moved over his chest, slowly making their way to his neck. They slid higher, the texture of his rough cheeks under my fingertips. I pushed them further into his dark wavy locks. I knew exactly what I was doing.

He pulled back for a moment, his hot lips pressing against my neck.

"I want to forget everything," I said breathlessly. I knew he wanted this, but...

His arms wrapped around me tightly as my assault moved back to his mouth. My assault only intensified as we moved back into the room.

He hadn't used the rings to manipulate me. Instead, this time I was turning the tables. My back hit the bed, and in a swift movement, without missing a beat, he pulled me up, the heavy weight of his form pressing into mine.

Nothing else mattered right now. I finally felt alive. This beast was taking control, and the raw power surging through my veins was almost overwhelming.

No...

I pushed Callon back. He hovered above me, confused, just as confused as I was. This wasn't right. It was the beast taking control. No matter what he'd done to me, he didn't deserve to be treated like this—ever.

"I'm sorry," I whispered. "I can't do this."

"Do what?"

My eyes wandered to the terrace doors. Why couldn't I banish my heartache out those doors forever? Why did I allow this beast control?

"Cheyenne?" a mumbled voice called from behind my bedroom door.

We stilled. Callon slowly looked at my door. He sat up and moved away, standing with his back towards me.

I lay still for a few moments, reminding myself why I'd allowed the beast control.

Another knock came. "Cheyenne?"

I inhaled and drew myself off the bed, straightening my clothes. Callon remained turned away.

"Come in," I called out and the door opened.

Dex entered slowly, his gaze moving towards Callon. "Everything okay, Cheyenne?"

I nodded.

He stopped before me and began rubbing his hands together. "If this is too much for you, sweetheart, you just need to let us know. Everyone understands..."

"It's fine," I cut him off. "I'm fine." Once again, I felt the cold touch of dark fingers draping across my shoulders. Guilt poured over me. I'd used Callon. He'd used the rings in the past to manipulate me, and now I was no different, manipulating him, playing with his heartstrings. Giving him hope for something I could probably never give in return—love. How could I tell him that I was afraid to love? That it was toxic? That everyone I'd ever loved had died—was killed—because of me. No, I just couldn't open myself up again. I wouldn't be able to face myself if Callon were ripped from my life like...

My lips twisted, and I glanced towards Callon. He was staring at me. The fire and passion I'd witnessed was gone, washed away and replaced with hurt. I wanted to apologize, but just couldn't.

I pushed past Dex and headed for the door. I'd have plenty of time to contemplate what had just happened, but for right now I needed to make an appearance. I'd be strong and I wouldn't allow love, passion, or friendship to slip in—I couldn't.

Callon and Dex followed me as I headed for the sitting room. I entered near the music area. Maes was once again keeping his distance from the others. He paced uncomfortably, but his eyes met mine before I passed. He moved towards me with the grace of a panther, until Dex stepped between us. They exchanged uneasy glares. Eventually Maes hissed and returned to his pacing.

Apparently he wasn't welcome here.

The group fell silent as I neared, and I kept my head level and steady. I wouldn't make eye contact, wouldn't open myself up. I stopped, staring at their shoulders.

"I'm sorry for my behavior last night," I said. "It was a bit much to take in when I wasn't expecting so many new faces. I thought I'd be given more time to grow accustomed to the idea before you arrived."

Koda moved closer, and I stiffened. I focused on Skylar's wild hair instead.

"This is my fault, Cheyenne," Koda said. "I shouldn't have insisted I come. I should have—"

"It's fine."

"But I can leave."

"No. I'm fine," I repeated. "It's going to be fine."

I stepped towards a small game table next to a large window. I took a seat, focusing on the sunshine breaking through the clouds. The uncomfortable silence began again, and I felt everyone's gaze on me. Daniel jumped to the open seat and moved a checker piece.

I sighed. Daniel, my one weakness...

"Your move, Chey," Daniel said quietly.

"I'm not in the mood, Daniel," I replied.

He was silent for a moment.

"But you're in the game chair seat. It's a rule: you have to play."

A dark shadow crossed behind me, Maes. My jaw clenched. It wouldn't take much to push me over the edge this morning.

"Here, let me move the first piece for you," Daniel said, his eyes not meeting mine, but instead staring at Maes.

"Hmph," Maes grunted. "Still need someone to fight your battles for you, Cheyenne?"

The hair on my neck stood on end. Maes was deliberately fueling my beast, wanting to see how far he could push things. I rose, the chair squealing in protest, then made for the door. I wasn't going to let him play his stupid mind games.

A hand grasped my arm, and I hissed, spinning around. Maes clasped his fingers tighter, and I growled.

"Touch me again, and it will be the last thing you ever do, Maes!" I yanked my arm away and headed for the terrace doors.

I heard murmurs as I passed over the threshold. The cool air met me and I inhaled, closing my eyes for a moment. I was quickly losing control.

"Wait, Cheyenne..." Lilly called out.

"Leave her be," Callon interrupted.

"But—"

The terrace door closed.

I moved towards a chaise on the far side and took a seat. I allowed my eyes to wander to the field and forest as I calmed the inner creature. No heart, no heartbreak, I reminded myself. I couldn't even allow Daniel in.

Callon's face flashed before me. I'd wounded him deeply. I'd been cruel and heartless in my actions, and yet I hadn't stopped it. I'd let it play out, watched him suffer and watched the beast enjoy it. I couldn't even speak, to ask for his forgiveness. It was too late now—I had no choice but to hold back any feelings of love. I'd do as they asked. I'd marry Callon, but I'd just be the weapon they all wanted. A weapon used in battle and abandoned when it was over.

A bright light hit my eyes, and I had to squint. I shielded my face with a hand, searching for the cause. Something was reflecting off the water. The calm undulating waves stirred an idea. A walk by the lake would help calm my anger, and then I wouldn't have to hear their murmurs of disappointment.

I slid off the chaise and hurried into the field.

"Where are you going?" a voice called out. I stopped, and turned back.

A woman had appeared on the terrace, and now she was heading towards me. I frowned, remembering she'd introduced herself as Andre. How long had she been watching me?

Huffing, I spun back towards the lake. I didn't have to answer to her. Annoyingly, her footsteps rushed behind, and she caught up with me.

"Pretty impressive words with Maes back there," she smirked. "I'm surprised he backed off. I've never seen him bow to anyone, but then again, if looks could kill, even he would've been fried on the spot by you."

I didn't reply, although the thought of Maes frying was appealing.

She snapped off a tall blade of grass and began playing with it.

"So do you always talk this much, or is it just me?"

"Just you," I said under my breath, though I instantly regretted it. I didn't mean to be so harsh. I just wanted to be alone. I twirled my fingers, causing the grass to sway around us, remembering Maes' words. I needed a distraction.

"Ah, good to know. Must mean you're a good listener."

I raised an eyebrow. What an odd thing to say. I quickly resumed my walk, finding the worn path to the lake. My eyes remained on the water. The solitude would be welcoming, but then again, I wasn't alone.

I stood at the lake's edge, the water lapping at my toes. Andre plopped down on the small beach, removing her shoes and curling her toes in the sand.

"It's been ages since I've done this." She smiled. "Something about feeling the cool earth beneath your feet. Well, what can I say?"

I nodded, completely understanding the want or need to be outside and just lose myself in nature. But that didn't matter anymore. All that lurked around every corner were shadows.

Letting out a deep sigh, I sat on the shore too. I followed the curve of the lake until it disappeared beyond the trees. One day, if given the opportunity, I'd explore more, but right now I knew I was still on a tight leash. And I didn't need more people guarding me twenty-four/seven.

"It's gorgeous, isn't it?" Andre pointed to the darker parts on the lake. "The calming sound the water makes as it laps against the shore. Can't beat it." She began chuckling, "Maybe that's because the rest of them drive me crazy at times."

I tilted my head. "They drive you crazy?"

"Hell, yes! Especially Koda and all his stupid jokes. Just you wait till he turns his attention on you."

"Oh great..." My thumb began to run over my Servak ring. Just what I needed, for Koda to act like Colt and tease me.

"I'll try and keep him away as long as I can, but he'll pester you mostly because he likes you. He couldn't stop talking about you."

My eyes narrowed. "He was talking about me?"

Andre raised a dark brow. "Yeah, even with what happened, he could see how great your powers are going to be. He said once you can control them, you'll be an unstoppable force."

"Right," I mumbled. "I'm nothing but a child who can't do anything right."

She shook her head.

"He didn't mean it like that, Cheyenne."

"No one ever does." I grasped my Servak ring. I'd made too many mistakes that day and the days leading up to it, and now everyone here was going to rub my face in it.

Andre rose. "I'm going for a swim. Want to come?"

"I don't have a swimsuit on."

"Neither do I." She smirked, stripping off her clothes. "Underwear works." She ran past me and dove into the water, gasping as she came up. "Holy crap, it's cold!"

I couldn't help but smile. I rose and neared the water's edge. I spread my fingers out over the surface and watched the ripples. I suddenly realized I was feeling weak. Was using small doses of my power causing it?

"Is it deep?" I asked.

"Nothing you couldn't handle," she replied.

The reflection from the sun hitting the water's surface nearly blinded me. I had to close my eyes. I stepped closer to Andre, wading deeper into the water, hoping to avoid the glare. Suddenly, the ground beneath my feet vanished, and I fell right into the water. I came up, gasping. The water was like ice!

"Well, if you were that prudish about getting undressed, you should've said something," Andre chuckled. "You okay?"

"Just fine," I said, gritting my teeth. "There must've been a ledge there."

"Whatever. Come on, let's go!" Andre began swimming away.

I followed, a strange feeling drawing me to the murky depths. Was it because it was as deep and dark as I felt inside? Or was it the chill, the same chill I felt with this angry beast inside me?

Andre stopped. She faced me, her eyes wide. "What was that?"

"What?"

"Something just ran over my foot—AH!" She disappeared below the surface before she'd finished her yelp.

"Andre!" I screamed. "Andre!"

I dove under, searching for her, pushing myself further down, but the water was too cloudy. Something had stirred up debris from the bottom.

A faint light began to emerge from the dark, and I swam towards it. If there was light, I could use it to find her. My fingers came to the bottom and I stilled, allowing the debris to settle and my eyes to adjust. The glow returned, and my eyes widened. I reached out towards the light, and my fingers struck something round and metallic.

A shiver ran down my spine; something wasn't right. A moment later, someone screamed above the water. Abandoning the light, I flew to the surface. Bursting into the cold air, I searched for Andre again.

She was gone.

Splashing caught my attention. I caught her hand before she went under, but her fingers slipped through mine. No, I had to save her!

I plunged down again and swam towards her last location. I held my breath, watching the water for ripples or bubbles. Three pops appeared about twenty yards away on the surface, and I hurried towards them. My chest tightened as something drifted over my arm, but before I could grasp it, it was gone. I searched for as long as I could, but fatigue took over, and eventually I had to come up for air.

The lake surface was peaceful now. Fear of losing Andre spiked my adrenalin, and I looked again. But with so much dirt below, I couldn't see more than a few feet in front of me, and the light I'd seen before had disappeared.

Suddenly husky voices bellowed from the shore. Callon, Koda and

Maes were there, about to jump into the water. I didn't wait for them, and swam deeper, exhausted or not. If only I could *see*! I clawed through the murkiness, wishing I could summon a hurricane and rip the water clean. But I didn't dare. Not after what happened last time.

My lungs burned, and I pushed myself to the surface. A pair of hands grabbed my shoulders, and I half-screamed.

"Where is she?!" Maes demanded, his hold so tight it left marks on my skin.

"I—I don't know!" I spluttered. "She was here and then she disappeared..."

"Where'd you last see her?" Koda swam ahead, scanning the depths.

"She was right over there," I pointed, struggling to remain calm. This was my fault again.

"Cheyenne!" Callon pulled me towards him. "It's going to be okay. We'll find her."

"I—"

A scream broke my concentration. A few hundred yards ahead, Andre appeared, and was fighting to stay afloat. Maes grunted and swam towards her, Koda directly behind.

Andre struggled hard, but her head slowly began sinking below the surface again. Something was dragging her down!

"Andre!" I screamed, trying to swim towards her.

"No!" Callon's arm wrapped around my waist. "Koda and Maes will get her. Just tell me what happened."

I ignored Callon, unable to tear my eyes from Andre. She couldn't die on me, not now.

Maes dived, then Koda. Moments passed, and the water grew still. Tears began to form in my eyes.

No, not again! My love wasn't toxic. I was!

Finally Maes burst from the water, Andre in his arms. Her head fell limply to the side but she began coughing. Maes and Koda started swimming towards us. Callon released his hold and yanked on my wrist.

"Swim!"

We paddled to shore, reaching the sand moments before Maes, Koda, and Andre. A group had formed on the banks. Lilly's hands were pressed to her mouth. I collapsed as Callon moved away, barking out orders.

"Nakari, get some towels and blankets," he ordered. "Lay her here, Maes."

Andre's face was pale and her eyes closed, but she was coughing. Callon rolled her to her side, trying to help clear the water from her lungs.

What had I done?

My hands began shaking, and my legs wouldn't allow me to stand. I crawled closer, peering through the crowd. Callon was speaking to Andre quietly as Maes held her head. Koda touched her hand and squeezed. Dex moved in closer, checking her pulse.

"Can't a girl have a swim when she wants?" Andre muttered between her coughs.

What had happened? I kept replaying the events in my head, but nothing made sense. What had dragged Andre away?

Maes's jade-rimmed eyes met mine. The veins in his neck were growing at an alarming rate.

"What happened?" Maes growled. Before I could answer, Nakari appeared with Daniel, towels and blankets in hand. Callon and Dex began wrapping Andre up.

"Daniel," Callon called out. "Take Andre back. Nakari, take Dex with you."

Within moments they disappeared. *Ah, Nakari could jump like Daniel.* Lilly began running towards the manor. With them gone, all the attention turned towards me.

Maes looked like he was about to hit someone. "Start talking, Cheyenne!"

"I—I don't know what happened." My lips trembled.

Callon pushed Maes aside, his hazel eyes etched with concern.

"Are you okay? Are you hurt at all?"

I shook my head.

"Can you stand?"

He grabbed my arm and helped me up. Koda moved beside Maes, wary he might do something aggressive.

"Cheyenne, what happened with Andre?" Koda asked again. His eyes had softened; those same icy blue eyes and blond hair now dangling over his lashes. I looked away.

"I've told you, I don't know. One minute she was there and the next..."

The group remained still, studying me. Did they think I was lying?

"Why didn't you do anything, Cheyenne?" Maes snarled.

My chest tightened. "You don't think I was trying? I searched the entire lake bed for her!"

"You didn't try hard enough!" Maes barked. "All that power at your fingertips and you're still worthless!" His eyes flashed. "The lost Kvech heir, our lost leader and salvation...what a joke!"

"I never asked for this!" I shot back. "You're the one who keeps piling expectation onto me. You keep saying I'm your hope. Well, I'm not! All I bring is death and destruction!" My hands began shaking.

"Cheyenne, calm down," Callon reached for my hand.

I backed away from him, breathing hard. I didn't want to give him my poisonous touch.

"You'd be better off with Marcus," Maes mumbled. "At least he'd put that power to good use."

Instantly my hands rose, the beast within wanting release. If Maes wanted power, a fight, he'd feel it firsthand. The ground began rumbling, mirroring my emotions. At once, Callon grasped my arms, pinning them to my sides.

"Cheyenne, stop it!"

I blinked as he stared down at me, and the realization hit. I had been about to give total freedom to the crimson-eyed creature. My body relaxed, and Callon loosened his hold. I lowered my head.

"Just leave me alone." My voice shook. I pushed away and headed back towards the estate.

What was happening to me? I was completely out of control. This wasn't like me at all. I'd always had a temper, but to be so willing to lash out...what if Callon hadn't stopped me? How many others would I have harmed or even killed?

I rubbed my eyes. Why should I feel guilt for Maes, or any of them, really? They were the ones who treated me unfairly. Telling me that grieving for Colt was wrong, that I had to marry Callon and destroy Marcus. That my own heart and free will meant nothing. It's not like they'd even told me how I'd destroy Marcus. What difference did it make if I followed their wishes or the beast's? Maybe the best thing I'd done was giving it total and complete control.

Gravel crunched close behind me, but I knew it wasn't Callon. I twisted. Clayton was there, slightly out of breath.

"I'm sorry, Cheyenne. They asked me to follow you back." He sounded afraid. "I—I—"

The beast growled, and I clenched my fist. Callon had sent someone else to take care of me. Once again I'd been pushed to the side. Once again he could have made a difference, could have talked with me, but he left me alone. Left me alone with this *thing* gnawing away further at my resolve. How could he say he wanted to help find me when he wouldn't come searching himself?

I didn't respond, and instead made my way up the terrace steps and to my room. Clayton stayed in the sitting area, waiting to make sure I had returned.

As I changed, leaving my wet clothes in a pile on the bathroom floor, I was surprised the cold hadn't affected me much. A massive difference from when Colt had dunked me in the river to cool my fever.

Before those memories could be dredged up, I headed for the balcony. I couldn't afford to get distracted. The group was still at the lake's edge, staring out at the water.

Today's events had only confirmed what I'd known to be right. I had to stay away from everyone. I was bad luck. Andre had only wanted to keep an eye on me. Instead I'd let her get caught and almost killed by whatever was in the lake. And for all my powers, I'd been helpless to protect her. Like I'd been helpless to protect Colt.

Maybe Maes was right. I'd be better off with Marcus.

My fingers clenched the railing. No, Marcus was what drove the beast inside. The hatred for all he'd taken away from me fueled it. Marcus would never have me; I'd never allow it. I'd die trying to kill him first. I'd see him suffer in hell for all that he'd done, both to me, and my family.

A soft knock caught my ear, and then my bedroom door opened. I didn't bother to turn as soft footsteps neared. Wouldn't they even give me a little privacy?

"Cheyenne?" Lilly said quietly. "Are you alright? I rushed off with Andre, and I feel horrible for not checking on you."

"There's nothing to check on. I'm fine."

Lilly moved closer.

"Cheyenne?" She hesitated. "You seem upset. Do you want to talk about it?"

I turned, my face completely void of emotions. "How's Andre?"

Lilly blinked. "She'll be fine. Just a little shaken up, is all."

"Did she tell you what happened?" I asked.

"A little. She said something grabbed her leg and began dragging her under the water. She couldn't see anything, but she got the impression that it was black and scaly..."

I nodded and pushed past her, heading towards the stairs. I couldn't let this continue. For too long I'd run away and hidden in my weaknesses. I'd relied on everyone else to defend me, and never stepped up for my own sake. No more.

Somehow I was going to prove my worth. How I was going to do it was another question all together.

CHAPTER 6

I entered the sitting room. Everyone's eyes focused on me.

"Cheyenne?" Clayton stood up. I quickly passed him. "Um, Callon wants you to stay here..." I ignored him, heading for the terrace doors. He followed.

Nakari was already there, her auburn hair fluttering in the breeze. Her green eyes caught mine as I hurried down the steps.

"Cheyenne, please," Clayton begged. "You need to stay here." His fingers brushed my elbow. I twisted out of his grip.

A second later Nakari blocked my way. She'd jumped. I stopped, staring at her indifferently.

"Callon's asked that you remain here, Cheyenne," she said coolly. I frowned. I didn't need to take orders from her.

I took another step, and she latched onto my arm. A smirk rose on my lips. Before she could stop me, I drew on her power. Goosebumps rose on her arm, and she let go. A second later, I was in the middle of the field; two seconds later, I was at the lake.

Callon and the others were there, staring into the water. I attempted to walk past them, when suddenly Callon turned on me. His hands clenched into fists.

"What are you doing here, Cheyenne?"

"I know what happened."

"Oh?" Maes snorted. "How come it's suddenly clear to you when half an hour ago you couldn't speak?"

Koda pushed his way forward, blocking my view of the green-eyed dog.

"What happened, Cheyenne?" he asked.

"Andre said something grabbed her leg and tried to drag her to the bottom of the lake. When I was underwater searching for her, something brushed over my forearm. Something that resembled tentacles."

Callon frowned. "Something touched you?"

"Probably a fish," Maes snarled.

"It wasn't a fish!" I shot back. "It was different."

"I'll take a look," Skylar added. Moments later he disappeared into the lake. I attempted to move closer to see what he doing, but Callon stuck out his arm, keeping me back.

"What's he doing?" I asked.

"Searching," Callon replied.

"How? I couldn't see anything down there. It was too dark."

"Skylar doesn't need light to see," Callon answered.

"Huh?" I asked.

"Skylar's power is something special," Koda explained. "He's good in the water." He flashed a smile, and my breath caught. I cast my gaze out to the lake again, trying to forget the image. He wasn't Colt, he wasn't Colt...

"So he can hold his breath for a long time?" I asked.

"It's more than that, Cheyenne," Callon said. "He has other abilities as well."

"Like?"

"He can detect things invisible to the naked eye."

"Like underwater sonar?" I asked.

"I guess you could look at it that way."

I nodded. Out of nowhere Daniel landed beside me, and I flinched.

"Sorry," Daniel said, shoving his hands in his pockets. "Andre's doing fine, Callon."

"Dex and Lilly are still with her?" Maes's eyes focused in.

"Yeah, she's resting."

Maes nodded.

"Cheyenne!" Nakari screeched.

I didn't look back; her tone of voice said it all. Still, while I hadn't meant to upset her, it was nothing less than she deserved. It was her own fault for thinking she could boss me around.

"Should have warned you to not mess with Nakari," Daniel

whispered.

"She doesn't scare me," I muttered under my breath. Sighing, I turned to face her, but the irritation I'd heard didn't show on her face. It was as if she'd lost her momentum. I narrowed my eyes, glancing at Callon. He was staring at her; an unspoken warning to back off. His hazel eyes switched to me, admonishing.

"Don't do that again, Cheyenne."

"Why'd you stop her, Callon? Still don't think I can fight my own battles?" I scoffed.

"No," Callon said. "You need to get a grip and calm down. You're completely out of control."

The beast flared within. *I* was out of control? The wind picked up, tossing my hair out of place. I raised my hand to brush it back, and before I knew it Callon was in front of Nakari, watching my every move. My chest tightened.

"Callon, do you honestly think I'd hurt her? That I'd hurt any of you?"

No reply came.

"Oh, I get it," I sneered. "You want me to trust you, but you won't do me the same favor?"

He stood immobile. Nakari touched his wrist, and he glanced at Daniel. Moments later Daniel jumped us further up the field, towards the forest. Anger rose in my throat, stirring the beast, and I swallowed it down. Once again I'd been proven right. I wasn't a human being, I was merely a weapon. A highly uncontrollable, volatile weapon.

"Chey," Daniel spoke softly. He made to wrap his arm around me, but I pushed him away. "You can't keep this up. This isn't you."

My voice cracked, unable to hide the emotions. "This is who I am, Daniel. Everyone had a part in creating me." And I now even disliked myself for what I was becoming.

Splashing caught my attention, and I glanced back to the lake. Skylar had returned.

"Did you see anything?" Maes demanded.

"Not really, but there's definitely something down there," Skylar replied. "I felt it." He shook the water from his hair.

"What do you mean you felt it?" Koda asked, kneeling beside him.

I attempted to move closer to hear better, but Daniel stopped me.

"There's some kind of presence, but I couldn't see or make sense of it."

So Skylar had felt the same thing I had.

"I don't want anyone in the water until we figure out what attacked Andre," Callon ordered. He turned towards me, and my jaw clenched. There was nothing but coldness in his eyes.

I took a step forward, only to find myself further away from the group on the shore. Daniel had a hold of my arm. I yanked it away and made for Callon again, but Daniel was quicker and jumped me even further away. I just wanted to help.

"Daniel, stop it!" I growled, trying to force my arm free again, but he didn't relent.

"No, Chey, I won't let you become this thing you say I helped in creating. If I helped in making it, then I'm sure gonna help get rid of it."

"Let's go for a walk," Koda's voice boomed behind me. He'd jumped up with Nakari, whose powers were restored. She didn't make eye contact as she released Koda and disappeared back to Callon.

"I was trying to go for a walk." I pulled my arm free again and glared at Daniel. "But Daniel won't let me."

"You were heading in the wrong direction," Daniel snapped.

Koda pointed towards the stables.

"It's really not safe to be around me," I muttered under my breath. I found the narrow path and began walking. It was obvious no one felt safe around me, and that frightened me.

Why was Callon doing this to me? He kept saying he wanted me whole, and yet he was the one continually hurting me. He'd brought in Koda, the one man identical to my Colt. The one man who would constantly bring up Colt's memory every time he laughed, smiled, and joked with Daniel. He'd surrounded me with strangers when he knew I coped best with faces I was familiar with.

Why was he so intent to destroy me?

My pace quickened as the emotions poured forth. Dusk was approaching, and I swallowed. The shadows would be coming out. They would join with the creature inside me and have their merry way with my heart. Filling my head with lies and destruction...

Soon my legs took over, and I began running.

My fingers tightened into fists. Callon had thought I was going to attack Nakari. He probably thought I'd already hurt Andre. A few tears escaped, and the beast growled at my weakness. I wasn't weak. I was hurting. I was hurting because I just couldn't let go. Why did I still want to hope even when I was so willing to give up?

I was out of control, spiraling into that black vortex, and I didn't know how to climb out.

I stopped running and threw my hands out to the sinking sun. I began twisting them above my head like a conductor directing a symphony. I closed my eyes and felt the crimson-eyed beast creep to the surface, but I kept it from coming out.

The anger, rage, fury at what was taking place around me tightened its noose around my heart, trying to crush it further. This wasn't me, I knew, but I couldn't find my way back, not without help. The only help I wanted was Callon's, and he kept abandoning me every time the seas became turbulent.

My hair was now whipping against my cheeks, and I pulled the winds in tighter so it felt like it was suffocating me, draining the life from my limbs, but I held on, pushing more out until finally I couldn't breathe any longer.

I fell to the ground, gasping for air.

"Are you done now?" Koda asked as he knelt beside me.

I couldn't reply.

"Daniel, start a fire," he ordered.

I remained limp on the grassy meadow, staring up at the darkening sky, wishing Colt were here with me. Wishing I had something to bring me comfort. Words were worthless. I needed his touch, and that could never be.

The fire crackled and its light began to chase the shadows away. Koda sat across from me and began stoking the flames. Daniel sat beside me.

"I won't run away from you, Chey," he said. "There's nothing you can do that would be so awful that I'd leave. Nothing."

"I like the power I feel, Daniel," I whispered, vaguely aware of what I was saying. "It makes me strong." I sat up, and he tilted his head. Surely this would open his eyes. "I don't feel weak anymore. I just feel angry. Angry at everything that's been dealt to me." Yes, this was it. Strength from anger.

"It's alright to feel angry, Cheyenne," Koda said, "but using that anger to have power is wrong."

"No, it's a gift. It's a way for me to grow stronger."

"No, it's a way for your destruction," Daniel argued. His shoulders sagged, and he lowered his head. "You used to love everything, and now..."

"And now I hate." I finished the sentence, feeling his pain. "Run away while you can, Daniel, and forget about me. Forget the old Cheyenne."

He shook his head, and his weary eyes met mine. "I won't give up on you—ever."

"You should. I've given up on myself."

"That's the stupidest thing I've ever heard!" Koda snapped.

I sat up straighter. "Easy for you to say. You haven't felt half the pain I have! You haven't had the ones you loved ripped away from you!"

The beast burst forth, and I stood twisting my wrists, turning the small fire into an inferno. Koda leapt back, his stance growing wider, ready for battle.

"Cheyenne, no!" Daniel yelled and leapt for me. I thrust my hand out and sent a burst of air, toppling him over.

I pushed the flames higher, but kept them tight within my hold, ready to move them when needed. Koda dodged to the left, and I moved the inferno, but suddenly he changed direction. Before I could react, he had knocked me to the ground. The fire dispersed.

He and Daniel stood towering over me as I caught my breath.

"Why are you fighting Koda?" Daniel pleaded. "You're supposed to be friends. You're breaking this family apart, Chey."

My chest tightened. "I—I..."

My family...

"You've got to stop." Daniel gripped my shoulders. "You can't live with all this anger inside you. You have to let it go!" He drew me in closer, his arms wrapping around me tightly, and I didn't fight him.

"I'm sorry," I murmured, "I'm so sorry." His hold grew tighter. I couldn't live like this. I'd eventually break apart everything that I held dear—my family.

"Colt wouldn't have wanted you to be this way," Koda said. "I know you don't want to hurt anyone." He moved closer, kneeling beside us. "Even with the small glimpse I caught of you, I could see the love and compassion you hold. You don't need to draw power from your anger. Instead draw it from your love, the love of your family."

71

He was right, but I was so far gone now. I needed to be strong, and I didn't know how to do it without the rage driving me.

"We'll help you," Koda said, as if he was reading my mind. "But you're going to have to do your part as well. It can't be one-sided."

"I love you, Chey," Daniel whispered. "I'd never let anyone take you away from us. You're the reason our family came together again after so many years apart. You're one of us, now, my sister."

He drew back, smiled down on me, and eventually moved over. Koda sat on my opposite side, and we stared at the fire. It was the calmest I'd felt in a long time. Maybe it was because Koda reminded me so much of Colt, or maybe it was because I felt I had a piece of Colt still with me. Or maybe it was because I was finally realizing what I'd been doing.

Koda began fiddling with his stick. "What do you call a boomerang that doesn't work?"

I raised a brow. Where had this come from?

"A stick!" He began chuckling.

I stared, dumbfounded.

"What do you get from a pampered cow?" he asked.

I shrugged.

"Spoiled milk!"

Daniel began laughing, and I couldn't stop my lips from twitching into a smile.

"What lies at the bottom of the ocean and twitches?"

"Uh, I don't know," I replied.

"A nervous wreck!"

I couldn't help myself. A snort came forth, which caused Daniel to laugh harder and drove Koda on.

"One day a blond was driving on the highway and got pulled over by a cop. The cop said, 'Why do you keep swerving?' The blond replied, 'I turn one way and there's a tree, I turn again there's a tree, and then there's a whole bunch more trees popping out of nowhere.' The cop replied, 'You dork, that's your air freshener!'" Koda began chortling loudly, and I started to giggle.

"Those are the stupidest jokes I've ever heard!" I exclaimed.

"I know!" Koda bellowed.

We continued laughing for some time before I rolled to my back and stared up at the stars.

"You're gonna be just fine," Koda said quietly.

72

I didn't reply, but held on to his hope that I would be.

Eventually we made our way back to the estate. I saw the crowd in the sitting room as we stepped onto the terrace. I stopped in my tracks. I'd been acting like a spoiled child since these clan members had arrived. I'd snapped at them and acted rudely. Yet another mistake to add to the growing list.

Daniel leaned in closer. "It's going to be okay, Chey. They're more understanding than you think."

Maybe I didn't want understanding, maybe...

I took a step back. Then there was Callon and what I'd done to him this morning.

"Colt would have wanted you to move forward, Cheyenne," Koda said as I bumped into his chest.

I was completely surrounded; they weren't going to let me turn back.

Daniel opened the terrace door, and Koda gently nudged me in. Silence fell over the room. Lilly rose and hesitated. Dex moved beside her, his hand on her shoulder.

"Cheyenne," Lilly called out softly. "Are you—"

"It's about damn time!" Maes snarled as he barreled into the dimly lit room. "Have fun with your little fire show did you? Feeling better now?"

He, no wait, *they* were watching what happened? The beast clawed at my chest, wanting its release again, and I clenched my fists. I couldn't allow this dog's cruel, cutting words to affect me. Daniel grasped my hand, and Koda blocked the green-eyed monster from my view.

"What's this? You now have your own bodyguards? I've never met anyone more—"

"Enough!" Callon growled. He stormed forward from the corner of the hall. Nakari followed behind him, her emerald eyes avoiding mine. She stopped just to the right of Callon, her shoulder touching his.

My chest tightened. Was she afraid of me? Did she still think I was going to hurt her, or was it something else?

"She nearly got Andre killed and you're not going to say anything?!" Maes demanded. His footsteps grew closer.

"She didn't do anything, Maes," Callon snapped. "You heard what Skylar said. There's something in the water. Cheyenne had nothing to do with it."

I inhaled a shaky breath, pushed Koda aside, and pulled away from Daniel. Lilly and Dex rushed forward, but I sidestepped them.

"I'm a total and complete failure, Maes." My throat tightened as I was fighting to hold back my rage. "Is this what you wanted to hear? I'm sorry I'm not following your rules and that I'm mourning Colt's death longer than you deem appropriate. I'm sorry that you think I didn't do enough to help Andre. I'm sorry for being such a horrid person since everyone arrived here." I met his green eyes. "I'm sorry I can't be what you want me to be."

"Stop apologizing, Cheyenne. We're not forcing all this pressure on you," Callon said. "Stop doing this to yourself." He reached for me, and the creature inside rose its head.

"How dare you, you hypocrite!" My hand rose and came down hard against his cheek. "The only way to defeat Marcus, the sole living Kvech heir...that's all you've said from the start! Don't even *think* about turning the blame onto me! You did this, you, you, you!"

I stared, shocked, afraid, and humiliated at what I'd just done. So much for wanting to start over. My hand began throbbing, and I ran from the room. I raced up the stairs, knowing Callon wasn't far behind me. I couldn't breathe by the time I'd reached my bedroom door and slammed it shut behind me.

What was I becoming? Daniel had just told me I was the one driving this family apart, and it was as if his words didn't matter. I sat on my bed facing the terrace, my breath still ragged. This anger coursing through me...it was too much. I couldn't control it.

The landing outside my door creaked. Callon was there, but he hadn't entered yet. Would he? Or would he walk away again when I needed him most? Why did my mind and heart feel like a jumbled mess?

The cool night air drifted through the opened terrace doors, and my bedroom door creaked open. He'd come inside, but did I truly want him here? I lowered my head, my shoulders slumped forward and I clasped my fingers together tightly. I'd made a mess of things again. I sensed his eyes on my back, waiting, unsure.

"Why can't you understand?" I whispered.

He moved closer, and I held up my hand.

"Don't come near me." I knew what I was doing, hiding, running to the only safe spot I knew.

"Cheyenne, why?" Callon pleaded. His hands ran through his hair. "All I want to do is help you. It's all I've ever wanted to do."

The beast surged again.

"Liar!" I clenched my fingers into fists as the whirlwind of the last few days came to life again. "You don't help me. You hurt me. You've never told me the truth. You've manhandled me like a piece of meat. You've never asked about my feelings or thoughts, and just treat me like a puppet to bow to your whims." The incident at the lake flew into my mind and tears began to pour without my consent. I couldn't stop my voice from quivering. "You were going to take Colt away from me, just so I could be yours. You've never tried to win my heart, only seize it. You're no better than Marcus..."

"Enough!" Callon roared and I flinched, curling myself away from him.

What was I doing?

He exhaled heavily and moved towards the terrace, stopping so he could see me through the glass.

"Forgive me," he sighed, but then hesitated. "Is this really what you think of me?"

I didn't answer. I couldn't. Once again I'd just blurted out what was in my heart without thought to what the consequences would be. My anger, rage, *the beast* had gotten the better of me again. I'd let it loose. And now I couldn't tell the difference. I was utterly lost.

I drew my knees to my chest.

"I don't know anymore," I whispered. "I'm drowning, Callon, and I don't know what to do." The cool air wrapped itself around me, and I shivered. I didn't want to be this cold-hearted shell. "I know...you want to help. You all do. But I don't know how you can." I swallowed and lowered my head further. "Or if I even want it."

Callon turned to face me. "What do you mean?"

I released a shaky breath, not wanting to meet his hazel eyes, ashamed at what I was about to admit again.

"When...When I saw Colt die, all I could feel was pure, hot anger." I held myself closer as I relived the memory. "I couldn't see, couldn't think. There was just this...rage. This all-consuming, blazing inferno that rampaged through every inch of my flesh. And for the first time in my life, I wanted to make someone suffer."

He walked to the bed and sat beside me, but he didn't try to touch me. Instead he rubbed his cheek where I'd slapped him.

"I wanted to make Marcus feel every bit of hurt he'd ever done to me." I closed my eyes as I began to shake. "I wanted to burn that pain deep into his heart, engrave it there so he'd never forget." I paused. "And I almost killed everyone because of it."

Callon drew his arm around me, and I didn't fight it.

"What am I becoming, Callon?" I whispered as I looked up into his weary eyes. "These feelings inside of me—they're out of control, and it scares me." I wiped the tears from my cheeks, remembering all too well the hurt and pain I'd caused him this morning. "I don't want to hurt the ones I love, I don't! But this darkness, this *beast* that's raging in my soul, it's eating at me day by day. One day there'll be nothing left but the hate, and then..." My breath caught, and I couldn't speak as the tears burst forth.

"Hush," he said, pulling me into a tight embrace.

I wrapped my arms around him as I began sobbing. I hated what I was becoming. He stroked my hair and gently began rocking me.

"Cheyenne, it's normal to feel like this..."

"How?" I sniffled. "How can it be normal to want to destroy everything!"

"No, that's not what I meant." Callon rubbed my shoulder. "When I saw Colt fall...it was like watching a dream. I couldn't believe it. My brother, my comrade-in-arms, my best friend, gone, just like that. And then Marcus started laughing."

His jaw tightened against my cheek.

"In that moment, I would've ripped him from limb to limb. I would've faced his entire army, fought against every Tresez and Tracker he had, if only to let him feel half the pain I felt."

Callon paused, as he seemed to relive the memory himself.

"I know what that kind of venomous hate feels like, because it's not the first time Marcus has hurt my family."

I stiffened and withdrew slightly so I could see his face. "What? He's done this before?"

He cupped my cheek. It was as if he was deciding to tell me the truth, the whole truth about him and his family. It was as if he was now ready to tell me his secrets. I held onto his arm, waiting.

"My sisters," he finally said. "They were living far from the front lines." He glanced away from me, staring at the bed sheets. "I never thought Marcus would find them, but he did." He swallowed. "He didn't spare my brothers-in-law, not my nephews and nieces. He slaughtered them all, and leveled their homes to the ground. And he did it for the sole reason of getting to me."

Callon's eyes narrowed before he closed them. He knew what I was feeling, the pain, and the agony. My fingers brushed his cheek, and he raised his hand and held it there.

"If they hadn't been related to me, Marcus wouldn't have cared," he said, still unable to hold my gaze. "He would've left them alone. But he tracked them down, hunted them, knowing he'd do so much more damage than if he'd attacked me directly." He tapped his chest. "He hit me here, and it was the worst pain I could ever imagine."

"Callon..." I leaned in and kissed his cheek. How could I have been so blind and selfish? "I—I had no idea."

His head rose as his hands came to rest on my shoulders. The intensity in his eyes...I couldn't look away.

"He's doing the same to you," he said. "He took Colt away to drown you in the darkness, suffocate you in your own hate. Because he's afraid of you, Cheyenne. He knows your power, and he's trying to screen your eyes from it, to limit your potential."

He leaned in closer as the reality of everything hit me hard. I'd known it, but I was refusing to see it till now. Our brows touched.

"I don't want you to go to that place I did," he murmured. "The darkness so deep you can't see where you've been or where you're going. Where your heart is so blackened you can't feel pain or joy. Where you want nothing more than to fade away because you think there's no reason for you to live anymore."

He knew...

"When you're drowning..." I whispered, "...and you're scared everyone's going to go down with you, so you try and make them stay away."

I ran my hands up his arms, resting them at the back of his neck. This was the Callon I needed, the man who knew my pain and could help me, but would he?

"Colt was my light, and now all I have is darkness," I breathed. "I—I don't, I—I can't..."

"Then let me be your lifeline." His cheek touched mine. "I'm not trying to replace your light. But let me keep you above the water." His lips brushed mine, and my lids lowered. "Let me keep the darkness at bay, so you don't have to see it all the time."

Another caress warmed the corner of my mouth, and I trembled.

The beast didn't resist. It was calm as Callon held me. It was as if it knew, needed Callon as much as I needed him.

"I know you didn't mean what you said this morning, Cheyenne. I know it was the anger talking."

"Don't desert me, Callon. You're my last hope," I whispered.

His mouth covered mine, and a tremor rocked me. This morning I'd been cruel and heartless, and he knew it wasn't me. I needed him like the air I breathed. He truly was my lifeline. If he gave up on me, all would be lost.

I pushed closer, needing every inch, every breath, every bit of life from him. I wanted to feel alive. I wanted to change the path that I was sure would cause more chaos and destruction than I could ever imagine.

Marcus wouldn't win. He wouldn't blind me any longer. My eyes were wide open now.

I'd have to learn to tame the beast inside.

CHAPTER 7

My fingers traced the pillow beside me. It was still warm. I hadn't been dreaming after all. Callon had stayed with me most of the night. His warm musky scent still hung in the air.

I needed him desperately, and he hadn't deserted me. Finally, I was beginning to feel some hope. Hope for our future, and the Timeless clans.

I stretched and threw the covers back. My feet padded against the cold wood floor, and I opened the terrace doors. The orange glow of the morning sun was just beginning to break through the overcast skies. I pulled the chaise closer and sat, watching the meadow come to life.

A lone black rabbit hurried over the worn path and disappeared into the forest. I heard the soft sound of grass moving before Callon came into view. He was walking towards the lake, inspecting it for the unknown creature, I was sure.

I'd heard his warning about staying away, but sooner or later I'd find a way to rid us of the creature. I had to, if only to prove my worth. I owed Callon that much.

The chill in the morning air washed over me and I grabbed the blanket lying beside me. Callon must have put it out here for me knowing I'd come onto the balcony this morning. I snuggled up in the soft fleece.

Callon disappeared into the trees, and I turned my attention elsewhere. The sound of the horses whinnying in the distance caused me to smile. My thoughts wandered to Mandi. I missed her. I closed my eyes briefly as I pictured my Palomino prancing around the corral, demanding her release. The moment Colt would open the gate, she'd be off in a flash, galloping through the meadow, but always, after a bit, she would turn and search for me. It was as if she wanted her freedom, but knew her heart belonged to me as mine did to her.

Soft footsteps caught my attention, and I turned to see Nakari stop and lean on the terrace rail. She was staring out into the meadow like I had.

A sigh escaped her, and she pulled a necklace from her blouse. Her fingers ran over it while she stared lovingly at something hanging off the chain. It was a white gold ring with a large diamond; it looked like an engagement ring.

She closed her eyes as she grasped it in her palm and pushed it to her chest. Her expression saddened as she curled her fingers tighter. A tear escaped and trailed down her cheek.

She was heartbroken, just like me, but over whom? Had she lost her love? Was he brutally taken away from her like mine? I'd been selfish and self-absorbed since everyone's arrival. I should have known others would have been through the same; others had suffered and sacrificed too. I couldn't change what I'd done, but I could at least make an effort to see other's hurts. I also owed her an apology. What I'd done was wrong.

Movement in the meadow caught my eye. Callon was returning. His gaze rose towards the upper terrace, but he wasn't looking at me. Nakari pushed the necklace back under her shirt, but her eyes never left Callon.

Did he see me and was still fearful for Nakari? Or was it something else? Suddenly his gaze moved to me, and I turned to see Nakari had disappeared.

A morsel of jealousy rose in my chest. Was there something between Callon and Nakari, or were my thoughts running wild and playing tricks on me? I shook my head. It had to be my mind playing tricks. I'd already been acting coldheartedly, doing things and hearing thoughts that weren't my own...it had to be.

I headed inside to the bathroom, changed and then headed for my bedroom door. The hall was empty, but soon I heard footsteps behind me. I glanced back to see Andre and cringed.

"Cheyenne?" Andre called and my pace quickened.

After what happened yesterday, my guilt over her accident and my behavior washed over me.

I headed down the stairs and stopped in the hall.

Voices echoed from the sitting room, and I found new clan members waiting. I paused. More had arrived?

"You can do this," Daniel whispered near my ear. I jumped. Where'd he come from?

My eyes narrowed. "You're not helping the situation here, Daniel," I grumbled.

"Sorry," he replied. "I really didn't mean to scare you."

I turned towards the crowd and found that I'd somehow moved closer.

"Stop it!" I snapped. "I'll move when I want to move."

"There you are," Callon said and walked towards me, his eyes wary.

He leaned in and kissed my cheek. "I want to introduce you to a few clan members."

Without allowing me to delay, he pulled me forward. My breathing hitched, but I didn't feel like I was out of control. Maybe just having Callon touch me was all I'd needed to help tame the beast.

Lilly burst from the kitchen, Dex following behind.

"Cheyenne," Lilly said softly, but suddenly stiffened as Callon glanced her way.

The room grew quiet as Callon moved us towards the waiting group. Maes stepped closer, his jade-rimmed eyes focusing on me. The creature inside began to rumble, but Callon squeezed my arm.

"Cheyenne, this is Brogan, Layla, and Quinn of the Laundess clan. They've come to help as well."

All attention remained on me, waiting for the explosion they'd grown to expect. I swallowed and stuck out my hand.

"It's nice to meet you, Quinn," I said calmly.

His brown eyes leveled with mine. He was the same height. A genuine smile breached his lips as his brown hand came out to grasp mine, and he bowed his dark head over it.

"It's a pleasure to meet you as well, Cheyenne," he replied, his Middle Eastern accent thick.

Andre moved closer and hugged Quinn as they spoke quietly.

A delicate woman stepped forward, capturing my attention, and I couldn't help but stare. I'd noticed Nakari's beauty, but it had a cold standoffishness to it. However, that was probably due to me being unwelcoming. But this woman, she had a presence about her, a softness that I was sure was a reflection of her inner beauty.

There was no hesitation as her blue-green eyes met mine and she gracefully moved closer, embracing me. Her coal black hair, braided to the side, pressed up against my cheek. I inhaled. She smelled of wildflowers, like my mom had.

"What a privilege to meet you, Cheyenne. I count it an honor to have the opportunity to become friends with you." Layla squeezed tighter, and I couldn't help but feel her words were genuine.

She drew back, smiling. "You truly are a gift to the Timeless clans."

"And I'm Brogan," a deep voice grumbled. I had to take a step back to look up at the sheer size of the man before me. Colt had been large, but Brogan...monstrous was the first thought that popped in my head. His dark brown eyes met mine with a coldness I hadn't expected, and he didn't extend his hand. Instead he brushed his thick fingers through his wavy brown hair. I caught sight of his clan ring. He was the leader of the Laundess clan.

"So you're the hope of the clans." He eyed me as if I was a speck of dirt on his shoe.

I blinked, and the beast inside growled.

Callon instantly moved closer, drawing me away.

"Yes, she is something special," he said quickly. "If you'll excuse us, I was going to take Cheyenne riding this morning."

Without another word, the clan members parted, and Callon and I made our way out onto the terrace.

"You thought I was going to explode again, didn't you?" I fought to keep my tone even as we stepped off the stone terrace.

"You just told me last night that you feel angry all the time." He reached for my hand and pulled me near. "I wanted to remove you from a potentially dangerous situation before the anger had time to surface."

"Brogan," I said quietly.

"Yes. I felt you tense up the moment he stepped forward."

"He doesn't think much of me."

"No," Callon agreed, "you'll have to earn it."

"Yeah, I got that impression."

We quietly walked along the well-worn path until we came upon the stables. The same two large black stallions that Lilly and I had observed a few days ago met us. Callon headed inside, while I waited outside. It wasn't long before Callon appeared with two horses in tow.

He smiled and handed me a set of reins.

"This is Minuit and Joree," Callon said, adjusting the stirrups. "The only way you can tell them apart is that Minuit has a tear in his ear." He raised his hand and stroked Minuit's ear. "He got it over a mare. Joree was jealous."

I raised a brow.

"Jealousy can lead to strange things," Callon observed casually.

I nodded, but didn't reply. I knew firsthand what jealousy did.

He extended his hand. "I want you to ride Minuit."

He helped me mount and was soon beside me on Joree. We followed the path towards the forest. We meandered through the tall grasses, crisscrossing stone walls along the way. Minuit was a good horse, calm and placid.

The sun peeked out from behind the gray clouds; warming me and causing me to long for the warmth of the sun back home in Montana and Idaho. I longed for those long summer days with Colt, days I'd never have again.

We remained silent, each in our own thoughts until mine began to drift to Nakari, and what I'd witnessed this morning on the upper terrace. There was no doubt in my mind that she'd lost someone she loved, but was that someone staring me in the face? Or was it just my overactive imagination, the beast within trying to cause more chaos and confusion? There was a fine line between reality and untruth, a line that was always blurring.

"What about Nakari?" I blurted out and cringed. I hadn't meant to be so blunt.

"What about her?" Callon replied.

"Is she a friend or..."

He turned and cocked a brow at me. "I've known her for a long time."

"So she's a friend?"

"Yes."

We rode for a few more moments in silence before I spoke again.

"She was holding a ring this morning, and she seemed sad." I stared ahead, my blond hair drifting across my face in the breeze.

No reply came.

"Did she lose someone?" I prodded.

"Yes."

"Did you know him?"

I shifted in my seat.

"It's not my story to tell, Cheyenne."

"Oh." I looked down at my hands. "It's just that you know so much about me, and I honestly know so little about you. I thought maybe she meant something more to you."

"Nakari and I are close, but you don't need to feel threatened by her. I'm betrothed to you, Cheyenne. I love you."

I sighed. I should have known I was blurring the lines.

I decided it was best to remain silent as we rode on, trying instead to focus on what was before me. I kept my mind on the calming scenery, like the soft rolling hills lush with greenery. Being in nature somehow always spoke to me; it always produced a quietness in my heart. It brought me back to happier times with the ones I loved.

The ones I loved…Callon. He was trying so hard and I was finally feeling hope. Hope that he'd help me tame the beast. He'd felt my anger rising, and he was the one who quickly removed me from a potentially dangerous situation, a situation where I'd cause more hurt and pain for others. But was I ready for a real future with him? Was I worthy of his love after all that I'd done to him?

There was also the issue of being involved. I'd begged not to be left in the dark and yet now I wasn't so sure I wanted to know everything. With knowledge came responsibility, and with this beast clawing to the surface every chance it got, I couldn't be responsible— not for myself or other clan members. I'd failed too many times already.

Hours passed before we emerged from the woods. The stables were now in sight. A tall gangly figure was leaning against the rail in the distance. Probably Skylar.

"Lilly is making a meal for us tonight," Callon said. "We should see if she needs help."

I stared at his hands. He was rolling the reins in his palms, his fingers clenching down and then releasing it. He glanced at me from the corner of his eye.

He was upset, but over what? Because I'd questioned him?

"Beautiful day for a ride, Cheyenne," Skylar cheerfully said, grabbing Minuit's reins. "Did you have a nice time?"

I nodded and faintly smiled, watching Callon closely. Skylar took Joree's reins as well and we dismounted. Callon didn't glance back as he and Skylar disappeared into the stables.

He didn't like me questioning him...that had to be it. I turned and headed towards the estate. I was sure we'd talk about it later. It was no use trying to bring it up with Skylar around. I'd already shown my temper one too many times. It was time for me to approach this calmly.

It didn't take long for Callon and Skylar to catch up. Callon's fingers locked over mine, and he began twisting my rings. I glanced up, but he kept his gazed steady on the horizon.

We entered through the terrace doors into the sitting room and immediately heard commotion in the kitchen. Koda and Daniel's laughter rolled along with Lilly's motherly voice scolding them. A smile rose as a fond memory of Colt surfaced. I was going to be okay...

Skylar headed for the kitchen, but before I could follow, Callon tugged me towards the stairs. I raised a brow.

"I thought..."

"Later," he said coldly.

The stairs and hallway were empty. He opened my bedroom door abruptly and forced me inside. Then he closed it, pushing me into the corner. His hands rested on either side of wall, caging me in.

"What are you hiding from me?" His eyes bore into mine.

"I don't know what you mean," I protested.

"We rode for hours without you saying a word. It's like I have to pry everything from you. Why won't you give your thoughts to me freely?"

"It's complicated, Callon."

"No, you make it complicated." He lowered his head. "Just like the fact that you still haven't said I love you. Is it so hard for you to say?"

"Oh," I swallowed.

"I'm committed to you. We have a destiny to fulfill—we have the rings. I've already told you I want to spend the rest of my life with you—loving you. Does that not say it all?"

I looked away, my throat tightening. He wanted words, words I wasn't prepared to say yet. Words I couldn't say yet...emotions I felt, but my lips wouldn't allow me to speak them.

"I—I—" I couldn't speak past the pressure in my chest, the lump in my throat.

"Is it that you don't believe me, Cheyenne?" His voice softened and fingers traced my cheek. "Do you not see my love? Can't you feel it? Do you not see that I want all of you, your thoughts, your desires?"

I looked up into his hazel eyes, eyes desperate to hear those words.

"Do you love me, Cheyenne?" he whispered.

"You know I do," I pleaded.

"Then say it."

My lower lip began to quiver. I knew I loved him. It wasn't the same way I loved Colt, but I loved Callon nonetheless. I'd promised myself to say the words so others would know, but now when it came down to it I couldn't. Why?

Because my love was toxic...

"You don't trust me." He lowered his head.

It was a trust issue...I didn't want to trust him with my heart. I didn't want to feel pain again, the unbearable sorrow that always came after I let myself love freely.

"I'm not going to leave you," he whispered near my ear and moved closer.

The tears I'd been fighting to hold back flowed.

"Colt made the same promise, and—," I barely spit out.

He drew me into his arms. A tender kiss touched my head.

"You can't live in the past, love. We have to live for the future. Our future."

"I'm trying."

I curled into his hold, absorbing the comfort he gave. One day I'd have to say the words...one day soon.

A sharp knock on the door caused me to jump.

"In a minute, Daniel," Callon said, and I looked up. His fingers brushed the hair from my eyes. "It's going to get better, I promise."

Another rap at the door, and Callon sighed heavily.

"Lilly say's it's time for dinner and that if I don't come back with the two of you she's going to be angry. She's scary when she's angry, Callon," Daniel's muffled voiced echoed in the hall.

"In a minute, Daniel." Callon faintly smiled. "I know you love me,

Cheyenne, and I know one day you'll say those words to me."

"I'm sorry," I whispered.

"No more sorrys, love, no more sorrys."

Over the coming days and weeks, the manor started to swell with guests. Clan members from all over the world were showing up, and my head spun trying to keep track of all the new names and faces. There were just too many to remember. I only noticed the cute brunette, Bree, because she was one of Daniel's friends.

Callon had been busy, organizing things with the clan members and sorting through his various duties, and I'd decided it best to let him have at it. I'd just be in the way, not that he didn't offer to have me involved. It had been ages since a gathering like this had taken place. It was all because of me, a gathering with expectations that I'd live up to the Kvech name and heritage. It was a large Timeless family reunion of sorts—with a family I didn't know.

I chose to remain secluded and instead tried to bury myself in practicing with my powers, shooting burst of air at designated targets. I quickly learned that it was draining. I didn't understand how could I create a fierce storm out of anger and not feel weak, but just causing the curtains to ruffle had me taking naps.

Out of sheer boredom, I'd asked Dex for some books on Timeless history. Now was as good a time as any to get myself acquainted with my legacy.

The first volume was really nothing more than a genealogical listing, who was married to whom and what children were born. It also included their births and deaths. I truly was the last Kvech heir; I didn't even have a distant cousin alive.

I dove into the second volume, and scanned over the pages until I came to my Servak grandfather, Jorell.

There wasn't a whole lot that was readable; parts of the writing had been blocked out. It was as if they were trying to record nothing more than his birth and death...and his alliance with the Sarac. From what I could make out, he'd been a strong leader at one time, but what had happened to change all of this? Why did they want to remove history? I sighed. I'd have to ask Dex for more information later. If he'd made mistakes, what's to say that I couldn't fall into the same trap if I didn't know about them?

I'd managed to keep my temper under control. I hadn't had another outburst; however, I hadn't been provoked, either. Maes had been preoccupied with Andre since the incident at the lake, and Brogan hadn't really been around to make conversation. He was busy enough planning and plotting with the other clan leaders.

And then there was Nakari. Callon said I shouldn't be threatened by her, but I couldn't help but see her in only one light. It was my fault. I'd started out on the wrong foot with her by stealing her powers. I'd have been angry too.

I'd been watching her when she wasn't paying attention, peeking from time to time from behind my books. She laughed and smiled while conversing with other clan members, and it was genuine. Clayton, Skylar and Quinn had no troubles fawning over her. Why wouldn't they? She was beautiful. But when her eyes would reach mine, everything changed. It was as if they held a mixture of regret, anger and confusion. It was no wonder she really didn't talk with me or I with her...something lay beneath the surface, but I just didn't know what it was or understand it.

The estate was bursting at the seams, yet I felt utterly and completely alone. The others all had connections with each other, even Maes, and I was on the outside looking in. A round peg trying to fit into a square hole.

Koda, Daniel and Bree rushed by me as I stood in the downstairs hall studying the portraits, and entered the library. Nakari, Andre, Skylar, Clayton and another I couldn't remember the name of stood stoic, their heads bowed.

I inched closer. Something was going on.

"You don't need to be here for this," Callon said. He pulled the library door closed. I moved towards the front door, but then turned and pressed my ear to the wall to listen.

"Did you find out anything about Bailee, Hayes?" Koda sounded nervous.

It was silent for a few moments. "I think you and Bree need to sit down," Hayes replied.

"What?!" Bree's voice rose. "What do I need to sit down for?"

"It's—it's that, well, it's Bailee..."

"Spit it out already!" Koda growled.

"Bailee, she's..." Hayes swallowed. "There was blood all over the house. It looks like she fought off her attackers, but..." He trailed off.

"But what?" Bree pleaded.

He sighed. "She lost the battle in the end."

My hand flew to my mouth in horror. I didn't even know this Bailee, and yet I knew she'd been someone important to them. Yet another life lost in this terrible war.

"No!" Bree cried.

"She could still be alive!" Koda protested.

"Her car's missing, but her computer and clothing bag were found at the house."

"That means nothing!" Koda bellowed.

"Did you have them check the other houses?" Daniel asked. "She could have run to them."

"They checked and found blood and tire tracks leading away."

"Koda," Bree's voice broke. "Koda, do you think she's gone?"

"They found a pool of blood at the bottom of the stairs, another on the couch. The entire house was coated in her blood with her hand and footprints. There were Tresez's prints as well," Hayes added. "I'm sorry, Bree, but Bailee is gone."

The library door flew open. Koda bolted past me and out the front door. My heart ached. How could I have said to him he couldn't understand my loss...

Callon's eyes caught mine as he rushed past. He didn't bother to hide his sorrow. It was another death, another needless tragedy that Marcus had orchestrated.

The estate fell quiet. A gray gloom had wrapped over all of us, and my thoughts couldn't help but turn inwards. Misery surrounded me, and it was hard not to let the memory of Colt's death overtake me. I couldn't deal with so much grief and heartache when I'd barely come to terms with my own.

I'd managed to hide myself away for brief periods of time, but I knew I needed an outlet. I needed to clear my head. I needed to be alone, away from the crowds of unfamiliar faces. I'd even tried sneaking down an unexplored corridor off the main hall, but found the metal studded doors locked. I had to find someplace of my own.

I rose early. The sky was dark and overcast, the clouds

threatening to release their tears. It was quiet as I peeked outside my bedroom door. The whole manor was probably still asleep. I continued into the hallway, sneaking down the stairs and out the front door.

The gravel crunched beneath my soft-soled shoes, and I headed towards the forest. I'd never have gotten away with this if Callon had been aware, but with Bailee's death, they were all preoccupied.

I passed the main fountain and stopped. Andre was sitting there. She tilted her head at me.

"You can't hide from me forever, Cheyenne," she said.

I looked away, pulling my coat closer around my neck.

"I'm not hiding," I replied, knowing full well it was a complete lie. Since the incident at the lake, I'd been avoiding her like the plague. I didn't need any more guilt in my life. I already had enough regrets as it was.

"Well, you've barely spoken to me since the attack, You won't make eye contact..." She began walking towards me. "...and I think if I said *boo* right now, you'd jump sky high."

"I wouldn't jump." I looked her in the eyes and then continued with my walk. She followed. "How long have you been stalking me?"

"A few days. You've been hiding inside, and I figured eventually you'd attempt to sneak out."

"You can read me that easily?" I asked.

"You're just doing what I would do." She shrugged.

"I'm sorry about your friend," I offered.

She sighed. "Well, it's all a part of war, I suppose. I just wish she'd have come with us in the first place instead..." she trailed off.

"It's not your fault."

"No, I know that, just like it's not your fault for what happened at the lake, regardless of what Maes thinks."

I rolled my eyes at the mention of his name. Andre smiled.

"He pushes you for a reason."

"It's getting old." I veered off, wanting to circle through the forest and emerge behind the stables to avoid being seen. My goal was to sit by the lake even with Callon's warning in place.

"What's getting old," Andre chuckled, "is Maes following me around. Do you know that he now thinks he's my self-appointed guardian?"

"Better you than me," I smirked.

"I heard you had experience with that too. How'd you get him to stop?"

I smiled. "You came along."

"Lucky me," she commented.

We continued at a brisk pace and soon we were in the forest. The crack of branches caught my attention and I stopped. I moved in front of Andre.

"What?" she asked.

"Did you hear that?" I tilted my head and listened again.

A branch crackled again.

"There," I said "Something's here with us."

I searched the dark forest and heard the patter of paws. Was it Maes or something else? I clenched my fists. I wasn't going to let Andre get hurt this time. I'd kill the Tresez if it attacked.

She touched my shoulder. "Relax, it's just Maes."

"How do you know?" I asked. "I can't see him."

"Because these grounds are guarded by an enchantment. No one other than those who are invited, namely Tresez, can set foot upon this estate."

I faced her.

"An enchantment?"

"Yes."

I stared, waiting for the rest of the explanation. "And?"

"Well, it's an enchantment that's been maintained by generations of the O'Shea family." She stared back.

I lifted a brow.

"They didn't tell you this?" she asked.

"No."

She shook her head. "Alright then. You know what an enchantment is, right?"

"Sorta." I hated to reveal how ignorant I was.

"It's a magical defense barrier that protects us from unwanted visitors. From the outside, all you see is the manor sitting about three miles away, and you'll always be walking towards it."

"So it keeps sending you back to the spot from which you came."

"Exactly."

"Interesting. So for each invited guest, Callon has to change the enchantment?"

"I'm not exactly sure how that works, but I guess something along those lines."

That might explain the bags under his eyes. It would drain him. I started walking again. At least I knew we were safe here, but if we left, we'd be vulnerable.

The patter of rain hitting the trees gave me a sense of peace as we made our way through the woods. My plan had been to circle the lake, but as we neared from a different angle, I realized the sheer magnitude of it. There was no way Callon would let me wander that far, and I had no idea where the enchantment boundaries lay. It wasn't worth the risk, no matter how desperate I was to be alone.

I found a fallen tree and sat as the rain stopped. Andre remained a few feet behind me, allowing me my personal space. I sat quietly, watching the raw beauty unfold before me.

The lake was serene. Not even a simple breeze moved the water's surface. My eyes followed the shoreline, taking in the tree-lined hills rising from the lake's edge. The depths of greens were amazing. How could one color vary in so many different ways? A lone bird flew low over the waves, searching for its prey.

The patter of paws returned behind me and soon it turned to footsteps. Andre sighed as I heard Maes sit beside her.

"I told you not to follow us," she murmured.

Maes gave no reply.

"You need obedience lessons, Maes."

Maes snorted, and I couldn't help but smile.

I stood up and moved closer to the water.

"Don't think about going for a swim, Cheyenne," Maes growled.

I narrowed my eyes and glanced over my shoulder. "It's a bit cold for a swim, Maes."

I picked up a rock and skipped it over the water. I followed the ripples as my mind ran to a memory of Colt. He was the one who'd taught me to skip rocks properly. He used to laugh at my throws. *If only you could see how far I'd come, Colt...*

"Not too bad," Andre said as she stood beside me. She ran a hand through her soaked hair. "Really, Cheyenne, you could've picked a better day to go for a walk."

"Aw, have I messed up your hair?" I eyed her matted locks. "You know, the wet dog look suits you."

"You're one to talk," Andre replied. "Your blond curls are bordering on a bird's nest."

I snorted. "And your mascara is running down your cheeks."

 Her eyes widened. "I don't wear mascara."

"Well then something else is slithering down your cheek."

Her hand flew to her face and Maes turned her to face him.

"Let me take a look."

I stepped towards the shoreline, my eye caught by one of the pebbles, when Maes moved beside me. We both stilled as we focused on a shimmering object in the water.

"You see it, don't you?" I asked.

He nodded.

I moved closer towards the lapping water until large fingers clasped onto my jacket.

"Can you part the water?"

I looked up and blinked. "I don't know."

"You've been practicing, right?" he asked.

He knew I had been, since he'd caught me several times, but this was something I'd never attempted and then there was the...

"Little bursts of power tend to weaken me."

"Then make it big." He turned away for a moment. "Andre, call Callon."

Maes's fingers latched onto the back of my jacket to hold me steady as I concentrated on the water. I pulled my hands down and spread them apart, watching in amazement as the water began to part. I was really doing it.

"Make it bigger and longer," Maes instructed, and I pushed forward.

I managed to open up about twenty feet of water, and we stepped forward onto the damp sandy surface.

"Do you still see it?" The water was now over my head, but Maes was tall enough to see over the crest.

"Yeah, get us another ten to fifteen feet..."

My eyes caught sight of movement in the water beside me, and I flinched. Was the creature lurking nearby?

"It's just fish. Keep moving." Maes nudged me forward.

I pushed out more power, but could feel myself weakening. I knew I wouldn't be able to maintain it for much longer.

A splash of water hit my cheek, and I froze. That wasn't a fish. A glint of red whipped past, and I felt its presence—the creature was here.

"Maes, I think…"

I glanced down when something that resembled a tentacle slinked into view. My breath caught as I watched it latch onto my ankle, and the water collapsed on top of us.

I was thrust through the water at a high speed, and any air in my lungs was ripped from me. My jacket peeled away like it was nothing. I fought to open my eyes and realized I was in complete darkness. My chest began to burn, and I forced my hands down towards my ankle, pinching and clawing at the slick skin. Whatever had a hold of me loosened, and I swam towards the surface, gasping for air as I broke through.

I barely caught the sound of Andre screaming when I looked towards shore and saw her pointing. I'd been dragged out more than five hundred yards. It only took a moment to realize her warning as a limb from the creature narrowly missed me. I spun around, dazed. My eyes grew large as I saw more tentacled limbs emerging from the dark abyss. My heart began to race. Now was my chance!

"Cheyenne!" Maes's frantic voice caught my attention. He was swimming towards me. Daniel suddenly appeared next to Andre on the shore. Andre had summoned help.

I turned back to the creature. Two tentacles crashed beside me, hurling me like a rag doll further into the lake. This time I managed to take a breath before being sent into the deep cold water.

The creature once again had me spiraling towards the bottom, and the murky water wrapped itself around me like a vapor. I stared into the darkness, trying to find it with my senses when something slithered across my neck, causing a stinging sensation.

Air was what I needed to fight this thing, air that was at the surface. Unless…

I began spinning my hands above my head, concentrating as hard as I could, trying to create a whirlpool.

A tentacle found my waist and began squeezing, cutting into my T-shirt and jeans, ripping into my skin. It had claws, tiny nails, thousands of them! I had to get away. Its hold grew tighter as I struggled; it was squeezing the air out of me!

A bulky arm snaked around my chest, and my head was turned as air was forced into my lungs. Brogan. The tentacles seized onto him, trying to pull us apart. Just before his grip left me, my fingers brushed his skin, drawing on his power. Strength, yes, this was what I needed!

As he was torn away from me, I grabbed onto the nearest tendril, severing it in half with my bare hands. I felt its blood warm the water, and I ripped away another piece, and another. A piercing shriek shook me as suddenly the creature vanished. My chest was about to burst; I needed air. Kicking my weary legs, I headed for the surface.

I sucked in all the air I could, pushing the pain from my fresh wounds down. I'd heal later. Before I could make a move, though, I was quickly surrounded. Brogan, Callon, Koda, Maes and Skylar were around me, making sure I wouldn't escape. Daniel must have brought them.

"What did you do to me?" Brogan snarled.

"Took what I needed!" I snapped. I should've felt guilty for stealing his powers, but I didn't. I needed them more than he did, and I'd put it to better use, too.

"Cheyenne, we need to work together here!" Callon swam closer and stared at the blood pooling around me. "You're hurt."

I pushed away from him.

"That's not important right now." I'd wounded the creature, but it was still alive. I had to finish it off while I had the chance. And the only way to do that would be...

"Koda, can you throw me in the air?" It wouldn't be an easy feat in the water.

"How high?" Koda asked.

"Just what are you doing?" Maes snapped. "It almost drowned you! If you think you're any match against it..."

"Shut up, Maes! I know what I'm doing."

"Cheyenne, no!" Callon grabbed my arm. "You're still bleeding. You can't..."

"You need to stay clear while I create a whirlwind," I said. "When you see the creature rise from the water, then we can kill it."

"But you're hurt—"

"I have Brogan's powers," I reminded them. "I'll be strong enough."

I didn't back down from his stare. Eventually Callon sighed and looked away.

"Skylar," he called out. "Take Cheyenne and Koda below and help get her in the air."

Koda pulled me to his chest and Skylar took hold of Koda. I inhaled a large breath. We made a rapid descent. They waited for a moment while I curled into a ball. I'd only have one chance to get this right.

Koda squeezed my arms, and I waited as we cut through the water.

I burst from the lake and immediately began twisting my wrists, forcing the air to obey. I glanced around. They hadn't thrown me high enough, and I was falling too quickly! I pushed my arms out, and began spinning, twirling like a ballerina.

My free-fall slowed, and I held myself just above the lake. I'd done it...now to control the water-logged whirlwind.

I moved myself and my handiwork further away from Callon and the others. I wasn't going to cause them harm this time. Now I just had to wait for the creature to appear again, which I knew would be soon. I couldn't afford any delay; I wouldn't have Brogan's powers for much longer.

I hovered, waiting for it to strike when I saw ripples in the water nearby. Suddenly the tentacles lunged from the water, straight for me.

I reacted quickly, pulling the funnel tighter, tangling the tentacles together. I closed my eyes as I poured out more power. My skin tingled as the spray from the wind-whipped water slashed over my exposed flesh. I pressed the funnel even closer the creature, squeezing the life from it as it had done to me.

It was my turn now to show my strength, to show Callon I was strong enough to fight Marcus and avenge Colt's death. To prove to Maes I was no longer the weak link...to allow this beast inside me some freedom.

I squinted through the howling winds, and watched the creature rise from the dark depths. It looked like a giant squid from my deepest nightmares. Black shimmering scales with thousands of razor sharp claws lining the inner side of its tentacles. Crimson eyes stared back at me, eyes filled with wrath, evil, and pure rage.

Crimson eyes...

It started out small, a high-pitched squealing that was more of an annoyance, and began to grow with intensity with each passing second. My body began to shake, vibrating with the noise the creature was pushing out. Pain began to radiate into my limbs, working its way up my spine and settling in my ears and head. I pinched my eyes closed, trying to fight through the misery, but it was no use, and suddenly I was underwater.

I opened my eyes, disoriented, as I took in my new surroundings. The surface was nowhere in sight, and soon it became clear that I wasn't even sure which way was up. The creature's tentacle slithered over my arm, drawing blood, and soon a dizziness began to overwhelm me. It was poisoning me with its venom now. Before it had just been toying with me. I had to get to the surface, but where was it?

Suddenly I was being pulled through the water at a high speed. The creature had wrapped its limb around my thigh. I fought to dislodge it, but Brogan's powers were gone. As unexpectedly as it started, it stopped. Once again, I was left to float in the darkness. I spun around and began swimming towards a dim light. It had to be the surface, but the closer I got, I began to realize it wasn't sunlight, but something glowing on the bottom of the lake.

How far down was I?

I swam harder, knowing I was running out of air. Where was the illumination coming from? It was similar to what I'd seen when Andre was attacked. Just like what Maes and I had seen earlier. I reached out and the loose debris began to cloud the glow as I fumbled around in the muck. My fingers latched onto something round and metallic, and I yanked hard, pulling it in front of me.

It was a ring.

The light began to grow brighter, and I squinted as I drew it closer, examining it. It had symbols carved into the sides. Where three ruby red stones should have sat, only two were present. Ruby red like the necklace Maes had given me.

My chest began to ache for air. Timeless or not, I could still drown, and the creature wasn't finished with me yet.

A muffled scream took the rest of my air as Skylar appeared and pulled me towards the surface. I gasped, pressing my eyes closed and clasping the ring firmly.

"Cheyenne!" Skylar's voice trembled as he helped hold me up. "Cheyenne!"

"I'm okay," I muttered and fought to regain some strength.

"Callon!" Skylar bellowed.

I knew what I needed to do. It was now or never.

My fingers wrapped onto Skylar's forearm, and a warm tingling sensation filled my veins. "I'm sorry, Skylar." I pushed the ring onto my thumb and pulled away from him, holding myself just above the water's surface. I struggled to take a breath, and began to see two of him. No, I had to hold on, just a little longer!

Skylar tried to grab me, but I disappeared beneath the surface.

I kicked my weak legs and flew down towards the dark depths. I didn't need to see the creature. I could sense it.

Even though I knew I could probably hold my breath as long as Skylar, his other senses underwater were incredible. I didn't see the black muck and debris, but instead there was a pattern of heat waves where the creature had been. I also moved through the water like a mermaid, quick and agile. I'd have a fighting chance now.

Coolness ran through my right side and then suddenly my left. This *thing* was circling me, waiting to strike. I stilled, waiting for it to make its move. By instinct, my legs kicked and I pulsed through the water, the creature directly behind me.

I veered to the right and down. A tentacle brushed the already open sores on my thigh, and I forced back a scream. I stopped, twisting to face the crimson-eyed beast head on. I lifted my hands, the ring illuminating the darkness.

Red eyes stared at me from the blackness, at the ring. Was this the treasure it guarded?

A limb rose slowly and a pulsing began to vibrate the water, penetrating down to my core. This creature wasn't going to win. Two could play this game.

I stretched out my fingers, forcing my arms down, and felt my own beast come alive within me as the lakebed began to shake.

Lightning quick, a razor-edged tentacle whipped across my cheek, and I cringed, feeling the warm blood flow. Blows to my thigh, calf, and forearm caused bile to rise in my throat. I pressed my eyes closed to prevent the spinning sensation and pulsed more power out. The hits were coming fast and furious as I held my ground. The boulders below me began to move. The water was clouded with debris as I opened my eyes.

My body began to shake as the power poured out of me. The creature's shrieks grew louder as more rocks and boulders lodged themselves into its scaly skin. I could feel the power draining from its life form as it fought to move away.

A tentacle lashed out against my neck, and I lost my momentum as another crashed into my side, tossing me aside like a pebble. I righted myself immediately and moved to a safe distance. It began emerging from the rubble. No time left for my own safety...I had to finish it, now!

I swam closer and dug deeper, pushing harder for the dark beast inside me to give me more strength. I was strong, stronger than this creature before me. I wasn't giving up till it was gone.

The high-pitched screams shook me, breaking my rage-driven trance, and I covered my ears. Hit after hit tore my clothes to shreds, and I opened my mouth to bellow out my pain.

Then a high and deafening shrill began to grow with each moment. The water began to pulsate, pressing in all around, crushing the creature. Red rage-filled eyes met mine, and then without warning, a blast sent me flying backwards and into the rocks on the lakebed. My head made contact, and intense pain crackled through my skull. My body was drained, and Skylar's powers were fading quickly.

I stared at the ring, when the darkness closed in and everything faded to black.

CHAPTER 8

Rage, pure and hot, flowed through my veins. My body pulsed with energy as I focused in on the one who'd killed my Colt—Marcus. He was standing there on the ravine, his eyes darkening with pleasure as he pointed his hand out towards Colt again.

"No!" My voice bellowed over the rocks and grasses.

Power, raw and uncontained flowed from my hands, and I watched Marcus fall to the ground. He wasn't going to win. I was going to save Colt! I moved forward, keeping the deafening flow of air focused on Marcus. I just had to move closer to Colt.

"Cheyenne!" Callon's voice broke my trance. "Stop! You're going to kill us all!"

"He's not dead!" I screamed back as I dropped the winds and ran towards Colt. "Colt, get up!" I yanked hard on his arms as he began to move. "Get up! We have to move!"

"Cheyenne!" Strong arms came around me, pinning mine to my sides. "Cheyenne, stop!" Warm breath puffed against my cheek, and I began to shake.

"He's alive...he's alive..." I choked. "He's alive."

"It's not real, sweetheart. It's not real."

I blinked, staring out in front of me. Colt was rising from the ground. He was okay. "He's alive, Callon. He's alive!" I cried.

"No, it's Koda. It's not Colt."

I blinked again, trying to clear my vision. Brogan and Dex were helping Koda stand, while Skylar and Clayton were nearby, blood running down their cut cheeks. Daniel appeared, his face showing an impending bruise below his left eye.

"It's okay, Chey. It's going to be okay," he said.

A hand brushed my arm. Lilly was there, her eyes misted with tears.

In the distance, I heard Andre's frantic cry.

"It's Maes!" She waved towards the forest. "He's hurt!"

Dex and Brogan took off, leaving Koda to stagger to a tree stump and sit down. His lip was bleeding.

What had I done?

I lowered my head, suddenly weak. Callon caught me, and lifted me into his chest. Warm blood began to flow down my cheek. What was happening to me?

"Callon, she's bleeding badly." Lilly's voice shook.

"I've got her, Lilly. Daniel, take Cheyenne back to the estate. Nakari, take me back and then help Dex with Maes."

I pressed my eyes closed as everything began to spin.

"I'm gonna help you, Chey," Daniel said, taking me from Callon. My body began to shake from the cold. "We're almost there."

Warmth suddenly surrounded me and gasps echoed at our arrival. We were in the sitting room.

"Layla, clear the dining room table," Callon ordered. "Bree, go get blankets and towels."

Footsteps rushed off in different directions, and I was laid onto the cold hard wood. It was difficult to breathe, and when I opened my eyes, I saw two of everything. I pressed them closed again.

"What do you need?" Daniel asked.

"Get my medical bag and then head to my office and get bandages and supplies," Callon replied. He began ripping the shredded clothes from my body.

"Is she going to be okay?" Bree asked as she dabbed my forehead.

"There's some sort of poison in her system, a venom. It's causing her to hallucinate."

"Is that what happened out there?" Bree asked.

"Yes."

Her breathing hitched. "Did anyone else get hurt?"

"Yes."

My heart sank. Once again, I'd caused those around me to get hurt. When was this nightmare ever going to end?

More voices rumbled in the sitting area and moved into the dining room.

"Have them sit there. Dex, I need your help."

"Koda!" Bree squealed.

"I'm fine," Koda said. "How is she?"

Hands began pressing against my wounds, but I was numb now. My thoughts scattered, and I felt myself slipping away into that dark abyss, but I wasn't scared. I had a piece of hope to hold onto. I had what I needed to make it another day, to survive this battle.

"Colt's alive," I whispered. "He's alive."

A damp cloth was pressed onto my forehead. The scent of fresh morning dew and wildflowers drifted in the air. My eyes fluttered open. In the dim lighting, I caught Layla's beautiful blue-green eyes. She smiled at me.

"You've been sleeping a long time, Cheyenne," she said. "How are you feeling?"

I tried to speak, but my throat was too dry. Coughing, I tried to sit up, but my head began to throb. Every muscle and joint seemed to contract at once, throwing me into a spasm. I cried out, and Layla pressed me back into the bed.

"Don't try and move right now," she said. "You've been through a lot, and your body still needs rest."

I nodded and caught my breath. I glanced around the empty room.

"Where's Callon?" I'd have thought he'd at least be here.

"I sent him, and the others, to rest. They didn't want to leave your side, but everyone was weary after what happened."

My brows creased as I tried to remember events, but only bits and pieces came forward. One image stuck out, giving me hope: Colt.

"Are they okay?"

She dabbed my forehead again. "They're going to be fine. They're more concerned about you than their own injuries."

I'd injured them...

"What did I do?" I looked away, not sure if I truly wanted to know.

"From what I can piece together, after your battle with the creature, it left behind a venom in your system. You weren't seeing things how they really were. Maes hit his head..."

Maes!

"Is he alright?" I grasped her hand. She squeezed my fingers.

"He's going to be fine."

"Going to be?"

She looked away and rewet her cloth. "Nothing to worry about, Cheyenne. He's had worse wounds in battles, I'm sure."

But this wasn't a battle. This was me out of control again. And she said I wasn't seeing things how they were. What did that mean? Colt wasn't alive? But it had felt so real. I'd felt Colt's presence. I still felt it now.

I rolled to my side and stared into the darkness outside my window. I wasn't as afraid of the night anymore, but the lack of light still brought me chills. A tear rolled down my cheek, and I brushed it away. As I did, something cold and metal caught my skin, and I glanced at my thumb. A thick silver ring with ornate carvings rested there. I ran my fingers over the red stones that ran in a perpendicular line to each other. The center stone was missing, but the rubies seemed oddly familiar.

I fumbled at my throat, my fingertips touching bare skin. My necklace was gone. I sat up, then winced as the pain shot to life.

"Cheyenne, lay down." Layla pressed her hands on my shoulders, but I pushed her off and stumbled towards the bathroom. "Cheyenne, please!"

My hands slipped from the bedding, and I tumbled towards the floor. Layla caught me.

"You're not strong enough yet."

"Just help me to the bathroom," I groaned.

Pulling my arm around her shoulder, she helped me stand.

"Callon said you weren't to get out of bed."

"I have to find something. Just help me."

We staggered towards the marble floor. I sat on the edge of the claw-footed tub, catching my breath. I looked down and realized I was a mess. Not only did I ache everywhere, but green and black bruises riddled my body. One open wound on my leg began oozing. Why hadn't it healed?

"Just tell me what you're looking for," Layla offered. "I'll find it."

I pointed towards the sink. "A red stoned necklace. I need it."

She moved away cautiously, keeping an eye on me while she searched.

"I don't see it."

I tried to stand, and promptly fell onto the white marble.

"Cheyenne!" Layla raced towards me. Another set of pounding footsteps approached outside. "Brogan, is that you? Help me!"

Moments later, Brogan appeared. He jerked me into his arms and whisked me off towards my bed.

My thigh began throbbing as Layla and Brogan began cleaning the wound. The room went spinning, and I pressed my eyes shut.

"Why'd you let her get up, Layla?" Brogan growled. "Callon said she was to stay in bed. I was only gone five minutes."

"Go get Callon," Layla snapped. Brogan frowned, but said nothing as he disappeared out the door. "It's going to be okay, Cheyenne. Take deep breaths."

I heard her words, but at the moment they meant nothing. The searing pain was growing, and I couldn't catch my breath.

"What's going on, Layla?" Callon stormed forward and pushed her aside.

"She got up..." Lilly trailed off.

"She wasn't supposed to move!"

"I know. She wouldn't listen to me..."

Callon sighed.

"Grab my bag on the table," he ordered.

The scenery around me began to change. The walls and curtains switched to sky and trees. I was back in the forest, but it wasn't in Idaho or Montana. It was here, near the lake. Rustling in the brush caught my attention, and I turned to see Colt emerging.

"Colt?" I called out. He looked towards me, smiling in relief. Tears welled in my eyes, and I lifted my hands as I ran towards him. "Colt! You're here, you're alive!"

"Cheyenne!" Callon bellowed. "Cheyenne!" A stinging sensation radiated over my cheek, and I blinked. "Breathe!"

I sucked in a breath and stared into hazel eyes, Callon's eyes. But I'd been in the forest with Colt. "Colt's alive," I whispered.

"No." He shook his head. "It's not real."

"I can feel him."

"No, sweetheart, it's the venom. It's making you think it's real. It's not." His hands grasped my cheeks, and I closed my eyes.

"Look at me, Cheyenne." He kissed my cheek. "Look at me. I'm real. I'm here now."

"But..."

"I know, but it's not the truth. Look at me," he whispered.

My heavy lids opened, and I saw the weariness he was holding back. He didn't believe me. I glanced about the room as it began to fill with the others. Their faces were sober, almost pitying. They didn't believe me, either.

"He's alive," I murmured.

"Shh, now, love. He's alive in all our hearts." Callon pressed in closer, his breath soothing against my ear. "Rest now."

A dark shadow neared. *Maes.* His presence seemed to clear the haze, and I fought back tiredness. Even in the dim lighting, I spotted the outline of a scar on his temple. Had I done that? He was also holding something in his hand. Wait...that was my necklace, the one he'd given me in Montana at Christmas!

"Maes!" I pulled the ring I'd found in the lake from my thumb. "The stones on the necklace, this ring has the same ones." My shaking hand lifted the ring. Before Maes took it from me, he stopped. His jade-rimmed eyes were wide. "Do you know what this is?"

Maes didn't answer. He just kept staring.

"Where did you get that?" he said at last.

"The creature in the lake had it," I said, blinking. "What is it? Is it related to the necklace you gave me?"

"It's the Quaysaar clan ring," Dex said. He slipped through the gathering, his hands clasped.

"Quaysaar?" I repeated.

"The cursed clan." Dex added.

"My clan," Maes broke in.

I frowned. "But I thought you were a Tresez?"

"Yes, but they weren't always trapped in that form, Cheyenne. The Quaysaar clan were amongst the most powerful of the Timeless," Dex replied. "And that ring is their long lost clan ring."

Callon grasped my fingers.

"Why don't you rest. We can talk about this later, Cheyenne."

"No!" I snapped. "I need to know this."

"But your head is clouded right now. You're hallucinating and..."

"I feel fine at the moment."

Callon sighed and nodded at Dex. I wasn't going to let this chance for information slip by.

"The Quaysaar were the first clan willing to serve the Sarac," Dex said. Maes listened, not daring to interrupt. "Your grandfather cursed them for this. Since they were considered cowards who ran away like dogs, he made them the Sarac's servants. Serving them on all fours."

"But the curse is weakening," I said. "Maes wouldn't be able to turn human otherwise."

"Yes, but unless the curse is lifted, they can never reclaim their place among the Timeless clans," Dex said. "Perhaps at one time they didn't want to. But the fact Maes is here with us, helping us protect you from Marcus, tells me that they don't want to be mere lapdogs anymore."

"So how do we break the curse?" I asked. I'd been stupid not to ask Dex about this before. Maybe now Maes would quit pestering me about it. "Does it have something to do with the ring?"

"I don't know, Cheyenne," Dex sighed. "I—I don't think your grandfather wanted it broken." Maes looked away. I couldn't read his expression. "I've pored over the old manuscripts for years now, studying for ways to defeat Marcus, and in all these years I've never come across anything related to the Quaysaar's curse. Except..."

"Except what?"

"That we are to be forgotten," Maes answered coldly.

Forgotten...

I stared at the ring again. The missing stone stuck out to me. Though it had given off some kind of light in the lake, now it felt ordinary. Not at all like my Kvech or Servak rings, or Callon or Marcus's rings, either. The lost piece must have something to do with the curse. Or was it really useless, and had no meaning at all? I had no idea. Then again, couldn't Maes use a ruby stone from the necklace and repair it? Would that give him the deliverance he was searching for?

Sighing, I stretched out my hand with the ring between my fingers. Whatever the answer, this ring wasn't mine. I'd find the solution later.

"Maes, take it. It's yours."

Maes frowned, though he couldn't hide the hope in his jade-rimmed eyes.

"It found you, *mon espoir*," he replied.

"And I'm giving it back to its rightful owner."

106

Maes hesitated. Then he stepped forward and knelt beside the bed. His hands swallowed my fingers as he squeezed. He'd come to a decision.

"This has been too long in coming," he said. "Unbroken curse or not, *mon espoir*, I pledge my life for yours. As fallen leader of the Quaysaar, I pledge my undying loyalty to the Servak and Kvech clans from which you descend, and to your family, all generations yet to come, from now and until I take my last breath."

He bowed over my hand, and I dropped the ring into his palm. A bright, blinding light flashed and suddenly I was thrown across the room. My back hit the wall and I slumped to the floor. Voices cried out, and I heard someone—Callon?—rushing to my side. He called my name, but everything was muffled by pain. Suddenly a jolt ran through my leg, and I arched my head back. The last thing I saw was Callon's worried look, before a black veil rolled over my eyes, and I passed out.

I sat on the soft chair in the sitting room, watching the gloomy skies drop their moisture from the clouds. I was growing tired of the Irish weather, and longed for the brilliant sunshine of home again. The wind began to howl, and the raindrops pattered against the terrace doors. I pulled my blanket closer and shivered. Fall was definitely here.

"Here, maybe this will help," Daniel said. He offered another chair and helped me sit in it, before pushing me closer to the fire. "You've had a rough few days."

I smiled faintly as he tucked the fleece around my legs.

"Thanks," I replied.

He wasn't wrong. Not only had the creature done a number on me, but something with Maes's ring had compounded it. The wound on my leg still hadn't healed, and I was full of new questions. I didn't know what had triggered the light, and I didn't know if anything had come of it. Callon had made it clear that no one was to talk about what happened. Once again, he was trying to protect me from something I needed to know. I needed to know if I'd broken the curse. I'd caught Maes a few times over the last couple of days, yet nothing seemed to have changed.

There was also the issue of *seeing* Colt. Callon had told me I'd been hallucinating, that the venom from the creature was doing this, but that wasn't it. If I was just hallucinating, then why did I *feel* Colt? I'd only ever felt like this when he was alive...

The clanking of a tray caught my attention. Lilly and Andre had appeared with mugs of steaming drinks. Andre moved the small table closer and Lilly placed the tray at my side.

"I've made you some of Layla's herbal tea," Lilly said. She smiled, carefully placing the mug in my hands. "Callon and Dex think they're closer to a solution for your wound, too." She sat in the chair beside me and grabbed a drink. "Layla and Nakari are working with them. They're both very good at herbal remedies." Her smiled broadened. "I've often told the two of them they could start their own beauty product line with their creations."

"More testing would need to be done first," Andre chuckled as she moved to the floor beside Lilly. "Remember when they turned my skin green?"

Daniel laughed, and Lilly waved her hand. "Oh, Andre, that was years ago."

"I still remember it." She grinned. "It took weeks before Koda stopped calling me Mrs. Frankenstein."

A soft laugh escaped me.

"I'm sure it would have been fun to see you like that," I said.

"Yeah, perfect for Halloween, Andre," Daniel chimed in.

Andre rolled her eyes. "I supposed I can't complain too much. It wasn't half as bad as what they did to Bree," she snorted.

"I heard that!" Bree whisked in from the hallway. "No more beauty products for me!"

I lifted a brow, now curious. "What'd they do to you, Bree?"

"She looked like a pumpkin!" Daniel chortled.

"It was artificial tan for carrots, alright!" Andre laughed.

"Worse," Bree giggled.

"Hey, what's with all the laughing?" Koda boomed. He entered the room, sitting on a footstool. His blue eyes had a twinkle to them. I looked down at my mug. He wasn't Colt.

"Just remembering the beauty trials of Layla and Nakari," Daniel replied. "I think Bailee was their last victim."

Koda's eyes dimmed, and Daniel suddenly stiffened.

"Oh, I—I'm sorry, Koda, Bree, I—I didn't mean..."

It grew quiet. Finally Koda sighed heavily.

"I know, Daniel. It's okay to have memories."

I sipped more of my tea, my heart burning. Memories, all the memories in the world couldn't replace the real thing...

"You feeling better, Cheyenne?" Koda broke my thoughts.

"I'll be fine. I just can't seem to get warm."

"I'm sure it'll get better soon."

I nodded, my thoughts drifting to Maes.

"So has Maes changed, Andre?" She glanced at Koda, unsure. "You can't hide this from me forever, and since he won't talk to me right now, I'd really like to know if giving him the ring made a difference."

"Nothing's changed, Cheyenne," Koda answered.

"Ah," I sighed. "I was hoping otherwise."

"We all were," Andre said.

"Is that why he's been avoiding me?"

"No, he's out on a mission," Koda replied.

"On a mission?"

Koda nodded, but didn't answer. My eyes narrowed.

"Seriously, we're going to play the game of keeping Cheyenne in the dark again?" I snapped.

"Callon doesn't want anything to upset you right now," Daniel chimed in.

"What's upsetting is that you all think I'm incapable of handling any situation!" I growled. "I'm the leader of the clans. I have the right to know what's going on."

"He's out looking for some plants for me," Callon answered. He and Dex entered the sitting room, Layla, Brogan and Nakari behind him.

"You sent him out alone?"

Callon shook his head, resting his hand on my blanketed shoulder.

"No, Skylar, Clayton and Quinn are with him. They've gone to find the last part of a remedy for your leg wound." I glanced at him, and the stress he'd been under flashed briefly, before he pushed it away. "I was the one who asked that nothing be said. You haven't been yourself. I'm sorry."

"Don't hide things from me, Callon."

"I'm just doing what I think is best."

"I know what's best for me, trust me."

"Of course you do," a low voice added.

I jumped; I hadn't expected Brogan to butt in. He stepped in front of the fire, forcing me to look up at him.

"You might have fought a decent battle, Cheyenne," he said, though his eyes told me otherwise. "But what you did was completely out of order. Stealing another's power and leaving them defenseless on the front line is selfish and unacceptable!"

My fingers grew tight around the mug's handle.

"I did what I needed to do to kill the creature." I exhaled slowly. The beast within stirred.

Brogan snarled.

"Acting like a spoiled child isn't doing what you need to do!" he roared. "If that had been an army of Trackers, or Marcus himself, would you have seized your comrades' power and leave them to be slaughtered for the sake of your revenge?"

"You weren't exactly putting that power to good use!" I shot back. "Someone had to."

Brogan clenched his fists, his veins bulging.

"Cheyenne, stop it," Callon said. "What Brogan's saying is that we needed to work together as a team..."

"The creature would have killed me if I hadn't found something else," I cut him off.

"We were right there with you!" Brogan boomed. "We told you to leave it to us."

I snorted.

"Oh yeah, so you can blame me for failing again? How can I prove myself and my power if you never let me be a part of anything?"

"We work together, not alone," Brogan growled.

Daniel grabbed my forearm. He could sense the beast waking up.

"We wouldn't have let you die, Cheyenne," he said.

My jaw tightened.

"Colt didn't get that chance," I said quietly. "I failed him. There has to be one stronger than the others to succeed."

"No, Cheyenne." Callon stepped closer. "Our strength becomes greater as we come together as one."

I blinked. Those words...I stared down at my mug. My dad had said those exact words to me many times, and only now did I realize what he'd been trying to teach me.

110

"Those words are your father's, Cheyenne. Qaysean's," Brogan said. "He knew to rely on his friends and not shoulder everything alone. A lesson you would do well to learn sooner rather than later!"

I fell silent, and the beast quieted, too. It had become so difficult to keep it under control...and it kept feeding my poor judgment. Of course Brogan was right. Going it alone was what had caused the whole mess. The fighting between Colt and Callon, breaking apart my family, and finally Colt's death; all because I'd wanted to do things myself. Was I going to repeat the past again and lose more people's lives?

"I'm such a fool," I whispered.

"You're no longer a fool if you learn from your mistakes."

I looked up. Maes entered the sitting room. He held up a cloth package, and Callon took it from him. His jade-rimmed eyes were solemn. "It's time for your healing to begin, Cheyenne."

CHAPTER 9

With each passing day, my strength returned. Whatever herbal concoction Callon, Dex and the two ladies had made for my wound was working. My spirit was growing stronger, too. I had something to hold onto, and I didn't care whether it was because of the creature's venom, as Callon claimed. I had hope, a new feeling deep down that Colt was still alive, and I wasn't going to let go of any trickle of light I could get my hands on.

Daniel landed just outside my bedroom door.

"You ready?" he asked. "I suppose so." I rubbed my leg before rising from the bed. Even though I'd come a long way, my thigh still ached.

"They're waiting in the field for us." He smiled, uncertain. "Are you sure you're up to this?"

I strode towards the door, grabbing a dark-colored jacket from the chair. "I'll be fine. It's just a flesh wound."

Daniel chuckled.

"Quoting Monty Python now are we?"

"Well, it's Colt's fault. He made me watch them."

Daniel's smile broadened. "Fond memories are good."

I nodded and placed my hand on his arm. "They are." Especially when I was now convinced he was still alive, somewhere.

We disappeared down the hall, stopping briefly at the top of the stairs. Callon walked through the main hall, pushing his way to the library. Lilly was at his heels.

"Callon." Lilly reached out and touched his shoulder. "Callon!"

Callon ignored her, shrugging off her hand.

"Callon, listen to me! I really don't think this is a good idea. Cheyenne's not fully..." The library door closed, and Daniel jumped us to the terrace. I sighed. I knew Lilly meant well, but I was sick of being locked up inside. It was time to move on and put a collar on this beast before it ran wild.

The cold air bit at my cheeks, and I zipped my jacket up. Dark clouds loomed overhead, and I could taste moisture in the air. It had been Brogan and Maes's idea to start some training, in a bid to get me to be more of a team player. Callon hadn't been too enthusiastic, yet he hadn't disagreed, either. Lilly had been the only one to voice her dissenting opinion, and I wasn't that surprised at her reaction. But she had to understand. I needed to learn to control the crimson-eyed demon. Anger was my trigger, and I had plenty of fuel for that. I had to practice keeping it within limits. That was easier said than done, though, as Marcus's face was never far from my thoughts.

The mere thought of his name made me clench my fist. He was going to pay so dearly for...

"Cheyenne?" Andre hesitated on the terrace stairs. I unclenched my fists. "I can feel it when you do that, you know."

I rolled my eyes. Great, just what I needed; Andre to be my anger detector. I forced a fake smile. "It's all good, Andre."

Her eyes narrowed slightly.

"Maes and Brogan are waiting for you out in the field."

I followed Andre and Daniel, still unsure what "training" they had planned for me. If it meant creating and throwing whirlwinds, then all would be good. I just had to remember not to let my anger feed the beast too much. The practicing I'd been doing would also pay off.

Almost all the clan members were out there, with the exception of Dex, Lilly and Callon. I was sure Callon would arrive soon. He wouldn't leave me to my own devices, not when I constantly got in trouble.

"Cheyenne." Brogan gestured for me to come stand beside him and Maes. I stood between them and faced the entire group, feeling like a mouse about to get pounced. They were both easily twice my height.

Brogan lifted a red strip of material and proceeded to tie it around my arm. I raised a brow. What was he up to?

"How are you feeling?" His brown eyes negated the kindness of his words. Even after killing the creature, I hadn't earned an ounce of respect from him.

"Fine," I replied.

"Good. Now I know how hard we can train."

"I figured as much," I muttered under my breath. I stared at the red material. "You had to tag me to remember who I am?"

Daniel snickered in the background.

"We're playing a version of Capture the Flag," Brogan said, clearly not amused by my little joke. "You know what that is, don't you?"

"Yes, you hide your flag from your enemy and they try and steal it away." I paused for a moment. "So I'm the flag? This doesn't make sense. You want me to hide?"

A very sly smile rose on Brogan's lips. "You're the flag, and we're going to come find you."

Oh, I understood. It was a game of maneuvers, tactics, except they wouldn't be after a piece of material. They'd be after a moving target, me.

"So who's on my team?"

"You're on your own."

"Wait, what? That doesn't seem fair." I glanced around the circle of clan members. "All of you against me?"

"You seemed quite happy to fight the lake creature alone," Brogan said. "Why the problem now?"

I clenched my teeth. That sneaky...

"Brogan, you're being a little harsh here." Callon strode into the field. "Fourteen against one is excessively unbalanced. Give her a few teammates."

I mouthed a *thank you* to Callon, knowing that I'd have gotten nowhere with Brogan. He must've been really upset that I borrowed his powers.

Brogan growled from the back of his throat. He wasn't happy, but even he couldn't talk back to the clan regent. "Fine." He paused, eying the group. "You get Nakari and Maes."

Nakari looked pleadingly at Callon, as if she'd been asked to clean the toilets. I frowned. Why didn't she want to be on my team, and why did she constantly look to Callon for approval? Jealousy surfaced, rekindling my anger. Wasn't I good enough? Or was she afraid I'd steal her powers again?

"I'll be on Cheyenne's team," Andre said. She stepped forward and gave Nakari a quick glance.

"No," Brogan replied, "I've already made the choice."

I looked across at Maes. He seemed pretty indifferent to the whole thing. "So now what?"

"Try not to get caught." Brogan looked very pleased with himself. I got the feeling he was going to enjoy this.

"So I can use my powers?"

"Limited use of powers, Cheyenne," Callon admonished.

I rolled my eyes. "I won't purposely try to hurt anyone."

"It's not the purposely I'm worried about," Callon said quietly to me, though I know the others heard him.

I ignored his comment and instead stared at the forest. Fall had arrived, though since the weather was still much the same, I hadn't really noticed. The leaves formed a mix of colors, from mustard yellow and crimson to burnt orange and gold. At least with my dark clothes and the cloudy skies, I could blend in better. Except for this red band on my arm.

"So what about everyone else then? Do they get to use their full powers?" I asked, still trying to establish the rules.

No answer came. I was the only one limited.

I blew out a breath. "So what are the boundaries, and how will I know when the game is over and I've won?"

"The boundaries are the enchantment barriers, and we'll play till dark. If you haven't been captured by nightfall, then you've won this round."

"And I just return to the terrace?"

"Yes."

"Sounds easy enough, but how will I know where the enchantment barriers are?"

Brogan scoffed. "You'll know."

"How long do I have before you come after me?"

"I'll give you fifteen minutes."

Nodding, I began walking towards the lake. That wasn't going to be enough time to find decent cover without use of my powers.

"This is serious training, Cheyenne," Brogan called out. "We won't hold anything back."

"Got it." I waved my hand in the air as Maes fell into step beside me, his hands in his pockets.

"Any ideas?" I asked. At least I had him to help out.

115

"That is not for me to say, *mon espoir*. I'm already well-equipped for battle."

"So your role is to sit back and watch?" I asked petulantly.

"My role is to make sure you don't kill anyone."

I sighed. Just what I needed, zero trust again.

"What about teamwork? I thought that's what we'd just discussed."

"This is purely tactical."

I stopped.

"Why? So Brogan can watch me hide like a rodent? Is this how he wants me to face Marcus?"

"No, it's to gauge your natural abilities so we can build on them."

Nakari suddenly appeared, looking annoyed. I glanced ahead. We still had a little way to go before the forest, and it had already been five minutes.

"Care to give me a lift, Nakari?" I asked.

"And let you steal my powers again? No thanks," she replied, her voice as cold as ice. Obviously she was still upset about that, not that I didn't deserve it.

Frowning, I decided to rely on my own skills and sprinted towards the forest. Maes ran beside me in his Tresez form, and Nakari jumped, always landing a few yards ahead of us. First and foremost, my priority was to find high ground. I needed to see where my enemies were coming from, as it was obvious I wasn't going to get any help from my teammates.

As I entered the trees, I veered to the left, away from the lake. The patter of feet behind me soon disappeared and Nakari and Maes vanished into the leaves. I stopped to catch my breath.

Cowards.

The crackling of branches brought me back to the task at hand. I glanced around, and spotted Koda emerging from between two birches.

"Dang, Cheyenne," Koda chuckled, flexing his fists, "you were supposed to make this a challenge."

Crap! My hands flew out before I had a chance to think and I shot a blast of air in Koda's direction. Koda went flying into a tree, cracking it, and he tumbled to the ground. I didn't have time to apologize before I took off through the forest again. This time I wouldn't make stupid mistakes.

Patches of dense brush slowed me down as I climbed a ravine. My wounded leg was throbbing, and I tried not to push it too much. I continued running uphill for another hour, alert for movement. So far, there hadn't been any more signs of the enemy, nor my so-called teammates. Still, every crackle and movement of the wind had me on edge. At the top, I stopped and stared up at the blackening sky. It wouldn't be long now till the rain started, and then the real fun would begin.

"Gotcha!" Daniel cried, suddenly appearing out of nowhere. On instinct I dove, but my footing slipped and I fell, branches scratching my cheeks. I didn't wait for Daniel to grab me. Instead I rolled to my side, burying myself further in the orange and brown brush. Then I bolted to my feet and ran into the trees. Daniel appeared in front of me, ready to catch me, so I changed direction. He jumped again, and his hand skimmed the fabric on my arm. Before he could rip it off and escape, I touched his knuckles, the icy cold feeling of his powers trailing up my fingers.

"Thanks!" I called, then jumped into the forest.

This was more like it; I could move much faster and cover more distance, though I wouldn't be able to rely on this later. Daniel would know not to come too close again, so I wouldn't get a second chance to steal his powers, either. Maybe I'd been too hasty...

"There she is!"

I gulped. That was Brogan's voice. I searched around the branches, trying to pinpoint his location, when suddenly half a tree hit the ground in front of me. I squealed, jumping out the way. The tree lifted itself, and my eyes widened as Brogan hauled the trunk upright and aimed for me again.

"Hey!" I ducked under, sliding in the dirt. "That's not fair!"

"Life isn't fair sometimes, Cheyenne!" Brogan roared, swinging the tree like a club. It hit the ground once more, causing a minor quake. I stumbled, catching myself on my hands. Was he crazy?!

"The game is capture the flag, not kill it!" I barked.

Knowing I couldn't hope to match his strength, I headed into trees on the right again. He came after me, but he couldn't drag his trunk through the narrow spaces. Eventually I felt I was far enough away, and I stopped to catch my breath. I inhaled slowly, despite the fact my lungs burned for air. I couldn't afford to be heard.

Quiet footsteps approached, and I crouched behind a tree stump.

If I could find out which direction they were coming from, I could jump to safety before Daniel's power wore off. I only had a couple of minutes left.

A dark brown jacket flashed briefly through the branches, along with wild hair.

"She's quick," Skylar observed, glancing around. "You shouldn't have let her take your power, Daniel."

"Don't be boring, Skylar," Daniel chuckled. "You'd be surprised how creative Cheyenne can get."

I heard Skyler laugh, and their voices grew distant again. They'd walked right past me. I kept perfectly still, straining to hear any signs of further movements. Five minutes slipped by, then ten. It seemed the others didn't want to continue the chase.

The silence loomed, and I rested against the tree stump. My mind began to swirl, running through the events that had brought me to this point. So much had happened, so much death, despair, grief and anger. Everything had changed; I wasn't the same person anymore. I was no longer the sweet innocent girl Colt had fallen in love with. My heart had too many cracks, and too much of the crimson-eyed beast had poured out. My powers made me strong, and I loved the feeling and purpose they gave me. I'd thrown Koda aside easily, and hadn't felt any remorse over it. I couldn't help but wonder, would Colt still love me the way I was today?

I drew my arms around myself. *Colt, my Colt.* Callon had told me I'd been having hallucinations, but I knew better. This feeling ran deeper, a connection I'd always taken for granted until I'd thought it was gone. It was too real to be a delusion.

Or was it? Was I only feeling his presence now because I'd been too wrapped up in my grief to notice? Was he calling out to me? Or was I completely losing my mind?

I shook my head. Perhaps I was still dreaming. Too afraid to let go of Colt's memory and be with Callon. I'd hardly gotten to spend any time with Callon since the clan members had gathered, not that it wasn't partially my own doing. I'd been the one to back off from the responsibilities. It was ironic, however. In the past he'd always been at my side, so in my face that I'd longed for some space. Yet now, a brief glance here and there was all I could hope for. I shouldn't have taken my time with him for granted.

A rustle caught my attention, and I began walking. I couldn't afford to remain in the same place for too long. My thoughts continued, mulling over what was to come. My days would be spent like this now, planning and strategizing, as Callon and the others trained me to become the weapon to defeat Marcus. Any tender moments would be few and far between. Maybe that was where the jealousy came from when I caught Nakari staring at Callon. That had to be the source, since he'd told me they'd been friends a long time and I had nothing to be threatened by. Although the jealousy could have come from how all the other clan members treated her. They adored her and feared me. Even Lilly had a close relationship with her, and I felt like I'd been left out in the cold. However, once again that had probably been my fault. I was the one pushing everyone away to protect my heart.

But then again, sometimes friends turned into something else...

The soft patter of water droplets hitting my nose broke my thoughts. The rain had started. I couldn't wander around daydreaming. I needed to keep moving, play them at their own game and prove I was capable of holding my own.

I tried to slip through a pair of narrow trunks when the red material on my arm got caught on a branch. I yanked hard, tearing a chunk off. Great! I twisted around and untied the cloth, before securing it around my neck. Brogan hadn't said I couldn't move it. Besides that would make it harder for them to see it too.

I headed back to the ravine again, stopping just at the top. It did provide the best view, after all. The forest had fallen quiet for some time now; they had to be planning something. I scanned the forest, but with the clouds, rain and dense brush, the visibility had grown limited. A large pine stood a few feet away, and I stared at it. I could climb it, but was it worth all the sap and sharp needles? Chances were it wouldn't improve anything. The best thing I could do was keep a low profile till nightfall came.

"You can't just hide, Cheyenne," Maes rumbled behind me.

My hand flew to my mouth, stopping my scream.

"Maes!" I snarled. "You just can't sneak up on somebody like that!"

I took a few deep breaths, trying to calm my racing heart. It was like the dog could read my mind at times.

"It's a game of tactics. You need to outsmart them and get back to the terrace without being captured." He crossed his arms over his chest, and a chunk of wet black hair fell over his eye.

"Don't you have to stalk Andre or something?"

"You're far too predictable," Maes scoffed. "They're all waiting at the bottom of the hill. You've just trapped yourself."

"Who's at the bottom of the hill?"

"Koda, Daniel, Skylar, Clayton and Andre. The rest will be coming up from the north side to cut off your escape. But you've still got one way out."

"Really?" I frowned. "Why are you helping me now?"

"I've been helping you all along, *mon espoir*. You just haven't seen me." He tilted his head. "Nice touch with the flag. It's still visible, but at least now it doesn't scream 'here I am.'"

I rolled my eyes.

He stuck out his hand. A chunk of red material sat in his palm. "You left this behind. You shouldn't make it so obvious."

I snatched the fabric back and shoved it in my pocket. When I looked up, he was gone.

"Men," I muttered and began heading south, or at least what I thought was south. I had no sun, moon or stars to gauge my direction, but I knew night would soon fall and then I could head back and declare myself the winner.

I kept to higher ground, so at least I'd spot them first. The drizzle continued, and I pulled my coat tighter around me. Little good it did. The braid Lilly had helped me with this morning was nothing more than a sponge, allowing the water to run down my back. A hot bath would really hit the...

I stopped. The scenery had suddenly changed. The forest had thinned, and a narrow path leading to a small stone bridge had appeared.

Brushing my loose hair back, I slid down the wet embankment and onto the leaf-covered path. Since the others were so keen to ambush me, I could let them wait a while longer. This was my one chance to explore the estate without everyone wondering where I'd run off to.

My fingers trailed over the moss-covered rail as I crossed the bridge. A small meadow filled with low stonewalls and gates told me they'd been neglected over the years. Callon and his family must have used them for livestock years ago. Would he have run through this meadow as a child? Would he or Colt have played here? I'd have to ask Callon to tell me about it. There was so much I didn't know about him, so much I'd pushed away.

I continued past the meadow and found myself at the foot of a round path. The trees, brush and ivy had grown thick, and only a tiny space in the middle was left open to pass through. I smiled and couldn't help but think of Alice in Wonderland. What lay in wait on the other side of this rabbit hole?

As I passed through the narrow opening, my eyes widened. I'd found an ivy-clad cottage straight from a storybook. Almost every peak and ridge was covered in a blanket of green, and only a small portion of the roof remained visible. Even the white-washed windows were smothered with it. A brightly colored yellow door drew me in, inviting me to stay for a while.

A sneeze captured my attention, and I scrambled to the side of the cottage. Low voices were murmuring. Ah, maybe they'd guessed I'd come this far and were lying in wait for me to step inside. Quietly I slid closer to the voices. Only Daniel could have reached this place without me noticing. He was probably waiting behind the building to capture me. Well, that wasn't going to happen. If I caught him first, then he'd be my prisoner, and the tables would turn. I could force him to help me.

I stopped at the edge of the stone and listened, trying to determine his location and who was with him. The voices echoed off the cottage and forest just behind. A dilapidated low-lying wood fence lay ahead of me. I got down on all fours and began to crawl, inching myself closer to the sounds. When I came to the edge, I peeked through the open slots. It wasn't Daniel at all.

It was Callon and Nakari.

That little traitor!

My fists clenched. I knew she wasn't fond of me, but she was supposed to be my teammate. She wasn't supposed to help the enemy. We were meant to work together...wait, unless she'd been captured. But that didn't make sense. She could jump like Daniel. There was no way she would allow herself to be caught. Besides, they were after me, not her.

I watched them converse, the stones muffling the words. What were they talking about? Callon moved to a tree, leaning his back against it while staring out into the forest. He had that far-away look in his eyes, the same one he had when something bothered him.

What was he thinking about so hard? I inched closer, trying to capture their words on the wind.

Nakari bent her head. Her wet auburn hair fell into her face. She looked hurt; her fingers rose and latched onto her necklace. The necklace that held her ring. My heart burned. Why did so many of us have to suffer? So much loss among us, so much pain and misery.

Callon took a step forward. He spoke too softly for me to pick out what he was saying, but his tone said it all. He was comforting her, just like he'd comforted me. He lifted her chin and brushed the hair from her eyes. Her fingers wrapped around his wrist. Tears streamed down Nakari's cheeks, and she closed her eyes. She pushed Callon's hand over her chest, over the ring.

"I know you feel it, Callon," Nakari said loud enough for me to hear now. "It's never gone away. I can see it in your eyes when you look at me."

"Nakari, please." Callon shook his head.

"There are still feelings there for me, I know it." She pressed both her hands over his.

Callon turned away, hesitating.

"Let me prove it to you, then. Let me show you how much I still care about you."

My throat grew tight. My chest contracted as if a heavy weight had pressed down. I watched her lean in, her lips parting. I slumped to the ground, shaking as waves of hurt rolled over, threatening to drown me.

Callon...how could he? Callon who said he loved me, who said his heart belonged to me...he was a complete liar! Every word he'd ever said—every touch, every kiss—it meant nothing! I was just a pawn in his game to win the grand prize!

Without a second thought, I ran for the forest, not caring where I was heading. Anywhere away from them.

"Cheyenne!" Callon yelled, and I ran even harder.

Flashes of blue appeared, and I caught sight of Nakari's coat.

I wanted to scream, to create a whirlwind so grand I'd rip every tree from its roots and split them in half like my heart. I wanted tens of thousands of splinters to fly through the air, to show Callon what he'd done to me.

Suddenly a pair of arms came around me, and I was forced to the wet cold earth. I gasped, trying to catch my breath, when I was thrown to my back and my hands were pinned above my head. I stared up into hazel eyes.

"Cheyenne," Callon commanded, "don't run away from me!"

The crimson-eyed beast roared as I brought my fingers together. I narrowed my eyes, allowing the power to build in my chest.

"Get off me," I said between clenched teeth.

"No! You need to listen to me..."

The beast burst forth, and Callon was thrown to the side. The wind began to howl, building and building around me.

"Cheyenne, stop!" Nakari cried. She jumped to Callon's side. Go ahead and run to him, Nakari—have him! No more! I conjured up more air, watching the trees bend almost to their breaking point. She'd provoked this. She could deal with the consequences!

Suddenly something struck me in the side, and the wind escaped my fingertips. I hit the ground with a gasp, mud splashing into my face. I tried to move, but found a massive paw on my chest. Maes had pounced, breaking my concentration. His jade-rimmed eyes were hard. Slowly he backed off, returning to his human form. I stood, shaking, while Nakari helped Callon to his feet.

Tears poured down my cheeks. What had I ever done to be forced to endure such heartache and pain? I'd never asked for any of this! All I'd ever wanted was to live a normal life, and be with the one I loved. Not to constantly be angry and want to destroy.

"Cheyenne!" Maes growled. "What the..."

His words were cut short as I raced past. I couldn't stay here. Callon was right; I was still out of control. I turned back to see if he was following when a bolt of electricity shot from thin air. It tore through my limbs, and I was thrown back. I collided with Maes's chest, and we tumbled down a small ravine, landing in a creek. My cheek lay in a pile of cold mud, and Maes lifted his head. A groan escaped his lips.

"You found the enchantment."

My head spinning, I looked up. Flickering iridescent lights were gliding across the ridge, like fireflies.

Footsteps neared, and I caught familiar breathing. Callon had come.

"Cheyenne, please, just *listen!* I can explain..."

I didn't wait for him to finish. I brushed Maes's hand, seizing his power. A moment later, I shifted, becoming a Tresez. Almost at once, my head felt like it was going to explode.

"No!" Maes shouted.

I stumbled to my feet, the forest whirling before me. Patches of gray, black and red drifted past. It looked like another world. I opened my mouth to speak, but only a low whine came forth. Bile rose in my throat, and my legs gave out. My head hit the ground, and I began panting.

"Shift back, now!" Maes pulled my head up. "You shouldn't have done that!"

A red aura glowed around his chest, while the rest of his body was shrouded in dark shadows. I turned to see Nakari and Callon had the same aura. Maes had heat vision.

My panting slowed as the dizziness subsided. Power, raw unleashed power, trickled through my veins. It was different than what the crimson-eyed beast provided. This was pure animal strength, mightier than even Brogan's.

I leapt to my feet, releasing a roar, and focused on Callon. He pushed Nakari behind him, and I opened my jaws. There'd be no summoning of the wind, only razor sharp teeth to leave a lasting impression.

Maes stormed in front of Callon. Pure rage radiated as his aura grew brighter.

"If you don't change back now, I won't hold back," he threatened. I blinked. I'd never seen him so mad before, not even when I'd been moping around in the manor. I'd pushed him too far, but no farther than they'd pushed me.

I took a step back, my legs tightening, allowing me to spring forward. I cleared their heads and sprinted into the dense trees. Running was the safest option right now. If I didn't leave, I'd do something I'd regret. I needed to control this rage.

My new instincts filled every pore, and I let them lead me back to the estate. Nightfall was coming. I didn't have to play this stupid game anymore, didn't have to deal with Callon's lies. Besides, I'd proven myself worthy. I'd evaded them all, and hadn't let the beast get the better of me. It had been close, though. I still had a way to go.

Of course there would still be payment for Callon's actions, but it would come from me, not the beast.

124

I jerked to a stop. A powerful scent had reached my nostrils. It was familiar. I lowered my head, following the trail. So this is what it was like to be Maes. The slightest change in the air, and I could taste the difference on my tongue.

My ears perked up. Rustling in the bush ahead caught my attention. I crept closer, watching for any sign of life. Something prickled across my back; my old Tresez nail wound.

Oh no!

Suddenly a small red glow began to emerge. A tiny drumbeat echoed in my ear. No, not a drumbeat, a heartbeat. I slid closer to investigate, when a black rabbit bolted from the brush and took off into the forest. So that's what rabbit smelled like to a dog...

Be careful, you fool!

I snapped my head around. Who said that?

I caught a scent mixed with hers. She's not alone.

Huh? Who was talking? Where were they? I crouched lower, my eyes searching the forest shadows. My nostrils flared. It was the previous scent again. Not rabbit.

Circle to the right. We have the advantage in the dark. Conall will have our heads if we come back empty handed.

Either way we're doomed. If we meet up with Maes...

Tresez! I had to warn the others! Wait...*I* was a Tresez! I had Maes's strength. I could dispose of these dogs myself.

If you want me, come and get me! I screamed in my thoughts.

Glowing eyes met mine, and I felt the hair rise on the back of my neck. A low rumble grew from within as I began circling the filth in front of me.

Maes?

I leapt, landing on its back and sinking my teeth into its thick fur. A moan rumbled against my lips as the creature began snarling. I shook my head, the smaller Tresez flopping around like a rag doll until I lost my hold and it broke free.

I was hit from the side, causing me to stumble when I caught sight of more glowing eyes moving through the forest. There were more than just two. I began moving back. I could take on one or two, but an army?

Well, what do we have here? Maes out on a patrol? one growled.

My heart began racing as the monstrous Tresez neared. It was almost the same size as Maes...wait, of me now. I had Maes's

125

strength, but not his skills. The one before me was a seasoned warrior; I'd only be able to fight him with *my* powers.

Fangs nipped my hind leg, forcing me to change direction. They were creating a circle, entrapping me.

What? Cat got your tongue, Maes?

He was waiting for a reply. If I said anything, he'd know it wasn't Maes.

He went on, *What's that you say? Cheyenne's got your tongue now because you only answer to her, traitor?*

It moved closer, its nose in the air.

She's never going to free you. The curse can't be broken. All you've done is waste your time believing in fairy tales that will never come true. A snarl escaped him and white fangs flashed. *Besides, Marcus only wants her powers. He'll dispose of her after he takes them.*

Fangs sunk into my neck, and a yelp escaped me. I turned and snapped at the attacker. Another bit at my front leg while yet another got a hold of my tail. Crouching, I attempted to leap free, but was quickly knocked down by the large one.

Snapping jaws were everywhere as I was pinned to the ground. There were too many!

What's this? The great and mighty Maes giving up so easily?

"If you want a fight, pick on someone your own size, Conall!" Maes boomed.

Instantly the heads turned, and I bolted free.

"Run, Cheyenne, run!" Andre screamed.

Ear-piercing howls broke through the air. I didn't wait for an encore and ran through the forest. I just needed to get clear so I could shift into my human form. I needed to fight them with powers I knew how to use!

I see you, and I'm coming for you, little one.

I slipped on the wet earth, and landed hard on my side. I regained my footing quickly, but not before teeth sunk into my shoulder, and I was thrown through the air. I rolled to my side quickly, as yet another Tresez appeared. This one looked different, though. One of his front paws and a narrow strip extending from his eye to his snout were pure white, sticking out against his black fur.

Hello, Cheyenne. I don't believe we've met before. My name is Conall.

He began stalking me. Pain radiated across my shoulder blade.

126

But I had no time to waste. This was my chance to shift. I closed my eyes and thought about shifting to my human form, but nothing happened. Maes had made it look so effortless!

Your time is running out, little one. Marcus is waiting for you.

The name sent white-hot flames through me. *Marcus...*

I charged at Conall, taking him by surprise. I leapt and knocked him from his feet. With lightning speed, I spun around and dung my fangs in deep between his shoulder blades. A deep rumble came from his chest as he suddenly rose up on his hind legs and smashed me into a tree.

Instant pain rippled up my spine, and I collapsed in a heap. His hot breath poured over my face.

You're not strong enough. You're weak, just like your mother.

The crimson-eyed beast flared, flowing out through every pore. I rose, howling, as Conall backed away. My lips exposed the razor sharp fangs I was about to tear him apart with. I ran full speed when an explosion ripped through my body.

"No!" The words formed on my lips as I fell—human—face first onto the wet earth. My time was up.

Fangs latched onto my arm, and I was jerked to the right. My left shoulder made contact with a tree, and I screeched. A low rumble started from the back of his throat. It sounded like a hyena's laugh. He was laughing at me!

I crawled to my feet, cradling my arm. I blinked, trying to clear the fogginess. The flash of a blue coat caught my eye. Nakari! She'd come to help after all. But while she did glance my way, a second later she was gone. My eyes scanned the forest, but she'd left me once again. Abandoned me like everyone else.

Conall shifted. He had a chiseled face, flecked with multiple scars, one running from his eye to his nose...just like the white streak when he was a Tresez. His lank hair dangled over his shoulders, and he wore a set of dog tags. His loud laughter filled the air. "Looks like you're on your own there, little one. No one to swoop in and rescue you!"

I stood my ground, sliding my fingers closer to my wrist. It was going to be difficult using my left arm, but if I hit him just right I could do it.

"I don't need anyone to rescue me."

He laughed louder. "You're a pathetic child. They've taught you nothing here, and I've come to bring you to your proper home."

"Ha!" I began circling him. "You said Marcus was going to take my powers and dispose of me."

The dark figure followed me closely.

"All everyone wants me for is a weapon," I went on. "Why don't you fight your own battles, you coward?"

Conall snarled, and lunged for me. I pushed my hands out, hitting his chest with a surge of power. A howl erupted, but not before he latched his hands around my wrists. We both flew through the air and smacked into the forest floor.

I sucked in a breath, fighting back the pain, and squirmed to get away. Conall yanked me to my feet. His face was inches from mine as he pinned me to a tree. The battle wounds scarred his face, and his black hair was filled with mud and leaves, making him look wild and dangerous.

"Did you think I didn't know about your little tricks?" He released my wrist only to grab my throat. "Did you think I came totally unprepared?"

He pulled me away from the tree only to smash me into it again. I lost my breath. I wasn't going to last much longer. His grip grew tighter, and I clawed at his arm.

"I have orders, foolish girl, and you're coming with me."

My knee flew into his ribs, but it had little effect. My air supply was running short, and his hold was only getting stronger.

"If you kill me," I whispered, "then all is lost."

A wicked grin grew. "I'm not going to kill you. I'm just waiting till you pass out."

Dark patches floated before my eyes. It wouldn't be long now, and I'd have failed at yet another task. My whole life had been riddled with failures, defeats, and utter despair. Why would anything change now?

I grew still, my eyes rolling to the back of my head when total weightlessness took over. It was as if I was floating.

A deafening roar burned my ears, and my eyes shot open. Maes was in his Tresez form and was now looming over Conall. I lay there still for a few moments, listening to the battle. Once again, someone was fighting for me, once again I hadn't held my own. All this power, and all I could do with it was hurt those closest to me...

Strength welled up inside me. No, I wasn't going to sit here and watch! I was going to fight, and I was going to defeat Conall! I wasn't the weak link!

Maes turned and roared as he saw me approach. Conall's gold-rimmed eyes locked on me. Sheer will and determination drove me on, and I lifted my hands above my head, creating a whirlwind. Trees began cracking, and their splinters mixed in the air. I just had to get close enough to Conall and get Maes out of the way.

As if Maes heard my thoughts, he suddenly dove to the left. Like a conductor, I scooped my hands, ripping a tree from its roots, before firing it like a torpedo at Conall. It grazed his side. He turned and began trailing me. I ripped another out and sent the missile towards him. Without warning, he leapt over it and knocked me to the ground. His teeth sunk hard into my shoulder, but not before one last tree found its mark, smashing straight into his face.

Cracking ribs and a wild howl shook my ears, before I watched Conall and Maes run off into the blackness. I rolled to my side, barely able to catch my breath. White-hot pain rippled down my side, the smell of blood and saliva mixing.

How had the Tresez gotten through the enchantment? Andre said they couldn't, unless someone let them in...

Nakari.

She'd left me several times. It was obvious she didn't care for me, but would she go as far as that? She wanted to prove her love to Callon, but was she capable of killing me?

Lightning lit up the night sky, and soon thunder echoed. The rainfall increased. I rolled to my belly and sat on my back legs.

"Colt," I whispered, "I need you." My tears mixed with the rain. I needed his strength, his love...I needed something to hold on to, to get me through this.

Squelching footsteps warned me someone was near, but I didn't move. My head hung low. I couldn't deal with Callon right now.

"Chey, it's me, Koda."

I didn't reply.

"Are you okay?"

I inhaled a shaky breath. I wasn't okay. I'd never be okay. I just had to survive.

I closed my eyes as he kneeled beside me, an arm coming around my shoulder. I tried to push him away.

"It's okay. You're okay now."

129

I fell into his chest as his arms cradled me. I didn't want to accept his help, but I didn't have any strength left. I just needed to be told everything was going to be okay, that I had friends who'd support me. I needed to know I could make it through another day. I needed to know I wasn't alone.

CHAPTER 10

Koda helped me return to the estate, carrying me after I finally collapsed from exhaustion. He'd also stayed while Dex and Lilly tended to my injuries. It wasn't the first, nor would it be the last time I'd take a beating from a Tresez. The evidence from the attack was clear. My neck was changing from black to a greenish blue with streaks of red from broken blood vessels. Also, just about every muscle ached, but I'd been fortunate this time around, as my jacket had prevented any deep wounds.

My mind kept wandering over recent events, mostly what I'd seen Callon and Nakari do—they'd kissed. Betrayal, broken promises...all the words in the world couldn't describe how I'd felt seeing her lean forward. He'd told me they were friends, that I had nothing to worry about, but obviously I was just being lulled into a false sense of security.

But worse than that, what I'd done was wrong. I'd stolen Maes's power out of rage, with the intent to harm Nakari. If Maes hadn't stepped forward...I shook my head, trying to erase the memory.

I'd also put every one of our clan members at risk, all because I couldn't control myself. I couldn't keep doing this anymore. I couldn't become this *ugly monster* the beast wanted. I was heading down the wrong path, and I knew it. Maes had warned me it would be dark and dangerous, that I wouldn't be able to crawl back out of this hellish pit unless I realized my mistakes. I had to change. I hated what I was becoming. And worst of all, Colt would've hated what I was becoming.

The fire snapped as I watched the sun rise from the sitting room. No one had returned yet, and it was probably for the best. I was positive they were hunting Tresezes; chances were that more than just the five had entered. I'd purposely kept my back to the terrace doors. I didn't want to see Callon's face yet, or anyone else's disappointment.

Dex clicked a small lamp on and pushed a chair closer as Lilly and Koda moved in around me. Whatever was on their minds was sure to be on mine soon enough. I pulled my legs in closer and curled the blanket around me tightly. I was sure I wasn't going to like it.

"We need to talk about what happened, Cheyenne," Koda said. "What happened with Nakari and Callon."

I stared down at my blanket. Great, not that I didn't expect them to find out, but so soon?

"Callon told me," Koda added.

Lilly reached out to touch my hand, but I pulled it away. Hurt flashed through her eyes, and I stilled. I was doing it again, pulling away and retreating into my dark hole. I pushed the blanket down and grasped her hand.

"I'm sorry, Lilly."

She nodded and blinked away the moisture.

"What you saw and what happened were two different things." Koda lowered his head, trying to catch my eyes.

"I saw pretty clearly what took place, Koda. Callon and Nakari kissed." My throat tightened. I was calm now, but for how much longer?

"Callon would never betray you like that, Cheyenne." Lilly squeezed my hand. "He loves you very much."

"He kissed her." My jaw clenched.

"You ran away before he could explain what happened." Dex moved closer. "You've got such a temper, sweetheart. Sometimes it blocks you from hearing what needs to be said."

"I've only gotten a temper since all these responsibilities, this weight that's been thrust upon my shoulders!" I snapped.

"Do you think the rest of us don't have responsibilities or weight thrust upon us?" Koda replied. "Do you see us acting out against everyone that wants to help?"

"Cheyenne, we know you're stronger than this," Lilly said. "You're allowing your emotions to control you…"

I cut Lilly off. "Emotions are all I have left to feel alive."

"You have the love and warmth from your family, from all of us here, if you'd just open up and let us in."

Tears grew in my eyes. "If I open myself up and lose another person I love, I won't be able to make it."

"So this is what it's all about? Fear of losing us?" Dex's voice sombered. "What I think you need to realize, Cheyenne, is that our fear of losing you is greater."

I looked up into his warm brown eyes.

"You're here with us, but we feel like we're losing you and can't stop it. Do you know what it's like to sit and watch another person destroy themselves, and feel utterly helpless to stop them? We've all had enough loss in our lifetimes to fill the largest of canyons, and there will be more, but what we have to do is move on for the sake of all the Timeless yet to come. We can't allow Marcus to defeat us outside of battle. We must have inner strength as well if we're to overcome."

"But how?" I whispered, near tears.

"We have to work together, rely on each other for strength when we need it most," Lilly said.

"The strength of a family," I barely uttered.

"The strength of *your* family," Koda added. "You've got a large one right here ready and waiting."

I'd been such a fool. I needed to make good use of the resources around me, starting right now. I pushed the blanket away and leaned into Dex and Lilly's open arms.

Warmth, real warmth, filled me for the first time since Colt's death. They loved me, cared enough to help me realize my mistakes without condemning me for them.

"We love you like our own daughter," Dex said.

Lilly kissed my head.

"I love you too," I breathed and knew I truly meant it. I'd held back too long my words of love. To them, others and another…

"Cheyenne." Callon's gravely voice sent goosebumps down my spine. Dex and Lilly drew back, and I stood.

Dark circles etched Callon's eyes, his face was scratched, and his wet hair was coated in mud and leaves. His wet clothes clung to his frame and his hazel eyes held a mixture of sadness and exhaustion.

He'd come straight to find me without getting cleaned up. He reached out to grasp my hands, and I flinched at the icy coldness.

"We need to talk. What you saw, what you thought, isn't what happened."

I remained completely still. I didn't want to give in to my anger, yet I had to give him the chance to explain. I owed him that much.

"Nakari was upset, and yes, I tried to console her. She's just as lonely and heartbroken as the rest of us and made a mistake. A mistake that shouldn't be held against her."

Not unlike the many mistakes I'd made since I'd met him. How many chances had I been given? Too many, and he deserved so much more. It was time to let him know.

"I believe you."

His eyes closed as he drew me into the full embrace of his arms, nestling his head on my shoulder.

"I would have never betrayed you like this. I love you, Cheyenne."

My eyes watered, and my lips trembled with the words I knew I needed to say.

"I love you, Callon."

He stilled, but his hold grew tighter.

"I should have told you sooner."

"Now is perfect…" he whispered. He inhaled a shaky breath and suddenly the full weight of his body began to topple us over.

"Callon!"

We hit the floor with a loud thump, and I struggled to push him off me until multiple hands pulled him away. Dex was already checking his pulse.

"What's happening?" I shook with panic. Callon was the strong one…

Brogan and Koda carried Callon away. I tried to follow, but Daniel appeared. He held my arm.

"Wait!" I cried. "What's going on? Where are they taking him?"

"It's okay, Chey." Daniel placed his hands on my shoulders. They disappeared into the hall, and heavy footsteps sounded on the stairs. "He had to make changes in the enchantment. It always weakens him."

"What? Make changes? Why?"

"Because the Tresez were allowed in."

The little traitor…

"Nakari! She let them in!" I shoved Daniel away and pushed through the crowd of clan members. Nakari simply bowed her head as I approached, when Andre stepped in front of her.

"Cheyenne, you need to calm down!" Andre said firmly. "She may have made a mistake, but she's no traitor."

"Then why did she leave me when I was fighting Conall? She could have helped me!"

"I went to get Maes," Nakari said. Her voice was weak. "I didn't want to leave you, but I didn't have a choice. Conall is too strong to fight alone."

I stood immobile. Was she telling the truth? Or was this an excuse? Regardless, I knew what I wanted.

"I don't want you here."

Nakari's green eyes flashed at me. She looked just as tattered as the others, and soaked to the bones. She turned away, but not before I saw the hurt she didn't bother to hide.

"No, Cheyenne. Marcus will kill her if she leaves," Andre protested. "Besides, you haven't exactly had a perfect record either, and no one's asked you to leave."

I blinked, caught off guard by Andre's frankness.

Bree moved to stand beside Nakari, her arm looping in hers.

"*I* never tried kissing another woman's betrothed," I replied.

"But you kissed Colt when you were betrothed to Callon," Daniel said quietly.

I froze. My anger, this stupid, reckless anger, was taking control again, clouding the truth before my eyes. I'd done no better than Nakari, and I couldn't condemn another to death.

"I'm sorry," I said, feeling my face flame with regret once more. "You're right. It's not my place to judge."

I headed towards the hall and ran up the stairs. I just needed to get away from her right now. Besides, I needed to see how Callon was doing. I'd make sure he was all right, find out more about the enchantment, and then deal with Nakari.

My fingers brushed Callon's forehead, pushing the loose strands of his hair aside. Koda and Brogan had managed to help him clean up. He lay in his bed, motionless, just as he had been for hours.

Daniel said it had to do with the enchantment, that Callon had to make changes, but what changes? And why did it weaken him so much?

I traced the dark circles under his eyes. He was bearing the burden for everyone. It was time I stepped up. No more moping around for what should have been. I needed to look ahead for what would be.

Grabbing the extra blanket at the foot of the bed, I crawled up beside Callon and lay down. My mind kept running over the scene with Nakari...I had to let it go. I believed Callon, but I didn't trust Nakari. If I'd been weak too many times with Colt, then surely Nakari could weaken again. It was a chance I wasn't willing to take.

I sighed, curling closer to Callon, my arm coming to rest over his chest. I smiled as I recalled our first encounter, the brick wall I'd run into at the cathedral. He'd been there looking out for me before I even knew he existed, before he even knew who I was. He hadn't once given up on me—ever. Even when I'd pushed him away, he waited. How he could have been so patient with me, I didn't understand, but now, things were going to change.

He'd no longer bear the leadership of the Timeless race alone. It was going to be a partnership, and I was going to accept destiny and grow into the leader I needed to be. No more hiding, no more running.

My blinks grew heavier as the patter of rain hit the windowpane. Its rhythm was soothing, and soon the weight of sleep pushed me under.

A feathery touch traced over my knuckles, stopping on my Kvech ring. Callon adjusted it so the stone was on top again. I exhaled, stretching slightly, and looked up to see his warm hazel eyes.

"You're awake." My voice cracked, and I tried to clear it. I started to sit up, but suddenly the aches and pains from my last Tresez battle decided to come to life. Callon gently pushed me back down.

"You don't need to get up yet." He eyed my neck, his fingers tracing the bruises. "Conall did this to you?"

"His idea of taking me quietly."

"I'm sorry. This is my fault. He shouldn't have been here."

"Daniel said something about the enchantment failing. What happened?"

"I don't know exactly." He lowered his head.

"Can you tell me how it works? How you created it? Maybe that will help." I rested my hand over the top of his.

He remained quiet, processing his thoughts.

"I don't want to sit back on the sidelines anymore, Callon. I need to be involved. We need to share this responsibility equally."

A small smile rose. "Do you know how long I've waited for you to say this?" He leaned in and kissed my forehead. "First you surprise me by saying 'I love you' and now this. I really don't deserve..."

"I don't deserve you." He wouldn't have left me, I knew that now. He took his responsibilities too seriously, but regardless of my previous feelings, he'd been the one who allowed me to make the choice instead of forcing me. He'd been patiently waiting. "Let me help you with this."

"Alright." He lay back down, staring at the ceiling. "I'll need to go back a bit. When we came here a couple of years ago, preparing for your arrival—"

I propped myself up on my elbows.

"You came here to prepare for me?"

"Yes. It was the week Gene and Alexis were murdered."

The blood drained from my cheeks, and sympathy flashed through his eyes.

"We'd sent Daniel ahead of time to get the house in order, but something happened to the enchantment while he was here." His face fell. "Colt didn't want to leave you, but you were supposed to have been in Hawaii at the time. Gene and Alexis were going to tell you about being Timeless, and possibly about us. They were supposed to let you know that you'd be moving to Ireland right after graduation."

My eyes welled with tears. "They were going to take me on a tropical vacation?" I whispered. I was instantly transported back to that week and the camping equipment lining the front hall. "And Colt was in on the surprise..."

"Yes." Callon's voice grew quiet. "Except everything changed when we left, and we had no idea what happened until we returned."

I wiped the tears from my cheeks, as the old wounds started to open up. No, I couldn't let them. I couldn't change the past, but I could make a difference in the future. I pushed back the dark shadows that wanted me to live out their death again.

"So what happened to the enchantment?"

Callon hesitated for a moment, unsure if he wanted to go on. "Daniel tried to fix some holes that had sprung up over the years."

"Holes?"

He sighed. "I hadn't returned here for a long time. The enchantment needs to be renewed from time to time. Otherwise gaps appear. Gaps that allow others in."

"Like what just happened with the Tresez?"

"Yes."

"But you fixed it, right?"

"I thought I had. What Daniel tried to do in actuality erased the old enchantment. It takes all the living heirs to create a new one."

"So you gathered all the heirs and created a new one?"

"Daniel, Colt and myself are the only descendants of the O'Shea family, so together we created a new enchantment, one I thought would be stronger over time."

"But something happened."

Callon sighed. "It just doesn't make sense," he said. "Enough time has passed since the enchantment was created for it to be stronger than the previous, and I've been checking every day to make sure there are no holes."

"Is that where you've gone on your walks?" And he always came back with dark circles under his eyes...

"Yes."

My eyes widened. "It drains you." Just as I had suspected.

Callon nodded.

"So how else could the enchantment have been broken?" I mused.

He turned towards me warily. "Only by a living heir."

I blinked, confused. "But only you and Daniel are left. And Daniel wouldn't open any holes, at least not on purpose."

He looked away. "I've already talked with Daniel. He's got nothing to do with the current holes."

That also meant Nakari couldn't have let the Tresez in. I sighed and lay back down. "I accused Nakari of letting them in." Yet another mistake I'd made.

"No, Nakari couldn't have." He sat up and shook his head. "The only other person who could've broken through would be..."

138

"Colt," I muttered, but hope didn't rise. Instead confusion set in. "But if Colt were alive, why would he let the Tresez in? He'd never do anything to harm us." I struggled to sit up, and Callon helped me. "My dreams. They're true, aren't they?"

Callon stood up and headed towards his windows. He pulled the curtains apart.

"I don't know."

My gaze moved to the wool rug, and I fought to push back any hope that Colt was alive for the sheer reason of not hurting Callon once again. I'd felt Colt, in my dreams, as if he were alive and calling out to me. I was treading on dangerous ground here. If Colt were alive, the fact still remained—we'd never be together. I knew that now, but the wariness I'd witness in Callon's eyes told me everything. He was fearful of Colt being alive and my feelings for him.

I moved towards Callon, turning him toward me and caressing his cheek. "I love you, Callon O'Shea, and Colt possibly being alive will change nothing. I know, I understand now, that we can never be together as I wanted, and although I can't ever stop loving him, I'm yours now. You and I are a team, and we need to be united on every front."

A faint smiled rose. He lowered his head, and my eyes closed as a tender caress was placed on my lips. "I love you too."

A knock at the door ended our brief moment.

"Callon," Brogan called out, "we need to talk."

"It's time you become a part of our meetings, Cheyenne. It's time you participate in the planning. There's a lot you need to catch up on," Callon invited.

I nodded and followed him to the door, reaching out and intertwining my fingers with his. I'd need Callon's strength, especially since Brogan would only look down upon me. He'd only seen me react out of anger, act selfishly and push everyone aside. It was going to be an uphill battle with him and another...Maes.

I sighed. I was going to have to make things right with him, if he'd even talk with me. He'd been right all along, and I'd ignored his warnings.

Brogan eyed me like a speck of dirt on his shoes as we entered the hall.

"Cheyenne," Brogan grumbled.

Yup, a long, slow uphill battle, one that I deserved.

Brogan led us down the stairs and into the library. Dex, Koda, Daniel, Andre, and Maes were waiting. The library door clicked closed, and I couldn't help but feel the pressure change in the room. I understood all the clan leaders being present, but what role did Andre play? It looked like she'd purposefully placed herself next to Maes, but why?

Callon led us to a couch, and I looked up at Maes. He was staring at Callon, but wouldn't make eye contact with me, not that I blamed him. Daniel sat beside me. At least I could always count on Daniel.

"Do you feel you've patched the enchantment, Callon?" Dex asked. He was flipping through an old manuscript on the table.

"It's been repaired," Callon replied.

"How'd we get a hole in it in the first place?" Brogan leaned against the table, his arms crossing over his chest.

"I thought that only one of the O'Shea's could change it," Maes stated. "And there's only two here."

"Daniel didn't do anything, Maes." Callon eyed him carefully.

"I wasn't accusing him."

Andre shifted uncomfortably. "We know that, Maes," Andre replied. "You were referring to the elephant in the room—Colt."

They knew, or at least had an idea, like Callon did. I was about to speak up, when Daniel touched my arm. A softness passed through his blue eyes. No, I needed to keep quiet and listen right now. I'd have plenty of time to speak up later, when I'd earned their respect.

All eyes remained on Callon, waiting for a reply.

"He may still be alive," Callon finally replied.

Koda stood up, his nostrils flaring.

"We watched him die on that ravine. There was no way he could have survived Marcus's attack! We would've brought him with us..."

"He had no pulse," Callon answered solemnly, "but that doesn't mean that Marcus couldn't have changed things. No one knows truly how vast his powers are."

"That would explain Marcus's lack of movements," Brogan added. "He's been quiet for too long. Even our spies haven't been able to get a handle on his whereabouts or plans."

"Colt would have never willingly handed over the estate, Callon," Dex pleaded. "You, I, we all know this. Marcus must be using him, forcing him to work for him."

My heart pounded in my chest. I wanted to scream out that we needed to rescue him, that we couldn't leave him to Marcus's devices...but instead I pressed my lips together tighter. I was part of a team now. I couldn't just do what I wanted. I needed to see where these conversations lead.

"We need proof," Maes stated. "Even if Marcus has Colt, risking our lives for the life of one...this whole thing reeks of a trap."

"Call in the twins," Dex answered, his gaze hardening into a well-seasoned war strategist. "Jayna and Tre are the best. Brogan, you can make contact with them, right?"

Brogan nodded, but he looked to Callon for the final verdict. Callon squeezed my hand.

"Contact them discreetly, Brogan. We can't have the Sarac know of our plans."

"Will do." Brogan quickly exited the room.

The meeting dispersed, and my heart couldn't help but ache for so many reasons. Just knowing Colt may be alive gave me hope, but knowing he'd been under Marcus's power for as long as he had...

Then there was Maes. I had to make this right now. I couldn't delay it any longer.

I headed for the door when Andre grabbed my arm.

"I don't know if you should talk to him right now." Her blue eyes studied mine. "He's very angry."

He'd made it very clear he was still angry with me, but I couldn't let it fester any longer.

"Why were you in the meeting, Andre? Everyone here has a leadership position except you, unless there's something I don't know," I asked.

She raised a brow. "I'm here because of the tension in the room. I can read it."

"Because I came to the meeting."

"Yes. When Callon told Daniel that you were coming, I was asked to be a 'mood moderator' of sorts."

"So you can read moods?"

"I can read moods, emotions, and can even tell if someone's being truthful."

"Just about anyone can read moods, Andre, and based on eye contact they can tell if someone is lying."

"True, but when you've lived as long as we have, it's easy to train

141

yourself not to give away the signs," she explained.

"How can you read me or anyone else?" I asked.

"The best way to describe it would be an aura."

"An aura?" I repeated.

"When you went out yesterday, your aura was red, which indicated your anger. It also had a black hue to it too, which showed your depression and withdrawal."

"And today?"

She smiled. "For the first time since I've met you, your aura is a pale blue mixed with specks of yellow and pink."

"And that means?" I sat on the arm of the couch.

"Blue tends to mean calm, content. The mixture of yellow indicates your concern, worry over the situation and pink, well that's love."

"You can see all that?"

"I see it all."

"What about Callon? Did you see his aura?"

"I don't kiss and tell. I'll tell you what I see in you, but not others, unless they give me permission or under direct orders from clan leaders."

I nodded. It was probably best, as it would cause problems otherwise.

I headed for the door. I needed to talk with Maes.

"I'd still advise against speaking with Maes right now," Andre called out as she followed me into the main hall. "Give it a few days."

I heard her words, but chose to ignore them. I'd take my chances. However, I needed to catch him alone. I didn't need to air all my dirty laundry in front of everyone. It was going to be bad enough in front of Maes.

I entered the sitting room. He wasn't there. The terrace doors were ajar, but when I peeked outside, only Bree and Daniel were there, talking. I tried the kitchen and found it empty. Passing the large studded doors just off the kitchen, I turned the knob once again only to find it locked. I'd have to ask Callon about this soon.

I climbed the stairs, pausing on the top landing. I had an idea which room Maes used, but I wasn't completely positive. I didn't want him to hear me knocking on the wrong door and vanish before I got a chance to speak.

I paused at the last door on my left and glanced back. It was about three doors down from mine, which was about right. He'd want to be close. In case anything happened, he'd want to make sure he'd have time to help if needed.

My knuckles rapped on the hard wood. I waited for a reply. When none came, I rapped again and waited a few moments before pressing my ear against the door.

The shuffle of feet on the hardwood and then padding on the rugs told me I'd come to the right room. Maes was pacing.

I twisted the brass knob, and met no resistance as the door silently opened. I stepped inside and closed it behind me. The pacing stopped.

No words were uttered as I slowly turned around. Only Maes' flaring nostrils produced any sound. I didn't need Andre's powers to know exactly how Maes felt. My body vibrated with his anger, and my fear that he'd never forgive me.

His teeth flashed a snarl, and the veins in his neck bulged. I needed to speak quickly before he shifted and ripped me to pieces.

I fell to my knees, my legs no longer able to hold me. "I'm sorry, Maes." My lips trembled. "What I did was completely wrong." I bowed my head, utterly ashamed. "I took your powers out of anger." I swallowed knowing what I was about to admit. "I wanted to harm Nakari, and it was wrong."

He didn't reply, but his breathing had slowed.

"I don't like this *thing* I'm becoming. You were right all along. You warned me that anger and despair would eat me alive, but I didn't listen. You told me not to go into those dark depths. You even knew the crimson-eyed beast. You tried to protect me from the same fate as you...and I didn't listen."

I inhaled a shaky breath.

"I came here to ask, no, beg for your forgiveness, but I understand if you can't grant it. I pushed you too far, and I'm truly sorry for all the grief I've caused you."

I swallowed. "Regardless of your decision, I also came to make a vow to you today. For however long, for however many heartaches I must yet endure, I vow to you that I will never give up fighting to find a way to free you of your curse. I vow this to you, and all your future generations—forevermore."

I waited for a reply, for anything, but nothing came. I rose and turned towards the door, pausing just before it.

"I was just lost, Maes. Misplaced..." I reached for the brass handle and pulled, but the door didn't move. I looked up to see a large hand holding it closed. His dark presence loomed behind me. I hadn't heard him move closer.

"You were never misplaced, *mon espoir*. Misplaced indicates something of no worth, like a pen, but lost...when something is lost, it is valuable enough to be found. The value of a masterpiece doesn't go down when it's lost—it increases. Just as your value as a lost soul only increased, and became priceless when found."

Maes had forgiven me. I turned and stared into jade-rimmed eyes. Eyes that now viewed me differently, eyes that trusted me once again.

"I'm sorry."

"I know."

I couldn't help myself as I hugged him. It was time to bring warmth back into this family again.

CHAPTER 11

The cold winds howled in the barren trees, and the dark skies threatened to release their heavy rains again. I pulled my jacket closer around my neck and adjusted my scarf, waiting for the others to catch up.

"Here," Andre said, handing me some gloves.

Koda winked and Daniel smiled at me. Skylar followed behind them. We all stepped off the terrace to begin our patrol.

It was Maes's idea to patrol the grounds, even though Callon assured him the enchantment had been repaired. Callon had also told me directly that Marcus hadn't come through. He reassured me that only the Tresez had; however, I was getting tired of surprises.

Each of us would take turns going out in groups of three, to ensure there were no Tresez still around. Maes had a suspicion that one or two still might be hiding, although we hadn't spotted any tracks.

Koda and Daniel had decided to tag along out of boredom, and I'd been placed in Skylar and Andre's group. "Strong with the weak," Brogan had said. At least I'd moved up a notch in his book. He believed I could handle myself now, but then again, he could have been referring to Skylar or Andre as the strong one.

The mood had changed again in the manor. We were waiting for the report from the twins, Tre and Jayna. Callon told me they had special skills, although he didn't really clarify. He said I needed to see it for myself. I was assuming I'd get to meet them soon. I wasn't the only one hoping Colt was alive; I'd seen a light in Callon and

Daniel's eyes, too. I felt like a weight had dropped off my shoulders, and the laughter had returned.

Just yesterday Andre, Lilly and I were folding laundry, when Koda brought in several heaping baskets. I smiled, because it reminded me of Colt. Just like Koda, Colt would have piled the baskets over his head.

It only took a second for Koda to hit a potted plant Lilly had been nursing on the window shelf. The pot exploded, sending particles of wet soil all over Andre and her clean pile of whites.

Lilly, Koda and I burst into laughter while Andre's flaming eyes sought out Koda. Within a moment, Koda had darted out the door and Andre was hot on his heels with a broom and a long list of trailing words. I couldn't help but smile.

My fingers traced the tips of the long yellow grass as we passed the edge of the meadow and entered the dark forest. My mind couldn't help but wander to the previous week, specifically, the incident with Nakari. We'd been avoiding each other, neither of us making eye contact. We'd both been wrong in our actions, she trying to kiss Callon and me accusing her of treachery. Though I'd been the one who went too far…

"We're going to head south," Koda said, breaking my thoughts. "You girls take the north side, and we'll meet back here in a couple of hours."

"Scream if you need us," Daniel chuckled, before he disappeared into the thick brush.

I eyed Andre. It was never a good thing when Daniel chuckled like that and used the word "scream" in the same breath.

Skylar shook his head.

"Watch out for Daniel today. I have a feeling he's up to no good. I heard Bree screaming before we left," I warned them with a faint smile. It had been a while since Daniel had played his jokes. I was starting to realize how much I'd missed it.

Skylar caught my expression and smirked. "It's good to have hope again, Cheyenne. It brightens everyone's outlook. It's contagious."

I nodded. With a final wave, Skylar and Koda disappeared into the trees. Andre and I turned right, though Skylar's words remained with me. Hope was contagious…

"What're you thinking so hard about?" Andre asked. Her pace had quickened as we trudged up the ravine.

"Just stuff," I replied. I glanced up and watched the wind whip her black hair around.

"What kind of stuff?" she pried.

She wasn't going to let it go. "What? Has my aura suddenly turned into a rainbow or something?"

She stopped in her tracks. "Actually, it's more a brown color."

I cringed. That sounded horrible. "Seriously?"

"Tends to mean muddy, unclear. I've never seen anything like it before. Just trying to figure it out."

"Oh?" Well, that would give her something to think about for a while, and I was sure she'd think aloud, too. I continued walking.

"So what colors mix to make brown?" she asked.

I didn't reply. She'd answer her own question soon enough.

"Yellow, red, blue..." She was counting them out on her fingers. Ignoring her, I pushed a large branch aside and held it for her to pass.

"Yellow is worry, red suggests anger, and blue, well it's calm..." She shook her head. "Makes about as much sense as a Timeless anti-aging cream."

My foot slipped on the mud, and Andre caught my arm.

"Thanks."

She studied my face. "What are you angry about?"

"Nothing?" I shrugged. I really didn't feel angry, at least not like I had in the past. Although, I was still upset about Nakari.

"There's anger mixed in there, but mostly worry."

She was right on the worry. I was stressing over a lot of things, mostly Callon. He'd regained most of his strength, but he still had the dark circles under his eyes, and I'd caught Dex giving him worried glances. I wasn't the only one concerned about his health. Just how much did renewing the enchantment drain him?

"Look, don't fret about Callon. He's going to be just fine."

I stared at her. "Don't tell me your other power is mind reading, Andre."

A sly smile perched on her lips.

"So I was right!"

She stopped as we reached the top of the ravine.

"So you're still angry with him?" she insisted.

I couldn't help but smile.

"You're not going to give this up are you?" I asked, knowing the

147

answer.

"Nope."

"Fine. I'm worried that the enchantment has taken too much out of him. He's still weak, and it's been a week. I'm still slightly miffed at Nakari, but I'm to blame also. I just need to learn to let it go. And I'm calm, or calmer because I'm learning to deal with my anger, and honestly…" I paused, unsure if I really wanted her to know. "You're the first female friend that I've ever had. I feel like I can be myself around you, and you're not afraid to tell me when I'm being stupid."

Andre stood still, soaking in my words, then shrugged as she walked along the small trail. "I always say what I think."

"No wonder Maes likes you," I muttered under my breath. "You're two of a kind."

"I heard that."

"I'm sure you did."

We continued on the trail, searching for any Tresez tracks, when the patter of rain began to hit the ground. I pulled my scarf over my head in hopes of preventing a complete soaking.

The scenery began to change as we emerged from the forest and a small meadow appeared. At the edge stood an old building that had seen better days. I slowed down as I caught movement on the far side.

"Andre, wait," I whispered. She stopped, turning to me. I pointed to the building. "Something's there."

"Yeah, I know." She continued to walk toward the building.

I grabbed her arm. "Let me check it out first."

She rolled her eyes. "It's Nakari."

I stiffened, and then the realization set in. "You knew she'd be here?"

"Yup." She pulled away and continued walking. "You two need to talk. I'll be waiting at the edge of the trees when you're done."

I scowled. "I really don't like you right now."

"You'll get over it." She waved her hand and disappeared behind the building.

Nakari appeared, her hair plastered across her shoulders from the rain. Her emerald eyes stared, intent.

Anger rose in my throat, but I swallowed it down. Better to get this over with now. I had to move forward. I stopped before her, staring down at the grass. No need to make eye contact. It wouldn't change anything.

"Cheyenne." Her voice was soft. "You were right in asking me to leave. What I've done is unforgiveable. I—I had a moment of weakness, and Callon was correct to push me away." She folded her hands together. "I came here not liking you, even though I didn't know you. My mind had already been set. You had a path of destruction lying in your wake. You'd ripped all my hope away, and I blamed you for tearing Callon and Colt apart. I—I blamed you for breaking my heart." She inhaled a shaky breath, and I looked up into her moist green eyes.

"You were angry when we came to help, and I can't fault you for that. What's been thrust upon your shoulders would be difficult for any Timeless, but you—you were thrown into the lion's den. I understood your anger at being dealt this hand. The cruelty of destiny to wave what you truly wanted before you, only to have it shattered into a million pieces. I could relate to that, and it angered me even more."

She swallowed, and a tear trickled down her cheek. "I remembered all those yesterdays, knowing that I couldn't ever touch or see him again. Memories that haunt you when you sleep and sometimes drive you to do things you know are wrong, regardless of the consequences. Grasping for just a small thread of hope."

My heart ached in understanding as I listened.

"I wish I could turn back time and change everything for us." She lowered her head, her auburn locks falling into her face. "I don't deserve what I am going to ask of you...your forgiveness."

My lower lip trembled. I knew what I needed to confess, to clear the air, but the words wouldn't form.

Nakari turned and began to walk away.

No! I couldn't keep pushing others aside, not after what she'd just told me.

"Nakari!" I called out. She halted. "If you're asking for forgiveness, then I need to ask the same of you." Her head turned slightly. "I was angry, but I was no better than you at one time. What I've done or thought about you was wrong. I accused you of betraying us—me. When you left me with Conall, I thought it was your way of ridding yourself of me." I hesitated, but forced myself to go on. "What's worse than what you did with Callon was my reaction to it. I—I took Maes power with the intent to cause you harm."

Nakari gasped. Her eyes hardened.

"If Maes hadn't stopped you..." she whispered.

"Let's just be thankful he did," I said. "I've had a problem with anger management, if you haven't noticed."

Nakari clenched her shaking fists.

"I can't believe you!" she hissed. "I might not have liked you but never to the point I'd want to *kill*..." She began shaking her head. "You really are a monster."

I flinched. Her words hurt, but I knew I deserved them.

She turned her back to me. "Forget everything I said. You're not deserving of my forgiveness."

"Now wait a second!" I protested. Andre emerged from where she'd been waiting, wearing a frown. She stormed forward, stepping between us.

"Nakari, Cheyenne's apologized. What more do you want from her?" she asked. "You can't hold a grudge forever. You need to move on as well."

Nakari sighed. For a long while she just stood there, listening to the rain, when finally she spun around.

"Alright then." She held out her hand. "Maybe we can make a truce."

Bowing my head, I stepped forward and clasped her fingers.

"Truce," I said. I might not have repaired the damage yet, but at least this was one step closer to it.

Nakari released my hand and quickly jumped into the shadows. I sighed. It would take a while to earn her trust. At least now we could tolerate each other, although the uncomfortable silences would probably linger.

Andre sighed, slicking back her hair. "Well, a truce is better than nothing."

I shrugged. "Whatever."

This time I led the way back into the forest. I didn't need Andre planning out any other surprises.

Our patrol turned up nothing, so we circled back around to meet up with Koda, Skylar and Daniel. I hugged myself tighter. The wind was colder, and the rain wasn't making it any better. I'd be glad to get back and warm up by the fire. Tonight was also our weekly meal. Having something hot inside would help fight the cold as well. As up-to-date as the manor was, it was still old and drafty. Even with the fire in my room, I'd wake up in the night shivering and have to search for extra blankets.

I caught a crackle in the distance, and then loud laughter. I looked up, and screamed as a large branch barreled towards us. Andre knocked me to the ground, and we watched it fly past.

"Koda!" Andre snapped. "You idiot! We're down here!"

I rose, brushing the mud from my sleeves.

"You couldn't hit the broad side of a barn, Koda!" Daniel's voice echoed off the trees.

"Hold still and I'll show you, you twig!" Koda bellowed back.

Andre moved beside me. "They're both morons."

"Daniel's gotten Koda a little worked up. Sorry for the missile," Skylar said, emerging from the trees. His scraggly blond hair was matted to his head. "Did you two see anything?"

I glanced at Andre, still not sure if I should be mad at her for forcing me to talk with Nakari. "Nothing of importance," I replied.

"Good. I don't know about the two of you, but I'm looking forward to the soup Lilly's making."

I smiled as we began our track back. "So am I," I replied.

Daniel suddenly jumped in front of us and my heart skipped a beat. No matter how long I'd know him, I'd never get used to his sudden appearances.

"Hey, ladies!" Daniel said cheerfully.

Andre reached out and shoved him aside. "Do you know how irritating it is to have you appear like that?"

"About as irritating as your whole 'aura' thingy," Daniel snickered.

"Seriously, Daniel," Skylar said, "are you sure you want to anger Andre? She's got Maes's ear now." Skylar winked at me.

Andre turned on her heels, her wet hair hitting her cheek. Her brows pinched together and her jaw tensed. "For the last time, I am *not* dating Maes!"

"Well, someone's a bit testy when it comes to her lover," Koda purred as he popped out from between two large trees. His blue eyes locked onto Daniel, and an evil smirk grew on Daniel's lips.

"You know she's always wanted a puppy," Daniel added.

"And this puppy is going to tear your throat out!" Maes growled.

I blinked. Where had he come from?

Daniel's eyes widened as Maes shifted into his Tresez form. A

151

moment later he was jumping through the forest, Maes hot on his tail.

Andre rolled her eyes, running after them. "I can fight my own battles, you dog!" she hollered.

"Told you she had Maes's ear," Skylar chuckled.

I couldn't help but laugh with Koda and Skylar. It'd been too long since laughter had filled my heart, and the fact someone else was getting teased for a change made it even better.

We finally crossed into the meadow by the lake, and the manor came into view. What I wouldn't have given for Daniel to appear and jump me inside quickly. Rain drenched my coat and scarf, and I started to shiver. I really needed to get a waterproof jacket like I'd had at home.

"We're almost there," Skylar said, encouraging me.

"And Callon said dinner will be ready in about an hour," Koda added.

"Good." Then maybe the popsicle I was becoming would defrost. A hot shower would work wonders, though the water didn't always heat up quick enough or last long enough. Another joy of living in an old manor.

It seemed like an eternity before we came to the terrace steps. The lights from the sitting room gleamed brightly against the night sky. Everyone had gathered inside, awaiting our arrival.

A burst of warm air hit me as Koda opened the door. Lilly was at my side within moments, helping me out of my wet jacket.

"Dear lord, she's soaked to the bone!" Lilly cried. She instantly turned on Koda and Skylar. "What's wrong with the two of you? You should have been back hours ago!"

I snuck past her and smiled at Callon as I passed through the sitting room and into the hall. First on the list was a change of clothes, with multiple layers to give me warmth. I was seriously lacking in winter clothing, but since I was confined to these grounds, there was little I could do about it.

I trotted to my room, changed and returned to the top of the stairs. I paused. The halls echoed with laughter, lots of laughter, including a deep, rich chortle that gave me goosebumps. I hadn't thought Brogan could make such a sound. I hadn't heard this sort of happiness for a long time. Rather, I hadn't wanted to hear it, too consumed in my own misery.

Sighing, I made my way down the stairs, halting inside the music area. Apparently the mock battle between Koda and Daniel hadn't ended, and now Skylar was in on it.

"You got nothing on me, Skylar," Daniel said slyly. He turned his head and a devious smile rose on his lips. He landed beside me, and I startled. I knew what that smile meant.

"Hey now..." was all I was able to get out before Daniel jumped us across the room. Koda lunged and I cringed, waiting for an impact that never came.

"You wouldn't hurt Cheyenne now, would you?" Daniel hid behind me.

Daniel twisted me to the right as Skylar moved closer.

"And you'd use a poor defenseless girl as a shield?" Skylar asked.

"I wouldn't call Cheyenne defenseless," Koda chimed in.

"Hey!" I grabbed Daniel's hand, touching his knuckles, but something blocked me from taking his power. Daniel wagged his finger at me.

"Not this time, Cheyenne. I need my powers, and you can't have them."

I glanced towards Callon, and he shrugged, smiling. He was enjoying this.

"Don't worry, Cheyenne," Koda said. He stealthily moved closer. "We won't hurt you, just Daniel."

"Good to know," I replied as we landed near the dining room table. My damp hair clung to my lashes, and I looked at the fire longingly. Within a second, we'd moved into the hall again. If this kept up, I was going to be sick.

"You've got nowhere to go now," Koda rumbled.

"And you say you know me," Daniel teased.

Suddenly, I was in complete darkness, and the soft whisper of a breeze told me Daniel had disappeared. He'd left me.

"So much for getting warm," I mumbled. I stuck my hand out and moved towards what I thought was a wall. My left shoulder made contact with a large object. "Ouch!"

Where had Daniel jumped me? I fumbled around for a few moments, until I found a door handle. The knob was cold as I twisted it and I stepped forward.

A shiver escaped me. This room was even colder, and pitch black as well. I twisted to my right, pushing my fingers against the wall.

There had to be a light switch someplace. Finally, I found it and flicked it on. Light flooded the room, and I flinched at the brightness.

I was in some sort of storage room. Sheets covered paintings lining the left side of the wall. Boxes were stacked in organized sections circling around to the right, and old furniture had been placed behind some chests and crates. I'd found a treasure trove.

I glanced towards the door. The hallway was dark. This must be what lay behind the metal studded doors just off the dining room. Apparently Daniel could jump me through walls if he knew what lay on the other side. I guess I wasn't going to have to pester Callon after all.

Moving further into the room, I ran my fingers over the sheet-covered frames. Might as well have a look while I was in here. I might not have the chance again. I paused in front of a frame larger and broader than me, then carefully lifted the sheet back. My eyes grew wide. A pair of icy blue eyes were staring at me.

Colt.

He had to have been about twelve or thirteen. He was dressed in what looked like black wool pants and had shiny black boots that ran up to his knees. A crisp white shirt stuck out from under his gray-buttoned vest and his blond hair was tied back with a black ribbon. He was much smaller, almost scraggly looking, with an awkward smile perched on his lips.

My fingers traced his outline. What would he have been like as a teenager? Surely he'd have had awkward moments like the rest of us...like me.

I soaked in his picture for a few more moments before I carefully covered it again and moved on. I studied the frames, deciding which to inspect next, when an oversized one with part of its sheet falling off caught my eye. It was buried behind some other paintings, so I worked on moving them aside before I could make enough room to pull away the sheet. It fell to the floor, and I stepped back.

It was a life-sized painting of the male O'Shea's—all of them. Callon, Colt, Daniel, and their father. I moved in closer to view the gold tag at the top. *Kieran*. So that was their father's name.

It was easy to see where they'd gotten their looks from. Kieran had black wavy locks, icy blue eyes and a frame that was just a tad bit larger than Colt's. There was also a softness to his features that resembled Daniel's.

154

Callon and Colt stood in the back, wearing black wool suits, black vests with white shirts and red ties. Kieran sat in a chair, dressed much the same, and Daniel sat with his arm propped over his knee, staring out into some forgotten place. I moved in closer. His eyes, those dark blue eyes that had always relayed warmth to me were filled with sadness, loneliness. Why?

I looked up at Colt's eyes. Had the artist captured something in his eyes as well? Distance...he was looking at the artist, but seeing beyond. It was a far off gaze, searching for something on the horizon.

I moved over to Callon. His shoulders were squared, his hand resting on the back of his father's chair. His eyes revealed strength, determination, and confidence. He was the first in line, his father's son, ready to stand in his father's place when the time came, and he longed for it.

I reached out, wanting to trace his jawline, wanting to feel what he felt, but pulled away at the last moment. All his strength, determination and confidence were wavering now, most likely because of my actions and things that had happened in his past. How could one live for so long, with so many changes, and yet still remain so loyal to a cause? I covered the portrait, knowing I'd probably never understand.

I sighed and turned around. Did I really want to explore this place? I could learn so much, but I'd probably only uncover more things to remind me of what was at stake here...the continuance of the Timeless race as they knew it now.

I stepped out of the small space and tripped on a piece of loose material. My hand caught the edge of a box and it toppled over. I froze as a familiar song began to play, and my eyes caught pink fabric poking out from a cardboard lid.

My heart ached, and I forced myself to crawl forward. I lifted a shaking hand and pulled the brown lid away. I blinked back tears as I reached for the small pink and white box and closed the lid. The melody fell silent. I traced the small dents in the lid, and the tear in the material on the lower left corner.

My jewelry box.

I sucked in a breath. This had been a gift from my mom and dad when I was six. I'd been frantic after my parent's death, searching the house for it. Colt had come to my home and found me panicked. He knew it was important to me.

155

"Cheyenne?" Callon's voice echoed down the hall. "Hey, what's going on?"

I couldn't reply.

"Sweetheart, what's wrong?" He moved beside me, his arm coming around.

I lifted the small pink box up.

"What's this?" Callon asked, studying it.

"My jewelry box." My voice shook. "It went missing after my parent's death. I'd wanted it so badly then..."

"You found it here?" He stroked my cheek.

I nodded.

He placed a tender kiss on my forehead, his hand coming to rest on mine. My thumb ran over the gold latch, and I delicately flipped it open. The familiar melody began to play again, and I stroked my Servak ring. I watched the small ballerina and my mind traveled back to when I'd received this gift from my mom.

The memory was crystal clear, as if it were yesterday.

The warm wind blew my ball past the playground and into the grassy field. Children's laughter and screams filled the air. I was happy. It was my birthday, and I was now six years old. I chased after the ball, smiling as I ran, because I knew my parents would be here soon to help celebrate with my classmates. My mom was bringing cupcakes, and soon everyone would be singing to me.

I paused at the edge of the field. A woman with long wavy brown hair was holding my ball.

"Is this yours?" she asked.

I nodded.

"Cheyenne!" my teacher called out, and I turned to see her waving me back.

"Cheyenne..." the woman repeated. "That's such a pretty name." She moved closer and handed me the ball.

"Thank you," I replied. "Today's my birthday. I'm six."

An angelic smile crossed her face, and her gray eyes grew watery.

"Happy Birthday, Cheyenne," she whispered.

"Sweetheart," a man just behind her called out.

I moved to see him. His blond hair fell into his eyes.

"We have to go now," he told the woman.

"Cheyenne, it's time to come in now," my teacher called out. "Your parents are here."

"I have to go now," I told the pretty brown-haired lady. "We're going to have my party." I smiled.

"Goodbye," she whispered, close to tears. "Be brave, Cheyenne, and always follow your heart."

The vision disappeared, and I felt my cheeks soaked with tears.

"Sahara..." I whispered.

Callon turned to me, his eyes probing. "What did you do?"

I blinked. "I—I didn't do anything...I don't know."

"You had a memory?"

"Yes, it was so clear, like it took place..."

"Yesterday." He finished my sentence for me.

"Why? How?" I couldn't form my questions into words.

"You took one of my powers, that's how."

"What?" I shook my head. "I don't understand."

He sighed and looked down, his fingers stroking my wrist.

"I'm able to enhance memories."

"Enhance memories?"

His hazel eyes met mine. "I can't create new memories, only bring old memories to the surface with clarity. And though I wanted to comfort you, I didn't help you produce this memory."

"It was my mother, Sahara. She came to see me on my sixth birthday..." I looked up, my eyes widening.

"What?" Callon said.

I pressed the small box to my chest.

"I received this on my sixth birthday." I swallowed, fighting to stop more tears spreading. "It held my Servak ring, Callon. My parents gave me this...my real parents, Sahara and Qaysean." I couldn't hold back, and I choked out a sob. "I got to see them...they were still alive when I was six."

Callon pulled me closer, and I curled into his hold, hugging the box tightly. Subconsciously I had known all along. It was one of the few gifts I'd ever received that wedged its way into my heart. Just having it around was soothing, and now I knew why.

Slowly, I calmed down. Wiping my eyes, I looked to Callon.

"You've done this before, helped me relive memories?" I asked.

"Yes."

"At the cabin, when I didn't want to get out of bed because I missed my parents." I drew back. "You brought me the memory with Colt on my birthday, and you got me to speak again."

157

A faint smile rose. "I did. I didn't know how else to help you."

"You've helped me in so many ways, Callon."

"Just as much as you've helped me," he said.

He leaned closer, his lips brushing mine. My fingers moved to his silky hair. He brought his lips to mine. It'd been too long since he kissed me like this—way too long.

"I—I never knew I could feel so much for you," he muttered against my mouth.

My eyes fell closed. I too didn't know I could feel so much for another after Colt.

His lips covered mine, and he pressed me closer, his hand sliding up the back of my shirt. Goosebumps rolled down my spine, and my breathing hitched as he parted my lips.

For too long I had held back from him, afraid of betraying Colt's memory, but now...now I needed to let go and give Callon back what he'd given me—life. He'd given me hope as well, hope that I, we, could move on.

He tilted his head, pressing the kiss deeper, and butterflies erupted in the pit of my stomach. Raw, untamed passion poured out from him as our breathing grew ragged.

Footsteps sounded in the hall, and Callon stilled. He drew back, a faint grin rising. "I think we've been found."

He pushed my hair behind my ear, and I looked up to see Daniel, Koda, Bree and Skylar standing in the doorway.

"Everything okay?" Daniel asked, glancing around.

"She found her jewelry box, Daniel," Callon replied.

Daniel's eyes grew wide and he knelt beside me.

"I'm so sorry, Cheyenne," he said. "I—I forgot that Gene and Alexis had shipped some of your things over here. The caretaker had told me, and I said to put it in storage...I—I just forgot."

"It's okay, Daniel," I whispered.

Daniel remained still. He was still fearful of pushing me over that edge.

Callon helped me stand and drew me into his side, and I wiped the remnant of a tear from my cheek.

"I didn't mean to upset you. I can bring the rest of your boxes to your room," Daniel added.

"There's more?" I looked around.

Daniel twisted a box around. "Anything with a big C on it is yours."

"I'd like that," I told him. "Thank you." It would be wonderful to have some of my own things.

Callon took my hand as I cradled the pink and white box close to my chest. The hall was no longer dark as we left the storage room, and I kept my head lowered as we passed Koda, Skylar, and Bree.

"We'll help Daniel," Bree offered.

I nodded and followed Callon out into the hall and up the stairs to my bedroom. I sat on the corner of my bed, waiting for the boxes to arrive. This was the last piece I needed to move on. I'd missed so many things from home; which may have been why I'd never really found the courage to move on completely. Now though, that would change. I wouldn't get caught in the past, but take it with me into the future.

CHAPTER 12

Five large boxes were delivered to my room, and I couldn't have been happier. Clothes, sweaters, jackets, scarves, gloves, jeans, boots and a few blankets lay at my feet. I'd finally have something warm to wear.

I smiled as I dug through the last box. I remembered packing some of these things with my mom; it's what we always did when the season was about to change. I just never expected that I'd have all this stuff here with me. But then again, my mom always thought ahead, was always the planner. For that I was grateful.

My fingers ran across something hard, and I quickly pulled it out.

"What is it?" Lilly asked, folding some of the sweaters.

I carefully unwrapped a book-sized package. Once the paper fell away, I gasped.

"It's a picture of my parents," I whispered. Tears that I thought had disappeared were fresh again.

Lilly moved and placed her arm around my shoulder. "And it's in a nice silver frame," she added.

I traced the outline of my mother's face, before sighing and setting it on the table beside my bed. At least now I had a picture.

"Alexis was very thoughtful in sending things here ahead of time," Lilly said while she tucked some clothes into a drawer. "The picture of her and Gene is sweet, thoughtful."

"It is," I replied, putting the last of the jeans away.

Lilly placed her hands on her hips, smiling. "Since we're done here, Dex has asked for you to meet him in the library."

"Oh?" What was this all about?

"He wants to make sure you're up-to-date with some Timeless history. We've made huge mistakes not sharing our heritage with you. It's time we fixed that."

My eyes lit up. It was about time! At last, I could finally learn more about my family and the clans. All the things Callon had promised were coming true.

I dashed for the door. "I'm on my way then!"

Lilly laughed, and I hurried through the hall and down the stairs, pausing at the library doors.

"Where you off to in such a hurry, *princess*?" Brogan grumbled.

I turned, giving him a blank look. "Me?"

"Yes, you, princess." He crossed his arms over his large chest.

Great, now Brogan had a nickname for me...

"I'm meeting Dex."

"And?"

What did he care? "We're going over some history."

A smirk rose. "It's about damn time somebody listened to me."

"That's right, love. We all need to listen to you," Layla swept into the hall and hung off his arm, her eyelashes fluttering.

"I think I should go with her and make sure..."

Layla cut him off. "Leave her be. I need help with some herbs."

His lip twitched, but when he looked down on Layla, his eyes filled with warmth. I had to blink twice to make sure I'd seen it right.

A sly smile rose on Layla's lips, and she led him towards the dining room. I swallowed. That was a disaster averted. I pushed open the library doors and walked in. Callon peeked out from behind a bookshelf.

"Hey there." A warm grin emerged. "Looking for me?"

"Always." I glanced behind him. "Is Dex here?"

"No." His head tilted, and he moved closer. "Is everything okay?"

"Oh sure, it's just that Lilly told me Dex wanted to see me in the library."

Callon chuckled. "He's in the other library."

"Huh?"

He grasped my hand. "I've been wanting to show you, but I needed to make sure you were ready." He tugged me along into the hall and headed towards the dining room. He stopped at the metal studded doors and pulled a key out of his pocket. Unlocking it, he ushered me inside.

This time there was more light, a trail of small hanging sconces lit the way. The corridor was windowless, and the gray stones made it feel like the walls were closing in. Our feet padded against the long red runner, its pattern more Asian than the other rugs in the manor.

"This is where I was last night?"

"Yes, this hall not only leads to the storage room, but a gym and another library," Callon explained.

The cool draft made me shiver, or maybe it was the gloom from the dark shadows...

"So why keep it under lock and key?" I asked. A gym and storage room didn't seem like it needed to be guarded.

"This library contains information that doesn't need to fall into the wrong hands."

I twisted to see inside a well-lit room as we passed. It had small, high windows giving it light. Gym equipment filled the space, and a punching bag oozing sand lay on its side. Had Colt come here to work out? I wondered how many other secrets the manor held.

"Like?" I asked.

"Like enchantments, things that protect the manor."

"Like?" I repeated.

"Secrets of the rings, Timeless information that Marcus could use against us, things like that."

"Oh."

We rounded a corner and stopped at another set of metal studded doors. They resembled something from a medieval movie. Callon touched the door with his hand and spoke just above a whisper. A lock snapped open, and he twisted the handle. Instantly I was hit with the smell of dust and leather. We stopped just inside the doorway.

"The door has a spell?" I looked at the tarnished handle.

"Of course." Callon pressed me forward.

Would Callon give me the spell someday? I felt giddy. It was my turn to learn, to understand about the Timeless. Would it make me happy, or bring more despair?

I looked around at my new surroundings. Dark wood shelving lined the walls, and several bookcases were neatly arranged in the center, all filled with books.

"Ah, here she is!" Dex rose from a chair near the fireplace. "I've been waiting for you, Cheyenne." A mahogany desk with a small green lamp lay behind Dex's chair. The light's pull swung back and forth.

Callon kissed me on the cheek. "I'll leave you to it. Have fun."

He turned and left, and the heavy doors clicked closed. Dex pointed to the upholstered chair across from him. He sat on the edge of his chair while he stoked the fire and added another log.

There were no windows in the room—to protect the information or preserve the books, I guessed.

"I assume Lilly's told you why we're here, Cheyenne?" Dex asked.

"To learn Timeless history," I replied. I was starting to feel the warmth from the fire and shifted my legs closer.

"Correct. I felt it was time you knew some of our most important secrets, given your position as Kvech leader." His hazel eyes softened. "I really wish we could've gone through this sooner. It might've helped. But we're here now, so we'll go through everything I think you need to know."

"I'd like that."

"If Lilly and I had raised you..." He trailed off, deep in thought, then released a heavy sigh. "Anyway, feel free to ask questions if you don't understand. I'll try and explain as best as I can."

I nodded, anxious to get started.

Dex dropped a large leather-bound book onto the small table and flipped it open.

"I want to start with marriages." He looked up. "I want you to understand your betrothal first, since that has caused you the most heartache."

I swallowed. Memories of that day in Dex's house after my trip with Colt rose to the surface. I quickly pressed them down. What was done was done. I couldn't dwell on it.

"It's not just some random thing, Cheyenne. There is purpose behind it, and it's deeper than you realize. The Kvech are the ruling clan for a reason. They bring stability to the Timeless," Dex said.

"What do you mean, bring stability?" I asked.

"You have seen for yourself what we—you—are capable of. Callon's ability with memory, Daniel's jumping, Andre's aura sensing, Maes' shifting, your own powers with air...these have all been inherent with the clans since their original founding. But over the last few centuries, and especially since the war with Marcus began, our powers have waned."

"Waned?"

Dex sighed.

"It is rare now for a Timeless to inherit powers. This becomes particularly important for the clan leaders, whose job it is to regulate the power between clans. They need stronger powers for this purpose, but in order for this to happen, they also need to choose strong partners. This is why marriages are arranged." Dex paused. "Are you following so far?"

"I think so," I said, rubbing my temple. It was quite a lot to take in. "How do the clan leaders control the clans' power, then?"

Dex offered his hand, showing his Coltooro ring.

"The rings," he said. "These allow us to merge our powers with the other clan leaders, so we can plug the weak gaps with strong ones."

I nodded. Strong with the weak; a theme Brogan loved to repeat. It made sense. It also explained why Callon had been so upset when I'd gone to open the safe deposit box in Helena. I always thought my Kvech ring was just a symbol of being Timeless. Yet both that and my Servak ring were far more important than I could've dreamed.

"Look here," Dex said. He pointed to the book again. "This is a listing of all the clan leaders throughout our history. It's a pairing, strong with the strong, though the Kvech lines are a bit more complex."

I pulled the book closer, scanning the page. The Coltooro and Consilador clans were listed with the most recent leaders, their spouses and children. There were also blotches beside some of the older names. I pointed to them.

"What are these?"

"At one time we had each leader's power listed, but it fell into the wrong hands and their powers were used against them." Dex lowered his head. "It was heartbreaking to know that someone we trusted would go as far as they did."

"Was Marcus behind it?"

"No. Makhi was."

"Makhi?" That name sounded familiar.

"Makhi was Marcus's father. He was a good man, once."

Dex quieted for a moment as he gathered his thoughts and moved back in his chair. I blinked. This topic seemed to have made him uncomfortable. Finally he sighed.

"What am I about to tell you is very important, Cheyenne," Dex said, his eyes intent. "You won't like some of the things I say, but hopefully it will help you understand."

I nodded and sat back myself, curling my legs beneath me in the comfortable chair.

"The Kvech are the Keepers of Power. Their rings are the strongest, but it wasn't always this way. At one time, the clans were equal, and there was no fighting. Powers were maintained through family lines, because they were arranged accordingly."

"So what changed?"

Dex hesitated. "Your grandfather, Jorell, Sahara's father. He was a very powerful Timeless, known for his abilities with enchantments. The original enchantment here was modified by him for Kieran, Callon's father."

I nodded.

"A long while ago, something happened between Makhi and Adalmund, Qaysean's father. They both wanted to stop the clans' powers from disappearing, but this divided the clans. Five of the clans gave a portion of their power to the Kvech, as Adalmund and his family were known to be pacifists. We trusted the Kvech to regulate the balance. Makhi was angry with this, as he felt he should have been chosen instead."

"So that's when the Quaysaar and Servak joined the Sarac," I whispered.

"Yes, and this was what would eventually lead to war. Makhi then convinced Jorell to experiment with his enchantments to increase their power...increase Makhi's powers. Makhi was determined to prove Adalmund was the wrong choice, and he wasn't afraid to do this by force."

"What happened then?" I sat up, captivated by the story.

"This is where the rings come in again," Dex said. "In addition to allowing the clan leaders to maintain balance, they also protect them, as otherwise they'd go mad. Jorell and Makhi's experiments bypassed the rings, granting them stronger power, but at the cost of their minds. Jorell eventually betrayed us, using the clan leaders' powers against them. This is how the Sarac have gained so much strength, and why we have struggled to defeat Marcus. He is draining all of us, and if he isn't stopped soon, we will have nothing left."

I sat back, absorbing everything that had been said.

"Why didn't you ever tell me this before?" My mind went back to my visit to their home. So much heartache and pain could've been prevented if only I'd known!

"Because you weren't ready to accept it," Dex said. "You'd barely learned you were Timeless. It would've been cruel to throw all these facts upon you as well. We all saw how strongly you felt for Colt, and Callon was going to break the news gently, but then you overheard us…"

He trailed off. I sighed. I wish they hadn't worried so much about what I could handle, but I had to take the blame for some of this as well. My pride back then hadn't let me ask the questions I needed to.

"In hindsight, we probably should have told you as much as we could, and for that I am sorry, but now I hope you understand something of the battle we've been fighting."

I looked at my hands and began twisting my Servak ring. If they'd relayed this information behind the marriages, I might not have fallen so hard for Colt. But even if they had, it would've been too late. I'd fallen for him long before my mind admitted it…my heart had known all along.

"You see, Cheyenne, your mother was betrothed to Marcus before Makhi and Jorell went mad. The Servak were the first to notice their powers waning, so they hoped an alliance with the Sarac would counter this."

"But she married Qaysean." I looked up. "So it was almost the same thing, right?"

"Essentially, yes," Dex said, "but Marcus has all the knowledge from his father's experiments. He knows how to subvert power, and has been punishing the Servak since." He pointed to my Servak ring. "The Servak are now weaker than ever, and if balance is not restored soon, they will lose their powers forever."

I bit my lip. "So if I marry Callon, I can bring the balance back?"

"Yes," Dex said "Both to the Servak and to the Consilador."

I blinked. "Consilador? But Callon's just as strong as I am…"

"It relates to Callon's father, Kieran," Dex said. "He was murdered, and the Consilador clan ring was lost for a time. By the time Callon retrieved it, it had lost a lot of its power. His clan, too, needs to be restored to its former glory."

I sat back and once again looked at my Servak and Kvech rings.

The puzzle pieces began to fall into place.

"You said Callon's ring lost power when it went missing," I said. "But my Kvech ring was hidden in a safe deposit box, yet it still has power?"

Dex twisted in his chair.

"Why don't we look at the rings as batteries," he suggested. "The Consilador ring and the others are like half-charged batteries. Their powers will drain away quickly. Whereas the Kvech ring is like a fully charged battery. It will take longer to completely drain it."

"So my ring has lost some of its original power?"

"Yes, but like all batteries, once it's on the charger, it will eventually regain full strength."

That made sense, but... "But Callon's had his ring for a long time right? Wouldn't it be recharged already?"

"He didn't always wear it when it was originally returned, and it takes longer the older a Timeless is."

"So how does a Timeless age? I mean, do your powers remain with you until the end?" I said.

"That's a bit complicated. You see, when we first become Timeless, we age one year for every one hundred human years, until we reach the age of four hundred, then it all changes. Once we're four hundred, then our aging switches to one year for every ten years. Got that?"

I nodded. "So like a Timeless menopause?"

Dex chuckled.

"I never thought of it like that, but yes, I suppose so. But that isn't the only thing. After four hundred years, we begin to lose our powers, and our rings lose their strength."

"So that's why Lilly said she used to talk to animals," I said, remembering our conversation while petting the horses.

"Yes, she did at one time, but her power has waned."

"And the reason why the rings need to be passed down..." I trailed off.

I rubbed my forehead. There were so many rules, exceptions and...I sighed. And Dex had no heir to pass his ring down to; Marcus had killed his son, I was sure, with this intent in mind.

"But you don't have an heir," I noted.

"I don't." His brown eyes saddened. "But I'm looking for a Coltooro heir that is worthy to step up," he breathed, "it will diminish my powers a great deal, but it won't completely take them. The clan will survive." He looked up. "The problem of this waning power can only be fixed once the Sarac stop draining the power of the clans."

There was so much more to being a Timeless than I realized. And then another thought hit me. All this power and restoration had so many implications.

"I was hidden away because you thought Marcus would see me as a threat. But in actuality he didn't—he saw me as a way to further boost his power. When you found me, I was a threat to you." I stood and moved closer towards the fire, staring at the flames. I understood now why Brogan didn't like me, why Maes pushed me the way he did...why Callon didn't give up hope.

"I'm a threat to the entire Timeless race," I whispered, "A highly volatile explosive weapon."

"You are a daughter, sister and friend whom we have come to love." Dex stood and pulled me into a hug.

"But if I fail, I'll bring destruction upon us all."

"You won't fail, Cheyenne. We won't let you."

He wouldn't let me, but honestly, the only way to prevent me from falling into Marcus's hold would require one thing. I stepped back.

"I have to marry Callon as soon as possible."

Dex sighed. "I wish it were that easy. Because you're Kvech, you can only marry under the summer solstice, which takes place in June."

"Why?"

"Because if a Kvech unites their power without the counterbalance of the sun, it would kill their partner."

I stared at him for a moment. Callon would...die?

Dex reached out. "Breathe, Cheyenne."

I inhaled, not realizing I had been holding my breath. I plopped into the chair. November had just barely arrived and June was months away. If Dex knew I could only marry under the summer solstice then...

"Marcus knows about this, doesn't he?"

"Yes."

"That's why he's been inactive. He's planning something."

"Most likely, but you're safe here."

"Not if Colt's out there and Marcus is controlling him," I said.

"The Tresezes passed through the enchantment, which means others could as well." Panic began rising. "We can't just hide out here and hope for the best, we—"

Dex held my shoulders. "We are working on it Cheyenne. Once we get word from Tre and Jayna, we'll have more accurate information. We can't just charge out of here because we think Colt might be alive. We need to have proof."

"And a plan of rescue."

I leaned over the table and began flipping through the manuscript again, stopping on the Kvech. My fingers traced my parents' names. What would it have been like to be raised by them? I wouldn't have had this huge gap, this misunderstanding about the Timeless race. I would've grown up knowing who I was and what was expected of me...and I would've either been killed or united with Marcus.

A shiver ran down my spine.

They'd done what they thought was right to keep me safe. I had to quit faulting them, and what had been handed to me. I just needed to absorb as much knowledge as I could before we faced Marcus. I knew he wasn't the forgiving type, and I'd promised myself no more failures.

The first thing I needed to do was talk with Callon. I'd been so naïve, always trying to rebel against his orders. But then again, he'd kept so much from me. It wasn't like I had the chance to make an informed decision. There were times in Montana when Callon seemed as though he wanted to tell me more, but I was too busy trying to find my own path, not realizing what truly lay before me.

"Thank you, Dex," I said. "I need some time to think things through."

"You're welcome, Cheyenne. I'd like to arrange a time to meet again, and we can go over more."

I left the library and found my way down the dreary hallway. The heavy doors creaked, and low murmurs echoed in the hall. I peeked around the corner. Andre and Maes were talking quietly in the sitting room. For someone who denied she and Maes were an item, she didn't seem to mind spending time with him.

I smiled. Maybe one day Maes could be happy. He'd suffered enough. It was time to make amends and fix the mess. Hopefully over time, his ring's power would be restored.

I headed down the hall and opened the main library door. Layla looked up from her book. She was snuggled up against Brogan, who was viewing a video on his phone. He didn't bother to look up.

"Are you looking for Callon?" Layla asked.

"Yes."

"I think I saw him heading upstairs."

"Thanks."

I quietly exited the main library, pulling the door closed behind me. Upstairs, Callon's door wasn't completely closed. I pushed it open, peeking around the corner. He was sitting in a chair near his fireplace, his head down.

"Callon?" I said softly.

He didn't reply.

I took a step inside his room and quietly closed the door. He must be concentrating, perhaps reading.

"Callon," I repeated. Again he didn't reply.

My soft-soled shoes made no noise on the thick wool rug as I neared, but a snap from the fire caused me to jump. Callon still hadn't moved. I stood to his side; he was staring at a picture of himself and Colt.

I kneeled down. He missed Colt so much. I reached out and touched his wrist, hoping to lend some comfort, when the world suddenly spun. I gasped as the fireplace melted away and my vision grew hazy.

Seconds later, I was somewhere completely different. Almost at once I realized where I was. We were in the Canadian forest again, trying to escape Marcus's trap. Callon was probing my wounded shoulder. He wasn't sure how much damage the Tresez had done.

"That still hurts?" Callon asked. *She should have healed already.*

I could hear his thoughts...this must be his memory.

"It's not awful, but it's not great either," I heard myself reply.

Callon glanced at Maes. "Should we have her try it out now?"

I watched my brow furrow. "Try out what?"

"We need to know if you can use your powers, Cheyenne," Maes said. "We can't fight Marcus alone, not when he wants you so badly. But I can't risk it here and now. I don't want to draw any more attention to us at the moment."

Callon nodded. *She needs to regain her strength. We're going to need her.*

"So we're taking orders from Maes now?" Colt growled. "You're seeking his advice over mine, Callon?"

Daniel moved closer and touched Colt's arm. Colt didn't even acknowledge him, staring at Callon with something close to hatred.

I moved closer to the misty vision, seeing the indifference in Callon's eyes.

Maes knows more, Colt. He was Marcus's right-hand man. We need to trust him, Callon said.

Ha! I can't believe you're falling for this, Colt spat. *He stole Cheyenne right from under our noses, and you're kissing his ass!*

She wouldn't have run if you'd only listened to me, if you'd have kept your distance and not forced your way into her heart!

Cheyenne gave herself willingly to me...she chose me over you, brother, Colt hissed.

NO! Callon snarled. *You're to blame here. You knew you needed to step back when we found out her true identity. You, Colt, are being selfish, just as you've always been. You've only ever thought of yourself and what you want, completely ignoring our responsibilities to the Timeless clans! You cannot change her fate, and if you try, it will destroy us all!*

And that's why I came back, to ignore my responsibilities?

You only came back because it involved a woman!

And you, dear brother, have always put the Timeless responsibilities above everything else! You never made time for us. You weren't there when Daniel was suffering. It was because of you our father was murdered!

Callon's eyes darkened. *That's it, Colt. I'm not going to tolerate you and your selfish ways any longer. The minute we're free from Marcus, you're banished. You are never to see Cheyenne again. You're banished from our family, our heritage. You're not my brother anymore!*

Colt clenched his fist, his arm shaking.

"You've taken everything away from me, Callon," Colt snarled. "Everything!" His nostrils flared like an angry bull. Koda stepped between the brothers, flashing a dark glare at Colt.

The ache in my heart doubled. Callon had been pushed to this point because of my relationship with Colt!

In an instant, the scenery changed again. We were on the ravine when a brilliant light flashed, causing me to gasp. I could taste it on my tongue before I realized the familiar dark rage. But this wasn't the red-eyed beast I'd known. This was Callon's own monster. Black, bitter and holding enough regret to fill an ocean. Anger, hatred, and despair swirled around him like a black mist, and I was terrified at its intensity.

I stood unmoving, watching Colt's death play out before me. Tears streamed down my cheek. An uncontrollable sob escaped me, and suddenly I was crushed against Callon's chest. The forest was gone, replaced by bedroom furnishings.

"Cheyenne, I—I'm so sorry. You were never meant..." Callon moaned.

I clung to him, pushing myself closer, unable to speak.

"I never should've banished him. I was just trying to do what was best," he whispered. "You shouldn't have touched me."

"How?" I cried. "How could I see your memory?"

"Your powers, they're so much stronger than we know. You shouldn't have been able to...I'm so sorry."

I curled myself into his lap further. I could have prevented so much if I'd only listened. I'd been acting just as selfishly as Colt, but I—we could change that now. If Colt were alive...

"Why didn't you ever tell me?" I asked. "We had all that time in Montana."

I drew back and stared into the warmth of his hazel eyes. He gently wiped the tears from my cheeks.

"I wanted to so many times, but you'd been through so much already. You'd lost your parents; you'd been ripped away from your home. You'd just been told you were Timeless, and there was no way to explain it all without overwhelming you. And your transformation...it nearly cost you your life. Colt was safe for you. You always turned to him. I just never thought it would turn out like this."

He paused for a moment.

"I always thought that through reliving memories, I could change what happened in the past," he whispered. "What I did to you, what I said to Colt..."

"But you can't," I said. "You can't dwell on the past. Neither of us can. We can only work on what lies ahead."

"If Colt's alive..."

"Then we'll find him together and make things right."

Callon drew me closer. "I just don't want to lose you in the process, Cheyenne."

"You're not going to lose me, Callon," I said. I pulled away, looking him straight in the eye. "I've made so many mistakes, so many failures against my name...but not any more. I understand now, clearer than ever, what I need to do." I paused, and took a breath. "I'm going to marry you."

CHAPTER 13

"You ready?" Callon asked as he stepped inside my bedroom. I'd been staring out the terrace doors, watching the rain again, waiting for him.

He pushed his fingers through his brown wavy locks and sighed. He was as nervous and anxious about this meeting as I was. It had been over a month since Brogan sent word to Tre and Jayna, and apparently he'd heard from them. I was told it took time before they could relay the data, whatever that meant.

"I can't wait for the rain to stop," I said, trying to ease the tension.

A smirk rose on his lips. "It always rains here, Cheyenne."

I leaned in and kissed his cheek. "Well, then at least I have you to cuddle with."

His arm came around my waist, and he escorted me down the hall. "I didn't know I was cuddling material," he chuckled.

"Not everyone qualifies, you know."

He squeezed my waist. "You have to qualify?"

"Oh yes."

We paused at the top of the stairs and he turned toward me.

"You're not going to be more specific?" A twinkle grew in his eyes.

"Well, first." I touched his shoulders. "You have to have broad shoulders. It makes for more snuggling room. Second." My fingers caressed his cheek. "These must be unshaven."

He smiled.

"Third." My lips brushed his. "These must be kissable."

"Three qualifications." He pushed the hair behind my ear. "Seems

I make them all."

"Lucky you..."

Daniel suddenly flashed beside us, and I gasped, slightly annoyed that he'd ruined the moment.

"Hurry up," Daniel said. He rubbed his hands together nervously, eager to get going. My heart softened. He'd been so jumpy—he wanted to know about Colt as much as we did. I knew deep down that we'd find him today, but it was going to be hard on all of us. Especially if our worries about him were true.

Daniel jumped ahead, landing at the bottom of the stairs, and gave me a restless glance. He disappeared again, and we headed down the stairs. When we reached the hall, I headed for the library, but Callon tugged my hand and nodded towards the sitting room. We were meeting there. As we headed inside, I soon understood why; everyone was here, and there wasn't enough space anywhere else.

Brogan leaned against the fireplace, conversing with Dex. He flashed me a dark glance, but I ignored him. I'd gotten used to it by now. The rest of the group was scattered on the sofas, talking in low murmurs. The tension in the room was thick, and I held Callon's hand tighter. He guided me to a spot that had been reserved for us, and we sat together. Daniel jumped beside us and sat on the arm of the chair, his leg bouncing nervously. Bree moved beside him and took his hand, her fingers interlocking with his.

Brogan cleared his throat, and the murmurs fell silent. He strode to the center of the room and looked at Callon.

"Tre and Jayna are here," he said.

Blinking, I glanced around the room. I hadn't noticed anyone new.

"I see," Callon murmured. He sounded distracted—he must have been thinking something through.

"Are you going to let them in?" Maes asked.

My brow creased. Let them in? He must have been referring to the enchantment. But Tre and Jayne were allies, right? It shouldn't affect them...

"That's irrelevant at this point," Callon replied. "Their powers won't work within the boundaries of the enchantment. If we want to know what Marcus has been up to, we'll have to meet them in the open."

Maes lower lip twitched, and he cast a sidelong glance at me. "Is that really a good idea?"

"We have no choice," Brogan broke in. "The Tresez have already crossed through once, and to get the most accurate information, we'll need both Callon and Cheyenne to help them. We have to risk the exposure."

I sat up straighter. Callon hadn't mentioned that I'd be so closely involved.

"Why us?" I asked. "If it's just information on Marcus, couldn't they simply tell us?"

"It's not quite as easy as that," Dex replied. "It's a bit hard to explain without seeing it, but look at it as having a camera in Marcus's back yard. They're able to project visions across vast distances, but they do have limitations. That's why we need to meet with them."

I twisted my Servak ring. It was pretty hard to picture something like that. What kind of power did these two possess?

"I don't like it," Maes said. "Marcus's army sits outside these walls, and we're going to just waltz out and say hello? We might as well hand Cheyenne over with a bow tied around her."

"You don't think we've thought about that?" Brogan growled. "We're going to take precautions."

Maes's eyes flared.

"Having your two most powerful clan leaders preoccupied like this is an opportunity for Marcus," he said. "You'd really endanger them for the sake of a little information?"

"Tre and Jayna can show us what we need to know," Brogan growled. "There's no other way."

Maes scoffed, his chest swelling. "*I* have a better idea of what the Sarac could be up to..."

"Like how you predicted the Tresez attack?" Brogan shot back. Maes bared his teeth, stepping forward, but Koda blocked his way. "This isn't my first rodeo, Maes. I'm in charge of this operation, and you can keep your *ideas* to yourself."

Maes's nostrils flared. My fingers tightened around Callon's as I thought Maes was about to shift, but then Andre pulled him back. I didn't need her aura skills to know it was getting red hot in here.

Callon stood up.

"Enough, both of you," he commanded. "I knew sending for Tre and Jayna would be dangerous, but I think it's worth the risk. If we don't find out about Colt, then that puts us in a tough position. We've already seen how the enchantment was manipulated. It can happen again, and next time I won't be strong enough to repair it." He sighed. "Then there really won't be anywhere safe for any of us."

I blinked. It had drained Callon that much?

Dex stepped closer, resting his hand on Callon's shoulder.

"Besides, from what I can tell, the Sarac's movements here appear random," he went on. "They're watching us, but not attempting to re-enter."

"How can you be so sure?" I asked.

"I can sense them, Cheyenne," Callon answered. "The enchantment isn't just a barrier, it also helps me see the surrounding area. This is our best opportunity to catch up on Marcus's plans."

"Well that's convenient," I muttered, wishing he would've told me sooner. Then again, he probably hadn't said anything because he didn't want me to worry. Every day he looked so tired; keeping me safe had really taken its toll on him. If only I wasn't so weak, I could've helped him...

"So how are we going to do this?" I asked. "It's like Maes said, we can't just walk out there."

Maes's jade-rimmed eyes focused on me.

"Maybe that's not such a bad idea," he said.

"What do you mean?" I asked.

Callon began pacing in front of the fire. "So you're saying we just leave here in broad daylight?" he asked.

"*We* will," Maes replied. He jerked his head at Koda. "Koda can keep Cheyenne hidden with his invisibility cloak. If Marcus's forces don't see her, they won't suspect anything. They'd never expect us to move so openly if we had her with us."

"A reasonable observation," Brogan said. "It could work."

"We could still run into trouble," Dex chimed, rubbing his temple. "Even if Cheyenne is their main goal, there's nothing to stop them from attacking us."

"But it's our best chance," Koda said, folding his arms. He turned to Callon. "What have you been sensing out there?"

Callon stopped pacing and stared at the fire.

"The usual suspects, Trackers and Tresez, but those aren't the ones I'm concerned about."

"Cloakers," Daniel said quietly.

"Cloakers?" I peered up into his worried blue eyes.

"Yes." His lips twisted uncomfortably. "You remember the Ghosters, right?"

I nodded, a shiver running down my spine. How could I forget those sparkling lights that ripped your soul from your body. "Yes. But I'm stronger now. The lights shouldn't affect me, right?"

"You'll be just fine with the Ghosters," Daniel said, "but the Cloakers..." He trailed off.

"You see, Cheyenne," Dex explained, "Cloakers are able to manipulate space. They can project themselves as black mist, and can travel as fast as the wind. But unlike the Ghosters, they can rematerialize on the spot as well. That makes them even more deadly."

"They can also take you with them, if you're alone," Maes added. "Avoiding physical contact is a must." He looked at Brogan. "Did you consider this little problem as well?"

"We can manage," Daniel spoke up. "We'll keep in constant contact with another by holding hands."

"But it only takes a second for the contact to be broken and for them to take a Timeless," Maes countered.

"Wait a second," I said, holding my hand up. "They won't be able to touch me if they can't get near me. I can blast them back with my powers."

"Possibly," Maes replied. "But some Cloakers are stronger than others. If Raina is out there..."

"Let me do it," Daniel said, his hand coming to rest on my shoulder. "I'll protect Cheyenne. If we run into trouble, I can jump us out of there."

Callon turned towards us, but remained silent. Daniel's fingers tightened on my shoulders, but then relaxed. They were talking it out.

"Honestly, Daniel," Koda said, "I'd be more worried about Callon."

"Callon?" I glanced to him, not sure I understood. "Is this true?"

Callon lowered his head. "I haven't regained all of my strength. Giving some to Tre and Jayna might leave me with nothing at all for a short time."

"Then don't do this," I said. "Let me."

"It has to be both of you, Cheyenne," Dex said. "Callon has the connection to Colt, and you have the connection to Marcus."

"What?" I raised a brow. "How do I have a connection to Marcus other than being betrothed?"

"It's twofold really," Dex replied, "You were with him, which gives a temporal connection, but mainly it's because of the Servak ring. It was in his possession for a period of time."

My thumb rolled over my Servak ring. These rings still had more to them than I knew. But if this whole thing was based on close connections...

"I still don't understand why Callon needs to do this too," I admitted. "I had a deep connection with Colt. Wouldn't that also work? And what about Daniel?"

"Callon's connection is stronger." Daniel's shoulders sagged. "And my powers aren't great enough."

"Your powers are great enough to help us in other ways, Daniel," Callon assured him.

Daniel gave a weak smile.

"How long will it take you to arrange a safe meeting place, Brogan?" Callon asked.

"Give me three days," Brogan replied. "In the meantime, we've got some training to do."

Leaning against the kitchen counter, I stretched and immediately cringed. When Brogan meant training, he hadn't been joking around. Everything hurt, and I sighed, touching my wrists. The finger marks had started to turn to bruises, but it didn't make them any less painful. Brogan, Maes and Koda had all taken turns reaching for my arms, and I had to learn how to break their holds. It made sense, since most of my powers involved my hands, and Marcus had been quick to tie me up the last time we'd met.

Then there had been Skylar's routine, which my legs were still feeling. He'd been teaching me how to "glide." I'd almost laughed when they said it like that, but after working with him, I understood why he seemed so graceful when he fought. There was a technique to his movements, allowing him to sidestep swings and attacks. It was a dance of sorts, choreography that I needed to learn.

"You okay?" Daniel asked. He was standing just inside the

kitchen doorway.

I blew the stray hair from my eyes.

"Yeah, just looking for some ice packs," I replied.

"Let me help you." He jumped beside me and grabbed some plastic bags from the counter. He moved again, landing before the freezer, and filled them with ice. He landed beside me. "Here."

"Thanks." I pressed the ice packs around my wrist.

"It'll be better by tomorrow."

I nodded, knowing tomorrow was when we'd leave the estate. I had faith in my powers, but my fighting tactics, well, they didn't come naturally. Fighting a human, hands down I'd be fine, but another Timeless with cloaking abilities...that was completely different. Everything I thought I knew flew out the window, and only having two and a half days to prepare didn't help either.

"We're both strong enough," Daniel reassured me, as if he could hear my thoughts.

"I'm not worried about my strength, Daniel."

"Nakari and I will be there. We're faster than them."

I sighed. "I know we have to work together as a team, and although I'm stronger now, I'm still the weakest link."

"Chey." Daniel touched my shoulder. "You're not the weakest link."

"But my powers aren't fully stable, and I've never encountered a Cloaker before."

"That's why we'll be there," Koda answered entering the kitchen. He stopped beside Daniel. "You've got more abilities than you realize."

"I just hope the risk we're taking is worth it." Even I was having doubts about leaving the estate. What if this was all just a trap? But I had to know if Colt was alive. If we didn't do this, I'd have even more regrets than before. I had to be brave and believe in my protectors.

I forced a smile.

"Come on," Daniel said and tugged on my arm. "It's been a while since we've played poker. It'll help take your mind off things."

I paced the floor in the main library, glancing out the window.

The sky was darkening by the moment, both because of the rainclouds and the approaching night. I swallowed. We would be leaving within the hour to travel to a town about thirty miles away. Callon wanted to stay away from villages and any smaller towns, believing a larger community would provide more safety, more human eyes watching. However, there was still a dense forest we had to pass through. That was going to be the most dangerous part of the trip, particularly on the drive back, and particularly with the storm rolling in.

I heard voices in the hall, and then Andre appeared, and tilted her head at me.

"You're a bit green, Cheyenne," she said.

I raised a brow. "Well, that's a nice thing to say."

"Your aura that is."

I continued with my pacing, waiting for her to tell me all about it.

"You're worried, but trying to remain calm."

I tapped my nose. I didn't need Andre to tell me how I was feeling right now. I was a bundle of nerves.

"Maes won't let me come with you."

"I heard." I paused and faced her.

She fiddled with her fingers. She was worried too.

"I think I'll hide in the back of the car. I don't need a dog telling me what to do."

"He's bossy."

Andre smiled faintly and rolled her eyes. "Slightly."

A dark shadow moved behind her, and she shrugged. She stepped away, but not before she and Maes exchanged glances. It wasn't her typical glance laced with sarcasm; this was woven with emotions she'd rather not share.

"Andre," Maes's grumbled. He too was hiding things.

"Are we ready?" I asked.

"It's time," Maes informed me with a curt nod.

Grabbing my jacket from the chair, I followed Maes to the hall. Koda was waiting there, holding his cloak. For anyone else, the cloak wouldn't have worked, but because of my powers, it did. Lilly had even altered the length so I wouldn't trip over it.

Memories of the last time I'd worn it crept forward, but I shut them out. I needed to do this. I wrapped the fabric around my shoulders, but kept my head uncovered for the moment. Koda

181

stepped out the front door, and I followed. Three black Range Rovers with tinted windows were waiting on the gravel drive. I glanced around. Why did we need three? Only eight of us were going.

"One's a decoy," Koda said. "The Campbell's are driving out before us."

I nodded and watched the first depart.

"Cheyenne!" Lilly called out, rushing down the front steps. She didn't bother to hide her anxiety as she hugged me.

"You need to be careful, do you understand?" Her voice trembled. "I need you to come back, and in one piece. All of you."

"I will, Lilly, I promise," I replied.

She kissed my cheek and drew back. Dex joined her, and he patted my shoulder.

"We love you, Cheyenne," he said. "Be safe."

"Love you too."

"Cheyenne!" Maes barked, nodding towards the second Range Rover. He opened the rear door, and I crawled in. Callon was already waiting inside. Daniel slid in beside me and Brogan took the driver's seat. Maes moved into the passenger side. I turned to see Nakari, Skylar and Koda get in the second Range Rover. Koda was our one-way radio link to the second vehicle.

Maes turned. "Wrap up and buckle in, Cheyenne."

I nodded and slipped Koda's cloak hood over my head. Now I'd be invisible. I quickly buckled my seatbelt. Moments later we were driving down the long gravel drive.

Callon kept his gaze forward, just like the rest. Our shoulders touched, but that was about all the contact we could risk. He had to pretend I wasn't here.

A tingling sensation ran over my skin as we passed the estate's main gates. I jerked slightly as the heavy raindrops began to fall. The storm had broken again.

The drive was quiet, but I couldn't stop glancing through the windows. We were out in the open, exposed, vulnerable. I could only hope the cloak would fool them. Without me, the Trackers and Tresez had no reason to pay attention. Still, if we took too long, they'd get suspicious. We needed to hurry.

"Breathe, Cheyenne," Maes said. "You're ready for this."

I pressed my eyes closed for a moment and inhaled. I swear at times that dog could read my mind. Calm, I needed to remain calm and aware of my surroundings. I returned to watching the landscape, searching for hidden dangers.

Rolling green hills dotted with low-lying rock walls and open pastures with farmhouses lay around us. Those walls could easily hide a Tresez in this ever-darkening rainstorm...or worst yet, Cloakers.

Several villages blurred past, their houses nestled tightly together. I shifted in my seat, trying to push down the nausea. I was working myself up too much. I took a few cleansing breaths.

"It's going to be okay, Chey," Daniel whispered. I could tell he wanted so much to touch my hand, to reassure me, but he couldn't. I wasn't supposed to be here. Despite the risk, I softly brushed my hand against his.

Finally the gloomy darkness of the forest appeared. The atmosphere in the Range Rover changed dramatically. Maes sat forward, while Brogan gripped the wheel tighter. Callon and Daniel had practically stopped breathing, alert for the smallest hint of trouble.

Within moments, we were completely covered in shadows. I didn't need to look at the speedometer to know Brogan had increased his speed. The headlights from the second Range Rover no longer lit the interior of our car; they were literally riding our bumper.

Maes spread his arms, one resting on the dash, the other on Brogan's seat. He was bracing for something when his head whipped to the left. He stared out past Callon's shoulder.

"Did you see anything, Maes?" Brogan snapped.

"Just a dog."

Brogan nodded, but Maes kept his eyes glued to the landscape for a while longer.

A bend in the narrow road was coming up. We came upon it, and a moment later an open patch of rolling hills appeared. The ruins of a moss-covered castle stood stoic in the downpour.

I stared at it longingly. This was about as much sightseeing as I'd ever get while in Ireland. What I wouldn't have given to be able to stop and view the ancient walls, to run my fingers over the old stones and dream about who had once lived there. Could it have been a Timeless like us, or perhaps a wealthy family that had lands and livestock?

"It won't be long now," Callon said, his gaze still locked on the trees. "Another five minutes, and we'll be out of the forest."

I nodded even though no one could see me. Almost exactly to the minute, the trees vanished and more rolling hills surrounded us. The hills turned to small cottages, at first spread out, but quickly gathering together as we neared the city. We were almost there.

The car began to slow and as we circled a roundabout, brightly colored buildings came into view, along with the city's name, Killarney. Even in the gloom, the cheeriness of yellows, reds and greens were hard to ignore. The buildings were compacted in rows, each linked to the next the entire length of the street. People milled about regardless of the weather; it was a Saturday after all.

We passed through several roundabouts when Brogan turned left and we stopped, parking in a larger lot. Koda parked beside us.

"Stay here," Maes said. He left the Range Rover.

I watched through the tinted glass while he ensured the area was secure. I glanced at the dashboard and saw it was now four o'clock. With the wave of his hand, we too exited the vehicles. I made sure Koda's cloak hood was over my head.

Callon pressed close, his chest brushing my back, while Daniel stepped beside me, holding an umbrella. Callon had barely spoken a word since we'd left, not that he needed to. The tension in his face told me everything I needed to know.

The sidewalk began to swell with weekend shoppers, and the sight of other people was comforting. At least we blended in.

We began walking. Daniel and Callon walked side by side, and I kept just a step behind them. I caught glimpses of the colorful shops, and the smell of fresh bread. The scent of spices and meat grilling caused my stomach to grumble, regardless of the fact I didn't need to eat. What I wouldn't do for a caramel frappe along with a blueberry scone. My mouth began to water at the thought, but that would have to wait for another time.

We followed Brogan, winding our way down a few alleys before we stopped at a rundown brick building near the edge of town.

Brogan slid a huge metal door to the side and ushered us in. Any light in the dreary building vanished when the door closed.

"Wait here," Brogan said. He disappeared into the darkness.

The sound of electricity crackled, and a dim light in the far corner of the warehouse appeared. Brogan waved us on, standing at the base of a staircase that led to a metal walkway.

I pulled down my hood and looked around. The stench of must and oil hung in the air. Dusty old machinery lay in the corners, and a broken-down delivery truck had its hood open. It must've been an abandoned garage or something.

The clanking of heavy footsteps echoed off the walls, and I looked up. Two figures were standing on the walkway, peering over the rail towards us.

"Glad you could make it," one said—a woman with a soft voice.

Tre and Jayna were here.

CHAPTER 14

We climbed the metal walkway. My shoe caught in Koda's invisibility cloak, pulling out part of the hem Lilly had made. Callon grasped my elbow.

"Careful," he admonished.

I nodded, too anxious to speak. This was it. We were about to find out if Colt was alive.

"Tre, Jayna," Brogan greeted them. He gestured to me. "This is Cheyenne."

I stepped closer and pulled my hand out of the cloak.

"Nice to meet you," I replied, shaking their hands. The twins smiled in response.

"The honor is ours," the man—Tre—said. "We only hope we can be of some help to you."

I couldn't help but see a resemblance in him to Quinn. In fact, both he and Jayna were of smaller stature, and had darker skin with black hair. Something about the shape of their face, the curve of the lips, too; they had to be related.

"We need to get started," Maes ordered. "I don't like what I'm feeling around here."

Brogan moved back. Tre and Jayna stepped forward, placing themselves between me and Callon.

"Did they tell you how this was going to work?" Jayna asked.

"Sort of," I replied. "From what I understand, it's like a camera?"

"It's based off memories, Cheyenne," Tre answered. "Jayna and I made a trip to Marcus's compound because we had to have a visual link to the *place*. What you're going to provide is a link to the *person*."

"Marcus," I said. "So what we're going to see isn't what's happening now?"

"No, it will be a memory, Marcus's memory," Tre replied. "But it will be a recent one, so it should give us useful information."

"We're going to need to hold your hands and borrow your powers," Jayna explained. "It's going to feel a bit uncomfortable once we lock on a memory, but I promise the feeling will ease within a few moments."

"Okay."

"We're then going to filter through both your memories to allow the connection with Marcus and Colt. Some of them may be duplicates because we can't have a connection to both at the same time. We'll start with Marcus first, then switch to Colt."

Tre and Jayna extended their hands, and I clasped them. Callon did the same. I couldn't read his expression.

"You need to close your eyes, Cheyenne, and think of Marcus. I know this is going to be hard, but if you can produced a happier memory, that will make the process faster," Tre said.

I frowned. Any memory of Marcus was laced with anger and hatred.

"You can do this, Chey," Daniel whispered.

I closed my eyes, trying to bring forth a happy memory. Almost instantly, I felt the wind. I was surrounded by trees, which were shaking from the force of the hurricane. I was on the hillside standing over Colt's body. Red-hot rage filled my veins, giving life to the crimson-eyed beast. I'd destroy them all!

"Cheyenne!" Callon screamed.

My eyes shot open, and I gasped. Callon squeezed my fingers.

"Cheyenne," he said again, but this time softly. "I know this is hard. I know where your mind wants to take you, but you have to think of something else. Try and focus in on how you met him. You didn't know who he was then. Before he..." He trailed off.

I exhaled, trying to clear my mind from the rage. Instead I focused on a time I'd seen him in a softer light. When I'd spent time with Matt.

"Cheyenne?" A hand touched the back of my head. *"Are you feeling okay?"*

I groggily lifted my head to see steel gray eyes staring at me in concern.

"Dinner's ready, but if you don't feel good..."

I sat up straight and realized I must have fallen asleep. "No, I—I'm fine." I forced a smile and stood up. Matt watched me closely.

I gritted my teeth, my anger stirring again. He'd been nothing but a lying cheat. He was never a friend. No! I snapped to myself. He was Matt then, a concerned neighbor. Nothing more.

"Is the kitchen table okay?" he asked.

I nodded and headed for the kitchen. He pulled out the chair for me. "Thanks." I sat and watched as he moved to the chair beside me. Sighing, I dropped the napkin in my lap and raised my brows at the full plate of pasta before me. "Wow, this looks great, Matt."

A smug smile spread over his face. "Thanks. Now dig in."

I rolled my fork with pasta and blew on the sauce to cool it down. The taste that touched my tongue was simply amazing. "Matt, this is fantastic!" I quickly shoved another bite in.

"It's an old family recipe."

"Don't ever lose it!" I smiled, meaning it for the first time in a long while.

We finished dinner, and I was once again shooed off into the great room as Matt cleaned up. I stared out the windows, watching the rain tumble to the ground. I hadn't realized truly how much I missed my trio until now.

"Penny for your thoughts?" Matt asked as he sat across from me in the chair.

I looked down and fiddled with my Servak ring. It had actually been nice having company around. But my thoughts were private, and the thoughts about what happened earlier were off limits. "It's not worth the penny," I replied.

He sighed. "I worry about you, Cheyenne. One so young shouldn't have to bear whatever burden you've chosen to bear."

"I didn't choose it. It chose me."

"I'm a good listener, you know."

I looked up and met his open face. "I'm sure you are, but I'm a lousy talker."

He remained silent for a few moments.

"What's your favorite color?"

I tilted my head. "Huh?"

"What's your favorite color?" he asked again and took a sip of his wine.

I shrugged, as I had no idea where he was going with this. "Blue."

"Favorite time of year?"

"Fall." It seemed simple enough to give one-word answers.

"Song?"

"I don't have just one."

"Fair enough." He nodded. "Okay, favorite instrument?"

I shook my head. He should know that. "Guitar."

He smiled. "All right, favorite food?"

"Mexican."

"Favorite outdoor activity?"

I grinned, knowing he expected me to say hiking. "Horseback riding."

"Really? It so happens I own some of the finest stallions in Canada."

Suddenly an excruciating pain ran up my neck and into my head. My legs swayed, wanting to give way, but I didn't fall. I was being held up somehow, floating in a vast sea of images...memories. We were racing across the sky, over the Atlantic Ocean, across the eastern coast of New York, and before I knew it, we were there.

Rugged mountains came into view, followed by dense forests and a crystal clear lake. Now that we weren't moving so fast, I spotted an army of Trackers and Tresez gathering behind thick, gray stone walls, the walls of a compound.

Smoke burned my nose and then cleared as we disappeared inside a large structure. I blinked, trying to focus in the dim lighting, when I heard him...*Marcus*.

"You failed yet again, Conall?!" Marcus bellowed. We were in a living space, a sofa and chairs arranged near a fireplace. The room vibrated with electricity.

"She's stronger than we realized," Conall replied.

"It was simple," Marcus growled. He stormed towards Conall, grasping his collar. "I told you how to control her—bind her hands! Without them, she's no stronger than a human!"

Conall's image became clearer; the same chiseled face, the same scar running from his eyes to his nose. The sound of dog tags rattled as Marcus shook him. Conall was larger than Marcus, yet he didn't fight back.

189

"It was Maes," Conall mumbled. "He interfered. We couldn't get him out of the way."

"That's no excuse!" Marcus roared. "I had the enchantment opened for you with the promise you wouldn't fail me! Why is it that a stupid dog like you has such a hard time following simple instructions?!" Marcus released him and turned away. "You're not up to this job. Get me..."

"No!" Conall yelled. "I'll get Cheyenne for you. Give me a second chance."

"Second chance? You useless fool, you nearly killed her!"

Conall stepped back.

"Did you think I don't know what happened? Did you think I didn't see you try and strangle her? You don't seem to understand what a precious gift she is!" Marcus growled.

"I can do this."

"You can't. I need someone stronger. Send a message to Ra—"

I didn't catch the rest, as with a jolt we were in a forest, dark and misty. I could see Callon; a wispy ghost floating before me. I followed him, when abruptly he reached back, his fingers intertwining with mine. My eyes caught the glow of a fire ahead, and I heard horses whinnying. A cold chill ran over my skin.

"Get him secured!" A raspy voice hissed in the distance. "I ordered you to use the chains of Mozary, you fool! He'll break through anything else!"

Our pace quickened, and we stopped just short of where someone lay on their side. His clothing was ripped and bloody, and his blond hair was dirty and matted. His arms and chest were covered in bruises, and there were fresh cuts on his face. My eyes went wide.

Colt!

My heart began to ache, and I fought to reach out and touch him, but Callon held me back. Tears welled in my eyes. After all the grief and pain, I was so happy to see him alive, but I felt my guilt rise. We'd left Colt to be captured. We'd deserted him...

Colt staggered to his feet. He was wearing the same shirt as he had that day, a huge hole burned through the chest where he'd taken the lightning bolt. His eyes filled with rage, and he attempted to step forward, but he was too weak and only managed to sink to his knees again.

From the shadows, Marcus emerged, looking smug.

"It's a nice show you put on, Colt," Marcus taunted, kicking dirt in Colt's face. "So ready to give up your life for Cheyenne, and for what? So she could run off with Callon and leave you for dead?"

A bellowing growl vibrated across the trees, and the muscles in Colt's neck began to bulge.

"Did you really think she'd fall for you?" Marcus went on. "Did you think I'd allow it?"

Colt's nostrils flared. He lunged forward, when a bright light flashed before us.

"No!" I screamed and broke free from Callon. I ran towards Colt and tried to help him stand, but every time I reached for him, his image vaporized. *It's a memory. It already took place...*

Several Trackers jumped on him, binding his arms behind his back and securing them with chains. They shoved him to his knees, and Marcus paced around him. I stepped back.

"You fool, you think you're strong enough to fight me?" he scoffed. "I should have left you for dead on the hillside instead of saving your pathetic life. You're only good for one thing..." He stopped mid-sentence, his head rising. A tingling sensation ran down my spine, when suddenly he looked straight at me. A cold smile flickered across his face.

"I see you, angel," he whispered, "and I'm coming for you."

My breath caught.

"Cheyenne!" a voice screamed.

I fought to free myself, pushing back the hands that held me down.

"Cheyenne!"

I blinked and panicked hazel eyes came into view. Callon...

"He knows," I whispered.

"It was a memory, he can't!" Callon protested.

"That wasn't a memory, Callon," Jayna said quietly. She kneeled beside me. "He broke in somehow."

"What?" Brogan growled. "Marcus broke into the memory?"

"We've got to leave now!" Maes snapped. "Get her up!"

Callon and Jayna helped me to my feet, and the warehouse began spinning. Despite knowing the danger, I felt as if a huge weight had been lifted off me.

"Callon," I said, "Colt's alive! We shouldn't have left him..."

"There was no way he could've survived that hit," Callon

answered. "Marcus has done something to him..."

"There's not time to speculate!" Daniel ordered. He'd jumped up the stairs and was reaching for my hand. "We have to go!"

"But we have to rescue Colt!" I cried.

"Daniel's right. Now is not the time," Callon said. "We need to get out of here. We'll have plenty of time to discuss this later." He nodded at Daniel. "Get her to the car."

"What about you?" Daniel asked.

"Nakari will help me," Callon said. He clasped my shoulder. "Cheyenne, don't try to rely on your powers. They'll be weak for a short while. Stay with Daniel, and he'll keep you safe." He pulled the cloak tightly around me. "Above everything, don't let yourself be seen."

"Okay." I nodded, then winced as the movement triggered a dull ache behind my temples. How much power had they drained from me?

Daniel pushed the cloak's hood over my head and grabbed my hand. A moment later, we were at the bottom of the stairs with Maes, Koda and Brogan.

"You know what to do, Cheyenne," Maes reminded me. "Keep clear of them or break their hold. We'll try to keep them distracted."

We jumped outside into the alleyway. It was totally dark now; we'd spent a long time in there. The cold air hit me hard, and I began to shiver. At least the rain had stopped, but for how long?

"Keep your arm straight," Daniel said. "I'll keep hold, but I need to make it look natural."

"Right," I whispered.

Hand in hand, we took slow, deliberate steps, trying not to draw attention to ourselves. I looked up. The moon was starting to break through the clouds, providing more light. Would it help us see the Cloakers or would it prevent us from recognizing the black mists?

It happened so fast I had to blink to catch it. A murky vapor materialized at the end of the alley. Daniel released my hand, and I drew it into the cloak, concealing my entire body. At least I knew what to look for.

"Just out for a stroll, darling?" a whispery female voice said. "I thought you might have a package for me." She stepped into the light; a slender woman in skintight black leather pants and strappy stilettos. Her Gothic duster fluttered in the breeze, and she began to stroke the black-feathered scarf around her neck. Her pale skin, dark hair and blue eyes stood out against the gloomy ensemble.

Daniel didn't reply, nor did he jump. He remained completely immobile, waiting for something, but what?

"Raina," Maes's low growl gave warning.

I took a step to the side and pressed up against the brick wall. Maes and Koda strode past. Koda had his fists clenched.

"Maes, *mi cielo*," Raina smiled. "I've missed you." Her vapor suddenly appeared before him, but he didn't move. Willowy fingers reached out to touch his cheek, but Maes's hand instantly clamped around her wrist.

I knew enough Spanish to know she'd called Maes *my heaven*.

"Glad to see nothing's changed, *mi cielo*." Her ruby red lips produced a crooked grin. "But I'm not here for you."

"The *package* you seek isn't here," Maes informed her.

My heartbeat quickened once more. I had to get away without being seen or heard. The Range Rover was only a short walk. I could make it. I glanced further down the alley. It veered to the left, but it was too dark to see what lay beyond. Would it take me out to an open street or a dead end? We'd crossed over three main avenues, right? I ground my teeth. I'd been too preoccupied with the smells and a growling stomach that now I wasn't sure.

The stare down with Raina continued until Maes pushed her away, and she stumbled back, her eyes searching behind them.

"I'll find her, *mi cielo*, and when I do there's nothing you can do to save her." Raina suddenly disappeared into a fine mist.

Maes, Daniel and Koda didn't move.

"Get to the car," Koda said, his eyes remaining focused on Daniel. "We need to leave."

Daniel turned and swallowed, his eyes searching the alley.

Maes nodded towards the sidewalk, and all three vanished from sight as they rounded the corner. I was on my own.

I took focused steps in the opposite direction; I couldn't afford to slip up here. If my foot ventured outside the cloak, Raina would be all over me. If I somehow moved a puddle, Cloakers would swarm me. How many Cloakers were here, anyway? I glanced up to the roofs. Were they watching now?

A black cat jumped out from behind a dumpster, and I shoved my hand to my mouth, holding back a scream. It hissed and then took off into the blackness. I exhaled, and then froze as the steam from my breath filtered out.

"Tsk, tsk, tsk, Cheyenne," Raina said. A misty figure drifted before me. "You'd have thought with all the time they've had with you, you'd have learned something."

The mist jerked to the right, but didn't materialize.

I stepped back and felt the dumpster's corner touch my shoulder blade. She was testing the waters; she didn't know where I was yet.

A vapor taking the shape of a hand reached out, and I leaned back, narrowly missing her touch. The corner of the dumpster dug into my back.

"Toby, get back here!" A child ran past the alleyway opening, and the mist drifted away.

I lunged forward and suddenly was thrown back into the dumpster. I yanked harder and heard the cloak tear. It only took a moment for me to feel their cold presence around me. I yanked the tie at my neck and bolted past.

"Get her!" a female voice screeched.

I cursed. I'd blown my cover too soon. Sprinting as hard as I could, I made it to the end of the alley and turned left. Three Cloakers suddenly appeared, blocking my way. I thrust my hands out and sent a burst of air. It was weaker than I wanted, but they scattered into tiny particles. I ran past.

The glow of streetlights came into view, and my hopes rose. They wouldn't appear in public, would they? They couldn't take me if I stayed on the main thoroughfare and mingled with humans. I kept my focus on the roadway. I just had to make it.

Suddenly something clamped around my torso, dragging me back. I tried to scream, but it was quickly squelched by a large hand.

"Shh!" Maes crushed me to his chest. Without waiting for an answer, he turned and grabbed my wrist, racing towards the busy street. "Where's the cloak?"

"It caught on a dumpster. I had to leave it," I replied breathlessly.

We rounded the corner when Maes stopped. Raina sat on a bench just beneath a jewelry shop. Its sign read *O'Shea's of Killarney*. Her red lips rose in a smirk.

Daniel brushed my shoulder, and we locked hands. We moved forward.

"And you said you had no package for me, *mi cielo*," Raina tsk'ed. "You were never good at keeping secrets."

We passed, and she moved directly behind Maes, her fingers stroking his black hair as we walked. She was taller than I thought, only a few inches shorter than he, though most of it must have come from the stilettos.

"I wish you'd come back, Maes," she purred. "It hasn't been the same since you've gone."

Maes gave no reply, but our pace quickened. She couldn't do anything in public, and not with our hands linked, either. Raina was forced back as the crowd thickened. The dinner rush was on.

Loud laughter broke out from a group of people gathered outside a narrow doorway. A construction barricade constricted the space on the sidewalk as the roundabout curved to the right. The sign hanging above the doorway lit up, Mustang Sally's Bar.

Maes's hold grew tighter on my wrist, and I had to move behind him to pass through the mass of patrons. I glanced back over Daniel's shoulder; Raina followed, and a few others dressed in the same black Goth coats were directly behind her.

"Don't leave my side," Daniel whispered.

I caught sight of movement across the street. More Cloakers were gathering. They were creating a trap.

Maes shoved me closer to the barricade, and then I saw why. Just ahead was an alleyway opening, large enough to push someone inside of...

A horn honked. The Cloakers were moving on the crosswalk, heading straight for us.

I clenched my fists. The drain on my powers should have worn off by now, although they hadn't told me how long it'd last. If I could just blast them away with a wind burst like before...

"Don't," Maes hissed, "too many eyes."

I blinked. Did he just read my mind?

Maes's pace quickened, and soon we'd crossed another intersection. Here stood a stone church with red metal fencing and stained glass windows. This wasn't the same street we'd walked before. I'd have noticed it. We circled around it, following the path. Where was Maes taking us? The crowd was thinning. Were we heading out of town?

Screeching tires caught my attention. Two black Range Rovers sped up the street and skidded to a stop. The doors flew open, and Maes shoved me in the rear seat. I collided with Callon. He secured his arm around my waist and drew me closer. Daniel never lost his grip on my hand and the door slammed closed.

Maes straddled the seat, his eyes searching behind the cars, and Brogan concentrated on the road.

Maes and Callon exchanged glances.

"Now what?" I asked, not bothering to hide the trembling in my voice. There were more Cloakers than I realized. Would I be able to fight them?

"The forest," Brogan answered.

"Marcus would have warned Raina not to draw attention to herself," Maes explained. "They're going to wait for the cover of trees to make their move."

"I can fight them," I said, my courage growing. "I hit some with a pocket of air in the alley, and they dispersed."

Callon's fingers tightened on my waist.

"I shouldn't have risked bringing you out," he lamented.

"I came willingly," I reminded him. "You didn't force me."

"You don't understand," Daniel replied. "Raina's here."

"I met her." I sat up straighter. "She doesn't seem any different than the others. If I can get her out in the open..."

"Don't even think you can match her," Maes shot out. "She's—"

The car jerked to the right, and I was thrown against Daniel. The headlights from the second car revealed the swarm of vapors outside the windows.

"Buckle her in!" Maes bellowed.

My eyes grew wide as I saw a large boulder about to hit the windshield.

Callon shoved me further into Daniel's side, and a second later, we were tumbling arm in arm down a grassy ravine. Something sharp skimmed the back of my head, and I cried out. I pressed my fingers to my neck, and they came away covered with blood.

"I've got you," Daniel whispered. It took a moment to recover from the fall, but soon we were on our feet.

Nakari flashed before us, her eyes filled with panic.

"Get her out of here," she yelled. "I'll get Callon!"

She vanished, and Daniel jumped as well. Soon trees were whipping past us so fast they began to blur. But where were the

Cloakers? Then I realized; the scenery was blurred because of the black mists. Daniel's arms grew tighter around me. They'd found us!

"Pull your arms in and hold onto my jacket," Daniel ordered, "It'll make it harder for them."

"But I can fight them, Daniel!" I was strong enough. I needed to help out.

"You don't understand!" he snapped. "This isn't—"

His words were cut short as I was ripped from his chest. I hit the ground hard, gasping to catch my breath. A wall of misty shadows covered me. On instinct my hands flew out, and I forced them away with a blade of wind, clearing a small path of escape. I just needed to get on my feet and create a whirlwind. That would get rid of them. I ran towards an opening in the forest and faced the misty figures.

I began to twirl my hands above my head, feeling the pressure change, and the wind whip my hair. The shadows didn't move, only hovered in the wind. I narrowed my eyes and forced more power out, allowing the crimson-eyed beast some freedom. They weren't going to take me anywhere I didn't want to go.

The shadows merged with the winds. Water droplets sprayed the air, and my fingers began to tingle with the power within them.

A low murmur started to grow in my ear, a buzzing that increased in intensity until it turned into screeches and wailing. I cringed at the sounds, but refused to give in. The wind-filled wall grew denser, blacker, and started to glow with specs of iridescent blue, like a flame.

Soon the shadows emerged from the winds, hands reached out, grasping at me. I pushed the winds further away, but it didn't matter. Their limbs grew, stretching to reach out. A vapory finger touched my neck, and a burning sensation instantly erupted.

I clenched my teeth as more and more touches tore into my skin; my clothing was no barrier at all. The scent of burning material, burning flesh, pierced my nose. They weren't cutting me. They were burning me alive!

I needed to make the winds stronger, but the more I fought to push out the raw power, the weaker I became. They were going to wear me out! If I kept the Cloakers in the winds, they'd scorch my flesh to pieces, but if I released the winds, they'd take me away. Soon, I wasn't going to have a choice...

A misty finger ran down my arm for just a moment and intense pain rippled down it. I screamed, my winds diminished and I crumpled to my knees. Tears brimmed near the surface. I looked up to see Raina standing over me, a sly smile on her lips. She reached out, when suddenly I vanished.

"Hold on!" Nakari screamed locking her fingers over mine.

"No!" Raina bellowed.

Nakari had saved me...

The shadowy vapors trailed inches behind us. Just like before, whispery limbs stretched out, and what was left of my jacket fell off. Each and every touch set my skin on fire like a thousand burning needles. I struggled to take a breath.

Daniel appeared alongside us. He and Nakari exchanged glances.

I blinked and was thrown in Daniel's chest; his arms came around me as my legs gave way. Nakari was gone.

"I've got you," Daniel whispered. "We're almost there."

I clawed onto his shirt and held on. I began shaking, and I couldn't control it.

A wild shriek echoed beside us. Nakari was covered with the mists.

"Daniel!" I screamed. "We have to help her!"

Daniel made no reply, only held me tighter.

A tingling sensation ran over me, and we suddenly stopped. Daniel's hold loosened, and we turned. The black forest was behind us, and the waters of the estate lake sparkled under the moon.

We'd made it back.

"Nakari..." I whispered, barely able to speak.

We both stood motionless, watching, waiting. Finally Nakari appeared. She collapsed on the grass, fighting to catch her breath. Her jacket was etched with burn holes, her normally neat hair tousled. She looked up, her face dirty and cut.

"Get her to the manor, Daniel," she said breathlessly, "The rest are waiting for you."

Daniel's arm around my waist held me up, and we disappeared. We were safe now within the enchantment's borders. We'd all made it back, but in pieces. We couldn't keep doing this, hiding, living in constant fear of being discovered. Sooner or later, I was going to have to face Marcus and end this once and for all...

"You were right," Daniel whispered. "Callon told me about the vision. Colt's alive."

I closed my eyes. In spite of our close escape, I couldn't deny it had been worth it. At last, I had proof Colt was alive. I hadn't been imagining it. But now he was Marcus's prisoner. How were we going to free him?

A horrible taste suddenly filled my mouth, and I doubled over. Footsteps rushed around, and I heard a gasp.

"Get her inside, Daniel!" Lilly cried.

The grass disappeared, replaced by the warmth of the manor hall. Seconds later I was taken from Daniel and carried to the dining room table. The taste got worse, and I felt my body quake. Bile rose in the back of my throat, and Dex grabbed my neck, tilting my head as I vomited a vile black liquid. I heard him shout, but I didn't make out the words.

Exhausted, sick and hurting all over, I sank down onto the table. Lilly murmured, stroking my forehead, while Dex began to check my injuries. My eyes closed, and I felt a hand wrap around mine. Peace filled me, and I squeezed Daniel's hand.

"Thank you," I whispered.

As sleep began to creep over me, I could only replay the vision I'd seen. Colt was alive. He was a prisoner and in danger, but he was alive.

And this time, I'd be the one to rescue him.

CHAPTER 15

My lashes fluttered, and I shivered from the cold. I was face down on my bed, and it was dark except for the dim light of a fire. I moved to roll over, then shrieked as pain ignited across my back. I collapsed, gasping. Footsteps neared.

"Be still, love," Callon said softly. He sat on the bed beside me and stroked my cheek. "Between the Cloakers' attack and the visions with Tre and Jayna, it took a lot out of you. You're not healing as quickly."

The battle in the forest with Raina and the other Cloakers floated through my mind, but it was still a little unclear. It had all happened so fast. The black mist, and that scorching smell...

"They burned me."

"Yes."

In answer, a sharp pain shot across my shoulder blade. Of all the things I'd encountered, from the Tracker's whips and the Tresez's teeth, the Cloakers had to be the most ruthless. I didn't doubt that Raina would have preferred to bring me back to Marcus in several pieces. I guessed that was why he'd tried to avoid using them, but I'd made him desperate.

"I really don't like them," I muttered. "How long till I get better?"

Callon tucked the hair behind my ear and sighed.

"Layla and Nakari are making new compresses for the burns. Things should start looking up soon."

I shivered again.

"I'm cold," I whispered.

"We had to cool the burns in the meantime," Callon explained. "They'll be here soon. These new ones will warm you up."

The floorboards creaked in the hall outside, and soon a shadowy figure appeared in the doorway.

"I brought more firewood," Maes said. He dumped a load near the fireplace and added some to the fire.

"How long have I been lying here?" I asked.

"About twenty-four hours," Callon replied.

"Is everyone else okay? What about Daniel and Nakari?" They'd been with me, attacked by the Cloakers as well.

"A little beat up and bruised, but everyone is safe. You seem to have gotten the worst of it."

"So much for me being *precious*," I murmured, remembering Marcus's words to Conall.

"They only know how to do it one way, Cheyenne," Maes said. He stood near the side of the bed. "They only know how to make one submit through pain."

"Obviously they haven't figured out I'm not the submitting type."

"Obviously," Maes muttered.

My mind wandered back to the incident...what Raina called Maes, *mi ceilo, my heaven.*

"Raina knows you well, Maes?"

His gaze grew dark, cold.

"She called you *my heaven.*"

He didn't respond. I pondered for a moment the significance of it, but let the thought drop. It was obvious I wasn't going to get an answer.

"So now what?" I asked. "We know Colt's alive. How are we going to rescue him?"

Callon stilled, his hands coming to rest on his lap. His expression was masked, hiding his true feelings. I frowned. I thought we'd gotten past this.

Before I could question further, Maes broke in.

"It's too risky," he said.

I closed my eyes again, fighting to push back the emotions rising up inside.

"Colt is Marcus's prisoner," I said through gritted teeth. "We abandoned him once. We can't do it again."

"And we have the entire Timeless race to think about, Cheyenne!"

Maes snapped. "We can't just run off and risk everything we've been fighting for in the hope that Colt's still alive. What you saw was a memory; it took place in the past. For all we know, Colt could be dead by now."

"No!" I snarled and fought to rise up. I knew in my heart, felt it in my soul. Colt was still alive and calling out to me. He'd always been there for me; I wasn't going to ignore him, either.

Callon pressed me back down gently.

"Calm down, sweetheart." He looked at Maes. "We haven't come to a final decision yet, Maes. We need to look at all our options."

Hope swelled through me. Callon wasn't giving up on Colt, either.

"It's risky having him out there," Callon went on.

"Because he altered the enchantment?" I blurted. I knew it wasn't a question any more. He was the only one who could have done it.

"That's one thing, yes."

Maes moved closer to the fire and began stoking it.

"I don't like any of this," Maes mumbled. "The only reason Marcus would've kept him alive is to bait you into a trap. The enchantment is only a problem to him if you remain behind it. He wants to draw you out and pick you off one by one. He can't do that here."

"Perhaps," Callon replied, "but until we sort through all the facts, we're not going to make any hasty decisions."

My heart sank a little. Sort through the facts...Callon wasn't completely sure what to do yet. Was Colt a captive, or did Callon think something else? What exactly was he willing to do? I knew I felt guilty over what had happened at the ridge, and I was sure Callon was as well. But would he allow that to factor into the decision, or would he turn towards the rules he'd always known?

Callon sighed and his hazel eyes looked at me again. His eyes were filled with worry and concern, and his shoulders heavy with the burdens of the Timeless clans. I didn't need him to say it, but if we were to rescue Colt and bring him home, that might change things between Callon and me.

I worried as well...

"Don't I have anything looser?" I cringed as Andre and Lilly tried to help me into a T-shirt. Even my bra straps were digging into my shoulders and back.

"You can't walk around topless, Cheyenne," Andre stated.

"Although I don't think there would be any complaints," Bree giggled.

"I wasn't thinking of going topless!" I snapped back. "It's touching my skin, and it hurts."

"Let's try something else then," Lilly said. She helped me out of the T-shirt and I leaned over the bathroom sink while she disappeared into the closet. A total of forty-eight hours had passed since we'd escaped the Cloakers, and yet these burns still hadn't healed. It was like a horrible sunburn, and I could feel the skin peeling at the edges.

"How about this?" Nakari suggested.

Looking up, I saw her reflection in the mirror. She was holding a men's blue button down shirt.

She stepped closer, and I saw the remnants of burns on her neck and hands.

"It's one of Callon's. He didn't seem to mind you borrowing it when I made the suggestion." She held up her other hand. "I've also brought you more ointment."

"Thank you." I leaned down with my head on the vanity, pulling my hair forwards.

"Here, let me," Layla said and began dabbing the ointment across my burns. "It should be better tomorrow."

I nodded, wincing every time her fingers ran down the wounds. I knew I had to hurry. Callon and the others were waiting for me downstairs.

Lilly and Andre helped me put the shirt on. I looked at myself in the mirror. I was swimming in Callon's shirt. I sighed at my reflection, but at least now I wasn't topless.

"Come on." Andre waited in the doorway while Layla, Bree and Nakari passed her. "I'm sure Maes is growing restless," she added.

"Big surprise there." I smirked.

"I think they're all growing restless," Lilly stated. "There's a lot to discuss."

There *was* a lot to discuss. Colt's future rested in our hands.

I had to walk gently to stop the shirt from rubbing the burns. I paused at the top of the stairs, and took a breath. Somehow I had to convince the other clan leaders that it was a wise decision to rescue

Colt. I looked down at my hand on the rail, my Servak and Kvech rings staring me in the face. This was no longer just about me. I couldn't run off and do this alone. As a leader, I needed to be open minded, listen to all the input and then make a decision. How much I'd changed…a year ago I'd have already run off to do things on my own. I was transforming right before my eyes.

"You okay?" Lilly asked, her hand coming to rest over mine.

I faintly smiled. "I'm fine, Lilly. I'm just noticing that I'm not the same anymore."

"No, you're not the same anymore, Cheyenne. You're developing into a beautiful young woman. You're becoming the capable leader that Dex and I have always seen in you."

"Thank you," I whispered.

We continued down the stairs. Callon stood in the library's doorway, a stoic look in his eyes.

"We're meeting in here, Cheyenne," he said.

I nodded and entered the library. Andre followed, but Lilly headed for the sitting room. He closed the door behind us. Apparently not everyone was a part of this discussion.

Koda rose from the chair and gestured for me to sit. Maes kept his back towards me, stoking the fire. Dex sat on the sofa; he turned and gave me a worried glance.

"It still hurts?" he asked.

"It's more like a sunburn now."

I sat in the chair leaning forward so my back didn't touch.

Brogan lounged in a chair, his feet resting on an ottoman. He lowered his book.

"About time, princess," he sneered.

"Brogan," Dex said, giving him a clear warning to back off.

Daniel appeared beside me.

"Feeling better?" His blue eyes looked hopeful.

"Getting there."

He moved to the sofa and sat beside Dex. Callon stepped in front of the fireplace and Maes rose, facing us and crossing his arms. Andre sat on the arm of the chair beside me.

"We've got a lot to discuss," Callon said. "Decisions have to be made, and it's not going to be easy." His gaze circled the room. "As I told you earlier, we've reason to believe Colt is alive and in Marcus's hold."

"What you saw was a memory. For all we know he could be dead by now," Brogan replied.

"Not so," Koda said. "Someone had to open the enchantment, and it wasn't Daniel or Callon. He's the only living O'Shea descendant. It must have been him."

"Colt would have never done anything without being forced!" Daniel exclaimed. His cheeks flushed; he hadn't meant to shout so loud.

"I'm not saying he did it willingly," Koda said gently.

Callon sighed.

"That is exactly what I think," Maes growled. "Without a doubt, Colt is being manipulated. Chances are that's the only reason Marcus hasn't killed him yet. He's a threat and should be handled accordingly."

My brows narrowed.

"He's a threat and should be handled accordingly? What does that mean?" I said.

"It means he needs to be removed by any and all means possible." Jade-rimmed eyes stared me down.

"No!" Daniel shouted. "Colt needs to be rescued, not removed."

"How do we know he hasn't already given out valuable information that would lead to our deaths, Daniel?" Maes shot back. "How do we know that—"

Daniel leapt to his feet, and stared up at Maes, his blue eyes on fire.

"Colt would never do anything to cause us harm! He'd rather die!"

"Then what do you call the break in the enchantment, Daniel?" Brogan growled.

"He sacrificed himself to save us, Callon," Daniel pleaded, grasping his brother's arm. "He held onto Cheyenne and took Marcus's hits even when we were both screaming at him to drop her. He gave his life for us so we could escape!"

"You don't know the powers Marcus has, Daniel!" Maes hissed. "You haven't witnessed how the mighty have fallen under his command."

"Colt would never..." Daniel lowered his head, tears brimming in his eyes. I leaned forward and grasped his hand, pulling him back. I knew in my heart, as Daniel did, that Colt would never betray us.

Callon cleared his throat.

"I think the first thing we need is proof that he's alive, but honestly I don't know where to start," he said.

"Do we have any spies out in the field that we could send?" Dex asked.

"And risk their life and possible capture for the life of one?" Brogan sneered. His fingers tightened on the book's binding. "Since when did his life become more important than the lives of the rest?" His brown eyes narrowed in on me. "And what does our resident princess have to say about this? Colt was her favorite, after all."

I gritted my teeth. Brogan wasn't going to get under my skin this time.

"Colt would have willingly risked his life to save any of you," I said, taking care with my words. "He's already paid a larger debt. He's trapped with Marcus. Death would have been easier." I knew this firsthand. "And if all you're going to do is sit here and tell me that all he sacrificed isn't worth a thing, then I don't want to listen anymore."

I stood and left the library. My heart was getting the better of me, I knew, but what there were saying was just cruel. Colt was out there and possibly under Marcus's control. I understood he was a risk, a threat that needed to be handled, but not in the way they saw fit.

I headed for the sitting room, the dim lights illuminating enough of the furnishing to tell me that I was alone. Darkness loomed outside the windows. I stopped before the fireplace and sat down, staring at the remaining flames.

It was a two-edged sword knowing Colt was alive. A two-edged sword that had the potential to leave even more wounds in our ragged clans, wounds that could hurt Callon deeply. But it had also cut through my despair. He was out there, waiting for me.

I couldn't just abandon him...

I glanced to my left where the music area had been set up. I knew this was Daniel's doing. He'd made sure I'd have it if I needed it. He knew one day I'd need a release, that one day I'd find all of me again.

I stood and took deliberate steps toward the piano. Sitting on the bench, I opened the lid on the baby grand, exposing the black and white keys. It had been too long since I'd allowed myself this freedom, too long holding things in and bottling them up. It was time to open myself up and allow Callon to know what my heart held for him. It was more than just a responsibility. I was choosing him.

I closed my eyes, resting my fingertips over the keys. It was time to let go.

The first note caused my body to tremble, the crimson-eyed creature waking. It moved inside, unsure of what was taking place. Soon my mind and heart took over, and I felt the notes wash over me, cleansing and healing. Trails upon trails of notes danced before me, spinning and twirling like ballerinas. Weaving in and out of the room, dipping and curving with each spike and tap of the key. The delicate rhythm finally wrapped itself around me, calming the crimson-eyed creature inside. I'd never let it take control again.

Colt's image, the last image I had of him in chains and resisting Marcus, came into view. There was pain and agony in his eyes, but the sheer will to fight on showed in his defiance. I wrapped what I could around him, giving him back a piece of me to hold on to. I knew now, regardless of this outcome, that I needed Callon. There was the obligation, but there was more to it now. He'd been the one who pulled me through; he'd been the one who never gave up on me. He was the one who now believed in me and loved me as I loved him.

Callon could never take Colt's place, but the love I felt for Callon surpassed more than I could have ever imagined. He held my heart firmly, he cared for it, he nourished it and treated it with dignity and honor. He'd given up just as much as the rest of us, if not more. It was only fair that I gave myself to him fully as well.

The notes continued to morph into songs, songs of love and admiration for Callon. Songs crying out and letting him know exactly what I felt inside. He knew me; he knew how I expressed myself. He knew what I was saying without ever having to say the words. He knew I was finally giving all of me to him for good.

The music slowed, the passage of time unknown as the notes drifted quietly to the ground like snowflakes. Fresh, new, and untouched. Whole and ready to be molded into the shape it was to become. My fingers once again hovered over the keys. It was done.

A gentle hand cupped my cheek. Callon's musky scent drifted over me. His warm breath ran over my cheek.

"You did this for me, didn't you?" He sat beside me on the bench, our shoulders touching.

"Yes," I whispered.

"You knew I needed this, to know where your heart lay."

"With you, Callon, with you."

He pulled my left hand closer and from beneath heavy lashes I watched him slide a platinum ring on my finger. My heart began to patter against my ribs. He had a ring for me.

"I've been waiting for the right moment, waiting for you to be ready." He leaned in and kissed the corner of my mouth and then slid to the floor, taking a knee. "Cheyenne Alexis Wilson, will you marry me?"

Tears welled up inside, tears of happiness and joy that began streaming down my cheek. He didn't just expect me to agree. He was asking me to.

"Yes," I whispered unable to utter anything else.

He slid back up on the bench, his hands framing my face and wiping my tears away. There was a light in his hazel eyes, a light I hadn't seen in a long time. A light of hope, love and restoration.

"I love you, Callon." My lips quivered as he drew closer, my eyes falling closed.

"I love you more than you can understand, Cheyenne," he muttered over my lips. "So much more than I thought possible."

A cascade of emotions poured over and through me. Soft, gentle caresses lingered on my lips, pulling me deeper into the moment. A stolen breath taken, but then given back as his mouth covered mine. A swarm of butterflies erupted in the pit of my stomach, sending goosebumps trailing over my skin.

His hand gently tipped my head back further, directing me how he wanted to deepen the kiss. My hand came to rest on his chest. His tongue ran over my lower lips, and my fingers slipped up through his brown wavy locks.

It had been too long since we'd shared a moment like this. It had been too long since he'd released the passion bottled up inside. Every twist and turn of his mouth only showed me how he felt, the man I was to marry.

He pressed even deeper, stealing away my breath as I stole his. Every twist and turn only made me fall more in love with him. He was the one I'd be sharing my life with, and it would be far from loveless. I knew this was only the tip of the iceberg with his passion. One day he'd show me more.

His kiss slowed, and he drew back, his fingers tracing my neck.

"You've given me everything I've ever needed, love. Thank you."

He placed a tender kiss on my forehead, and I leaned in closer, snuggling into his chest. He gently placed his arms around me so he wouldn't hurt me, but I didn't care anymore. I'd take the pain and suffer just to feel his love surround me and give me strength.

I leaned closer to the sitting room window. It was a rare day for sunshine, and my engagement ring was sparkling in the sun's beams. I stared at the intricate design. Had it been in Callon's family for years? It looked vintage, and small imperfections were etched into the band itself. The ring felt heavier than expected. I was guessing the diamond was at least a carat if not more.

"I believe it's called a European cut," Dex said.

I smiled and examined the ring closer. The center stone was accented with four smaller single cut diamonds placed on each side.

Dex sat across from me at the small game table extending his hand.

"May I?"

I lifted my left hand for him to inspect the ring.

"I'd say around 1930s if I were to guess," he added thoughtfully. "I think it's been in the family for a long time." He smiled.

"Old is good," I replied.

"Congratulations." His hazel eyes softened. "I know this hasn't been easy on you, Cheyenne, and I just want you to know that Lilly and I are very proud of you."

"I said yes because I wanted to, not because I had to."

His smile deepened. "That's exactly what I wanted to hear."

"Cheyenne?" Andre's head peeked around the corner from the main entrance.

"Over here."

"I've been searching all over the place for you."

She'd pulled her black hair back into a ponytail, and she had a pretty blue sweater on. She'd done her makeup, too. I couldn't help but giggle.

"What?!" Her right nostril flared slightly.

"You look nice. That's all."

"Is there a crime in that?" She smoothed down her sweater.

"The only crime committed here is you looking pretty," Dex said with a grin.

Andre rolled her eyes.

"Your fiancé wants to see you in the library, Cheyenne."

I couldn't wipe the grin off my lips. Andre was dressing up for Maes, though she'd never admit it.

"He'd like you there too, Dex."

Dex and I followed her into the hall, but she didn't stop at the library doors.

"I thought you said the library?"

"The private library."

"Oh."

We continued through the hall to the metal studded doors. Andre pulled a key from her pocket and unlocked it.

"You have a key?" I asked.

"No, it's Callon's. He just gave it to me to bring you here."

We continued down the dimly lit hall. Even with the lights on, it still was too dark and gloomy for me. A cold breeze drifted by, and a shiver ran down my back.

We stopped at the library doors, and Dex moved between us. He whispered a phrase, and the door unlocked, just like it had done before when Callon spoke the spell.

"Ladies," Dex said and opened the door, ushering us in.

Callon immediately rose from the desk and neared, placing a kiss on my cheek. For just a brief moment I witnessed what looked like distress flash through his eyes.

"Love," he greeted me.

Callon led me to a chair and had me sit next to the fire. Andre disappeared back into the hall, but within moments she was back again, Maes, Brogan, Koda and Daniel following. What was going on?

Callon exhaled and moved back to the desk. He sat and opened a drawer. He hesitated a few moments, but then reached in and placed a small brown package on the tabletop. I sat up straighter, trying to see it better.

"A package arrived today. The Campbell's brought it over." Callon's voice was devoid of any emotion. "It's addressed to you, Cheyenne."

His hazel eyes met mine, and the distress I'd witness earlier had returned. I blinked.

"I have a package?" I asked.

"Yes."

Maes, Brogan, Dex, Koda, Andre and Daniel gathered round, inspecting the package.

"That looks like..." Daniel trailed off deep in thought.

Callon stood and moved to the ottoman between the two chairs, holding the package in his hands.

"You need to open this, Cheyenne. It's addressed to you."

I nodded, still confused about who would send me a package. No one knew where I was except...my hands began to tremble. I read the label, and I pressed the Servak ring into my palm. I knew this handwriting. I inhaled a shaky breath.

"It's...it's from Colt," I murmured. Daniel appeared at my side, holding my shoulder.

"Yes, it's his handwriting," Daniel said.

I blinked back the tears. How? Why? What was it? My fingers traced the words and I looked to see the return address—the cabin. It was postmarked from there too. I pushed the package onto the ottoman.

"What if it's a trap?" I looked up at Callon, begging for some sort of judgment.

"That's why we're in the library," Callon replied. "We're protected in here."

"It's safe then?"

"Yes."

"What if something leaps out and attacks us?"

"I'll whisk you away, Cheyenne," Daniel said, squeezing my shoulder.

I stared at the package, my thumb rolling over my Servak ring. Colt would never do anything to harm me, but Marcus would do just about anything to get me. Callon said we were protected...I had to find out what Colt sent me.

I lifted the small square box and gently pulled the brown paper away, revealing a cardboard container. I carefully peeled away the tape and opened the lid. A small black velvet jewelers box sat protected by packing peanuts. I set the box down and slowly pulled the black velvet box out. I hesitated, not sure what to expect.

My heart raced, and I tried to still my shaking hands as I opened it. A single glance was all it took. I lost all ability to breathe and dropped the box, spilling the contents. I blinked. Daniel had jumped me further away, near the entry, his arm around me.

"It's okay," he said.

Callon strode over, picking up the fallen item.

"It's—it's my bracelet," I murmured. Callon nodded, his fingers tracing the stones.

"What is it?" Brogan stepped closer. "It looks like a harmless piece of jewelry to me."

"It is." Callon turned towards me. "It's a bracelet Colt gave Cheyenne last Christmas."

"I left both halves of it in Montana," I said. "I...It was too much to bring it with me."

"So it's a trap," Maes said.

"No, it means we know where to start looking for clues," Koda countered.

"Clues that will lure you into Marcus's grasp," Maes growled.

"Wait," I replied. "Why would Marcus care what was in the cabin? He'd know Callon wouldn't have left anything behind." I swallowed. "These wouldn't have had any meaning to him."

"He could have forced it out of Colt," Brogan broke in. "I agree with Maes. Marcus is trying to bait you."

"Enough!" Callon said. "Cheyenne has a point. I don't doubt Marcus would have had the cabin searched from top to bottom to find something to use against us. They wouldn't have bothered with the bracelets." He glanced at me. "There's a chance Colt must have found a way to send this, to let us know he was alive. He wouldn't know we saw him through Tre and Jayna. He probably wrote the address himself so the information wouldn't leak."

Maes scowled.

"I still don't buy it," he said. "If Colt found an ally, why wouldn't they have made themselves known to us?"

"Who cares?" Daniel blurted. "It means Colt's still on our side, and he's asking for help!"

"We can't just ignore him," I added. "He must've risked a lot to get this to us."

"So Callon," Brogan said, "what will you do? How much are you willing to risk for your brother?"

Callon was silent for a long while.

"We're not in a position to do much right now," he said at last.

"But Callon..." I began.

"Cheyenne, this isn't something we should rush into," Callon interrupted. "The bracelets might have come from the cabin, but we saw that Colt was in the forest with Marcus. It could be the forest near his compound. We need to gather more data."

I clenched my fists. We had the proof we needed, and he still wanted to wait around?

Daniel bent close to my ear.

"I know, Cheyenne," he whispered. "I want him back too. We'll bring him home." He kissed my cheek. "I promise."

CHAPTER 16

Helena, Montana. I typed in the arrival destination on the flight search. I tapped my fingers impatiently on the kitchen counter, waiting for the details of the search to pop up. Rain splattered on the windowpane, and I stared out into the dreary landscape. What I wouldn't have given for a good snowfall. The monotonous months of fall and winter were dragging on. I could only hope spring brought some sunshine.

It had been weeks since Callon had sent Quinn, Skylar, and Clayton out to dig up more information, weeks that had passed with little to no contact. Weeks that we could have been doing something, anything, except sitting here and twiddling our thumbs, as my mom used to say.

I knew where I'd start looking—the cabin was the most obvious place—but they wouldn't listen. I thought with my heart; they thought with facts. I wasn't going to win this battle easily. Yet I had to start something. I was going crazy just waiting...

The kitchen door swung open.

"What are you up to?" Koda asked.

I jumped and slammed the laptop closed. Hopefully he hadn't seen the search window.

"Stop scaring me like that!" I snapped, brushing the hair from my eyes. If I was caught trying to do this on my own, I'd never hear the end of it. I could hear Brogan now, *"Well, our little princess thinks she can just run out and save her knight in shining armor..."*

Koda strolled closer, his eyes on the laptop.

"Whatcha looking for?"

I averted his gaze.

"Stuff."

"Like?" He raised a brow.

"Wedding stuff."

He crossed his arms over his chest and leaned on the counter.

"Don't lie. It doesn't suit you."

I looked down at my hands. I shouldn't have lied, but...

"I was searching for a new invisibility cloak."

Koda let out a bellowing laugh. At the same time, Daniel pushed the kitchen door open.

"What's going on in here?" he asked, a smile plastered on his lips.

I cringed, now I had to deal with the two of them.

"Cheyenne's searching the internet for an invisibility cloak for me," Koda snorted.

"Oh?" Daniel stepped beside me, his eyes filled with laughter.

"I felt bad that I'd lost it."

"Any luck?" Koda chuckled.

"Maybe." I pressed the laptop to my chest. "Now leave me alone." I took a step when Daniel swiped the laptop from my hands.

"Hey!" I reached for it, but he'd already jumped to the other side of the kitchen island.

"Let's see what you've found," Daniel said and opened the laptop.

I ran around the island, trying to close it, before he saw what I'd been searching for.

Daniel grew still, and I stopped beside him. He was staring at flights times to Helena, Montana. Koda leaned over my shoulder.

"Well, I didn't really think you were searching for invisibility cloaks," he said. He turned me to face him. "Nor did I believe it was wedding stuff."

I looked down, my thumb running over my Servak ring. I'd been caught.

"Did you think you could just walk out of here, Chey?" Daniel asked softly. He pulled his sweater sleeves up, exposing the scars on his arms. "You do remember how we got these? You think Raina and the others won't swarm you the minute they get the chance? Not to mention the fact that you don't have your passport. Callon does."

I kept quiet. There was nothing more I could say.

"We've been sitting here when we could have been searching for

Colt, Daniel," I sighed. "I just want to do something. He'd have done the same for us."

"You may think we've just been waiting, but we've been planning," Koda replied.

"Then why haven't I been told?" I argued.

"You've been told, but you're not listening. You've had your mind locked in on one thing and one thing only," Daniel said.

"It's not fast enough."

"And you need to have some patience," Daniel added. "Don't you think Callon and I are just as anxious to find Colt?" Daniel drew me into a hug. "I promised, Chey, and I won't break it. We're going to find him and bring him home. So no more searching for flights or invisibility cloaks."

I managed a smile.

"Wasn't having much luck in finding a replacement anyway."

"Come on." Koda tugged on my elbow. "Let's see if we can torment Andre about Maes. That always provides great entertainment."

We left the kitchen and found Brogan and Layla in the dining room.

"Evening, Princess," Brogan said dryly.

Layla elbowed him.

"Cheyenne, we were waiting for you," Layla said. Her long dark braid tumbled over her shoulder as she stood.

"Oh?"

Koda and Daniel moved on.

"With so much going on, and the fact that you can't really leave the estate, I wanted to offer up my services to you. I'd like to make your wedding dress if you'd allow me."

I blinked. Despite my earlier lie, I hadn't even thought about wedding preparations, I honestly didn't know if they would want to risk hosting anything elaborate.

"So I get to wear a wedding dress? I—I guess I just thought it would be nothing more than Dex marrying us in a simple ceremony."

"Well, if we were under different circumstance, this would be the wedding of all weddings," Layla said. "We haven't had a clan leader marriage in a very long time. However, even though it will be a small simple ceremony, it's just that I, no, we..." She looked up at Brogan. "We want to make it as special as we can."

I couldn't help but feel a bit of warmth swimming inside me. This was what family did for each other, loved and tried to make everything that was important as special as they could, regardless of the circumstances.

"So you'd make me a wedding dress?"

"I am a good seamstress. Andre, Lilly, Nakari and Bree can attest to it. Of course I'd show you some drawings first after we figure out what you want."

I smiled. "I'd love for you to make me a dress."

Layla's blue-green eyes lit up, and she rushed forward, wrapping me in a hug.

"Thank you, Cheyenne. I won't let you down."

She stepped back, and I looked at Brogan. He had his usual brooding expression, but at least now he didn't eye me like a speck of dirt on his shoe. Maybe I was making progress with him, but then again...

"How long have you and Brogan been married, Layla?" I asked.

She smiled lovingly at Brogan. "A very long time."

"Was it an arranged marriage?"

"Yes."

I smirked. "Well, I think you got the short end of the stick on that one."

Brogan's lip twitched, and it almost looked like he was about to smile.

"Yeah, I know I did," Layla replied, and I couldn't help but laugh.

"Hey now," Brogan grumbled.

I turned and headed for the library. I needed to tell Callon the good news, although chances were he'd asked Layla to make a dress for me.

The library door was open, and as I stepped in I found Callon on the couch. A few large books lay open on the ottoman. He turned and smiled, but it didn't reach his eyes. I moved closer and leaned over the back of the sofa, placing a small kiss on his cheek.

"Hey," I said softly and eyed the books. "Doing some research?"

"Always." He patted the seat beside him. "Why don't you join me?"

I stepped around the front of the couch and plopped down beside him. He lifted my hand and placed a tender kiss on my knuckles.

"You and Layla talked?" he asked.

"Yeah."

"She asked me if you'd be open to the idea," he revealed.

"Ah, I thought maybe you'd asked her."

He brushed the hair behind my ear. "No, this was all her idea. She really is quite talented. I don't think she'll disappoint you."

He pulled a large book into his lap, and I leaned in closer, trying to see what he was reading. It looked like a medical journal, but not a modern one. The pages were yellowed, and corners tattered, like they'd been folded over at one time or another. Even some of the text seemed to be smeared with a brownish substance.

"You searching for something?"

"More of a review if anything."

I lifted a brow. "Review?"

He placed his arm on the back of the couch, his fingers touching my hair.

"The magic Marcus uses is ancient. At one point in time, we knew how to treat certain ailments or injuries caused from it. If we're going to battle him again, I need to make sure I have as much knowledge as possible to help where it's needed."

"This has the potential to be bad, doesn't it?"

"Yes," he said grimly. "I don't want to repeat what happened on the ridge."

He sighed and then opened his mouth to continue, but then closed it.

"What?"

He shook his head.

"Callon, don't hide things from me."

His hazel eyes held such turmoil.

"Please, Callon, just tell me."

He stroked the back of my head.

"I don't want you to get your hopes up, Cheyenne, that Colt will..." He looked down.

I pulled his stubbled chin towards me. "Will what?"

"That Colt will be the same. Honestly, I'm not sure what to expect."

"You think Marcus has damaged him?" I worried.

"No one leaves Marcus untouched, no one."

"But don't you think that we can bring him back?" I pressed.

"I want you to be prepared for what you may see."

"You don't want me heartbroken again."

"Yes."

218

I stroked his cheek. "It's going to be okay. We're going to find him, bring him home and have a complete family again."

Callon held my hand against his jaw, and nodded slowly. We spent a moment in comfortable silence, when the library door opened.

"Callon, Cheyenne," Koda said anxiously. "Clayton's sent a message."

Almost at once, I jumped up and hurried towards the sitting room, Callon directly behind me. The room filled quickly. Koda stood in the center.

"Clayton says he's got proof that Colt is still alive and that he knows where he's being held prisoner. They'll be back in about three days."

"Where?" I moved closer, my heart racing.

"Montana."

Daniel jumped beside me and squeezed my hand. "See, I told you," he whispered.

It was just as I'd been telling them all along. I knew Colt was in Montana, and it wasn't just from the package's postmark. He was calling out to me, to us, and soon we would be bringing him home.

"Where in Montana?" Brogan asked.

"Possibly the cabin," Koda replied.

"Possibly?" Maes rose to his feet. "We're supposed to go on possibly?"

"They've been moving around a lot. It's hard to pinpoint, but we have proof."

"So how are we going to leave here? We had the element of surprise last time. I don't think it will work again," Brogan said.

"Quinn's had the helicopter repaired. It'll give us enough lead time to board the airplane and be on our way," Koda replied.

"He has a helicopter large enough for all of us?" I asked. "I mean, I thought more than just three of us would be going."

"It's large enough, Cheyenne," Callon said. "I'm assuming he has all the clearance paperwork done for the jet too, Koda?"

"A jet?"

"Yeah." Daniel smiled. "There are perks to being Timeless. Private jets, helicopters, estates in foreign countries."

I blinked. I had no idea, but it shouldn't have surprised me. My parents had always been able to afford a comfortable home for me. A private jet wasn't that much of a step up.

"So, we leave by means of the helicopter," Maes said, "and board the jet. Then what? Marcus is going to be right behind us."

"He'll be right behind us alright." Koda smirked. "Hours behind us. Quinn's been keeping an eye on activity at the airports, not just the ones in Ireland. We'll know the moment his team departs."

"But won't he know that we'll be heading to Montana?" I asked. "I'm assuming that Quinn will have to file some sort of report stating where the jet is heading."

"Like I said before, Quinn has helpers out there. A false report will be filed," Koda said.

"Giving us enough time to get in and get out," Callon added, his eyes focusing on me. "Cheyenne, you've been telling us all along Colt's in Montana, and so far you've been right. Where do you think we're going to find him, at the cabin?"

Warmth welled up inside me. Callon was showing more faith in my abilities.

"You're asking our resident *princess* here?" Brogan snarled. "She has zero planning and strategizing experience, and we're to go off her senses and good feelings?"

Daniel's chest swelled. "She hasn't been wrong yet!"

"Calm down," Dex stood and moved between us. "Cheyenne may not have all the experience and knowledge you do, Brogan, but unless we allow her to step up, she never will."

Brogan's hands flew in the air. "I give up. Let's all get ourselves killed. In fact, let's make a party out of it!"

"Brogan," Callon commanded, "calm down. If we play this right, I think this rescue is possible."

"I can't go on *think*," Maes grumbled. "I have to know it's going to work." His jade-rimmed eyes bore into me. "Where, Cheyenne?"

"The waterfalls." The words blurted from my mouth without warning.

"The falls?" Daniel's eyes narrowed.

"The ones on the way to Dex and Lilly's?" Callon asked.

"Yes." I sighed, knowing why Colt would be there.

"Why there?" Koda asked.

I looked down at my Servak ring and twisted it. I didn't need to look around to know all eyes were on me and what I was about to say.

"Because that's where I first knew I loved Colt," I whispered. Tears brimmed near the surface and Daniel's arm came around me.

"Great!" Brogan snapped. "Now we're off on a wild goose chase because the *princess* thinks life is a fairy tale and Colt will magically appear!"

"What gives you this idea, Cheyenne?" Dex asked. "Why the falls?"

He pushed his hands through his hair. Lilly moved beside him, her fingers sliding through his.

"The bracelet." I turned and looked at Callon. His mask was on again. "Colt risked sending it because he knows it was a place I'd never forget."

Callon looked away, and I felt a twinge on my chest. He knew I'd forever have feelings for Colt. I couldn't just push them away. However, even if Colt returned, I'd have to ensure Callon knew where I stood—always.

"It's not far from the ridge," Maes said and rubbed his chin.

"The ridge where I jumped in the river?" I asked.

"Yeah," he replied.

"What's the fastest route?" Koda asked.

"Balsom Pass," Andre answered.

"You know the area?" Maes questioned.

"Probably better than you." A sly smile rose on her lips. "No excuses to leave me home this time, puppy."

Maes rolled his eyes, and I couldn't help but smirk.

"Then it's settled." Koda looked towards Callon. "I'll make the arrangements for the horses and gear at the closest entrance to Balsom Pass. Brogan can get the vehicles situated and we'll be good to go."

Callon nodded.

"But what about the Cloakers?" I asked. "Won't they be in Montana?"

"Possibly," Maes replied. "Cloakers operate in colonies, like bees or ants. They have to follow the queen, the queen being Raina. Raina's here, which means they're all here now, but if she travels, they'll follow or die."

"Follow or die?" I said.

"The colony can't survive without the queen. And unfortunately, we can't prevent her from traveling," Dex added.

"So the risk remains," I murmured.

"We leave in three days," Callon said. He left the room, heading for the library.

"It'll be okay," Daniel murmured. "He's under a lot of pressure."

I sighed. The pressure I was creating wasn't helping either.

I headed for my room. I had plenty of time to pack, but being alone was probably best at the moment.

"Cheyenne," Callon called out from the library.

I stopped and changed direction. He had his back turned towards me, but his hand extended.

"Here," he said.

He was holding my bracelet.

I plucked it from his fingers, unsure what to say.

"Callon..."

"It's fine. I have a lot to prepare for, so I'd like to be alone."

I sighed. What'd I said about my feelings for Colt had hurt him. It would have hurt me as well.

"Thank you."

I slipped the bracelet on my wrist and headed for the stairs. Koda, Brogan and Maes's voices murmured through the hall. Dex and Lilly stood near the dining room conversing. At the top landing, Bree and Daniel talked as well. There was a lot at stake here, an awful lot.

I entered my bedroom and left the door open. Crawling on top of my bed, I snuggled up between the pillows. My fingers ran over the dark stones of Colt's bracelet. I'd given him back the other half, the other half that glowed when the two touched. He'd given it to me as a reminder, that no matter how far apart we were, I could always bring them together to remember our love. A love that haunted Callon.

Callon's words from the library echoed in my mind, and I swallowed. He said I needed to be prepared, that Colt might not be the same...or was it that Callon who wouldn't be the same? Would having Colt around cause problems? Would they fight like in the past?

I pressed my hand to my chest. I knew deep down that I wouldn't be able to handle it if they did. It would only break my heart to have to tell Colt to remain distant, to push him away after bringing him home.

A tear trickled down my cheek. Whatever happened was going to shake things up. I just had to make sure it didn't shake me over the edge.

My small pack sat in the hall just outside my bedroom door. Dawn was arriving; we'd be leaving within a few hours. I entered my closet one last time, searching for a pair of gloves.

"Hey," Andre said. I turned to see her in the doorway. "You ready?"

I nodded, too afraid to speak. My stomach was in knots, and I was a bundle of nerves. I left the bathroom and glanced around my bedroom. Colt's bracelet sat on my bedside table; I couldn't forget to bring it. I cleared the distance and placed the stoned bracelet on my wrist. I pulled my sleeve down to cover it and turned to meet Andre's intent blue eyes.

"Be careful, Cheyenne," she said.

I looked away. I didn't need any explanation of her warning, I knew what she was referring to, what all of them had made reference to. I needed to guard my heart. But most importantly, I needed to guard Callon's too. He was my fiancé now, and I'd have to keep my distance from Colt. If I hurt Callon, I'd have the wrath of others to deal with.

I headed out the door. Someone had already picked up my pack.

Daniel's arm looped in mine. A nervous grin rose and quickly disappeared. He'd been warned just like I had. Colt may not be the same, but neither he nor I wanted to believe it. Colt had sent us a message to come find him and that was what we were going to do.

Daniel jumped us down the hall, stairs, and into the sitting room where our group was gathering. He jumped to Bree's side, while Brogan, Koda, Maes and Callon stood near the terrace doors, reviewing our plans. We'd been through it hundreds of times, but it still didn't make it any less stressful. One mistake could cost us dearly.

Nakari gave me a sidelong glance as Andre joined her. At least I wouldn't be alone with her. Andre acted as a buffer, though things had gotten better between us. Both Nakari and I had wordlessly agreed that we weren't going to be best friends, but we'd tolerate each other. She'd keep her distance from Callon, and I'd keep my distance from her.

"Cheyenne," Lilly said. She reached for my hands, tears forming in her eyes. "I need you to promise me that you'll be cautious. I know what you want, both you and Daniel, but..."

"I know, Lilly," I replied. She didn't need to remind me.

She drew me into a hug. "Please be careful. I want you back in one piece."

"I will."

Dex neared, stress and worry filling his hazel eyes. "Don't use all your power at once, Cheyenne. Conserve them. Chances are you're going to have a fight on your hands, and Callon will need you. Anticipate your enemies like you've been trained, and remember that you're more than capable."

"Let's go," Koda called out.

Dex leaned in and hugged me, placing a kiss on my cheek.

"We love you."

"Love you too," I replied and headed for the terrace doors.

Brogan lagged behind, speaking softly to Layla before he followed.

The hum of a helicopter hung in the brisk air. We were meeting it in the field by the lake. Koda held up his hand in the predawn light, and Callon moved beside me, his fingers locking over mine. He had two packs over his shoulder, one of which was mine.

The winds whipped up loose debris around us as the mechanical beast settled on the ground. Within moments Koda had the side door open and was ushering us in. There were six seats in the back. Brogan, Maes and Andre took the seats facing us. Callon had me sit in the middle, and he and Daniel helped me buckle in. They dumped the packs on the floor. The door closed, and Koda climbed in the front seat as Quinn lifted off the ground. Nakari sat on the floor and wrapped her arm around my leg. Callon pushed his arm behind the buckles, securing his fingers onto my waist while Daniel grasped my hand.

Cloakers or no Cloakers, I wasn't going anywhere.

The red horizon loomed before us, and I felt the familiar tingle over my skin as we left the safety of the enchantment. It was a race against time now.

Nobody spoke. I couldn't even hear a breath as the misty green landscape flew by. Everyone kept their gaze to the sky, ready for just about anything.

A flicker of black caught my eye, and I tensed. They'd assured me that Raina wouldn't be able to fly this high. She did have limitations.

"It's alright," Daniel whispered. "It was just a crow."

I nodded, but still kept my vision on every speck that seemed out of place.

Soon, though not soon enough, the whine of the engine changed. We were landing.

Nakari rose to her knees, and everyone snapped open their buckles. Callon pulled me tighter against his side, and Daniel kept hold of my hand. Koda had already jumped out of the helicopter before it was properly seated on the helipad.

The side door flew open, and we piled out. Everyone formed a tight circle around me. My heart began racing faster. We only had a short window to get off the ground and not draw attention to ourselves.

Maes and Koda led the way and stopped just outside of a hangar. Koda held up his hand, and we paused. Maes disappeared around the side, and we waited.

I searched the runway. It wouldn't take much for Raina to appear. Misty clouds had moved in. She could easily disguise herself in them.

"Let's go!" Koda said and we ran towards the hangar.

As we rounded the corner, a jet came into view, and not just any jet. The code AJ318 was splashed across the tail. I knew what 737's looked like, and this was just a tad smaller. It could easily seat at least twenty comfortably. A staircase was propped up beside it, and two men stood holding it, ready to move it after we were safely inside. Maes stood inside the doorway, waiting for us.

Koda bounded up the stairs and quickly turned as Callon pulled me alongside. As I followed him down the aisle, the smell of leather and polish hit my nose. The bright interior came into view. We hurried through the spacious walkway and quickly sat down. I heard the exterior door slam close.

The jet jerked to life, and I fell back into the leather seat, struggling to buckle in quickly. Within moments, we were out of the hangar and taxiing down the runway.

I glanced around the cabin. Skylar twisted in his seat and gave me a smile. An interior door opened, exposing the cockpit, and Clayton moved to take his seat. There was plenty of room; this was a luxury jet. It even had a couch and what looked like a bedroom in the back.

Koda and Brogan settled opposite us, on the other side of the table. Daniel sat on our right, an arm's length away. He leaned over and touched my shoulder.

"We made..."

"Raina!" Maes hissed, cutting him off, and a second later Raina's black mist materialized in the aisle. She lunged forward and I gasped, but she never made contact as Koda and Brogan blocked her. Callon's hand tightened on my waist.

"You've made a bad choice, Raina," Maes rumbled. "Stick around, and you'll lose all your mindless workers."

Raina's black mist appeared again, her face plunging forward. I pressed back in to the seat, my breath suddenly gone. An awful hissing sound left her lips before she disappeared from the jet.

Maes pushed Brogan and Koda apart, his jade-rimmed eyes on me.

"We won't have the enchantment to run back to this time, Cheyenne. Use your skills wisely. Your very life will depend on it."

I nodded.

Don't forget to breathe... a voice whispered in my mind, and I blinked.

Maes turned and took his seat while I inhaled a shaky breath. Had he just spoken to me?

The whispery clouds surrounded us as I stared out the jet window. Callon's grip loosened, and I adjusted myself in my seat. The threat of Cloakers was gone at the moment, but it would return when we arrived in Montana. I had no doubt that Raina and her minions would be there at some point, and I'd have to be prepared. I'd have to do better than I had with our previous encounter. There was no invisibility cloak to hide me, or an enchantment to seek refuge in.

My mind couldn't help but run back to the moment when Raina lunged at me, and the voice I'd heard in my head...or at least I thought I had. Maes was staring at me, but now I couldn't remember if I saw his lips moving. Was I completely losing it? Chances were I was losing it.

"I'll show you around once Quinn gives the okay, Chey," Daniel said. "It's much nicer than the commercial airlines." He rubbed his hands together nervously. He was trying to distract himself.

"That'd be nice," I replied.

Callon's shoulder touched mine as he pulled a book from his pack. I stared at the old worn leather binding. It was the medical book he'd shown me before. Within moments he was fully immersed in it.

I twisted my engagement ring on my left finger. How was Colt going to handle our engagement? It wasn't like he hadn't known it would happen, but he'd been gone for so long. I sighed. So much had changed—I had changed. I wasn't the same Cheyenne he'd fallen for.

Maybe it was just as well...

CHAPTER 17

I shifted nervously in the SUV, adjusting the seatbelt for the millionth time. We were so close to reaching the cabin, I could almost smell fresh pine burning in the fireplace and see white smoke bellowing out of the chimney.

Callon grasped my hand, his fingers intertwining with mine.

"We're going to find him, Cheyenne," Daniel said quietly near my ear. "We're going to bring him home."

I weakly smiled at Daniel and glanced at Callon. He'd barely spoken to me since leaving for Montana, since returning Colt's bracelet to me. I could only imagine all the emotions and burdens whirling through his thoughts. The pressure he was under...and the warning to Daniel and me about Colt—the condition we might find him in.

Maes turned in his seat, stretching his arm out, his eyes searching the forest.

I glanced back as well. Andre and Nakari had been put in the third row seat. We needed both Daniel and Nakari nearby for our safety. Andre shrugged her shoulders.

"Did you see something?" Koda asked.

"No, it was nothing," Maes replied.

Koda slowed and turned onto the gravel road leading to the cabin.

Maes's jade-rimmed eyes met mine. He didn't have to say a word as I took a breath. I'd been holding it again without realizing it.

"You really need to stop doing that, *mon espoir*," he grumbled.

"Sorry my breathing bothers you," I replied.

"You need to learn to control your emotions as a leader. Holding your breath shows your weakness."

I rolled my eyes, staring out the tinted windows. It wouldn't be long now.

The SUV rolled to a stop and Maes jumped out. Daniel's fingers locked around my elbow. Patches of snow remained on the ground. I leaned forward, watching Maes shift into his Tresez form and dart off into the forest. Had he seen something?

I turned around. The second SUV had also arrived, and Brogan stepped out. Nakari moved in the backseat, her hand coming to rest on Callon's shoulder. Callon unlocked his hold on my hand. Although the tension between Nakari and me had lessened, watching her touch Callon made me uncomfortable. Nakari avoided eye contact.

"He's back," Andre said and pointed out the window to distract me.

Maes jumped in the SUV.

"Old tracks," Maes said. Nodding, Koda continued down the drive.

I strained to see between the front seats. One more turn and we'd be there...one more turn, and we'd be closer to finding Colt. I twisted my Servak ring with my thumb. Would he be here? Would it be that easy?

Our trip had been smooth so far, with not a sign of a Tracker, Tresez, Cloaker or Ghoster. Quinn had planned it out perfectly, and we'd remained ahead of Marcus. Brogan's spies had led them on a wild goose chase, as my father would have said, and hadn't been caught yet. How long our luck would last, well, that was unknown.

The SUV came to a stop, but Callon held my arm, preventing me from getting out.

"Wait till they clear it," Callon said.

I blew the hair from my eyes as we watched Maes transform again. He circled the house while Brogan and Koda stepped up on the front porch, disappearing from sight. Clayton moved beside our SUV. My leg began to twitch. I just needed to get out and look around.

Koda's head appeared from the porch, and he waved his arm. I blinked and found myself outside with Daniel. The familiar gravel crackled under my boots, and I stopped midstride. My old Jeep lay just ahead, covered with a tarp.

Memories soared in my mind...the day I met Callon at the cathedral, how he'd come to help me when I couldn't drive. The fight I'd had with the Jeep to get my laptop and the months of teasing afterwards. The snowy day I slid underneath it and found the tracking device they'd planted...

"Cheyenne?" Callon broke me from my reverie. "Come on."

I followed him up onto the porch, warmth flowing inside me. I remembered all the games played around the table, laughter from teasing, movies watched. The smells of leather and wood hit my nostrils as we entered the cabin. Callon paused. His fists tightened slightly before he relaxed them. I moved beside him.

Dust coated the kitchen table and side tables in the great room. No one had been here since we'd left, at least not that I could tell. Daniel disappeared into the bedrooms, and I followed, heading towards Colt's room.

I hesitated at Colt's doorway, staring at his dresser. The other half of my bracelet was gone, along with the note I'd left him. Moisture stung my eyes. He *had* been the one to send it. He'd read my note...

Brogan and Koda entered the room.

"Is anything missing?" Koda asked.

I pointed to the dresser, as Daniel appeared beside me.

"The bracelets I left there are gone," I said.

Both Brogan and Koda examined the dresser, opening the drawers. They didn't find anything, though. As I debated whether to mention my note, I heard the clack of claws hitting the hardwood in the hallway. Maes padded towards me, sticking to his Tresez form.

"Here," Brogan pointed to the dresser.

Maes sniffed the air and then the side of the dresser, moving up along the drawers till he reached the top. He stayed there for a long time, then suddenly bolted from the room.

I chased after him, bumping into Callon in the hallway. Maes had disappeared into my old bedroom. We'd barely made it to my room when he ran out to Callon's room. What was that crazy dog up to? Could he locate Colt completely by his scent?

Maes trotted back out to the hall, resuming his human form.

"He's been here," he said.

"How old is the scent?" Callon asked.

"A few weeks, maybe two or three at the most."

Daniel jumped beside me, hope in his blue eyes.

"See," he whispered. "I knew it!"

Callon nodded towards the great room; he wanted me to follow.

"Give me a minute," I said. "I want to grab a few things from my room."

"Sure." Callon stepped close—he wasn't going to let me go alone.

I headed straight for my closet, finding a small pack on the floor, and stuffed a couple of sweaters in along with a pair of jeans. I dug through the plastic container that held winter socks, hats and gloves. I knew it was going to be cold on our ride, and I needed more than what I'd brought with me.

Callon hovered in the doorway.

"Grab a few extras for Andre and Nakari too."

I nodded. When I was done, I handed the bulging pack to Callon and reached for a jacket. All our jackets were a bit on the thin side for where we were heading. I shoved my hand in the pocket and paused. There was something hard and smooth inside.

"What?" Callon moved closer. I looked up into his worried hazel eyes.

My fingers brushed the familiar stones and I slowly withdrew my hand, revealing the other half of Colt's bracelet. A slip of paper had been caught in the clasp. Callon's eyes narrowed.

"What's this?" He reached for the dark stoned bracelet and yanked the paper free.

"I don't know," I whispered. My hand began to shake.

Daniel appeared, his eyes intent.

"Open it," he said.

Callon unfolded the small scrap of paper. Only one word had been scrawled across it.

Come.

My heart leapt. It could only mean what I'd already known. Colt knew I'd find this, and that I'd know where to head...*come* to the waterfalls. He was waiting for me there.

"Cheyenne?" Daniel touched my shoulder. "What does it mean?"

"The waterfalls," I said. "He's waiting at the falls."

Callon shoved the pack at Daniel.

"Wait in the great room," he ordered.

Daniel disappeared.

I clenched the bracelet tightly in my palm. Callon stepped forward, his hands pulling my chin up to see his eyes.

"Are you sure?" he asked, his voice soft.

I nodded.

He looked away for a moment, but not before I saw it...the worry, stress and anxiety over the whole situation, his distress over losing me again. I knew he'd been quiet, trying to hide his ever-growing fear of having Colt back in our lives again. Of what it would do to me, to *us*.

I stepped forward and wrapped my arms around him. He needed to know...I needed to know, to say it out loud, to confirm it again for both of us.

"I love you, Callon," I whispered.

He sighed and placed a soft kiss on my head.

"I love you too."

A throat cleared, and Callon drew back. He grabbed a glove from the floor that had fallen out of the pack, before he took my hand and headed for the great room. Our rescue party was waiting.

"Let's go," Brogan ordered, and we followed him out the door. Daniel must have already told them about the falls, confirming what I'd said at the estate.

We loaded the SUVs and began our drive. I turned and watched the cabin disappear, my memories fading into the trees along with it. Callon's arm came around my shoulder, pulling me into his side, his head touching mine. I closed my eyes to rest. I was going to need all the strength I could to do this—we all would.

"Cheyenne." Callon nudged me and I peeled my weary eyes open. "You fell asleep."

I stretched and sat up, blinking as I looked around. Several horse trailers sat around us, and we were parked at what looked like a trailhead.

"How long did I sleep?" I asked groggily.

"You were tired. You haven't been resting much." He pushed the hair from my cheek.

I knew I hadn't been resting; my mind wouldn't shut down long enough.

He continued, "Now that we're here, you need to be on your guard at all times. You need to trust your instincts."

I nodded.

He sighed and opened the SUV door. We headed towards the others. Skylar and Quinn had stayed back to guard the jet, but there seemed to be more here than the nine of us. Blurs of bodies and horses rushed past. Everyone seemed to have a job except me.

Nakari and Andre stood to my right, each holding two horses. Both had put on the extra layers of clothing I'd brought. Snow was still on the ground, but the late afternoon skies didn't look threatening. Clayton nodded as he passed, a black horse in tow—a very large black horse. *Midnight*...Koda's horse was here? Would that mean...

I hurried past the side of the black SUV and around the corner to one of the horse trailers. Immediately a blond mane flashed before me and whinnying ensued. I burst into a grin. *Mandi!*

I rushed to her side and threw my hands around her neck. She pushed up against me. I stroked her chest.

"Mandi!" I whispered. "I wasn't sure I'd see you again." I hadn't realized how much I'd missed her, how much she meant to me. She'd been a gift from the boys, a special gift that had stolen my heart. She stomped her foot in response. She understood me, always had, regardless of my gift of speaking with animals.

A nose nudged my back. I turned to see Sam, Colt's brown beauty, demanding his share of attention too.

"Hey there, Sam." I rubbed his nose.

"They've missed you," a young voice said.

I looked up to see a small red-headed child untying Mandi's reins, a faint smile on his pink lips.

"I've missed them too," I replied.

He handed me Mandi's reins, but where I'd expected to see youthful eyes, instead they were weathered, telling me a different story. He was a Timeless. But why did he look so young? He should appear in his twenties, at least.

"I think they want you over by Andre and Nakari." The boy pointed. "Can you take Sam too?"

"Sure."

I took the reins and headed towards Andre, but then stopped.

"Have you been caring for them?" I asked.

"Yes," he replied.

"Thank you."

He nodded and turned back to his duties without giving me his name.

I pulled Mandi and Sam along, then stood by Nakari and Andre, waiting for our departure. Daniel appeared with Charlie and Bo. He rolled their reins in his palms and stared into the forest.

The rest of our rescue party neared. Brogan took hold of one of Nakari's horses, mounting in a swift motion. I was about to mount when Callon touched my arm.

"Here," Callon said, wrapping a black scarf around my neck. He pulled a hat from his pocket as well. "I want you to stay warm."

"Thanks," I replied and slipped the hat on over my braid. My ears were already starting to feel the chill.

"You must tell me if you get too cold," he ordered. "It's already late afternoon, and we're going to be riding through the night to get to the falls."

"I will."

He sidestepped and threw a small pack over Mandi's saddle, securing it in place. He then took the reins from my hands as I mounted. Once everyone was set, we set off into the forest, Andre and Maes leading the way.

Our pace was steady, and eyes alert to every movement. Callon and I rode side by side, Daniel and Nakari just an arm's length away. No one spoke, and I only heard the thud of hoof beats and the horses' heavy breathing.

As the sun tucked below the trees, I adjusted my scarf, pulling it up and over my nose. It appeared they'd had an early spring with only small patches of snow remaining, but I knew that could change within the blink of an eye. When night fell, the temperatures would drop even lower.

I glanced back. Koda, Brogan and Clayton rode behind us, watching our backs. Clayton was holding Sam's lead rope, guiding him along. I sighed. Soon Colt would be riding him back with us. We'd bring him home at last.

I took a cleansing breath, trying to push the nervousness down. My stomach had already been churning somersaults. I'd heard Callon's warning—all their warnings, but deep down I knew he'd be the same Colt, the same man I'd come to love...that we all loved.

Darkness fell over the forest. I zipped my jacket higher; I was becoming colder as the night wore on. A shiver escaped me, and I fought to keep my teeth from chattering. Callon rode closer.

"You're cold."

"Maybe a little," I admitted.

He glanced at Nakari and rode ahead, trotting alongside Andre. We came to a stop.

"We need to warm up," Callon ordered.

At least it wasn't just me this time.

Within moments we'd dismounted. Clayton and Koda disappeared while Callon moved closer and rubbed my arms.

"We'll have a fire soon."

"I though as a Timeless I wouldn't be affected by the cold as much," I said.

"True, but we've been in Ireland. We have to acclimate to an area first," Callon replied. "I'm not as warm as you might think," Callon admitted.

Andre and Nakari huddled beside us.

"Thanks," Andre said. "I didn't want to be the one to slow us down, but it's colder than Antarctica here."

"It's not that bad," I said, regardless of the fact that my teeth were chattering.

Andre scoffed.

"Oh, give me mass flooding and daily rain any day!" she joked. "If it gets any colder right now, there'll be icicles warmer than me."

"So melodramatic," Nakari said and rolled her eyes.

"I have acclimatization issues. Is that so wrong?" Andre shot back. "You're not exactly looking so warm yourself, Blue Cheeks."

"I was in a rush. I didn't realize which blusher I used," Nakari answered.

I brought my fingers to my mouth, partly to warm my hands, but mostly to hide my chuckling. I'd never known Nakari to have a sense of humor. Then again, that was hardly a side of her she'd want to show to me...

Soon the boys had built a crackling fire, and we hovered beside it. Callon, Maes, Koda and Brogan stood in a huddle nearby, going over the plans again, I was sure. It was a get in and get out sort of plan; we wouldn't have time for anything else if we wanted to beat the Trackers, Tresez and Cloakers. They'd even talked about using *other* options with Colt as well, if they thought he was under Marcus's influence. I wasn't exactly sure what those *other* options were, but

I'd seen Callon bring along syringes and bottles.

"Are you getting warmer?" Clayton asked, adding another log to the fire.

"Getting there," Andre replied.

Even Nakari inched closer to my side. She must have been desperate.

"Thanks for the extra layers," Nakari said quietly. "I appreciate you thinking of me."

I nodded, deciding not to tell her it'd been Callon's idea.

Steam poured from Nakari's mouth like she was going to speak, but nothing came out. I gave her a sidelong glance, but she looked away.

"Just say it, Nakari," Andre said.

I looked at Nakari again; this time her green eyes fought to hide her apprehension.

She sighed and stared into the fire.

"I know just about everyone had given you warnings about Colt, Cheyenne, but I've kept quiet because of our...unique relationship. I just want to ask one small thing. Please don't break Callon's heart."

My throat tightened. She thought I'd crush him.

"I'm not as coldhearted as you might think, Nakari!" I snapped.

"I'm sorry. It's just that I've known Callon for a long time...I know what he's been through in the past, and I can't bear to watch him travel down that path of despair again."

I blinked. She was convinced I'd hurt him. I turned on her.

"I love him. I'm going to marry him, and I have no intention of breaking his heart or allowing past emotions to get the best of me. We're out here to rescue Colt because he is an important part of this family—nothing more."

Even as I said the words I knew the untruth to them...Colt was more than a part of this family, he was a vital part of me. But I knew I'd have to suppress any and all emotions of romantic love for him—I had to for Callon's sake, for mine and for the Timeless clans.

"Thank you," Nakari whispered. "I just needed to hear it from your lips."

Callon paused in his discussions and looked over at us. He'd heard the conversation, heard what I'd said. His eyes drifted to Nakari; her head was lowered. It'd taken a lot of courage for her to say those words to me. Words I mostly likely needed to remember and heed the warning.

Brogan, Koda, Maes and Callon stepped closer to the fire, warming themselves. I looked around, but realized I hadn't seen Daniel in a while.

"Where's Daniel?" I asked.

"Here," Daniel replied. His shoulder brushed mine. "I was just securing the area."

"Thank you," I replied.

As soon we'd warmed, we mounted and were riding once more. I knew that by midday we'd make the falls, as long as the weather held up.

I shivered off and on for the remainder of the night, but when the sunlight began to break through the trees, warmth spread through my limbs again.

"It won't be much longer now," Daniel said. "Just be sure to stick close, just in case we need to make a quick escape."

I nodded. They'd been drilling it into my head; running was just fine for now. We'd stand and fight later. My safety was their first and foremost concern.

"Remember," Callon added, "go for the water. If Cloakers are here, they can't touch you there."

I remembered what he and Dex had told me earlier. Water was the Cloakers weakness. They needed to have a solid surface to land on before they could grab someone. It would be like pouring coffee grounds into water, they wouldn't be able to stick together. At least that was the best explanation Dex had given me.

"Yes, got it," I replied.

My fingers tightened on the reins and Mandi whinnied. She knew something was up. She felt just as anxious as I did. I stroked her neck.

"It's alright, girl. It's going to be alright."

She nodded in agreement and kept up her steady pace.

A pile of blackened ash and partially burned logs lay slightly uncovered beneath the snow. I glanced around. While the snow on the ground made the forest look slightly different, I knew exactly where we were. This was the campsite we'd used on our travels to Dex and Lilly's. I kicked Mandi's side and rode ahead.

Callon and the others didn't try and stop me, and Maes allowed me to lead. My legs tightened in the stirrups as a large log came into view. Mandi leapt over it with little effort, landing in the small stream. Her hooves found solid ground again as we cleared the bank, and my breath caught. Soon the falls would be coming into view.

I heard it first, the gushing gurgling of the river and then the pounding of water hitting the rocks. We were close now, very close. Within the blink of an eye, the gravely beach beside the small pool came into sight. Brogan, Callon, Koda and Maes pushed ahead, and I slowed Mandi to a walk. Nakari, Clayton, Daniel and Andre stayed back with me.

I searched the forest, looking for any movement, any sign of Colt. My heart raced, pulsing with energy. He was here, nearby.

Koda, Callon and Brogan dismounted and Maes disappeared into the surrounding trees. Callon waved us forward. When I stopped, he held Mandi while I dismounted.

"I don't see anything, *princess*," Brogan grumbled. "No tracks…"

"You've only glanced around from horseback, Brogan," I said. "Colt wouldn't want to be found by anyone else. He'd make the clues hard to find."

Brown eyes bore into mine.

"We have to search on foot," I insisted.

Callon waved Brogan off, but not before a nasty glare etched his eyes. Back to feeling lower than pond scum…

"Spread out," Callon ordered. He squeezed my hand.

Daniel jumped beside me, and I headed for the water's edge. His fingers latched over mine. We had to stick together, no matter what.

I followed the shoreline, walking slowly, examining every detail, searching for a hidden clue—a boot impression in the sandy surface, rocks out of place—anything. The spray of icy cold water brushed over my cheeks, and I stared at the falls, taking in their beauty once again.

Anxiety welled up inside me, making my heart race even faster. I was here again, here at the falls where I first knew I loved Colt. I watched the misty images form, Colt standing before me as I sat, his fingers brushing away my wet hair. The feel of his bare chest against mine…

I fought to push down the emotions, the feelings of warmth and happiness, as I knew they were a lie. It'd been nothing but turmoil since I'd met him, nothing but heartache, but still…

"Cheyenne?" Daniel squeezed my hand.

I blinked.

"Are you okay?"

"I'm fine, Daniel."

I focused again on the details, on the spot where I'd sat with him. It was different somehow. The water flowed over what appeared to be rocks, yet I was sure nothing had been there last time.

"Daniel, take me to the falls."

"Chey?" He raised a brow. "The water..."

"Just do it!" I tugged him forward.

Daniel jumped us to the falls, to the ledge where I'd sat before. The icy cold water was pushing at my shins; the spring run-off was starting already. I fought to remain standing as I tried to walk closer to the edge.

Daniel gripped my arm, trying to pull me back.

"Chey, you'll fall in."

"Look!" I pointed to the watery surface. Large stones were arranged in a pattern. Daniel's eyes grew wide.

"It's a word!" he shouted above the roar of the falls.

We both moved closer, my eyes trying to make out the clue.

"It says '*Come*'!" Daniel exclaimed. "It's a clue!"

He turned to jump us to shore, wanting to tell the others, but I shook my head.

"Wait." I took off a glove and pulled one of the bracelets from my pocket. "Help me lift a rock."

His brow furrowed.

"I want to leave Colt a clue that we were here, in case something happens."

Daniel nodded. I bent down, placing the stone bracelet under one of the large rocks. Satisfied, he jumped us back to the shore.

"What'd you see?" Koda asked. The others gathered around, eager to hear.

"Colt gave us a clue. He spelled '*come*' with rocks, like he said in his note." I pointed to the falls, to the rock shelf where Daniel and I had just come from. "He's been here. And he's still close by. I can feel it."

"Spread out then," Koda ordered. "Callon, Nakari, head north. Maes, Andre, you take south. Daniel, Clayton and Cheyenne, head west, and Brogan and I will head east."

Daniel, Clayton and I began heading west when Koda called out again.

"I want us all back here within the next two hours, no later."

We dispersed into the woods. We didn't want to miss any clues that might be lying on the forest floor.

Daniel jumped ahead, while Clayton and I kept our eyes out. A broken branch, or rocks in a grouping...Colt could have placed anything for us to find.

Time ticked by, and still nothing appeared. I had no idea how much ground we'd covered, but soon we would have to go back. Clayton glanced at me nervously. He knew too, but didn't want to say it.

Suddenly, I caught the smell of burning wood. I stopped, trying to locate the source. At the same moment, Daniel reappeared.

"Do you smell that?" I asked. Clayton sniffed, and shrugged.

"Smells like a campfire," he replied.

Daniel nodded, then pushed us behind a large tree trunk.

"Stay here," he instructed. "Let me check it out first."

I tried to reach for his arm, but he disappeared before I made contact. I wanted to go with him. Clayton held onto my elbow.

"Don't," he whispered. "Daniel will come back for us. We don't know what might be waiting out there."

As much as I wanted to yank myself free, I knew I needed to listen. We needed to work together.

Daniel reappeared.

"It's a Tracker party..." he hesitated. "Colt's with them."

My heart raced, Colt was so close! I took a step forward, but Clayton pulled me back.

"Wait, we need to get the others," he said. I looked to Daniel, pleading.

"Can't you just tell Callon?"

Daniel shook his head.

"We're too far," he said. "It won't take long to head back. The three of us aren't enough to get Colt out, anyway. We can't ruin our only chance."

"But if we take too long, they'll get away!" I protested. "We can take them..."

Daniel sighed and grabbed my hand.

"If I show you, will that be enough?"

I swallowed. "Well..."

"I won't take you if you can't promise to stay hidden."

I sighed. He was right. I had to keep my head.

"Alright."

He jumped through the forest, Clayton running behind us. Within moments, we were perched behind some trees. I peered around the corner, and my heart leapt in my chest. Colt was sitting on a tree stump. He was wearing the same shirt I'd seen in the vision, and thick chains were wrapped around his arms. Tears of both relief and love escaped my eyes. He was alive!

"I think those chains are enchanted," Daniel whispered. "He'd have broken free otherwise."

My hands began shaking. We were so close.

Daniel grabbed my shoulders, forcing me to look into his worried blue eyes.

"I don't think I can jump him out of here. If the chains are magic, chances are it'll prevent me from jumping with him. They'll block our powers."

"Then how do we get him out?"

"We don't!" Daniel hissed. "We need Callon and the others."

"But..."

"You promised, Cheyenne!"

I shook my head.

"I'm not going to abandon him like I did at the ravine," I said. "Besides, what if the Trackers find Clayton's tracks? They'll run out of here before we can catch up again. We've got to do this now. If you can distract the Trackers, I can get to Colt." I flexed my fingers. "I should be able to break his chains with my powers. Then, with him on our side, the Trackers won't stand a chance."

Clayton looked torn.

"It could work," he said, "but I don't want to risk anything. If they capture you instead, Cheyenne, they won't care about Colt or any of us. They'll drag you straight to Marcus."

I clenched my fists. I knew I'd be putting myself in danger, but it was no less than Colt had done for me. If only I could convince them...

A shout from the trees on the opposite side of the clearing made me jump. Soon a pair of Trackers appeared, muttering to each other. They must have been on patrol. One pointed towards us, and I gulped.

"We're going, now." Daniel gripped my arm and we disappeared. Clayton made to follow, but unfortunately he stepped on a twig, and a loud snap echoed. The Trackers yelled, running towards the sound.

"No!" I fought to shake Daniel off. "They'll get Clayton. We have to go back!"

"You're more important!" Daniel shot back.

"But if they catch him, they'll send out a party to search for the others," I said. "Leave me behind Colt in the trees. They won't think to look for me so closely. When you've got Clayton out, come back for me."

"Chey..."

"Please, Daniel!"

Daniel sighed. I knew he really didn't want to follow my plan, but eventually we jumped again. I blinked; we were behind the trees surrounding Colt. His broad back filled my vision. Before I could whisper my thanks, Daniel was gone. I prayed he would get to Clayton before the Trackers spotted him.

Colt shifted a little. Had he heard us?

"Hey!" one of the Trackers shouted. The clang of metal falling to the ground shortly followed.

"Watch him!" another yelled, and footsteps pounded in the forest.

I rounded the tree, and stopped. A scraggly looking Tracker eyed me nervously; he'd been hidden by Colt's frame, and I hadn't seen him. I wasn't afraid. I spread my arms out, summoning the wind, and the Tracker turned tail and ran. It was a far cry from the men who'd kept me under guard when I was with Marcus...

"Cheyenne?" Colt murmured weakly.

I twisted on my heels, and my breath caught. Colt had stood up. His shirt was caked with mud, his cheeks dirty and sunken, and a hollowness echoed in his icy blue eyes. Still, I caught the flicker of hope within them as well. He'd been waiting for me!

I threw myself into his arms, his chains rattling in protest.

"You're here," I breathed, his heartbeat echoing in my ear. "You're really here!"

"Oh, Cheyenne," Colt whispered, smiling. "I knew you'd come for me!"

CHAPTER 18

"You're alive," I whispered. His warmth beneath my cheek, his strong arms around me...he was right here with me. "I knew it. I felt it in my heart." I inhaled. He smelled of pine, dirt and sweat. Eventually he pushed me back, and his shoulders sagged.

"Did you come alone?" Colt asked.

I shook my head, suddenly reminded about Clayton and Daniel.

"No, and we don't have much time," I said. "We need to go now."

"Yeah." Colt stretched his arms, causing the chains to jingle. They'd cut into his wrists, leaving blackened scars caked with grime.

"Let me get those off first," I said. "They'll slow you down."

"Good luck," Colt snorted. "They're enchanted. They've been draining my strength since Marcus forced them on me."

"I'll fix that. Hold out your arms."

Colt obeyed. I grasped each shackle. They felt normal enough. I closed my eyes, focusing my power to the palms of my hands. The chains began to rattle, and grew warm beneath my hand. Suddenly a tingling sensation ran up my arms and into my shoulders, and I couldn't let go. Snarling, Colt shoved me away.

"Don't!" he snapped.

"Why?"

"The magic trailed up your arms. It'll weaken you like it has me."

"But we have to get them off..."

Loud howls bounced off the trees. I froze. I knew those howls ...Tresezes!

"Over here!" A deep voice rumbled.

243

Trackers too!

"Forget the chains. Run!" Colt shouted.

He pushed me in front of him, and we sprinted through the forest towards the falls. Pine needles brushed my jacket and cheeks as we wove through them. I glanced up. It wouldn't be long till nightfall. My thoughts turned to Daniel. He must've told Callon by now. I could only hope the Tracker patrol here wouldn't find the others too quickly. Otherwise...

Colt stumbled, his foot catching on a tree root. I held out my arm to help catch him, but we both collided with the hard soil. Any air in my lungs escaped me as Colt landed on top of me. I winced.

Colt didn't move quickly. I wiggled my way out from beneath him and helped him to his feet. He shook his head slowly. His footing was unsteady. My heart ached seeing him like this; this was not the strong Colt who'd carried me across the ravine. How much damage had these chains done to him?

The thundering footsteps were getting closer, and the panting breaths of the Tresezes weren't far behind. I shivered as I remember their awful scent...dead rotting flesh. There were more than we'd anticipated. They must have been hiding.

Run! A familiar voice screamed in my head. *Run towards the falls!*

My eyes widened. There was no question now. It *was* Maes! Somehow he was able to speak to me through my thoughts. I'd have to figure out how later. Right now I just needed to listen.

I yanked harder on Colt's chains and glanced back at him. He was breathing heavily, his face pale and his pace becoming more and more unsteady. He must have hurt his leg. Please, Colt, we just had to make it a little farther!

Suddenly Koda appeared. He shoved his shoulder under Colt's arm and pushed him along.

"I've got him!" Koda barked. "Get to Brogan now!"

I nodded, running faster. Brogan came into view, just at the bottom of the small ravine. He pushed me behind him, pressing me against a boulder. Colt and Koda landed safely behind us, hidden from sight as well. Brogan's back tensed. The Trackers had paused at the top of the ravine.

"This way!" one shouted. Their footsteps soon faded.

I stared at Colt. He lay on his side on the cold, hard ground, his chest heaving. Koda held onto his shoulder, his eyes filled with worry as he stared at the chains.

"Did you try and remove the chains?" Koda asked.

"I can't. Colt said they'd drain me of my powers."

"Maes may know a way," Brogan said. "Let's get him to the falls."

Both Brogan and Koda helped Colt to his feet. I was surprised Brogan wasn't angry that I'd rescued Colt alone, but maybe he was saving the lecture for later. First we had to get Colt free.

We set out quickly, checking the shrubs and trees for hidden movement. We wouldn't have much time before the Tresezes picked up our trail. I kept my hand around Colt's, squeezing gently.

Soon the roar of rushing water caught my ears. We were back. Callon and the others were sitting by the pool, looking tense. The second Callon saw us, he shot to his feet and bolted to Colt's side.

Koda and Brogan eased Colt to the ground, and he sat against a boulder. I knelt beside him, still holding his hand. Daniel appeared beside me and didn't hesitate to wrap Colt in a hug.

"Chey and I knew we'd find you, Colt. We knew it!" His voice shook.

Colt didn't reply, his head hung between his knees. He was still trying to catch his breath. What had become of him? Would he ever get his strength back?

"Can we do anything for him, Callon?" I pleaded. "Can you give him something, anything, so he's not so weak?"

"There's nothing we can do," Maes said. He stood to the side of Brogan and Koda, studying Colt. "At least not here, not now."

"We can't stay here," Brogan said. "We have to get moving."

He went with Koda and the others to prepare the horses.

"Help get him up," Callon said.

I leaned forward and pushed up under Colt's arm while Daniel and Callon pulled him to his feet.

"Stay here, Cheyenne," Callon ordered. "I can at least patch him up a bit before we go." He nodded to Daniel, and they headed over to Bo.

I ran my thumb over the back of Colt's hand.

"We'll bring you home," I said. "Then you can forget about this nightmare."

Colt's head slowly rose. He looked at me, a new brightness in his icy blue eyes. A smirk perched at the corner of his lips.

"Interesting choice of words, sweetheart." His voice was low, gravelly. "But there's something I have to tell you, first." He pulled his arms taught and then slammed his wrists together. The chains clanked, and he caught them in his fist. I stood unmoving, my gaze locked on his face. "Is this my nightmare, or yours?" The sunken patches under his eyes filled in, the dirt on his clothes and cheeks disappeared. He rose up taller, the muscles bulging beneath his tight shirt.

"Colt..." I could barely speak, unsure what was happening. Why was he looking at me like that?

"I just needed you to come to me, and you did, like always. You're so...*predictable.*"

He lunged forward, the chains wrapping around my waist and pinning my arms down. My skin tingled, and my head instantly throbbed. The chains began to illuminate a bluish hue...they were draining me of my powers!

"No!" I screamed.

He crushed me to his chest, my feet leaving the ground.

"No, Colt!" Callon bellowed and rushed forward, but he abruptly stopped as Colt tightened the chains around me. Daniel yelled, jumping to my side, but Colt smacked him away like a mere fly.

"Colt, stop it!" I cried. "He's your brother!"

In seconds, everyone was back. Brogan, Koda and Maes surrounded us. Clayton, Andre and Nakari made a second circle.

"Colt, what the hell do you think you're doing?" Callon growled. I caught a flicker of despair in his hazel eyes.

I moaned. It felt like the very life within me was being drained away. Tears pricked the corner of my eyes. Why was Colt doing this?

"Let go of Cheyenne," Callon said. "Marcus must still have a hold on you. You don't want to hurt her."

"No, Callon, no one has a hold on me. Not Marcus, not you, not our father. I'm free for once in my life, and I'm doing exactly what I want."

"You don't know what you're talking about!" Daniel pleaded, wiping the bleeding cut on his face. "You're hurting Cheyenne!"

"She'll be fine." His cheek pressed against mine, and he raked his fingertips through my hair. "She'll be treated better with Marcus than with any of you."

"He'll drain her of her powers and kill her!" Brogan growled. "You've really overstepped the lines, Colt. You're making yourself our enemy!"

"Ha, like your empty threats mean anything!" Colt shot back. "You've been fighting a losing battle for years. Now I've finally seen the light. Marcus has shown me the truth, and Cheyenne deserves to know as well!"

"The only truth Marcus knows is his greed and lust for power!" Callon shouted. I'd never seen him so angry. "Let her go, Colt. I won't ask you again."

Colt chuckled. "And still you keep feeding her with your lies," he said.

"What are you talking about?" Callon's eyes were livid.

"You know what I'm talking about. All the half-truths, all the history you've deliberately hidden from her since the start. All so you can control her, so you can take her powers just like you claim Marcus wants!" He turned my head towards Nakari. "Callon never told you about Nakari, did he?"

Nakari's eyes grew wide.

"Colt..." Callon warned.

"You didn't bother to inform poor Cheyenne that you were engaged to Nakari, did you, brother?"

Nakari's lower lip began to shake, as her green eyes locked on me. I could only stare back, shocked. I knew they'd been close in the past, but...Callon had been *engaged* to her? Is that why Nakari was so wary around me? Had she feared what I'd do if I ever found out? I'd already admitted to her once that I'd wanted to harm her.

The chains grew tighter, and my body grew weaker. I couldn't even speak.

"What pathetic excuse will you give her, Callon?" Colt jeered.

Callon clenched his fists. His hazel eyes looked to me, filled with sadness, but also defiance.

"I didn't tell you, Cheyenne, because I knew how you'd react. I knew you'd take it the wrong way, and you were struggling with your grief. I didn't need to make it worse." Callon's eyes narrowed. "The past is the past. It can't be changed or denied. Our future is what matters."

Koda snarled; he'd heard enough. Without warning, he charged, his hand coming around my arm, but Colt jerked me sideways and slammed his elbow into Koda's chest. Koda groaned, stumbling back.

"Marcus has brainwashed him well," Koda spat as he regained his balance.

"No," Andre spoke up. Callon looked to her.

"What?"

"He's not under Marcus's control," Andre said, averting her gaze. She didn't want to believe her own words. "He's doing this on his own."

She knows, Cheyenne, Maes's voice rumbled in my head. *She can sense when others tell the truth.*

No...this couldn't be...it couldn't be!

"No," I sobbed. "Colt, no!"

Dark forms moved in the shadows, and low growls erupted. Colt had laid a trap. He stepped back with me still pressed to his chest. The rescue party that had come to save Colt had fallen apart within mere minutes. They stood stunned, speechless as the Trackers and Tresez moved in.

"Colt, please," I begged. "Don't do this!"

"You'll thank me later." He turned, and we headed back towards the ravine.

"This is your family," I murmured. "We love you."

"You know nothing of love, child."

His words cut deep. What had Marcus done to him? Marcus had him believing in his own lies to the point it was now the truth for him. How could I help him see...

"Kiss me," I whispered. "Kiss me and tell me you don't know what love is, that I don't know what love is."

He stopped. The muscles in his arms tensed, and he turned me around so I was facing him. His thumb ran over my lower lip as hard eyes stared at me. He leaned in closer, and my eyes fell shut. He was close enough that I could feel his breath on my cheek, and my heart began to race. *Just a kiss, Colt, just a kiss...*

His warm lips touched the corner of my mouth.

"The thing is, Cheyenne," he murmured, "kissing you will change nothing."

The heat disappeared as he lifted his head and began walking again. I didn't bother to open my eyes as the tears fell. *My* Colt was gone, just like *his* Cheyenne was gone—too much had happened to ever restore us, to give us back what we once had.

"You got her?" a feminine voice said.

My eyes shot open. *Raina!* How had she caught up with us so fast?

"Of course I did. You doubted me?"

Her black mist drifted in front of my face, and a slender finger ran down my cheek. My skin hissed, and I screamed from the burn.

"Leave her be, Raina!" Colt barked. "Marcus said no harm was to come to her."

"Psft," she hissed. "Marcus isn't here right now."

I was dropped to the ground as Colt lunged forward, grasping Raina by the neck. She squealed.

"You forget who's in charge." She vaporized and reappeared a few feet away. "You're not to touch her—ever."

Raina's blue eyes filled with rage. "Your time will come, Colt."

"As will yours," Colt answered. "Now leave."

Her upper lip curled into a snarl, and she vanished.

Colt yanked me to my feet, and I gasped as the chains once again tightened around my chest. The blue aura had successfully removed my powers, and I felt weak, disoriented and confused.

How had it all gone so wrong?

Colt grabbed my jacket as he dragged me to a horse. He mounted, taking me with him, when something flashed across the way. He lost his hold, and I crashed into the hard ground, losing my breath. Seconds later I was off through the trees, a gentler pair of hands around me.

"Daniel!" Colt bellowed.

Wind whisked over my face and my head rolled back. Daniel...

"Hold on," he said. A bruise was forming on his jaw where Colt had hit him.

Blurring flecks of red danced above me. Finally Daniel stopped, and green eyes came into view. Nakari.

"You've got to get the chains off her," Nakari said. "They're sucking the power out of her!"

I was rolled to my belly as they fought to remove the metal.

"I can't. They're too powerful," Daniel moaned. "I'm not strong enough."

"Brogan!" Nakari called, and a moment later we were moving again.

The pine trees began to swirl together into a single green mass, and then everything stilled. Brogan appeared, and grabbed the chains. I felt the change the moment they were broken. A surge of power returned so strong it rippled across my skin, threatening to tear me to bits. I opened my mouth to scream, but no sound came out. Instead a blue shimmering cloud lingered in the air above me, dancing with the sunshine, and then without warning it dove back down upon me.

A violent tremor raked me. My body jerked for a few moments before a peace settled over me. I blinked to clear my vision. Daniel was holding my hand.

"Get her up!" Brogan ordered.

Daniel and Nakari helped me to my feet.

"The horses are just south of the falls. Andre's waiting."

Once again, the forest whipped past us at lightning speed. Mandi started whinnying the moment she caught sight of me. I leaned on her for a moment.

"It's okay, Mandi," I said. "I'm here."

Daniel helped me mount.

"You're gonna have to ride, Chey. I'm sorry," Daniel said.

I nodded.

He smacked Mandi's backside, and Andre, Nakari and I disappeared into the forest. My hat flew off, but I didn't have time to care. My heart ached for the one I loved. It would have been better for Colt to remain dead than for me to see him like this. It would have been better for me to mourn him than fight him...I didn't know if I had it in me to hurt him.

I hung low to Mandi's chest, allowing my fingers to intertwine with her mane.

"Keep me safe," I whispered. "Keep us safe."

Mandi's body rippled with strength, my words empowering her.

I heard them first, the thundering paws. A flash of black streaked by, then another and another. The smell of wet matted fur stung my nose. They were surrounding us, the Trackers, Tresezes, and Colt. Where was the rest of our group? Had Callon and the others already fallen?

We're here, Maes said in my thoughts. *Circle to your left. We're just ahead.*

I pressed Mandi on, moving past Nakari and Andre, pushing them to where Maes and the others were. They came into view. They'd formed a barrier with the horses and their bodies leaving just a small opening for us.

Mandi knew what was going on. She ran full speed until we were within the safety of the circle and then stopped abruptly. I fell off from the sudden halt.

Daniel had me up almost instantly and jumped me beside Callon and Koda. Callon's chest heaved. He'd been fighting. Dirt and mud covered his jacket, and a twig was stuck in his hair. Relief passed through his hazel eyes as he hugged me.

"I thought we'd lost you," he said.

I fought to push back the tears and sorrow. Now wasn't the time, not when we were surrounded, and Colt had his eye on me. I knew what I needed to do.

I pushed Callon away and slid between the horses before they could stop me. Trackers on horses and foot were just ahead. Tresez milled about, snarling and snapping. Colt slowly walked his horse to the front of the line, a smirk building on his lips. The rest of our rescue party stayed behind me.

A lone Tresez, one with a white streak running from his eye to his jaw, moved towards Colt. He shifted...*Conall.*

Together they stood, just a mere thirty feet in front of me.

I widened my stance and removed my gloves and scarf, dropping them to the ground. If they wanted a fight, I was sure as hell going to give them one.

"You going to fight us alone, little one?" Conall snickered.

I said nothing, but kept my eyes focused on him. My fingers began to tingle as the power grew in my chest and hands.

He's going to trick you, drawing your attention elsewhere before he attacks, Maes said. *Keep your eyes on him at all times. Don't watch Colt. It's Conall who'll have the lethal advantage.*

I nodded to show Maes I'd heard his thoughts. Conall's head tilted in curiosity and a brow rose.

"Are there other talents we don't know about?" He began pacing back and forth. "Marcus would be pleased to know you've undergone some additional training. You were sorely lacking in that area."

I still made no movement and no reply. Their horses grew restless, but I kept my attention on Conall.

"You know you're no match for me, little one." A sly smile rose on his lips.

"Awfully big words for someone who hasn't moved yet," I replied.

251

A fire lit his gold-rimmed eyes, just as a fire lit within me...a crimson-eyed fiery beast that had been itching for a release. Conall shifted mid-air, and I threw my hands out as an all-out attack began.

A wall of air hit Conall sending him flying backward into Colt. But I didn't stop until the group of Trackers and Tresezes had also been knocked out of their formation throwing them back into the forest. I swung my arms to the right and scooped up trees and branches, using them as lethal weapons, fastening some of the Trackers and Tresezes to trees. I twirled my hands above my head and then threw them down as the gale-force winds pinned the rest to the ground.

Behind you! Maes yelled. *Duck and spin to your right!*

I did as he said and caught a Tresez in its side, sending it flying. I stepped back, closer to our group, and twirled my hands above my head again. I slowly lowered them, creating an invisible barrier between them and us. They may have gotten Colt, but they sure weren't going to get the rest of my family.

A large hand touched my shoulder, and I glanced back. Brogan stood beside me, his gaze on the Tracker party. He'd never tell me in words, but it was his way of showing support.

"We need more time to formulate an escape plan. You think you can hold them for a bit?" Brogan asked.

"I'll try," I replied. I knew it was the best I could give him for the moment. Marcus wasn't here, but that didn't mean the Trackers didn't have their own tricks up their sleeves. I'd lacked knowledge and experience previously; I wouldn't make the same mistakes now.

"They want Cheyenne," Callon said just behind me. "They made that clear by their method of fighting."

"They backed off when they should have been aggressive," Koda added.

"Raina's not here..." Maes started to say.

"She's here," I called out over my shoulder, cutting him off. "Colt sent her off, but chances are she'll return."

"You saw her?" Maes asked.

"Yes."

"Cheyenne won't be able to ride alone then," Brogan said. "It'll slow us down."

"Midnight's more than capable of carrying us and not slowing down," Koda replied.

Movement caught my eye. A pack of Tresezes began circling. They were going to test the barrier.

Hold steady. They can't get through, Maes said in my mind.

My fingertips began to tingle in anticipation. The voices behind me turned to murmurs. It was as if everything else around me faded. It was just my invisible barrier and me. A lone Tresez pushed ahead, pausing just before my wall. He nudged his nose forward and then jerked back. I'd felt it, like the smallest of prickles on my skin. Soon more joined in, the prickles turning to stings, but it wasn't anything I couldn't handle.

Colt stood in the background, studying me. He called out to Conall, and then they both eyed me carefully. Conall reached into a leather pouch tied to his side and pulled out a small semi-circular object. He tossed what looked like a rock up and down, his palm swallowing it each time.

What were they up to?

The last remaining trickle of sunlight flickered out of sight. Night was falling; we were going to have a big fight on our hands.

The Tresezes and Trackers moved back behind Conall, and he stepped forward.

"Now, little one, no more games. It's time to go," Conall said.

Don't breathe it in! Maes screamed.

My eyes grew wide as Conall threw the rock at my wall. My body jerked violently as a bolt of energy ripped through me. A yellowish brown cloud of smoke billowed around me. I collapsed to the ground and coughed. It smelled of decaying leaves and burned my throat and eyes. I couldn't prevent the smoke from entering my lungs, but I could prevent it from reaching the rest behind me. I struggled to sit up, sending a surge of wind carrying the mist back towards Conall and Colt.

Callon dragged me back into our protective circle. I sat dazed as Andre held me up.

"How much did you breathe in?" Andre asked, panic clear in her voice.

"Enough," I choked out. It hurt to swallow and my lungs burned. "You didn't..." I couldn't finish my sentence as a coughing fit took place.

"You blew it away."

A leg hit my side, knocking me further into Andre. She grunted.

253

They were fighting, fending off the Tresezes and Trackers. How were we going to escape?

The horses began to scatter, and our protective circle began to break down. A Tresez broke through the barrier, its black eyes focused on Andre and me. I tensed, waiting for the attack, when Mandi reared up and smashed her hooves into its skull. The Tresez lay unmoving; Mandi released a wild snort and stood over us protectively.

Andre's hand shook while she pushed back her black hair. We were both defenseless on the ground. We needed to move.

"Help me stand," I said.

I winced. My chest stung with the exertion. Andre helped me to my feet, and shoved my arm over her shoulder to support me. We slowly inched our way back as the fighting drew closer. I glanced around. Everyone was engaged in battle. Daniel and Nakari were jumping around and landing deadly blows. Nakari wasn't large or all that strong, but the element of surprise and a log played well to her advantage.

I caught sight of blond hair, blond hair I knew too well. Colt was slowly inching his way closer to us, his hand clenched tightly around the chains. The chains began to turn red, like they were on fire, but no flames burned them. The red turned to deep amber and drops of melting metal dripped from them...like molten lava.

I pushed up against Andre.

"I see him," she said.

Did she see what was in his hands? If the chains hit her, they'd burn her. If Colt wrapped them around me again, I'd be burned alive!

"The chains!" I hissed. "They'll burn us!"

Andre's eyes narrowed, but she didn't say anything.

A Tresez crept closer. I blinked. It had two heads.

"Do you see that?" I quaked.

"Use your powers, Cheyenne!"

Andre jerked my hands up, and I recoiled from the pain. The forest, and the Tresez, began spinning violently. I didn't have to see clearly to know how close the Tresez was...I heard its low growl. I planted my feet firmly, opening the palms of my hands. No two-headed Tresez freak was going to harm us.

I flicked my fingers and watched a blue flash of light hit the

Tresez, throwing it into a grouping of Trackers. I stumbled back, stunned. Koda caught me.

"Well that's new," Koda said. "Think you can do it again?"

"I—I don't know." I wasn't even sure what had happened, other than the forest stopped spinning, and the Tresez vanishing. Was I hallucinating? Was it from the yellow smoke?

"Let's try."

Koda helped me raise my arms, and I shot another burst of blue light towards a group of Trackers. If I'd been bowling, I'd have gotten a strike.

"Yes!" Koda hollered. "Another!"

Before I had time to reply, he had me turned towards another grouping. This time Colt was directly behind them, his molten chains swinging in the air. I released the surge and crumpled in Koda's arms. It was taking too much out of me.

I inhaled a shaky breath.

"Chey!" Koda turned me towards him. "Damn! Callon!"

My head rolled to the side. I didn't have enough strength to hold it up.

Koda carried me towards Callon when he was hit from the side. I flew to the ground and winced as my cheek made contact with a tree branch. I lay still. Warmth ran down my cheek and there was a taste of metal touching my tongue...*blood*.

I blinked. Night was falling. The last bits of sunlight streamed through the tree branches...I blinked again. Why were the branches moving like that? There was no breeze, no wind, but the limbs seemed to dance, swaying back and forth...*snakes!*

A strangled scream left my lips, and I fought to catch my breath. My chest wheezed. I couldn't bring in enough oxygen. Six sets of gold-rimmed eyes came into focus, and I tried to crawl away.

"I told you it was time to go, little one," Conall said. His hand latched onto my ankle, and I stared at him, stunned. He had three heads!

This wasn't real! This wasn't real! I kicked to no avail.

"Save what energy you have left. The more you use your powers, the more you will suffer. Only Marcus has the antidote."

The yellow smoke...

"No!" I screeched.

With a rush of energy, I lunged forward and touched Conall's arms. I'd rather die here than be taken to Marcus. The crimson-eyed beast surge from my palms, Conall's lip twitched, his eyes rolled back into the back of his head, and then he was gone.

I dropped back down, staring up at the starry skies. All the sounds became whispers, and Mother Nature's cold fingers drifted over me. I shivered, my lungs clamoring for air as they fought to suck up every last drop.

Auburn hair and caramel eyes blurred above me, familiar somehow.

"Cheyenne," his whispery voice said. "It's Jahlem. Darrien and I are here to help you." One ripped open my jacket, while the other placed his fingers on my neck.

*Jahlem...Darrien...*They'd showed me kindness before, while with Marcus.

Jahlem's eyes darted about.

"Do it," Darrien said. "She's not getting enough oxygen."

Jahlem raised my head, while Darrien opened a small vile. They were about to pour something into my mouth when Darrien suddenly dropped the vial. It shattered on the ground. A moment later, they were gone.

"I've got you," Daniel said and lifted me into his arms. "They've cleared a path for us. Whatever was in the smoke is starting to affect them too. They're dropping like flies."

My eyes fell shut, too heavy to keep open. Strong arms came around me, and soon, the rhythm from hoof beats darkened my world even further, rocking me into a dark, deep abyss.

CHAPTER 19

I woke to a heavy weight crushing my chest. My hands flew out, struggling to dislodge whatever was there, when fingers came around my wrists. I gasped, trying to suck in air, and my eyes flew open.

"Cheyenne, it's okay. You're safe!" a voice cried out.

I blinked, trying to focus, but all I saw were blurry images. *Daniel?* I pushed at the silhouette. Why where they crushing me?

"Cheyenne! You're safe. Calm down!" This time I knew the voice, Callon.

I struggled even further, my body jerking forward. I needed air.

Cheyenne...

I stilled. The voice was inside my head. *Maes.* Why couldn't I see him?

The smoke, Cheyenne, Maes said. *It's poisoned you.*

My ragged breaths turned to panting. Callon's strong arms eased me back, my head resting on his chest. His fingers touched my neck, and I closed my eyes. Where was I? Above my struggled breathing, I heard the hum of tires and wind against windows. We were driving now. I'd been out for a long time. The last thing I remembered was our group riding away from danger, from Colt. My heart ached at the thought of him.

"Her breathing is getting worse," Callon said.

"It's going to get worse before it get better," Maes replied. "I know which stone Conall used, and the antidote is complicated to make."

"Once we're on the jet, we can work on it." Callon's voice was calm and serene, but his heartbeat told me otherwise. "I'm going to need to stop for some medical supplies in the next town."

"Stopping for anything other than gas is risky, Callon," Brogan rumbled.

"I don't have a choice. She needs oxygen."

"I can get it, Callon," Nakari said. "I can get in an out before anyone knows what's going on. I know what you need." Obviously, she was feeling guilty over Colt's revelation about her and Callon's engagement.

"I'll help too," Andre added. "She just looks so pale."

"Thank you," Callon replied.

Without my consent, my eyes fell shut and darkness swallowed me.

I breathed deeply. Finally I could breathe without feeling like I was being crushed. I inhaled again, sucking up the sweet air. Something was pressed up against my face, covering my nose and mouth, and I heard a hissing sound. I lifted my hand.

"It's okay, love. It's an oxygen mask," Callon explained. His fingers began to stroke my hair.

My lashes fluttered. My vision was still blurry, but I knew where I was and who was with me. We were still driving, and I was pressed up against Callon's chest. He was holding me. An oxygen tank sat beside us, where I should have been sitting.

"Are you feeling any better?" Daniel asked. His blue eyes came into view as he leaned in. "You can't see me very well, can you?"

I shook my head.

"Are you cold?"

I didn't have time to reply when he pulled a bulky jacket up around my shoulders.

"There, that should help." He sighed. "Callon will make you well again, Chey. He's already been talking with Dex and Layla. Maes know what needs to be done." His eyes saddened. "I just don't understand why Colt would allow someone to harm..."

"Colt," I murmured, and tears stung too near the surface. He knew what Conall had thrown, was a part of it...he'd betrayed us all.

"Shh." Callon kissed my head. His hand squeezed mine. "Finding Colt the way we did wasn't what we wanted, but we'll make it through this too, love."

It wasn't right, none of it. It was all Marcus's doing. Once again he'd taken away what little happiness I wanted—stolen it like he'd stolen everything else from me. The man was ruthless, and now he was trying to kill what he considered precious—me. I couldn't stop the tears once they started.

I clung to Callon, my fingers burying themselves into his shirt. I clung to him like he was the last lifeboat. I needed to be in his arms. I needed his strength at the moment to keep me from falling. I knew all too well what the pits of despair looked like, knew the crimson-eyed creature would welcome me again. I couldn't go back. Callon was my last lifeline—I'd do anything to keep him safe.

My tears eventually faded, and just the hissing of oxygen was heard in the SUV. Hissing that reminded me of a snake—Marcus.

The SUV began to slow, and regardless of my hazy vision, I knew we'd reached Helena. It wouldn't be long till we could board the jet and be on our way home—away from this misery-ridden hellhole we'd just crawled out of.

We passed through the security gate with no questions and parked beside a large hangar. I knew the jet had to be just inside. I'd overheard them talking while we drove. Quinn and Skylar would be ready to depart once we arrived.

The sun hung low in the sky. Another night was about to fall. Just how many days had slipped by?

The SUV's doors opened, and I immediately started shivering. Callon adjusted his coat over me and lifted me out. The cold swirled around us. The tubing from the oxygen mask drifted loosely in the wind. Daniel walked behind us, carrying the tank.

"We're almost..." Daniel didn't finish his sentence as Callon abruptly stopped.

Callon's hands grew tight on my limbs. I turned, but couldn't see what stopped him.

"Take her with you, and she'll die, Callon." A familiar voice called out.

Marcus!

Anger swelled inside me. My jaw clenched and the bitter taste of copper flowed on my tongue. Blood. I swallowed.

Brogan and Koda's large frames stepped before us, blocking any view.

"First it starts with hallucinations," Marcus said clearly. "Then each and every time she uses her powers, it weakens her. Next comes the labored breathing, and oxygen won't help. And finally, the worst of all, a deep, dark, lonely coma. It will be a long, slow painful death."

We slowly began to move again, a circle of bodies around us.

"If you get on that plane, Cheyenne, you'll die. I'm the only one with the antidote. Come with me, and you'll live. Go with Callon, and you'll die. I can offer you a life without running in fear. What can he offer you?"

The bodies parted enough for the shadowy figures to come into view. I didn't need to see clearly to know Colt and Conall were with Marcus. Colt should have been coming home with us...Marcus stepped forward with his hand outstretched.

"Come with me, Cheyenne. I can make you whole again. I can give you everything." It was the same tone he'd used on me before, soothing, caring and a complete façade.

I pulled the mask away, speaking just above a whisper, "I'd rather die than spend another moment with you!"

I knew he'd heard me because in the next moment Daniel's hand latched around my ankle, Callon's grasp became tighter, and our pace increased. It was apparent my words had angered him, enough that my protectors thought he'd use his powers, even in public.

The warmth from the jet's interior hit my cold cheeks. Brogan pulled my oxygen mask back into place. I closed my eyes. We were safe now. Callon laid me down on something soft, a pillow placed under my head and a warm blanket wrapped around me.

"Get my bag, Daniel," Callon directed. "I need to check her vitals."

A small wisp of air moved my hair, and my hand was lifted out from under the blankets. From under heavy lids, I watched Callon clip a small device over my finger. It emitted a beeping sound.

"I'm measuring your oxygen level, Cheyenne. You seem to be breathing better now," Callon said.

I couldn't help but wonder if there was some truth to what Marcus had just said. So far everything he described had happened, except for the last.

"Will I die?" I whispered.

"No," Maes replied. His dark figure stood behind Callon. "Marcus doesn't want you dead. He wants you scared so you'll conform to his wishes." He hesitated. "I'm not going to lie. This won't be pleasant for you until we find the antidote."

How much worse could it get?

The jet's engines roared to life, and Quinn's voice broke over the intercom, telling us to prepare for take off. Callon secured a buckle around me and then sat beside me on what appeared to be a couch. Obviously I needed to be near everyone instead of back in the bedroom. He brushed the hair from my face.

"I'll take care of you, love. I promise."

I closed my eyes and allowed the hum of the jet to pull me into a peaceful rest.

My eyes flew open at the screeching of tires. I blinked. My vision was back, and the cabin was dark. I inhaled; Callon had removed my oxygen mask.

"It's okay," Andre said. She was sitting on the floor beside me. "We're just landing in Chicago to refuel."

I tried to reply, but my lips wouldn't move. It was strange. I couldn't move my arms or legs either. What was going on? Was this the coma Marcus was talking about? But he'd said I'd go into a coma, and I was awake...panic began to well up inside. How was I supposed to tell Callon if I couldn't speak? I started to hyperventilate.

"Cheyenne?" Andre leaned up on her knees. "What's wrong?"

I fought to force my lips to move. I wanted to scream, but nothing came out.

"Callon!" Andre screamed.

Hazel eyes met the panic in mine. Callon was beside me in an instant, his hands holding my face. "What's going on, Cheyenne?"

When I didn't answer, he took a visual assessment. He quickly took my pulse. Then he lifted my arm and then released it. It fell limply to my side. He flashed a light in my eyes. In another moment, he opened my mouth and pressed a tongue depressor at the back of my throat.

I gagged, and tears formed in my eyes.

Callon placed the small device on my finger again.

"It's happening," Maes said.

"What's happening?" Andre pleaded. She stood up and grasped his arm. "What's happening?!"

"She's in what you would call a vegetative state," Maes explained.

"She can hear, see, smell and feel, but she can't move or speak. Marcus put her in a coma of sorts."

"Why?" Andre asked, and I saw the recognition before Maes answered. "He did it to immobilize her, makes it easier to travel."

"Yes," Maes replied. "Once she has the antidote, her condition will improve slowly."

Maes bent down, his calloused fingers wiping the tears from my cheek. *It's going to be okay, mon espoir. We're working on the cure.*

Callon replaced the oxygen mask and left the monitoring device on my finger.

"Stay with her, Andre. Help keep her calm," Callon instructed. "I'll be back to check her levels soon." He then stood and called out for Daniel.

Another large shadow loomed nearby in the dimly lit cabin. Brogan.

Koda passed by, his worried gaze upon me.

"Go with Daniel, Koda. I'll stay here and watch over her," Brogan said.

Koda nodded.

Where were Daniel and Koda going?

Brogan lifted my weighted legs, plopped down on the couch and rested them upon his lap.

"Sorry, princess, but I need to ensure you don't go anywhere. We're not taking any chances with Raina."

Andre held my hand. "It's going to be fine. Maes knows what he's doing. He won't let you down."

My head had been slightly turned, and from the corner of my eye I caught sight of long auburn hair. Nakari was hovering near one of the seats. She seemed unsure. Another figured loomed behind her as well. It was too dark to see clearly. It was either Skylar or Clayton or both.

"You look like a bunch of stalkers," Brogan grumbled. "Just come sit over here if you want to be near her."

The three sat on the floor beside me. Their wary glances didn't do anything to calm me. I shut my eyes, trying to block them out, but I could still hear their breathing. The only thing I could do was pray Callon and Maes figured out the antidote soon. Staying in this condition would slowly drive me insane.

Too many thoughts began to wander through my mind—dark

thoughts. Thoughts about bringing vengeance to Marcus, thoughts I knew I needed to keep under control. My breath shook slightly just remembering his words before we boarded the jet. I didn't need to see him to know what intent would have been in his eyes. He was growing desperate, threatening everything around me. He'd even stolen Colt from us, from me, just as he'd stolen the lives of my parents, my life, everything. He was fighting to control me and my powers, and I refused to give in.

We'd lost Colt, but we'd lose no more. I would not have my heart shattered again. Callon and Maes would find the antidote, cure me, and then we'd plot against Marcus—plot to end his reign of terror.

There was a loud pop, and then a hissing sound erupted. My eyes flew open. Brogan's grip on my legs tightened, and Andre's leg hit my side as she jumped up beside me. Her long black hair dangled close to my cheek as she leaned in protectively.

The scent of chemicals burning, then smoke filled the air. Fire alarms pierced my ears, and Quinn ran by. A swooshing sound was heard, like a fire extinguisher and then coughing. I cringed inside. Something hadn't gone right.

"Skylar, Clayton," Quinn called out. "Help me clear the smoke from the cabin."

A high-pitched vibration jolted my eardrums, and if I could have jumped I would have. The smoke began to dissipate, and Maes inched closer. Andre and Nakari ran to him. His shirt was blackened, and remnants of black smoke streaked his face.

"What happened?" Andre quaked.

She and Nakari pulled Maes to a seat nearby. Nakari turned over his hands and then disappeared.

"Explosion," Maes coughed. "Didn't quite go as planned." He was wheezing.

Thankfully we weren't in the air, or it would have been disastrous.

Nakari returned with a bowl of water and a cloth. Andre began cleaning his face and hands, revealing burn marks.

Callon! Where was Callon? My eyes franticly searched the cabin for him, where...

"Maes, are you alright?" Callon asked and kneeled down beside him, taking the cloth away from Andre.

Callon's clothes were blackened too, but it appeared Maes had taken the impact from the explosion.

"I've had worse," Maes replied.

"Nakari, get me some salve." Callon nodded to the back room. Nakari disappeared.

My heart sank. I knew what happened now. The antidote that they'd been working on had failed—failed in a big way. Callon had promised to take care of me, but I didn't want to be immobile the rest of my life. A few tears escaped and trickled down my cheek.

"It's just a small setback, Cheyenne. It's going to be okay," Brogan said softly.

I closed my eyes. I'd brought this upon myself. I had been the one who begged we send a rescue party for Colt. I had been the one who believed he was calling out to me...only to find out he was calling out to destroy me. He knew I'd come and bring everyone along. He knew I'd risk it all for him—I'd risked everyone's lives and was paying the price for it. Just another failure to add to the list.

"What happened?" Daniel quaked. "Callon...Maes, are you okay?"

"We're fine, Daniel," Callon replied. "Did you get what I asked for?"

"Yes, but..."

"But what?" Maes growled. "We needed those supplies!"

"Hold on, Maes," Koda spoke up. "We may have stumbled across something even better."

My eyes shot open, and my heart raced. What had they found? A cure? They were huddled together around Maes.

"What's this?" Callon held what looked like a small vile in his hands.

"It was a gift," Daniel replied.

"A gift from whom?" Maes stood and took the vile from Callon.

"I have my own ideas, but they wouldn't reveal themselves," Daniel said. "They said it's the antidote for Cheyenne."

Maes's teeth ground and his jade-rimmed eyes narrowed.

"No. Marcus would rather keep her like this than allow her to be healed."

"It wasn't from Marcus," Koda said. "It was from someone who wanted to help."

"It's a trap," Maes snarled. "No one wants to help—ever."

"You did," Daniel replied. "You know there are others out there from both sides helping out with intel and such. Why would this be any different?"

"It was too risky for *whomever* to get this to you. Marcus would have only allowed it if there was a way to bring Cheyenne to him," Maes snapped. He clenched the bottle in his hands as if he wanted to crush it.

"Don't," Callon's voice rippled with authority, and he stuck out his hand. "We have nothing else to go on now. I think it's worth the risk."

Daniel smiled and looked over at me. A moment later he was at my side. He lifted my hand.

"It's going to be okay. This antidote is going to work. I can feel it," Daniel said.

Daniel moved aside as Callon sat beside me.

"We don't have any other options, love. Are you willing to try?" he asked.

I wanted to scream yes, but I couldn't. My breathing increased. He pulled back the oxygen mask, his hazel eyes softening.

"I need you to blink twice for me if you want to drink this."

I quickly blinked twice.

"Alright."

Callon gently tilted my head, and a sweet tasting liquid touched my tongue. It smelled of oranges and peppermint, and then burned my throat like when my dad had given me a taste of whiskey. I was on fire! I struggled to scream, to lash out, anything to remove it from my mouth. I began choking, gagging, and part of the liquid spewed from my mouth before it was clamped shut. I struggled not to swallow, but had no choice. Soon everything faded to black.

I took a deep breath. It smelled of lilacs, and I smiled. I loved the scent of fresh cut flowers. My mom always had them in the house. Lilacs, and tulips in the spring, then she'd move on to wildflowers bouquets. I could picture an old blue canning jar sitting in the front room. Dad and I always tried to talk her into using vases, but she insisted the blue mason jars were much more decorative. I stretched and rolled to my side.

My eyes flew open. I could move!

I sat up only to have the room spin. I fell back down and pressed my palm to my forehead. Pain rippled across my temples. I lay still for a few moments, waiting for the ache to dissipate.

The antidote had worked—besides the headache.

This time I slowly opened my eyes and looked around. I was in my bedroom in Ireland, and traces of what appeared to be the morning sun trickled through the terrace doors. We'd made it home.

The chirping birds outside my window made me smile. I inhaled again, taking in the scent of the fresh flowers sitting on my bedside table. I was sure Lilly had put them there. She was like my mom, and had a knack with flowers and plants. Anytime she could cultivate a living thing, she did—including me.

My bedroom door creaked open, and brown eyes searched the room. Dex smiled. He and Lilly entered my room.

"Morning, Cheyenne," Dex said softly. He pulled a chair up beside my bed while Lilly sat beside me.

Lilly took my hand in hers. Her blue eyes showed the relief she felt inside.

"We've been waiting for you to wake up," Lilly said.

"How long have I been sleeping?" I asked.

"Long enough," Dex replied and then stared down at his hands. "We weren't sure what was going on for a while, but then last night you became restless. Callon and I figured it was a good sign."

Lilly reached out to touch Dex's arm.

"And now you're awake," Lilly said. "Honestly, sweetheart, you're making me age faster than a Timeless should." She gave a weak smile and brushed her black hair behind her ear. "You're not leaving here until after the wedding. I can't handle anymore of this stress."

"I—I'm sorry..." my voice crackled, and I tried to clear it. A small coughing fit took over. Dex helped me sit up while I took a sip of water. Whatever was in the antidote must have caused burns in my throat. It was suddenly painful to talk or swallow.

Lilly brushed the hair from my eyes as I lay back down.

"Callon told us about Colt." She sighed and began to fiddle with my comforter. "I'm sorry. We're all heartbroken over it."

I nodded and looked away, staring at the streams of sunlight dancing on my wood floor.

"Cheyenne," Dex said. "It's going to be okay. We'll get through this just like we always have in the past."

"You have your wedding to worry about now," Lilly added, trying to change the subject. "I know it'll be small, but we can make it just as spectacular and special as it should be."

I had no doubt in my mind that when Lilly put her mind to something, she'd do just as she said.

"Thank you," I whispered.

Now it was my turn to fiddle with my comforter. It was probably best that Colt wouldn't be here for the preparations and wedding. It most likely would have affected my relationship with Callon, and I needed to focus on him. My heart would always be broken. A piece of me always belonged to Colt, regardless of his choice. It's just that his choice made it all the more painful. I should have left him as a memory instead of pushing for what I wanted. I'd only caused more heartache for Callon and Daniel. Brogan was right. I was a princess, always thinking she could get her way.

"Callon and the rest are resting," Dex added. "We told him we'd take care of you when you woke. They're all a bit...beat up."

At least I knew where everyone else was, that everyone had made it back without anymore incidents.

"Layla will be up soon, with some warm tea and broth." Lilly touched my hand again. "Right now we need to focus on your health. Maes said it would be rough here for a bit, that it would take some time before you had your strength back."

I gave a faint smile. Strength was what I needed to make it through the next few weeks. Regardless of not knowing what day it was, I knew spring was here and that meant our wedding was about three months away.

"She also has some drawings for your dress if you want to see them." Hopefulness lit Lilly's eyes. "Callon doesn't want you out of bed for a few days anyway."

Callon may have not wanted me out of bed, but I knew from the feel of my grimy hair, I needed a bath or shower.

"Can I take a bath?" I croaked.

Lilly hopped off the bed and headed towards the bathroom.

"I'll start the water while Dex helps you up."

Dex stood, and helped me walk the few feet to the bathroom door. At least I'd be clean when Callon came again, and a bath would help me wash away those awful memories of Colt. I wanted to remember him like I knew him before, when I loved him.

I needed to have a long conversation with Callon about Nakari too. If I was going to take my vows with him, I needed to make sure there were no more secrets between us. I'd had to reassure him with my feelings for Colt; it was time he did the same for me.

CHAPTER 20

My health was slowly returning to normal and so was our family...whatever normal meant anymore. Colt had betrayed us. The wound was deep, and it wasn't just me that was hurting. Callon and Daniel valiantly tried to hide their pain, anger and sorrow, but the fact that Colt—someone who had at one time been so caring, loving and kind—had now turned into a monster was still unreal. I knew, just as they knew, the wound would always fester.

It also didn't help that I'd found out about Callon and Nakari. At least that explained the ring around her neck. I'd yet to bring the topic up with Callon. I'd been waiting for the right time. I didn't want a fight. I just wanted some understanding.

I adjusted my blanket and resituated my book. I'd taken to the library lately, following Callon's sudden immersion in his research. I knew it was his way of dealing with Colt's betrayal, and Lilly's distraction was to captivate me with wedding preparations and gardening. I was thankful for her support, but nothing could distract me for long. Luckily, it wasn't raining, and she had other things that needed her attention besides me.

The sound of papers shuffling on the desk caused me to look up. Callon's lip twitched. His head rose, and hazel eyes peeked out from under his brown waves of hair.

"Sorry," he said.

I gave a faint smile and pretended to read, waiting for him to return to his task. I watched his deliberate movements, the muscles flexing under his blue T-shirt as he stacked books to the side.

I studied his face. He'd taken to shaving again, and Lilly had been threatening him with scissors. He was required to get a haircut before the wedding, she'd said, or else. His appearance hadn't changed that much since I met him. He still looked like he was in his early twenties, but his eyes had changed.

He'd always tried to hide his emotions from me. He didn't want to worry me, but the mounting pressure, constant setbacks, and Colt were taking their toll. Looking into his hazel eyes told me a different story, a story of just surviving.

I was torn. Should I let this whole Nakari situation be swept under the rug, or should I finally just ask? Curiosity won me over. I was beyond being hurt by it anymore.

"Callon, can I say something?" I asked.

"Sure," Callon said, not looking back as he continued to replace books on the shelves. "What about?"

"About Nakari."

Callon hesitated for a brief second, but quickly resumed picking up books.

"What about her?" he replied.

"You were engaged to her, and you didn't tell me."

He paused, studying a book cover, yet he didn't answer me.

"It hurt to find out through Colt," I went on.

The muscles in his neck tensed. "I'm sorry. I should've let you know, but at the time there were too many other things to deal with. It seemed like the right decision."

"You had the opportunity when I asked about her engagement ring," I said.

He turned and leaned on the bookshelf, his hazel eyes fighting to hide his irritation. "And you had opportunities to tell me plenty of things in the past too, Cheyenne, and didn't. I'm not holding anything against you for that, and you shouldn't hold anything against me either. We've made a lot of mistakes. If I had a second chance, I'd make better choices, as would you. We need to let this go."

"I'm not holding it against you. I just wanted to know why."

"I told you in Montana," Callon answered. "You were emotionally vulnerable, and you would've used it as an excuse to lash out further. At least, that's what I felt. Whether it was true or not isn't the point. You know now." He glanced to the desk. "Like I said, the past is the past."

Before I could respond, Daniel appeared in the doorway.

"Hey, Chey," he greeted me. "Koda and I were going to play cards. You in?" He gave me a boyish grin. He'd also been trying to hide his pain by playing poker with me—teaching me new tricks, as he called it. It was better than hiding in books like Callon had.

"I suppose so." I glanced at Callon. He'd moved to the desk again. He waved me off without looking up.

"If I need you, I'll come find you," he said.

He was still irritated that I'd asked, but he was right. I—we needed to let this go. We had enough worries to fill the Grand Canyon, no need to add more to the pile. I also didn't need to have ill feelings for Nakari. She'd been dealt a lousy hand in life and love too. I set my book on the small side table and folded up the blanket, laying it over the back of the couch.

Circling around the couch, I stopped beside Callon's desk and gave him a peck on the cheek. He squeezed my hand and but didn't look up. He'd get over my questioning just like I'd get over the admission. Besides, in just a few more weeks, we'd be married. In just a few more weeks, I'd have a husband. I sighed. Callon would love me, and treat me well, I had no doubt, but marrying at twenty? I'd wanted to wait, but I had a responsibility to the Timeless race.

Daniel waited patiently in the doorway, his arm laced in mine as he led me to the dining room. Koda sat at the table, shuffling cards. A warm smile spread over his face, reaching all the way to his eyes. The way Colt used to smile at me. He'd been the one to get me to play poker in the first place at Dex and Lilly's. My chest tightened. It made it hurt even more knowing Colt had made this choice himself. There was no rescuing the unwilling.

"No cheating today, you two," Koda said and winked.

I gave a faint grin. Koda was insistent that there was no way as a beginner I could win as many hands as I had. And he was right. Daniel had been sneaking me cards. There was an advantage to his jumping skill, especially when it was used to torment Koda. It was only fair since Koda had been telling me lame jokes for months now.

Koda tapped the chair beside him, pulling it closer.

"I'm watching you, Chey," his voice was low. "I'll catch the two of you. That's a promise."

I shrugged. He could try all he liked, but the chances of catching

271

Daniel were slim to none. Koda dealt the cards.

I studied my hand as the play continued, drawing and discarding. I was aiming for a straight flush; however, Daniel was pointing me in a different direction. And by the way Koda had slouched in his chair and his lips twitched, I knew he had something good.

I lifted my hand, my thumb mindlessly rubbed over my Servak ring, Daniel's sign. I discarded and drew a new card. I forced my lips into a straight line. Daniel had given me an ace.

Koda's lip curled, and he spread out his cards.

"Straight F-l-u-s-h." He drew the words out.

Daniel let out a loud sigh and threw his cards down.

"I'm out," he groaned.

I bit my lower lip.

"Whatcha got, Chey?" Koda teased. "You're not going to beat me this time."

I blew the hair from my eyes and glanced at Daniel. A slow deliberate smirk rose on my lips. One by one I lay down each card, watching Koda's jaw drop further each time.

"Royal F-l-u-s-h." I drew out the words just as he had.

His icy blue eyes grew even larger, and then he blinked. A moment later he pushed his hand through his hair and then he rubbed his chin, staring at the cards on the table.

"How?" he mumbled. A moment later he was on his feet, his knees hitting the dining room table and jarring me back into my seat. "Cheaters!" He shoved his finger in my face.

"That's an awfully mean thing to say, Koda," I reprimanded. I pushed my chair back and stood, stepping away from the table. He looked like he was about to lunge at me at any moment, like Colt had done with me playfully in the past. "Did you see anything?"

His eyes narrowed, and a lock of his hair fell onto his forehead. He was past due for a haircut too.

"The two of you did something, I know it! No one is that lucky!"

"Well, you two are the ones teaching me to play poker. Obviously you're a better teacher than player." I shot him a playful grin.

Koda reached for me, but I was ready. I jumped back and ran for the front entry. He followed on my heels.

"You're not getting away with it anymore, Cheyenne!" he roared playfully.

I couldn't help but giggle. It had been a while since any of us had let loose and laughed.

"Run, Chey, run!" Daniel cheered. Bree was scolding him as I ran by.

I reached the marble floor and slid around the corner, making contact with an entry table. The large vase of tulips crashed to the floor, and water spilled over the marble. Koda stopped in his tracks.

"Oh, you've done it now, Chey. Lilly's going to kill you for that one." Koda crossed his arms.

Crap...he was right, Lilly had been watering it for weeks.

Daniel and Bree moved behind Koda, grinning.

Callon emerged from the library, and I slowly stood. My socks were drenched, and glass crunched under my feet as I tried to move.

"Hold still, Cheyenne," Callon said and moved closer. "Let me help you."

Callon carefully stepped onto the glass and lifted me off my feet.

I kissed his cheek.

"Ah, my knight has come to rescue me!" I giggled.

He shook his head and carried me over the broken glass and water. We were heading towards the library.

"Koda, you get to clean up the mess," Callon called out over his shoulder.

"Wait! What?" Koda's eyes narrowed and his head shook. "Daniel..."

Daniel and Bree suddenly appeared at the top of the stairs.

"Oh, I'm sure you've got it, Koda," Daniel called out and then in another blink they were gone.

Koda grumbled as he headed for the kitchen.

Callon and I entered the library. He set me on the couch and carefully removed my wet socks, discarding them in the trash. He lifted each foot, inspecting it closely.

"You don't feel any cuts, do you?" he asked.

"Not that I can tell."

"Good." He sat before me on his knees, his hands running up my legs and stopping on my thighs. Butterflies erupted in my belly, and I couldn't help but lick my lips nervously. Apparently he wasn't irritated anymore.

He'd been a bit distant lately—we all had—but that was why I was following him around like a lost puppy. We both needed reassurance; and he needed to know how much I loved him. We both needed to know it was going to be okay, that we could go on even with Colt's choice.

"We haven't really talked about *other things*," he said, his hazel eyes softening. "I think we've both been a little distressed about finding Colt in the manner we did. It hurts." He sighed and grasped my hands. "Honestly, it would have been better if we still thought he was dead."

I pressed my eyes closed, tears close the surface. I knew exactly how he felt. We both loved Colt dearly, and wanted him back the way he was, before Marcus changed everything.

"He's a threat now, love," he continued, lowering his head. "A threat I'm not sure how to deal with."

My heart sank even further. I knew Callon had been talking with Brogan and Maes. He'd purposely left me out of those meetings. He knew I'd still defend Colt, even though I shouldn't.

"What are we going to do?" I whispered, my voice cracking.

"There's talk of elimination." His finger began running over my engagement ring.

A tear trickled down my cheek. I tried to blink the rest away.

"How much more harm can he cause us, Callon? We're safe here with the enchantment. You've changed it so he can't access it, right?"

"Yes, but the problem is that he knows things about us. Things about other Timeless that could be damaging, and result in..."

"More deaths." I finished his sentence for him.

"Yes."

"You don't think he'd try anything before the wedding, do you?" I wanted to trust my instincts and say no, but after what had happened, after he assisted Conall in causing me harm, I couldn't or wouldn't put anything past him.

He looked up, not bothering to hide his wariness.

"I don't know," Callon sighed, "and then there's the wedding itself."

"I don't understand," I told him.

He moved onto the couch. His arm came to rest behind me. I turned towards him, and placed my hand in his.

"I've been wanting to talk to you about the ceremony so you'd understand. I wanted to wait until I knew we could secure everything, but I can't wait any longer. You need to know the potential risk for both of us."

"A risk? Dex said something about us marrying during the summer solstice so we would counterbalance each other. Is that it?"

"It's more than that. During the ceremony, we are united with the *Braid del amour,* the braid of love. The Braid is placed upon us, binding our hands and arms together, then the ritual is performed to show we're united in power and love." He hesitated for a moment.

"What?"

"We'll lose our powers for a period of time. We'll be completely vulnerable."

I blinked and then quickly recovered. "How long will we be without powers?"

He looked down at my hand, caressing my fingers. "We don't know for sure."

I tilted my head. "Why not?" My mind began spinning. "Dex and Lilly were married, and so were Brogan and Layla. Why can't you ask them?"

"It's different for everyone. It's only used for clan leader marriages, and honestly, it all depends on the power of the couple uniting. If they're weaker, it may just be hours or days; if they're stronger, days or weeks."

I began twisting my Servak ring. Both Callon and I were considered strong, which meant it could be weeks before our powers were restored. Weeks in which Marcus could plan an attack and slaughter us all, but my parents had taken the risk too.

"What about my parents? Their marriage was the most recent. Dex would have married them."

"He did, but right after the wedding they went into hiding. He never got the opportunity to ask."

Of course...but someone had to know. If they were in hiding, they would have been guarded.

"Who guarded over my parents during this time?" I asked.

Callon was quiet for a moment then replied, "Dex might know. I'll ask him, and then maybe we can get a closer estimate."

I nodded, still distracted by the thought of losing our powers.

"We're working on ensuring our safety," Callon added.

I knew he was, but things could happen, unexpected things.

"Where's the Braid now?"

"Hidden."

"Do you know where it's at?"

"No, Dex is the keeper of the Braid."

Dex kept the Braid hidden; at least that was a plus. But being completely vulnerable didn't set well with me.

"Who performs the ceremony?"

"Dex."

"Can anyone else perform the ceremony?" I stared at the red and gold area rug beneath my feet.

"Yes, one other."

"And let me guess...he's with Marcus?"

"Yes," Callon replied.

He drew me into a hug, and I soaked up his musky scent. We were risking our lives just by marrying each other, a risk that had to be taken, just like my parents had. Both the Servak and Consilador clans' power had weakened over the years. Dex had told me that. We needed to marry to restore the balance before it got completely out of control.

"I'll always come for you, Cheyenne, always," he whispered in my hair.

But if Marcus came, would Callon come too late?

"Cheyenne?" Lilly's voice echoed in the front hall. Her footsteps paused at the library's entry. "I'm sorry to bother you, sweetheart, but when you're done, Layla and I need you for a fitting."

I glanced behind me. Her blue eyes twinkled with excitement.

"We've only got a few more weeks till the big day."

"I'll be right there, Lilly," I replied.

A bright smile flashed over her lips and then she disappeared, but not before calling out, "We'll be up in your room waiting."

I snuggled back into Callon's hold, if only for a few more moments.

"You'd better go, love. You don't want to keep Lilly waiting." He kissed my head.

I sighed. I'd rather spend the afternoon in his arms than be fitted for a dress that I might die in. He drew back and stood.

"I've got more research to do. We can have some alone time tonight if you'd like." A warm grin appeared.

"I'd like that," I said softly.

With one last glance at Callon, I headed for my bedroom. Might as well get this over with sooner than later.

I entered my bedroom to find Bree, Andre and Nakari. Bree and Andre greeted me with a smile, but Nakari clasped her hands and looked down. She'd been like this for weeks now, since I'd found out about the engagement. I honestly couldn't tell if she wanted to be here or not, not that I cared anymore. But if it was uncomfortable seeing me in a gown, knowing I was marrying the man she loved, well, I completely understood. I'd have felt no different if the roles were reversed. It was time I just let it go and made an attempt at friendship.

I stopped beside Andre. Her blue eyes were wary at first, then turned to understanding.

"Nakari," I said softly, "if this is difficult for you to be here, I understand, but if you want to stay, I'd like you to."

Slowly her auburn head rose and green eyes stared at me with a mixture of emotions. Bree grasped Nakari's arm in support.

"I'd like to stay," she replied.

I nodded.

"Well, someone wore her big girl panties today." Andre's sarcasm made me grin. I looked over my shoulder, she raised a brow.

"Well, I just found some laying around and thought I'd give them a try," I replied.

The room erupted in light laughter.

Lilly and Layla appeared from the bathroom doorway and headed towards the bed. A large wooden framed full-length mirror was propped up against the wall nearby.

Layla's blue green eyes lit up. She'd been working very hard to create a dress that I'd love, but from her drawings, it was hard to say what it would look like on me.

"Over here," Layla called out and motioned for me to come beside the bed. "We've got your dress ready." Her smile was contagious, and I couldn't help but grin.

Lilly looped her arm in mine as she met me halfway. "It's going to be beautiful, Cheyenne."

A pile of white silk lay on my bed. Layla and Lilly carefully lifted the dress up, revealing its simple beauty. It gave the appearance of a ball gown, but what Layla had done to it was utterly amazing. She dropped the waistline and had buttons running down the full length of the long train. A small band of rhinestones and crystals embroidered the bodice, and there was a tulle halter strap that would help hold it in place.

"Come on," Lilly tugged at my hand. "It's time to try it on."

I was in complete and utter awe as I undressed and then allowed Lilly and Layla help me put the gown on. The room grew silent as I turned towards Bree, Andre and Nakari.

Bree's hazel eyes watered. She brushed back her long brown hair and smiled a genuine smile.

"It's beautiful," she whispered.

I gathered the skirt up in my hands and walked towards the mirror. I was completely speechless. It was even more beautiful than when it had been lying on the bed. This was my wedding dress, but I was marrying someone completely different than who I thought I would be. Colt should have been here with us. He should have been reunited with his family...

"I think you've outdone yourself this time, Layla," Andre said thoughtfully, bringing me back to the here and now.

My fingers traced the rhinestone and crystals, such a simple addition that made it sparkle. And the tulle halter was flattering and feminine. I twisted to see the back had a semi deep plunge that revealed my back without going too far.

Without a word, Layla and Lilly began tugging at the side seams, adjusting the tulle around my neck and pinning where they thought alterations should be made.

I caught Nakari as she tried to hide her watery eyes. My heart ached, regardless of the fact that we hadn't been the best of friends, or even friends. She was hurting, and it was because of me. She didn't have to be here. She could have left, and I wouldn't have thought anything of it, but the fact that she stayed made me realize truly what type of person she was. She was sacrificing, just like the rest, but she did it with more dignity and honor than I ever had.

"I'm sorry," I whispered.

She blinked, but recovered quickly.

"It's no one's fault, Cheyenne. It's just the way it is," she replied quietly.

I nodded and turned back towards the mirror. We probably would never be the best of friends, but knowing we could accept each other was better than the anger and hatred we'd been feeling before.

"Here," Layla said breaking the moment. "We need you to try on your evening gown too."

"What?" I asked in surprise. No one had said anything about an evening gown.

"Regardless of the fact that this will be a small family ceremony, Cheyenne," Lilly said, "it's tradition to have a wedding dinner."

"A dinner?"

"Yes," Lilly replied.

"If it's just a dinner, then why the evening gown?"

Layla, Bree and Andre began tugging at my dress to get it off.

"Ouch!" I snapped as a pin lodged into my skin.

"Sorry," Andre snickered.

"It's a wedding dinner that will include music, and dancing. It's the celebration before the celebration, of course," Lilly stated like I should have known about it. "This would have been a bigger deal if the clan members could be here for it."

"Then why hasn't anyone told me till now?" They removed the remainder of my wedding dress, and I stood there in my underwear and bra, crossing my arms.

"Callon said he'd tell you." Lilly began tapping her foot impatiently and her jaw squared. "I should have known he'd leave it to the last minute," she huffed then waved her arms. "Men!"

Layla and Bree had already brought over a blue silk gown and were helping me into it. Lilly hauled me forward once it was on, determination etched in her blue eyes. She pulled pins from her mouth, and she and Layla were pinning again before I'd even had a chance to view the dress.

It figured that Callon was supposed to tell me and had forgotten. That in and of itself was forgivable, but the fact that Lilly said there would be dancing made me antsy.

"I don't know how to dance," I blurted out.

Both Layla and Lilly stood.

"Didn't you go to dances in high school?" Andre asked.

"No."

"Were you an ugly duckling or something?" she snorted.

I narrowed my eyes.

"Andre!" Layla said and gave Andre a glare. She turned her attention towards me, grasping my hands. "We can teach you."

"Skylar and Clayton will teach you, starting tonight," Lilly stated and then twisted me around.

Bree and Nakari grasped my arms to prevent me from falling.

They began removing the dress, and I was left standing once again in my bra and underwear.

"Callon and I were going to be alone tonight," I said and then reached for my jeans lying on the bed.

"Well, you'll have hundreds of years to spend alone!" Lilly snapped. "Tonight is your first lesson."

With those words, she disappeared out the bedroom door with the blue gown while Layla followed with the wedding gown.

"Here, let me help!" Bree called out and ran after Layla and the trailing white silk.

I pulled my jeans and T-shirt on, shaking my head.

"I'm not a dancer," I mumbled under my breath. I was going to make a complete fool of myself. For someone who was musically inclined, I should have had some sort of rhythm, but it was like I had two left feet. Colt had tried to teach me once and we'd ended up on the floor laughing. I didn't need any more memories floating around in my head constantly reminding me that Colt betrayed us— me.

"We'll stick with you," Nakari said.

"If Skylar could teach Koda to dance, then surely he can teach you," Andre added.

I sighed. I had no other choice.

CHAPTER 21

One, two, three. One, two, three.

The count floated in my head as I moved with Skylar around the sitting room. They'd cleared the furniture, making a dance floor of sorts. Initially we started out slowly, focusing on hand positions, moving my feet properly to offset my partner's legs, keeping my head up...

Then came the more complicated stuff. In the second and third week, I had to put it all together—easier said than done—and to place the icing on the cake, I needed to remember the steps for each dance. Although Nakari and Andre had promised to "stick with me," they'd been overruled by Lilly. She needed them elsewhere. And why we couldn't have done it in my room or another more private place was beyond me. Apparently I still needed to be harassed about my lack of abilities.

Today didn't sit well with me. Despite all the practicing, falls and stubbed toes, I still hadn't gotten the hang of it. And the wedding was only days away.

"Keep your head up," Koda said, interrupting my dance so he could tilt my chin up. "You're not looking over his right shoulder. You're going to trip each other up."

I ground my teeth. Koda and Brogan had taken to watching my progress, adding in their opinion whenever they felt like it, and I'd had about enough. It was hard enough to remember everything and keep my steps in line, but their constant harassing was going to push me over the edge.

I tripped on Skylar's foot, bumping into his chest.

"Ow!" Skylar flinched. "Careful, Cheyenne."

"Sorry," I muttered.

He helped me upright again. His wild dark blond locks looked even messier since he'd started teaching me. He kept running his fingers through his hair. He'd been more patient than I could have ever been.

"It's okay. It's a bit hard to dance with heels on," he reassured me, but his green eyes said something completely different. Like, *you should have gotten this by now, Cheyenne.*

I looked down at my shoes. I'd stepped on his toes more than once with the stilettoes. He was right on one thing; wearing strappy heels to dance in took some getting used to. I couldn't help it; I'd always preferred flats.

"You're getting it, Cheyenne," he added. "By Friday night, you'll be ready." He leaned in a little closer. "Besides, Koda was way worse than you to begin with."

I couldn't help but grin.

"Thanks," I whispered, but knew I was still a long way from feeling comfortable with dancing.

Daniel started the music again, and Skylar extended his hand. We were ballroom dancing now, which I had to admit was a bit easier. It was more flowing action, and all I had to do was follow Skylar's lead.

We circled around the room when once again the dancing twins felt they needed to add their commentary.

"Your arm looks like a limp noodle, Cheyenne," Koda said above the music.

"Any limper and it might collapse," Brogan added. "Better start pumping some iron."

I forced Skylar to stop. My eyes narrowed, and I quickly crossed the room. Koda and Brogan were leaning against the wall, arms crossed, smirks on their lips. I poked Koda in the chest.

"Okay, twinkle toes, if you're so good, show me how it's done!" I snapped.

"Gladly." Koda yanked on my arm and tried to drag me to the dance floor again. I shrugged him off.

"No, not with me. I need to *see*, remember?"

He rolled his eyes.

"Fine, I'll just call Nakari..." He yelled her name, but I put up my hand.

"Ah ah, not so fast."

He looked at me, speculating. "You want a solo number?"

My own smirk rose.

"Nope. Your partner's Brogan."

"What?!" Brogan marched over. "I'm not dancing with Koda."

"Chicken?" I taunted.

"Listen, *princess*," he grumbled. "I don't..."

He was cut off as Koda grabbed his arm.

"She wants us to show her, so show her we will," Koda said. "I'm man enough for the challenge. Are you, Brogan?"

Brogan eyed Koda for a moment, then switched his glare to me. His eyes bore into mine, but I could tell he'd accepted the challenge.

"Fine," he said. "Let's show this amateur what she needs to aspire to."

"Music!" Koda commanded. He stuck his hand out for Brogan to take.

A sly smile began to grow. I couldn't believe they were going to dance for me.

"You're not leading, Koda, I am," Brogan said.

"No, I will," Koda argued.

"Listen, *girls*, we don't have all day," Daniel chimed in and started the music.

Brogan shoved his hand in Koda's, allowing him to lead. As they started to get into the rhythm, Nakari emerged from the door. Her green eyes filled with confusion, but that quickly dissolved into a grin.

"Someone called..." She started giggling. "I thought they were supposed to be teaching you to dance, Cheyenne."

"They told me they could do better, so I told them to prove it," I answered, folding my arms.

Brogan stumbled over Koda's foot. Koda frowned slightly.

"Careful, Brogan," I taunted, "your other left foot is getting in the way."

They whisked by, Brogan snarling as he passed.

"They're actually not bad," Nakari said. "I'm surprised."

"Whoa!" Andre's giggle echoed from the hall. "This is a first! Maes!"

At first Maes look as baffled as Nakari had. Then a smirk formed on his lips.

"Careful, Brogan, Koda's been known to grope his partners," he joked. "Wouldn't want Layla getting jealous now."

"Does this dance come with a skirt? 'Cos one of you needs one!" Daniel added.

Koda and Brogan abruptly stopped.

"Alright, enough homophobia," Koda said. He took two strides towards me and grabbed my hand. "Your turn, *princess*."

I could only squeal as he pulled me into his arms and then he was dancing me around the floor, faster than Skylar had ever done. I struggled to keep up.

"Slow down!" I pleaded, but Koda was having none of it.

"If you can master a hurricane, this should be no trouble," Koda said quietly. I blinked. Why was he referring to my power over air? It wasn't like I could blast Callon around the room...

My eyes widened. Wait, that wasn't what Skylar meant!

I adjusted my grip around Koda, regaining my footing on the floor. Rather than try and match his moves, I closed my eyes and felt the movement of the air around me. Now that we were moving with speed, I could feel it all around me, understanding my position much better. My eyes couldn't keep track, but my other senses could.

Using the rhythm of the air, I started to move my feet. The pulse of the music took over, and I drifted from note to note. I opened my eyes again, and to my amazement, I was matching Koda toe to toe. My confidence grew, and soon I was dancing with my eyes closed.

Koda slowed, and brought us to a gentle stop.

"See," he said, smiling. "I knew you could do it."

Icy blue eyes shone down on me, icy blue eyes that should have been Colt's. I looked away. Colt would have encouraged me like this. He'd always believed in me, but now...

Koda squeezed my waist.

"Just remember, you owe me a dance now."

I nodded, but kept my gaze away from his face. It would only bring back memories of a Colt that no longer existed. The Colt that couldn't be there for the wedding.

"Well, good job, Cheyenne," Skylar said. "Apparently you just needed a challenge."

"You know she only does well under pressure," Maes said.

I rolled my eyes at him. Skylar chuckled.

"I'll remember that for next time," he said. "Rest for a few days. You'll be doing plenty of dancing on Friday."

I nodded.

"Thanks, Skylar. I couldn't have done it without you."

"You're welcome."

He waved his hand to have the furniture set back into place. I sat in the music area and removed my heels, stretching my toes. It was a reminder why I didn't usually wear them. Standing on the pads of my feet all day made them ache.

While Koda and Brogan lifted the sofa, Daniel flashed by and left through the front door. I frowned. It wasn't like him to leave without a word. What was he up to?

I waited for a few moments, then followed him out. Grabbing my shoes was probably a good idea, but he might disappear by the time I found them. The stone on the front steps was warm—the sun had finally decided to show itself after all these rainy months. I relished the warmth for a few moments, before carefully stepping onto the gravel. Daniel was sitting on the ledge of the front fountain by himself. He was staring into the distance.

"Daniel?" I called out.

He turned, and gave me a half smile. I slowly walked over to him, stopping to dig a pebble out of my foot.

"Is everything alright?" I asked, plopping down beside him. A slight breeze cooled my skin.

"It's nothing," Daniel replied quietly. A little too quietly. He picked up a small round stone and skipped it down the road. I sighed. Something was bothering him. He'd been keeping to himself more over the last few days. I sat beside him, silent. Daniel was never a good one for secrets. Eventually he'd cave. He couldn't hide things from me, just like I couldn't hide things from him.

"Do you think he's out there?" Daniel said, his voice somber.

Ah...I thought that was what was bothering him. Colt. The person that had been bothering all of us.

"He's with Marcus now," I replied.

Daniel shook his head.

"I didn't mean it like that," he said. "I mean...is *our* Colt still out there? Trapped inside that..." His voice shook. "I just want to know why he's acting this way. We've been through so much in the past. I can't imagine what it would take to make him betray us."

I touched his shoulder.

"I don't know, but…" I swallowed. "Andre said he was telling the truth. It wasn't a trick."

"I don't believe it." He picked up another stone and threw it. "Andre must have gotten it wrong. Colt never…he'd never side with Marcus, ever. I know he wasn't around all the time, but he was always there for us when he needed to be."

"I don't want to believe it either," I said, "but we both saw it with our own eyes." Even saying the words pierced my heart. I didn't want it to be the truth either.

"He should be here with us." Daniel clenched his fist. "He should be a part of the wedding."

I looped my arm in his and leaned my head on his shoulder. Colt's betrayal ran deep. Marcus knew it would. How Colt could have fallen under Marcus's sway was beyond belief. He'd been fighting him for hundreds of years, but then again Callon had accused Colt of wandering, doing his own thing…maybe it had started long ago and no one knew. Maes's thoughts had started to change once he was around us. Why couldn't Colt have changed his mind in the same manner?

"He *should* be here with us," I said, my mind still whirling through the *why*. "But we can't dwell on the past. We can't change what he is now, Daniel. What we have to do is move on." I said the words, but in my heart I didn't mean it.

"I'm tired of moving on, Chey," he whispered. "So tired. He'll always be my brother, and I…I want him home."

He hid his face from me, but I still caught the glisten of tears. We were all tired of the changes, the constant struggle to move on after another senseless tragedy. Daniel and the others had seen far more than I had, but the most heartbreaking thought was that it wasn't over yet. There would be more death and loss before we'd find peace.

"I know, Daniel."

The crunch of tires on gravel caused me to look up. In the distance, an old yellow truck was slowly approaching. Who was coming to see us? Daniel felt me tense.

"It's okay. It's the Campbell's. They're bringing Lilly the things she asked for." He gave a weak smile. "Wedding stuff."

"Oh." *Wedding stuff...*I cringed. I'd forgotten to go see Lilly after my dancing lesson. She was probably searching for me by now. She'd been a little testy lately. I got the impression she wanted the wedding to be as perfect as possible. Several times I'd had things taken away from me when I didn't do it right, which was completely out of character for her. But we all dealt with stress differently.

The yellow truck stopped in the circle drive. A man with slicked back sandy-blond hair stepped out.

"Hey there, Danny-boy!" His Irish accent was thick. The man circled the truck as Daniel stood and shook his hand firmly. "And who might this be?" He winked.

"Cheyenne, Callon's fiancé," Daniel replied.

"Aye, so you're the one, are you? I'm Ryan Campbell, It's good to meet you finally. I've seen you hiding around and figured I'd meet you when I met you." He gave a broad smile and looked towards the house. "Looks like the weather might just hold up for the next few days." He turned back. "Is Lilly around? I have the things she asked for."

"Sure, let me get her," Daniel said and gave me a quick glance. He disappeared into the house, and I inched closer to the truck, taking a peek in the back.

White canvas and metal poles were rolled together, circular tables and white folding chairs were leaned up against the side. Boxes labeled *china, lights,* and *glasses* were pushed towards the back. Pillars and other miscellaneous things were piled together.

"It's going to be a beautiful sight," Ryan said thoughtfully. "Lilly described what she wanted it to look like."

I looked up and smiled. Lilly had given me a few hints, but she wanted it to be a surprise.

"My family has served the O'Shea's for many generations," Ryan said, "and we look forward to many more generations of Campbell's continuing on." He hesitated for a moment. "I'm glad Callon has found himself a bride. That there will be more O'Shea's around in the future."

"I'm glad he found me too," I replied. My life would have had a very different future if they hadn't—a future that mostly likely would have involved Marcus.

The front door closed. Lilly's pace was brisk and her eyes focused on the truck's contents. I moved back.

"Ryan." Lilly pulled him in for a hug. "I think you might have outdone yourself!"

Ryan blushed and shrugged. "Just doing what I was told, ma'am."

"Let's get this truck moved to the back of the manor to unload then, shall we?"

Ryan nodded and headed for the driver's door.

Lilly turned on me and looped her arm in mine, guiding me back to the manor.

"You were supposed to come and find me, Cheyenne," she reprimanded.

"Sorry, I got distracted." I decided it best to keep my focus on the ground.

"I see."

We paused at the front door.

"I'm sorry," she said. "I know that I've been a bit pushy the last few weeks. I hadn't realized how bad I've been till Dex pointed it out to me. I didn't mean to..."

I squeezed her hand.

"It's okay, Lilly. I know you want to make the wedding as special as possible."

She shook her head. "No, it's not the wedding plans that have me on edge." She looked down, her eyes tearing up. "It's Colt's betrayal. I've just used the wedding as an excuse." She pressed her eyes closed, her black hair falling into her face. "It's so unlike him, so out of character, that I'm still so shocked and angered by it."

Now it was my turn to look away.

"I've known him since before he turned Timeless," she whispered. "He was very different to Callon and Daniel—and not just physically, with his lighter hair. He had such an adventurous spirit. But he always put family first. He loved his brothers and his father more than anything." She touched my cheek. "And I could tell he loved you just as much. I just can't believe he'd..." She trailed off, and we stood in silence for a few moments. Memories of Colt teased at my mind, and I had to wipe a stray tear that had escaped. It all should have been so different...

The truck's engine roared to life, and Lilly pulled away.

"I'm sorry, sweetheart." She wiped her own tears from her cheeks. "We need to focus in on happy things, like your wedding." She forced a smile. "Come on. I'll have you work on a few small things, but you're banned from going out the back terrace or peeking till the big day. Got that?"

I nodded, and arm in arm again we entered the manor.

Tomorrow was the day. June twenty-first, the day I would marry Callon. I started towards the terrace doors in my bedroom, only to stop. Lilly had asked me not to peek out onto the back terrace as they were setting things up. She wanted it to be a complete surprise.

I blew the hair out of my eyes. I'd been banished to my room now that the final touches were being added. It was funny; whether it was in the cabin in Montana or here, it seemed I was always a prisoner of four walls. I'd gotten too used to my recent freedom, and now I was about to go stir crazy. No one could keep me company, either, because Lilly needed them to assist. Not even Callon could come because he and Dex were working out the final details for our security.

I returned to my pacing, my feet padding on the wood and then carpet. I'd wear a hole in the carpet soon if time didn't pass any faster. I'd already tried reading, listening to my iPod and even strummed a few notes on the guitar without success...my mind kept running to Colt when I should have been thinking of Callon.

I stopped and pressed my eyes closed for moment. My throat grew tight, and pain knocked at my heart's door again. If it had been anyone else, I'd have been upset and angered, but with Colt it was ten times worse. I'd given him my heart in the past, and he'd been careless, yet I'd forgiven him. I thought my heart was crushed forever when I watched him die, but then I found out he hadn't. The hope I held on to shattered with his betrayal, destroying everything I believed in. This was beyond forgiveness.

He'd casually crushed each and every member of his family without a second thought, and we were expected to move on...

A soft knock at my door drew my attention. I wiped away the few tears that had fallen. I needed to be happy; my future was here with Callon, with my family.

"Come in," I called.

Layla, Andre, Bree and Nakari entered, their brows moist with sweat. Apparently Lilly was working everyone hard. A twinge of guilt set in. I should have been helping too.

"It's time to get beautified, Cheyenne," Bree beamed as she pushed past Andre and Nakari, carrying a basket of what appeared to be beauty supplies. "First up on the list is a pedicure and manicure."

After hours of being alone with my own thoughts, I was grateful for the lighthearted, happy conversation. Even Nakari seemed to be enjoying herself; there was a different side to her that I was finally seeing. A lighter, carefree side.

"Geez, Andre," Nakari said with a twinkle in her eyes. "I'm gonna need sandpaper for your heels! When was the last time you had a pedicure?"

Andre pulled her foot from the tub of water and splashed Nakari.

"I don't recall asking for your opinion, Miss Still-Living-In-The-Seventies." Andre crinkled her nose and then pointed to her toes. "I think blue polish is the *in* color for the season."

Nakari snorted. "What would you know about *in* colors? The last time you painted your nails was back in 1950!"

Laughter broke out.

"Just because I don't find it necessary, that doesn't mean I don't know fashion," Andre replied. "I just choose not to voice my opinion all the time, unlike some people." She stuck her tongue out.

"She's only doing it now because of Maes," Bree chimed in. "She wants to look good for her puppy."

"Listen, Mrs. Daniel O'Shea-wanna-be, at least I know where I stand with my puppy," Andre replied.

Bree narrowed her eyes.

"So you're admitting you have a thing for the dog, huh?" Nakari's green eyes lit up as she stopped scrubbing Andre's feet.

"I'm admitting nothing. I just said I knew where I stood with him," Andre replied and pretended to busy herself with the bottle of polish.

Nakari and Bree giggled under their breath.

"Andre, the one who swore off all men..." Nakari trailed off.

I smiled. Andre was in deep with Maes, whether she wanted to admit it or not.

"All done, Cheyenne," Layla tapped my hand.

I took in my finger and toenails. They were the same blue of my dress, or at least close enough. It had been ages since I'd taken the time to paint my nails. I'd been too preoccupied with other things.

"Thank you, Layla," I replied. "They're lovely."

Layla turned. "You're up, Nakari," she said, "Cheyenne needs her hair styled, and we all know you and Bree are the best. I'll finish up old troll toes over here."

"Hey now, they're *vintage*," Andre replied with a small grin.

"This way." Bree pointed to a chair they'd set up near a small table and mirror. Irons, pins, brushes and combs had been carefully laid out, along with a good supply of makeup.

"Don't worry." She touched my shoulder while I sat. "We'll make you look beautiful."

I gave a faint smile, not knowing exactly what her words meant. Apparently I was a mess now.

My head was pulled from one side to the other as Nakari and Bree took turns curling, pinning and arranging my blond locks. Before I could catch a glimpse of what it looked like, they started with the makeup, and it was easier just to keep my eyes closed. I knew I was finally done when I heard Lilly sigh.

"Oh, Cheyenne," she beamed, "you look stunning."

I smiled and was about to look in the mirror when I was whisked away. It was time to put my dress on.

"Don't worry," Andre said. "You'll get to see the whole package when we're done."

Carefully I undressed with their help so I didn't mess up the creation they'd just completed. I stepped into the icy blue silk dress and waited patiently for them to help me get it all set into place. I leaned on Andre and Bree while Layla and Nakari assisted with my strappy heels.

They all stepped back, warm smiles spreading across their faces.

"Now you're done," Nakari said and pointed towards the mirror.

"We're going to get ready ourselves, so stay put until Callon comes for you." Lilly squeezed my hand. "We'll see you in a bit."

I watched them depart without looking into the mirror. I wanted to wait till I was alone to see what they had done.

My breath caught when I finally saw my reflection. I didn't recognize the woman before me. The dress was simple yet exquisite, regal yet refined. It had an empire waistline and a simple v-shaped halter. The bodice flowed seamlessly to the floor and hugged my shape just right, giving the appearance I had curves. I turned to see the low cut back. The silk shimmered as the late afternoon light touched it.

When I finally looked up, I saw that they'd given me a partial up-do. Not a hair was out of place, each curl placed with care. My fingers grazed my neck. They'd even left a few ringlets to dangle off my neckline.

I stood and stared at the stranger before me, wondering how she'd gotten to this point, wondering how much she'd overcome. The journey had been long and hard—and was far from over, but she'd made it this far. Scratched and bruised, clawing her way to the light...she'd made it—barely.

A knock drew my attention, and the door opened. A tall, dark figure loomed in the hallway, fingers grasping the doorknob, staring. Callon.

He stepped forward, and my heart began to beat faster. I'd never seen him like this before, so breathtakingly handsome. He wore a black tuxedo with a crisp white shirt and white tie. His vest was the same color as my blue dress. He'd shaved, and his hair had been cut like Lilly threatened. He'd slicked it back with his natural waves showing their texture. His lips curled in a partial smile, and his eyes danced like I'd never seen before. The mixture of brown, green, and amber were spellbinding tonight. And he didn't bother to hide his admiration of me.

He lifted my hand, placing a kiss on my knuckles, and I nearly lost my breath. I couldn't take my eyes off him.

"There are no words to say what I'm feeling right now, Cheyenne," Callon's low voice rumbled. Goosebumps raced up my arms. "To tell you how simply exquisite you are." He reached into his tuxedo's pocket. "So I brought you a wedding gift to express my love and gratitude even with my loss of words."

He lifted a long black velvet box and turned my hand over.

"Open it," he said and I did.

My breath caught. It was a necklace, but not any necklace; it was made of a blue oval gem that resembled a diamond, and it exactly matched the color of my dress. My finger outlined the large gem and then followed the platinum chains attached to it. They contained smaller gems of the same icy blue color. A pair of blue oval shaped gem earrings lay in the box as well.

"They're Blue diamonds," Callon added knowing I wasn't sure. "Very rare." He eyed me as I stared at them. "Here, let me help you."

Callon took the box from my hands and stood behind me. Ever so slowly he lifted the necklace and placed it around my neck. His fingers lingered on my back while an involuntary shiver rippled through me.

I stared at him through the mirror, as he reached around and adjusted the diamond so it sat perfect around my neck, resting on my chest. His fingers traced the oval, and I found myself leaning back up against him as they too followed the smaller diamond down the trail of the chain.

Butterflies erupted in my stomach as he stopped just at the neckline of my dress and a warm kiss touched my shoulder. I closed my eyes, afraid of, and yet thrilled at what might come next.

"Stunning," he whispered near my ear as he kissed my earlobe.

He placed an earring in each ear before another sultry kiss touched my neck. He stepped away, his warmth leaving me, but not before his hand ran down my bare back and stopped at the plunge.

"Shall we?" He leaned in closer and kissed the corner of my mouth.

My eyes fluttered open to see the warm satisfaction in his. I wanted to speak, but his kisses were still too warm on my skin. I nodded instead; afraid my quivering voice wouldn't answer.

"Tomorrow," he whispered once again near my ear as his hand on my bare back pushed me forward. "Tomorrow we'll be together, forever."

CHAPTER 22

With one hand around my waist, Callon and I headed down the darkened hall. We paused at the top of the stairs. The warm glow of candles lit the entry and gave everything a soft glow.

Lilly had adorned the rails with wildflower garlands; the scent of daisies and cosmos lingered in the air. I stood still for a moment, admiring their simple beauty, before Callon nudged me forward.

I lifted the corner of my dress while Callon maintained his hold, and we descended the stairs. Soft music reached my ears, along with the low murmuring of voices. We rounded the corner into the sitting room, and the last rays of the evening sun streamed through the terrace doors.

Regardless of the fact that this was just family, my stomach was still doing somersaults. I'd never been to a formal dinner with dancing, let alone a whole event planned out in honor of Callon and me. I gripped his hand tighter as we stepped onto the terrace and blinked, completely amazed.

We passed through an arbor overflowing with bleeding hearts that draped down in a mixture of deep pinks and ferny green leaves. A sweet scent swirled around us as the flowers kissed my shoulders.

The music continued in the background, soothing and elegant. We took the terrace steps slowly, ensuring I didn't trip, and I was in awe of the canvas tent in front of us, holding a dance floor and seating for our dinner. I smiled and looked up as we passed through the tulle covered entrance. Hundreds if not thousands of small twinkling lights hung from the ceiling, creating a dazzling glow that created the most beautiful pallet of colors.

Lilly had again taken the wildflowers and created garlands that adorned the pillars, along with small simple arrangements on the tables. She had outdone herself. I inhaled the sweet scent and looked up at Callon. He smiled.

"Lilly did this for you, Cheyenne," he said quietly. "She knew, just as I did, that you loved wildflowers."

Tears swam near the surface; they'd done this for me.

Andre and Maes stepped closer, and I had to blink twice to take in Andre's shimmering lavender gown. Her skin glowed with color, and her black hair had never looked more beautiful with it pulled up in ringlets. Her blue eyes danced with warmth and radiance.

But Maes was an even bigger surprise. His jade-rimmed eyes, normally harsh and warrior-like, had softened into something I'd never seen before, something that appeared to be affection and love for the woman whose hand was resting on his arm. *Andre.*

Maes wore a tux just like Callon's with a crisp shirt, and black tie, but his vest was the same lavender silk of Andre's dress. His black hair was pulled back neatly into a ponytail. He smiled and it reached his eyes.

"Mon espoir." His accent thickened. "I don't think I've ever seen you so beautiful."

I was stunned into silence as he bowed slightly before us.

I looked at Callon, who had his own twinkle in his eyes.

"You should probably say thank you," Callon chuckled.

"Don't worry, Cheyenne, I had the same reaction when I saw him too," Andre giggled. "I was wondering where he'd found such a good poodle salon."

"It's amazing how much the Irish love their pets." Maes winked. "I can't say I was too disappointed with my date, either."

I smiled, still unsure what to think of the new Maes when the rest of the family began to gather around us.

Layla swished forward in her pale yellow silk gown, which brought out more of the gold tones in her bluish green eyes. Her black locks were pulled up on the side and pinned with pearl-coated combs that were probably a family heirloom. Brogan followed close behind her, he too wearing a tux and a vest matching Layla's dress.

"You look lovely, Cheyenne," Layla said, the warmth showing in her eyes.

"As do you, Layla," I replied, finally able to speak again.

Brogan nodded, but said nothing as he gently pulled Layla back, allowing others to greet us.

Clayton and Skylar escorted Nakari, whose green silk dress hugged her body, accentuating her already perfect curves. Her long auburn hair drifted down her back in long cascades. Skylar and Clayton's tuxedo vests matched her dress as well.

"Cheyenne," Nakari said, bowing her head slightly.

I nodded, but didn't reply, uncertain how I felt about the glance Callon had given her. He approved obviously, or the smile wouldn't have emerged for me to catch out of the corner of my eye. He made no other gesture, but that was enough to bring back my insecurities.

Skylar stepped forward, his blue eyes holding a tad bit of mischief.

"Don't forget," Skylar said winking, "you owe your instructor a dance tonight."

"Of course," I replied.

"I may not have been your instructor, but I get one too," Clayton added and squeezed my hand. "It will be a fun-filled evening indeed."

They stepped back with Nakari, but not before she gave Callon a second glance.

Daniel jumped himself and Bree before us next. Bree wore a stunning burnt orange gown that looked like the deepest, richest sunset I'd ever seen. The golden hues shimmered in her eyes, and I couldn't help but see the spark she held for Daniel.

Daniel leaned forward and kissed my cheek.

"In another day you'll officially be my sister, and I can't tell you how happy that makes me," he said.

I squeezed his hand, his warmth and peace spreading through me.

"I couldn't be happier myself," I replied. I looked towards Bree. "And I look forward to having you as a sister-in-law one day too."

Bree's eyes grew wide, and she glanced at Daniel. His face flushed, and quickly they disappeared further into the tent. Whether Daniel wanted to believe it or not, I'd seen the way he looked at Bree when she didn't notice. He had strong feelings for her, but didn't know how to express them yet. It was cute.

I caught sight of Lilly as she began directing waiters to the tables. She was in party planning mode, and nothing was going to distract her at the moment. Her gray flowing gown swished as she moved back and forth with purpose, her fingers brushed back the stray black hair that fallen down already from her up-do. Her blue eyes caught mine for just a moment and she smiled, before returning to her task.

"She won't stop till later, Cheyenne," Dex's voice said behind us.

We turned. Dex too was in a tux with a silver vest matching Lilly's dress. His brown hair was combed back.

"She wants to make this perfect for the two of you, especially since we couldn't invite other clan members." He stepped closer and drew me into a hug. "Your parents would have been proud of the woman you've become. I'm proud of the woman you've become." He pressed a fatherly kiss to my cheek and pulled back slightly. "I wish I was the one walking you down the aisle, but I know Daniel will do a grand job."

"Thank you, Dex," I said, feeling a bit of his sadness. "I wanted it to be you as well, but you can't be in two places at once. You're the holder of the Braid and that's more important."

He nodded and Callon squeezed my waist. They'd explained that Dex had to hold the Braid in secret until right before the ceremony. Daniel had offered to escort me in his place, and I accepted.

I searched the tent. Someone was missing.

"Where's Koda?" I asked.

Callon grinned. "He was fighting Lilly until the last minute about getting a haircut. She didn't hold him down, but came close to it."

"If there's one thing I've learned over the years with Lilly," Dex added, "it's that if she wants something, she won't give up till she gets her way."

Both Callon and Dex chuckled.

"Champagne?" a petite woman asked. She carried a tray holding several glasses.

Callon took two and handed one to me. I stare out after the waitress and Dex till she disappeared and Dex stopped at Lilly's side.

"She's a Campbell," Callon said confirming my unspoken question. "All the help is," he added.

I lifted the fluted glass, the bubbles tickling my nose. I took a small sip and then crinkled my nose. It wasn't sweet like I was expecting. It was actually a bit tart.

"It's your first taste of champagne?" Callon asked.

I nodded. "Not what I was expecting."

He smirked. "Never is." He placed his hand on my bare back again and instantly heat tingled down my spine. He gestured to a table.

He pulled out a chair and we sat, Daniel and Bree joining us, and I couldn't help but notice one extra seat not yet taken.

Just as I was about to ask, Koda appeared. He smiled, taking the empty seat. My mouth went dry, and without warning tears pushed their way forward. I blinked them back, and a shiver escaped me.

Callon leaned closer. "Are you cold?"

I shook my head, unable to remove my eyes from Koda's face. Lilly's haircut had shortened Koda's blond locks, enough to make him identical to Colt.

Callon reached under the table and squeezed my hand. He was staring at me like I was staring at Koda.

Koda wore a black tux like the rest, with a white shirt and black vest, but his tie was the same blue of my dress. He adjusted himself in his seat and looked up. Sympathy instantly rippled across his face, and his lips parted to speak, but nothing came out. I looked away.

There was nothing he could say. It wasn't his fault that he and Colt looked so much alike. It also wasn't his fault that Lilly forced him to get a haircut and wear the blue tie. It was just like always...circumstances that put us here in this situation.

A dinner plate filled to the brim was placed before me. It should have appealed to me, should have been delicious, but without Colt here with us, everything was bland. I poked around the plate and managed to take a few bites. Koda, Callon, Daniel and Bree tried to carry on a light conversation, but I had no words for the moment.

Dessert came and went, and I fought to put on a happy face like the rest. I wasn't the only one who noticed Koda. We all did. I'd even caught the expression of sorrow on Lilly's face. She hadn't realized what she'd done till now.

Music had continued to play in the background throughout dinner, but now it changed. The tempo was different, and then I began to realize the song playing was a waltz.

Callon stood, extending his hand towards me.

"May I have the first dance?" he asked.

I placed my hand in his, and we moved to the dance floor alone.

Ever so slowly he drew me closer, our palms locking together. My free hand moved to his arm, while his free hand stretched out across the flesh on my back. Waves of heat ignited, and I looked up into hazel eyes that hid nothing from me.

There was sympathy at first. Sympathy that I'd once again been reminded that Colt wasn't here with us. But then sympathy quickly faded into graciousness. He'd worked hard. We'd both fought to get us to this point, and we both understood the sacrifices made. Graciousness ebbed into love and commitment.

He loved me, loved me with his whole heart, and had fought long and hard to earn it. He didn't prize it, but revered it. He knew, like me, that things could change in an instant, and our love was to be cherished for as long as we were together.

We didn't speak. We just absorbed the moment. After tomorrow, everything would change again, but it would be a renewal, a deepening and understanding of each other on a different level. One that would have far-reaching effects.

The music slowed, and we came to a stop. He drew me closer so I was pressed against his chest. His eyes had softened even more when he leaned down, his lids lowering, and warm lips brushed mine.

"Save the last dance for me," he murmured over my lips and left me with a soft kiss.

He drew back, amused, knowing what an effect he had on me.

I narrowed my eyes playfully.

"Your time will come, Callon," I said.

"I'm sure it will." He looked up and twirled me around. "But right now you have a line waiting to dance with you."

Skylar stepped up, brushing past Daniel.

"Hey!" Daniel said in protest.

Skylar put his hand up. "I instructed, therefore I get to have her second dance."

With a wink and a grin, Skylar whisked me across the dance floor like I was dancing on air. Others joined us now, and the whole atmosphere changed. Laughter and smiles adorned faces, and I was happy to see my family celebrating.

Our danced ended, and Koda immediate took Skylar's place. I didn't even have time to protest before we were moving around the floor. I stared at his shoulder, unable to look into his eyes.

299

"I'm sorry," Koda said.

"It's fine," I replied and focused on moving with the air.

"It's not fine, Cheyenne." He squeezed my hand. "I fought Lilly hard about not getting a haircut just for this reason, but she wouldn't give up."

"Well, she knows now." I'd seen her sorrow, knew she meant no harm in it.

"It's why I was so late. I didn't want to upset you and was trying to figure out any way around this."

"I told you, it's fine." We waltzed past Daniel, his worried gaze meeting mine.

"Then look at me." He stopped us in our dance, but the others continued on.

Slowly I lifted my head. Icy blue eyes that held sorrow met mine.

"We all miss him."

"I know," I whispered, tears once again rising to the surface.

He pulled me into the dance again for which I was grateful. I didn't need to be crying, not on the eve of my wedding. I needed to focus on the here and now—focus on Callon.

I glanced around the tent. He and Nakari were talking quietly at one of the tables. He was leaning in towards her, and a jealous tinge ran over my skin. Why was he talking so privately with her? They'd had plenty of time to air things out in the past few months.

We suddenly stopped again, but this time Maes had tapped Koda on the shoulder.

"My turn," Maes said as he eyed me.

No smile crossed his lips as he turned me out onto the dance floor, moving us further away from Callon and Nakari.

Let it go, Maes's voice rattled in my head, and I looked up. "There's nothing for you to be jealous over. Let it go," he said aloud.

There were plenty of things to be jealous for...Callon had been engaged to Nakari for one thing, showing there had been an attraction at one time. Second, regardless of me trying to push the past behind us, she'd kissed him not that long ago.

You've made mistakes too, need I remind you? Maes said and I sighed.

It really was getting annoying have this dog read my thoughts so easily.

Glad I can still annoy you, mon espoir.

I rolled my eyes.

Daniel wriggled his way in next, spinning me across the floor with ease, bringing laughter to my heart. Somehow he always had a special way, a way to lighten and brighten my mood just when I needed it.

"My turn," Brogan's rough voice startled me. He'd come up from behind, and I hadn't seen him.

I stared blankly at him for a moment. He held out his hands.

"I've seen you dance with everyone else, so I know you can do it, princess."

I awkwardly placed my hand in his and the other on his arm. I kept my eyes just off to the left like Skylar had taught me. I didn't need to mess up now. Brogan would be quick to jump all over it.

"You surprise me, princess," Brogan said, but there was no sarcasm laced in his words.

"I have that effect on people," I replied, not sure where this conversation was leading.

"I didn't think much of you when we arrived."

I didn't answer, but knew quite assuredly that he thought I was no more than a speck of dirt on his shoes.

"They say eyes are the window to one's soul," he continued. "And when I looked into your eyes, I didn't see the strong leader of Qaysean. I saw the weakling Sahara, who ran from her destiny."

I looked up, my body stiffening. If he was trying to pay me a compliment, he sure was missing the mark.

"Well, Sahara *changed* her destiny!" I snapped, my eyes narrowing. "Don't ever call my mother weak."

He lifted a hand and a small smirk rose. "Easy now, princess. Let me finish."

My jaw tightened, but I kept dancing.

"I admit I misjudged you. I didn't like the fact that Callon and the rest were pinning their hopes on someone so young." We paused in our dance. "You are both your father and mother's daughter, and you combine their strengths and abilities far beyond anything we could have ever hoped for."

I stood silently, staring up into sincere brown eyes. Eyes that no longer showed distrust or anger, eyes that told me he, Brogan, believed in me.

"You are a rare gem, princess. One worth protecting. And I am proud to call you our leader."

"May I cut in?" Dex asked, his hazel eyes unsure.

Brogan nodded and stepped away, leaving me stunned.

The music changed, and Dex pulled me into the dance. At least dancing with Dex didn't give me a neck ache from looking up.

"Brogan doesn't pay compliments easily," Dex said quietly. "You have earned a great gift, Cheyenne. You've proven yourself to him."

"I can see that." I stared off after Brogan.

"He's right," Dex said, drawing my attention to his warm smile. "You are a rare gem."

"Thank you," I replied.

Dex didn't need to say another word, none of them did. Brogan's words alone told me how everyone felt...and I couldn't help but feel the love and warmth of my family around me.

Family was what helped me through this, family who stayed loyal. Family was all I needed to make it through everything.

Our danced ended, and Dex hugged me.

"I love you, Cheyenne, like the daughter I never had." He placed a kiss on my cheek and slowly walked away.

My skin vibrated with electricity the moment Callon's fingers touched my back. He moved in closer, his fingers tracing my spine.

"It's time for our slow dance, love," he whispered near my ear.

Goosebumps once again rolled over my skin, and I allowed him to turn me into his arms. His eyes danced with delight, and I soaked up every moment of it.

We moved around the floor as if we were floating on a cloud. My eyes never left his. Gone were the thoughts of Colt and jealously over Nakari. Only the man before me now was the center of my attention, the center of my universe.

He drew me closer, his fingers sprawling across my bare skin until I could scarcely breathe. I rested my head on his shoulder as his hot breath ruffled my hair. I sighed. What this man's touch could do to me just wasn't fair, and he hadn't used the rings once since we'd arrived in Ireland.

The music slowed, and the evening had waned into night. We stood still for a few more moments, taking in each other's presence. Tomorrow would be different, tomorrow I'd be married.

A shiver escaped me, and I smiled.

"Let me take you inside," he murmured. "You're cold and need your rest. Tomorrow is going to be a big day for all of us."

He pulled back and kissed my forehead. Taking my hand, he led us through the maze of tables, but not before I caught the glance between him and Nakari once more. This time, I didn't acknowledge the jealousy. I couldn't change the past; I could only work for my future.

We entered the sitting room, and I hadn't realized how cool my skin was until the warmth from the room wrapped around me. It had been a magnificent evening, everything had gone to plan and I'd spent such a lovely time with everyone...yet something wasn't quite right. I couldn't put my finger on it.

We took the stairs slowly, Callon holding my arm while I lifted my dress, ensuring I didn't trip. We made it down the dimly lit hallway and paused outside my bedroom door.

My stomach began to churn nervously and the questioning in Callon's eyes came into view. I'd been quiet, too quiet for him, and he knew something was bothering me. He stepped closer, his hand coming to rest on my neck, playing with the loose locks of hair.

"What's wrong?" he asked.

I could lie and say nothing, or I could tell him what was on my heart. I went with my heart.

"Are you sure you want to marry me?" My voice shook with the unknown.

A gentleness I'd never seen before washed over his face, and he leaned in closer. His eyes lowered and he focused in on my lips. I couldn't help but lick them.

"I think you know the answer, love," his voice was low and sultry.

My heart stuttered in its beat, and I couldn't help but focus on his lips too.

"It—it's just that I—I want you to be sure," I stuttered.

"Oh?" His lips brushed mine and my knees felt weak. "Well then," he murmured over them. "Let me show you."

My lids fell shut the moment the fullness of his lips covered mine. His fingers firmed around my neck and drew me closer so he could spread his molten hand across my back again. My skin caught fire with his touch, and I pressed into him more as his tongue caressed my lower lips. I parted my lips with a sigh, and he surged forward.

I was hungry, desperate for his touch to fill me again. It made me feel alive and wanted. His fingers moved lower down my spine, and my heart slammed against my ribs fiercely. He tilted my head to the side and deepened the kiss.

His tongue dueled with mine, slashing and breaking down all the defenses I'd erected to protect myself. Callon was the one, the one who loved me as a woman, not like the child I had been. He'd torn down all my walls and helped me rebuild them with his love and affection, his adoration and strength. He'd been the one to bring me back from the pits of utter destruction. *Callon...*

His fingers began to trace my neck, his thumb brushing my cheek, and my pulse thundered in my ears. I fought to catch my breath as his hand slipped lower still, moving just inside the seam of my dress to grasp my hip.

I pushed my fingers through his hair, willing him to kiss me more, to deepen it further. Tomorrow wasn't soon enough. I wanted his touch now.

Voices echoed in the hall, and his kiss slowed. He drew back slowly, his mouth lingering over mine.

"Does that answer your question?" he whispered and pressed his forehead to mine, still trying to catch his own breath. His fingers caressed my cheek, and he sighed, standing straighter.

I wanted to answer, but the words had been removed from my mouth. My chest heaved, sucking in the precious oxygen.

He leaned in placing a soft kiss on my lips once more.

"I love you, Cheyenne. I always will."

He opened my bedroom door and I entered, turning back to catch one last glimpse. "Tomorrow," I whispered, repeating his words from earlier. "Tomorrow we'll be together, forever."

CHAPTER 23

My hands were trembling, and no matter what I tried, I couldn't shake this nagging feeling in my gut. I leaned over the toilet for the third time, emptying the contents of last night's dinner. All night I'd been tossing and turning, unable to calm myself to sleep, and now the nausea had become too much. What was wrong with me?

"You're just a ball of nerves," Lilly said sympathetically. She stroked my head pulling my hair back. "It's going to be okay, sweetheart. We all get nervous about walking down the aisle."

I wasn't afraid of walking down the aisle. I was fearful for what might happen to Callon and me afterwards. We'd lose our powers, be defenseless, but that wasn't the only thing. Something else was very, very wrong, and I didn't know how to explain it. Callon's words the previous night should have taken away any of my final doubts, yet this feeling still troubled me. I didn't dare share it with Lilly or the others. It was pointless really; they'd only keep reassuring me it would all be okay. What had bothered me the most was that it hadn't been this bad earlier in the week, but now that the day was here, the worry had grown worse.

"Any better?" Andre poked her head into the bathroom. "Want me to get you something, Cheyenne?"

I shook my head and lay it back down over the rim of the toilet. Maybe it was all in my head...maybe it was just nerves.

"Do you want me to get Callon?" Lilly asked hesitantly.

"No," I moaned. "I can't see the groom before I walk down the aisle. It's bad luck."

"Well it's going to be bad luck if we can't get you down the aisle without puking," Andre added, then put her hands on her hips. "When was the last time you slept?"

I turned away, allowing my hair to fall over my eyes. I'd been doing a great job hiding the dark circles till now. They'd all been too busy with the wedding to notice. It had been at least a week, maybe longer. I couldn't even remember anymore. My mind just didn't want to shut down long enough to allow me rest, which was probably why I was this worked up.

Mon espoir? Maes called out.

My head shot up, and I narrowed my eyes. "You called Maes?!"

Andre slithered away from the bathroom door, and a tall dark figured appeared. It was bad enough having Andre read my moods, but now she had to send in the mind reader too? How had I been so blessed?

Lilly stood, touching my head one last time. "We'll be back in a few hours to help you dress." She exited the bathroom leaving me alone with *him.*

You are blessed. His lips curled slightly. *You're not well?* He kneeled down beside me.

"Is it that obvious?" I said sarcastically. "What gave you the first clue?"

He studied me for a few moments, his eyes looking deep into mine and then, without warning, he scooped me up.

"Hey!" I yelped.

You need fresh air.

He took me out onto my terrace and set me in the chaise, but he didn't leave. He sat beside me.

Why are you afraid?

"You can speak out loud," I said.

"What are you afraid of, *mon espoir*?" he asked again, gently.

I could have lied, could have denied everything, but this was Maes, and he'd be relentless until I confessed.

"I'm nervous."

"About marrying Callon?"

"No," I hesitated. "About our safety."

"*Oui.*" His rough hand rubbed his chin. "That's an understandable fear to have, but I promise you, like I've promised you in the past, I'll always protect you." Jade-rimmed eyes looked deep into mine. "You've got an army of warriors here ready to battle for you at a moment's notice."

I knew that, but it still didn't ease my nerves.

His hand closed over mine, swallowing it.

"Would you like me to stay with you until Callon receives you during the ceremony?"

I knew I could defend myself quite well before the ceremony while I still had my powers. "I'm not worried about the before, Maes, it's the after."

He raised a brow.

I rolled my eyes. Did I have to spell it out? "When I'm powerless."

"I see."

I lay back against the chaise and allowed the gentle breeze to cool my skin. I stared out towards the forest. The sun was dipping further into the sky. Within a few hours I'd be walking down the aisle to Callon, at sunset.

Birds chirped madly and swarmed over a small group of trees. A lone black crow suddenly emerged from the branches and flew by, the sparrows chasing it away.

"It's a sign, Cheyenne," Maes said thoughtfully. "The sparrows are chasing away your fears. Let them go and enjoy your day."

Maybe it was a sign, like he said. Maybe I just needed to let them go.

Maes moved to the chaise beside me and we sat silently, taking in the lush landscape around us. Before long my eyes grew heavy, and I found myself drifting off. Perhaps the sparrows had chased away my fears...

"Is she awake yet?" a voice whispered nearby.

"We need to get started," another replied, sounding like Andre.

I stretched and opened my eyes.

Bree and Andre were leaning against the terrace rails, staring at me.

"Feeling better?" Bree asked eyeing me carefully. "We could get Callon or Dex if you want."

"I'm fine," I croaked and cleared my throat.

I glanced out over the horizon. The sun was lower than it had been when I first closed my eyes. I stretched again and sat up. I paused for a moment, a hand on my stomach, waiting to see if I was going to have issues again.

"You look better," Andre said, evaluating me closely. "Maes said you slept for a couple hours. Not enough, but at least now the dark circles aren't as noticeable." A sly smile rose. "Might not have to use all the plaster I brought after all, Bree." She nudged Bree's arm and they both chuckled.

"Ha, ha, ha," I replied. "Very funny."

"Of course it's funny. I said it," Andre said.

I stood and headed for my bedroom. At least the weather was cooperating. The evening was going to be warm and beautiful, a rarity here in Ireland.

The table that had been carefully stocked with beauty supplies last night was once again set up and waiting. Nakari stood to the side. She gave a faint smile and then looked down.

This wasn't easy for her, the whole wedding planning and preparation, but she'd been more regal than I'd have been in the same situation. Regardless of my jealously, she was strong, and I admired her.

I sat in the chair once again and allow Nakari and Bree to work their magic on my hair. They'd left the bulk of it down this time so long ringlets fell down my back. Pieces here and there were twisted and pinned, with delicate pink flowers finishing them off. Layla took over when Bree and Nakari were done and added my makeup for the final touch.

Lilly arrived, and she and Layla helped me into my wedding dress. I stood before the mirror, once again admiring Layla's creation. The dress was even more beautiful than I remembered. The way the silk reflected in the light causing it to look like shimmering stars amazed me. My fingers traced the embroidered band that ran across the top.

Lilly stepped behind me and placed a simple but elegant necklace around my neck. It consisted of freshwater pearls that were twisted together with what looked like sapphires, forming a seamless string. She handed me matching earrings too.

She moved in front of me and adjusted them, her eyes tearing slightly.

"This is your something old and something blue," Lilly said, trying to hold back her tears. "It was Sahara's. She would have wanted you to have it."

Emotions welled up inside of me that I fought to push down. My fingers traced the necklace. This was my mom's. Lilly didn't need to say it for me to know it. I felt it. How I wished she was here to see me now, and Alexis, too.

Gentle fingers touched my elbow. Nakari had something clenched in her hand. She pressed something small and warm into the palm of my hand. Her mouth opened to speak, but then closed, unsure. I opened my hand to see a silver charm bracelet with a single heart-shaped charm attached.

"It's something borrowed." She swallowed. "You need something borrowed." She looked down and locked her hands together.

My fingers ran over the metal, the ache in my heart tightening. I handed it back to her. Confusion filled her eyes and then I lifted my wrist.

"Can you help me put it on?"

A tearful smile rose, and she helped me latch the bracelet in place.

"Thank you," I whispered.

Nakari, Layla, Bree and Andre quietly left the room while Lilly remained at my side for a few more moments.

"You're not the same girl I met two years ago, Cheyenne. I—we are so proud of you."

I nodded and kept my eyes averted. I didn't need to shed tears now.

"I wish Sahara and Qaysean could have been here..." she whispered trailing off and then sighed. "Daniel will be here soon. Your bouquet is waiting at the bottom of the stairs." She leaned in and kissed my cheek. "I love you, sweetheart."

"I love you too."

My bedroom door quietly clicked closed, and I was alone.

I stared at myself, the woman before me still a mystery. She had scars running down her back from a Tresez attack, and her chest still contained remnants from the burns. How she'd managed to get to this point would probably be one of the wonders of the world. In just a short period of time, I would be walking down the aisle. I'd become Cheyenne O'Shea...no longer Cheyenne Wilson. What I would have given to have my birth and adoptive parents here to see me walk down the aisle, to have shared in my life for longer than what I'd had. But if they hadn't been taken from me, would I have become the woman I was today? Or would I have been weak, and relied on them instead of stepping up to claim the destiny that had always been mine?

A cruel twist of fate had changed everything, and I'd never know the answers. But the only thing that mattered now was that I was marrying Callon, and I was fulfilling what destiny had lain out before me.

I'd kicked and screamed the entire journey, endured heartaches no one should have, but I'd lived to see another day...and we'd end this tyranny with Marcus soon.

I turned away and looked at my nightstand. I knew what lay in its small drawer, Colt's bracelet. I'd brought back the other half on our failed rescue attempt. I couldn't help myself; I wanted to touch it one last time. My steps were purposeful, and I sat on the bed and opened the drawer. The black stone bracelet looked dull and drab sitting there, all the life and brightness it once knew now gone because its other half was missing. Just like our other half was missing—my other half. I sighed. It was time to give up childish dreams and come to grips with Colt's choice. He wasn't one of us anymore.

A soft knock drew my attention. I closed the drawer, shutting out those emotions, locking them away forever. I stood. The door opened, and Daniel entered, a warm smile spreading as he stared at me.

"Wow," he said, his eyes dancing with happiness. "I think Callon's going to be pleasantly surprised."

He jumped beside me. He was wearing the same black tux as last night, but today his vest was black and his tie white.

"You're not looking so bad yourself, Daniel."

"But I'm not the one on display for everyone." He winked, but then turned serious. "Bree told me you weren't feeling well earlier." He hesitated. "Nerves?"

I nodded, knowing it was a lie. I still had that underlying feeling something was off, but Maes had told me to let it go, and I had. I needed to focus on walking down the aisle and saying my vows...and losing my powers for who knew how long.

He shoved his hands in his pockets and looked down.

"I just want you to know, you're the closest thing I've ever had to a sister. And now that it's official, I just wanted to say..." He paused and took a breath. "I just wanted to say I love you an awful lot, Cheyenne. You're one of the best things that ever happened to us, my brothers and I. And regardless of the fact that Colt's not here with us anymore, you were the one who drew us together as a family again. You completed us."

He leaned in kissing my cheek and embraced me. His warmth spread through my limbs and calmed my nerves.

"You were the ones who completed me, Daniel," I whispered. "And you're the best brother I could have ever hoped for. I love you too."

He held on for a few moments before he stepped back. He tried to hide the fact that he brushed a stray tear from his eye, but I saw and it touched me even more. I was the lucky one. I was gaining not only a loving caring brother, I was gaining Callon too. A man who could move me like no other. I was gaining a husband who'd love me no matter what. The same way I'd love him back.

"Shall we?" He extended his arm, and I looped my hand through it.

The silk of my dress swished with each step. We paused at the top of the stairs so I could take in the beauty of the garlands wrapping the staircase and the candlelight in the entry.

"Ready?" Daniel asked and I nodded.

I blinked, and we were at the bottom of the stairs. I smiled. At least I wouldn't trip down the stairs. We moved towards the sitting room, and stopped at a small table so I could pick up my bouquet.

It was a beautiful collection of brilliant pink and white zinnias. The stems were wrapped in a white silk with long flowing silk ribbons attached. They were simple, and yet elegant, like everything else Lilly had planned. We waited in the sitting room until Lilly came and motioned for us to wait at the terrace doors.

My heart began to race, its beat rattling in my ears, drowning out the soft music. Daniel's fingers touched my arm, and I took a deep breath.

"You okay?" he whispered leaning closer.

"Nerves," I murmured back.

Clayton and Skylar stood guard to the entrance, their eyes on us. Lilly motioned, and they slowly drew back the tulle-filled entry, parting the way for Daniel and me.

The music changed, and my knees grew weak. I leaned on Daniel as he escorted us off the terrace steps and into the tent.

The tables were gone and chairs were lined up in their place. I took in the beauty around me. The rows were draped with wildflower garlands along with the tent posts, and thousands of twinkling lights illuminated the ceiling. I followed the rose petals that continued their

311

trail to the front. The sunlight was disappearing over the horizon, and the soft hue was creating a warm glow. The lights sparkled.

My attention locked on Callon, and at that moment, nothing else mattered. He made me forget about everything else.

His warm eyes took me in, while goosebumps trailed over my skin. His black tux made him look regal, like he had been made for this moment, to stand and wait for my arrival. A stray lock of his wavy brown hair fell on his forehead; his chiseled jaw was clean shaven. His full lips beckoned me to come closer, to kiss them wholeheartedly.

Callon stepped forward as Daniel squeezed my hand and raised it for Callon to take. My pulse quickened even more, but any fear or doubt I might have had washed away with every step we took. We stopped in front of Dex. Callon raised both my hands in his, and placed a tender kiss on each without ever losing eye contact.

A shiver filled with pleasure and promise escaped me.

"I'm the lucky one," he whispered as he leaned in and place a kiss near the corner of my mouth. "The lucky one indeed."

I heard Dex begin the ceremony, but I didn't take in all the words...I absorbed all of the man that was before me, my soon to be husband, Callon.

Lilly stepped beside me and took my bouquet; it was time for our vows. We each turned, facing each other, and locked wrist over wrist. Lilly next held a carved metal box with a simple latch. Dex raised the lid and revealed what looked like an old, worn leather braided rope. *The Braid del amour, the braid of love.*

Reverently he pulled it from its velvet-lined case and began to wrap it around our connected hands. He then began to speak.

"As the *Braid del amour* is wrapped around your arms, we are reminded this braid, as our lives, is twisted together in a myriad of different ways. You each bring in your own parts, and combine them together to form one union. One union that shall forever remain strong, one union that will eternally remain united in love."

Dex focused his attention on Callon now.

"Callon repeat after me," he said. "I, Callon Michael O'Shea, of the Consilador clan, pledge my love and my life to you, Cheyenne Alexis Wilson. To forever be your partner in life and your one love. I will cherish each moment I have with you more each day than the day before. I will trust you and rule with you, I will laugh and cry with you. I will love you faithfully no matter the outcome, regardless of the trials we shall face. I give you my heart and my soul from this day forward as long as we both shall live and until death we should part."

I listened as Callon repeated his vow to me, and then watched in awe as the Braid began to give off a bluish hue. I looked up, listening to the love and sincerity flowing from his voice, and the firm grasp of his hands told me of his commitment. Dex turned to me now, and he read the same vow. It was my turn to repeat the words.

"I, Cheyenne Alexis Wilson, of the Kvech and Servak clans, pledge my love and life to you, Callon Michael O'Shea." My voice grew stronger, knowing the words I was pledging to him. The Braid's glow began to grow. "To forever be your partner in life and your one love. I will cherish each moment I have with you more each day than the day before..." I hesitated, blinking my eyes. My vision was growing blurred, lights flashing around the edges. I looked down. The Braid's blue hue was growing darker. A tingling sensation tickled my skin. My powers were draining. Were they going into the braid? They hadn't told me what would happen during the ceremony. They just said our powers would unite. Why hadn't I thought to ask more detailed questions? I inhaled and forced myself on.

"I will trust you and rule with you, I will laugh and cry with you. I will love you..." I paused again. A strange stinging sensation pinched at my flesh. I shook my head; the lights around Callon's body were growing brighter. I couldn't see his face clearly now, but felt his grip tighten. I went on.

"Faithfully no matter the outcome...regardless of the trials we face..." I sucked in a wild breath, starting to become light-headed. "I give you my heart and my soul..."

The pain was becoming intense, and I shook. This wasn't right. I tried to focus on Callon again, and then realized my mistake. The lights; they weren't from the ceiling. They were shimmering speckles, the same ones that had appeared during our ride to Dex and Lilly's. Where Callon had first kissed me to break their hold on me.

No...not here...not today! This couldn't be happening!

"Cheyenne!" Callon's voice broke through.

"The lights," I whispered, scarcely able to get the words out. "The lights...*Ghosters!*"

They'd been here the whole time, and I was staring straight at them...they were around Callon's face!

With every ounce of energy I possessed, I fought to shut my eyes. But it was too late. They had me, and I couldn't stop them. They must have waited until I was at my weakest during the ceremony, when my powers would start to fade...but how'd they get through the enchantment? Had Colt let them in?

I watched in horror while I floated above my body in a ghost-like state, my vows unfinished. There was an eerie silence as I watched my family frantically race to my side. It was as if all sounds were blocked out. I could see their lips moving, but I heard nothing. I grew cold, colder than I'd ever felt, like I was freezing. The warmth my skin provided no longer insulated me. I exhaled, and steam rose from my mouth only to cause me to start choking. It was as if the air was freezing on contact—freezing me from the inside out!

Dex ripped the glowing Braid from our arms. In desperation, Callon pushed his lips to mine, fighting to bring me back—to focus on him. I reached out, struggling to force myself back into my body, but it only caused more agony. I wailed as thousands of needles pierced my limbs and saw, in the last moment before I was ripped away, my limp body in his arms—my eyes wide open and lifeless.

The more I struggled, the more misery I was in. The needle pricks turned into stabbing pain. I willed myself to still. I watched the forest fly past as I was sucked away by some invisible force. My soul was ripped from my body, only to be joined back when I arrived at the Ghoster's side. I was at their mercy—I'd be in Marcus's hold. No!

Powerless, I could only watch the scenery fly past. Trees flew by in a blur as they blended together. Dark shadows mixing with the leaves...what else was out there? The night sky gave way to a glowing figure in the distance. As I came closer, I saw the Ghoster, and Raina was standing beside her.

I hit what felt like a brick wall, my body slamming to an abrupt stop and my head pounding. I gasped and lay on the cold forest floor. Pain came in waves that rippled through my limbs and I shook, completely incapacitated.

Slender fingers grasped my wrist, and the searing pain of flames ignited. Raina was burning me. But without my strength, without my powers, there was nothing I could do to fight back.

I didn't have to rise or even look up to know we were moving again. Strips of her black mist licked at my face like whips snapping in the wind. I lay crumpled at her feet, dragged through the forest again. The sounds of my dress ripping to shreds as it caught on the branches echoed exactly how I was feeling at the moment. How...how had they come for me?! Maes had promised me everything was going to be alright, that everyone would fight for me, and yet Marcus's forces had snatched me with barely a second thought. My mind whirled. Had someone else chosen to betray us? But why? Everything around me, everything I'd fought for and loved was once again ripped away.

It was over. We'd lost.

A scream captured my attention, and I search the darkness, frantic to see who it was. Nakari's ivory gown stood out in the night, but she wasn't standing anymore. A fight was taking place, and she was surrounded by misty shadows that soon blocked her from sight.

"Give her back!" Nakari screamed.

"Nakari!" I cried, knowing I could do nothing to help her. I could only pray she'd survive.

Another black shadow stirred between the trees, blurring as it moved and then suddenly became clear...Daniel! He neared, and I struggled to reach out, trying to break Raina's burning grip.

Time seemed to move in slow motion as the moon's rays shone down through the trees. I pushed back the agony and forced myself to my knees, shoving myself into Raina's legs to knock her off balance.

She hissed and glanced back. Daniel reached out, and suddenly Raina's fingers dug into my scalp. She yanked me forward, and I screamed as white hot pain rippled through my head. I lost my breath, and I felt my eyes rolling back into my head.

I was quickly losing consciousness. Raina's grip was taking its toll. Without my powers to protect me, she could very well kill me if she didn't release me soon.

The moonlight faded, and soon lights outlining a city clipped past. She was circling us around the city, avoiding populated areas. She had to be taking me to the Dublin airport.

We stopped, and I was dropped, my cheek hitting what felt like concrete. My breaths were short and labored. Heavy footsteps neared.

"I told you not to hurt her!" an angry voice snarled. A voice that sounded like Marcus.

"She's breathing, and she's here. It's more than the others have done for you!" Raina snapped back. Her words were cut off by a yelp.

"Don't try me, Raina!" he hissed. "I only keep you around because you're useful, but that doesn't guarantee your safety. Now release her!"

Her petite body slammed onto the concrete beside me, her blue eyes burned with a wild animal's rage. A moment later, she was shoved away and Marcus rolled me to my back. His fingers brushed the hair from my lashes and sympathy etched his face. I growled. How could the man who'd inflicted so much pain on me dare look at me like that!

Carefully, he adjusted the remnants of my torn silk dress and scooped me up into his arms without saying a word.

"You're mine now." I hadn't the strength to stop him—to stop what was now taking place. Everything around me began spinning, and I pressed my eyes closed trying to prevent the nausea from taking over.

"Marcus!" Callon's voice boomed with fury.

My heart began to race. Callon was here! I opened my eyes, enough to see that we were inside a dimly lit hangar and just feet away from a jet. Marcus halted, turning to face him.

"It's been done, Marcus," Callon said. "We've already united our powers. She'll do you no good. Let her go."

Callon and Daniel stood side by side. Their eyes were hard and piercing, their stances rigid and firm, ready to do battle.

"Do you take me for a fool, Callon?" Marcus asked.

"You are a fool if you think you can leave here with Cheyenne," Callon's reply was laced with warning.

"...from this day forward, as long as we both shall live, and until death we should part," Marcus said.

My eyes went wide. The vows! I didn't finish my vows, but Callon had!

Marcus shook his head. "Your vows were not completed. It's too bad really, you were so close."

Daniel's eyes focused on me and then he vanished. Marcus's head twisted to the side. Daniel was next to the plane, but below us. He had been blocked from jumping where he wanted to go. He blinked, confused, just as confused as I was. Marcus laughed.

"You're the fool, Callon," Marcus sneered. "You can't admit defeat even when it's right before your eyes. I've won. The Consilador clan will be destroyed, and you're completely powerless to stop it." A gut-retching laugh rose from the pit of his stomach. "But I must thank you for giving me your clan's powers, as well as Cheyenne's. Such a kind wedding gift. I'll be sure to treasure it forever."

Callon stood motionless, his eyes lost in a sea of emotions as he stared at me. My gut recoiled in horror. What had we done?

Colt's looming shadow appeared, and he held up a silver etched box. No...the *Braid del amour!* The box was glowing that same blue hue, and Marcus had it. I struggled to reach for it, but was crushed to Marcus's chest.

"Hush, my angel," he said against my cheek. "There's nothing you can do outside of marrying me to gain access to your powers again...or to give the Consilador's back theirs."

I was whisked inside the jet and the door secured. A moment later, Raina appeared, and Marcus set me to my feet, still holding me up.

"Take her," he growled. "But harm her again, and it will be nothing compared to the punishment I'll unleash on you."

I blinked, and we disappeared, only to reappear in another jet, larger than the last, but similar to the jet we'd flown on to rescue Colt. While Callon's jet was bright and had life, the colors in this jet were dark and gloomy. Raina shoved me into a seat and then Darrien took hold of my arm. Seconds later Marcus and Colt appeared. The jet engines roared to life, and they began to prepare for take off.

I kept my eyes locked on the floor as Marcus buckled me in. Tears began to stream down my cheeks, tears I could no longer control. I couldn't believe it. We were so close! I cried for Callon and Daniel, I cried for Lilly and Dex, for Nakari, Koda, Skylar, Brogan; everyone. I cried for all their preparations, all their precautions. I cried for the Timeless race. But more than anything, I cried for myself. This was my ultimate failure, and there was no way to mend it.

I'd lost.

CHAPTER 24

I clamped my hands together, trying to stop the tremors. My breathing was erratic, and my lower lip shook. I was hurting not only on the inside, but the outside as well. My wrist throbbed where Raina's fingers had been, and I could feel the wound swelling. Blisters were forming on the now bright red skin. I knew as a Timeless it should heal soon, but she'd purposely harmed me. It was evident after she moved me the second time; I had no burns from then.

Blood dripped from my cheek onto what was left of my wedding dress. It had been torn to shreds in the forest. What was once white and flawless was now stained and ragged, not unlike me.

A voice came to life over the intercom. "You may now move about the cabin."

Marcus leaned over and unbuckled my belt. He helped me stand. The gray interior of the cabin began to spin, and my legs grew weak.

I heard a woman's gasp and what sounded like the rustling of material.

"Don't touch me, you beast!" she hissed. I caught sight of an ivory dress, and my breath caught.

Nakari!

Marcus's arm came around to hold me up, and he led me to a couch where I collapsed. A moment later Nakari was over me, hugging me tightly.

"Cheyenne!" she whispered. "Oh no, I'm so sorry...I was too late!"

My heart ached and yet I felt some small relief. Nakari was alive, but what were Marcus's plans for her? There would be no need to keep her now that he had me...or would he use her as bait to draw Callon and the others in? Would he kill them all?

She drew back, tears in her eyes. There were no words for her to say. I saw it in her eyes. Failure...we'd all failed.

Her auburn hair was filled with leaves and twigs, dirt smudged her face and her lips were swollen and crusted with dried blood. Her left eye looked puffy, and bruises were forming on her pale skin. Her dress had rips, along with mud and bloodstains. She'd fought hard, but in the end it didn't matter.

Marcus towered over us, but he didn't push her away. Instead, he gently helped her to her feet when Darrien arrived with supplies to tend to my wounds. Jahlem, Conall and Colt stood nearby, silently watching. I refused to make eye contact with Colt; I wouldn't have been able to handle it. I was already too emotional as it was, and looking at him would push me over the edge and right into the jaws of the crimson-eyed beast.

Darrien and Jahlem had Nakari sit nearby as they gave her a wet cloth to wipe her lips and face. I stared at her. Her expression had turned to worry and despair. She knew, as I did, that her chances weren't good. Her fingers traced metal bands around her wrists. Had she been wearing those before?

Marcus shifted, blocking my view of Nakari, and sat on the edge of the couch. Darrien and the others moved away, taking Nakari with them. Marcus focused on my wrist, gently wiping the blood, then spread a salve on it. Finally he wrapped it with gauze.

I studied his face for a few moments. It was different somehow. A scar ran from his brow across his right eye and then stopped at his cheekbone. He'd never had a scar there before, at least not that I'd remembered.

He turned his attention to my face. Raina's cloak had given me scratches, and I glanced around, searching for her. She was nowhere to be found. Had he left her in Ireland? He dabbed the blood away and then focused on my neck. His long fingers traced the necklace, taking time to caress the pearls and sapphires. His gray eyes met mine, quickly masking any emotions.

"It's an exquisite piece of jewelry, Cheyenne." He paused for a few moments, eyeing it closely. "Where did you get it?"

"Lilly gave it to me. It was my mother's," I muttered.

His gaze seemed to be lost in a memory, but then he spoke again. "I thought as much. Did you know *I* gave this to your mother as a wedding present?"

My throat tightened, and when I didn't think my heart could sink any lower, it did. Marcus let out an amused chuckle.

"How fitting that you now wear it, Cheyenne. It seems your mother's destiny has caught up to you, too."

I shook my head. Every turn I made, every fight with destiny kept bringing me back to him...why? Callon was my destiny. I'd constantly been told that it was Callon, and believed it with my whole heart. But if Callon was my destiny, then why did Marcus keep showing up? Were we wrong all along? Was I wrong?

No, everything about Marcus was wicked. He'd killed, murdered in cold blood to get where he was today. We couldn't change his past...but could his future change just like mine had?

I tried to turn away, but he pulled my chin back.

"You won't turn away from me anymore, my angel. We'll face each other head on, eye to eye. No more running."

He was right on one thing; I had nowhere else to run.

Gently he helped me to a sitting position, and the room began to spin again. I fell forward into his chest, unable to stop myself. His arms came around me as his fingers slowly worked their way up my spine. A tremor escaped me. My stomach grew nauseated. If I could have fought him off to keep him from touching my bare back, I would have. His hands stopped at my neck, and he unlatched the necklace, pulling it away. He then removed my earrings and shoved them into his pocket.

His hands returned to my back, caressing my skin. He stopped when they ran over my Tresez scar; he traced the wounds then lowered his head.

"I'm sorry that you've suffered so much at my hand, that I've brought you so much grief." His warm breath trailed over my forehead. "But it had to happen this way, Cheyenne. I had to pull you from the poison they filled your mind with. You'll see, just as Colt did. In time you'll forgive me and know I was right."

It was just as Dex had told me. Marcus, his father and my grandfather had dabbled too much with their powers, and it was affecting their minds. How could he say he was sorry for all the pain he'd caused me? He'd been the one to order the attacks! He'd tried to kill me and succeeded in completely destroying my life! Poison he said...*they'd* poisoned me? How could they have poisoned me when all they'd done was show compassion and love? How was that poison? And Colt? How could he have fallen for such stupidity? How had Marcus brainwashed him into thinking he was right?

Forgiveness would never come from my heart. Marcus had wounded me too deep, but now I was in his grasp and powerless. The Braid held my powers along with Callon's, Daniel's...and mostly likely Colt's. I was responsible for the Consilador clan's demise. I fought to keep the tears from falling. I was trapped with no way out.

Marcus drew back and then sat beside me on the couch. He guided me to lie down, my head resting on his lap. The cabin lights dimmed, but not before Colt rose and draped a blanket over me. He returned to his seat, but I felt his cold gaze on me.

He'd done this, taken part in my capture, and there'd be no forgiveness in my heart for his betrayal. It ran deep, this crevice in my heart, revealing the crimson-eyed beast that had been asleep all this time. He would pay for this.

Marcus began to remove the flowers and pins holding my hair. They dropped to the floor, like every hope and dream I'd ever had. It all lay in a crumpled pile to be swept away and never seen again. I closed my eyes and willed myself to sleep, hoping to wake up from this nightmare, but I knew I never would.

The soft whisper of someone humming caused my breath to catch. It was familiar, masculine and soothing. I blinked and looked up. Marcus's lips weren't moving, but the sound was coming from him. His gray eyes softened as he twisted a strand of my blond hair between his fingers. I remained still, listening, when I realized why I knew it. It was my melody, the melody I played when I wanted to think, sort through things...the one I played when I was with him in the forest. He'd remembered and was doing it to soothe and comfort me.

I closed my eyes again. I wouldn't fall for his tricks. Instead, I concentrated on how to restore Callon's powers. There had to be a way, regardless of my being trapped here.

"Cheyenne! Wake up!"

I blinked, confused and dazed. The cabin was dark, and Nakari was standing over me.

"Hurry!" She yanked my arm and dragged me off the couch.

"They'll be back soon!"

I stumbled after her, unsure what was taking place. The cabin was empty, and we were heading towards the back of the jet. Quickly I managed to snap out of sleep and take faster steps.

"There's a rear access panel to the baggage compartment that we can crawl out of." She pushed open what looked like a storage room door.

"But I thought the baggage door could only be opened from the outside?" I stared at the small narrow door.

"It's open, I heard it. They were loading supplies, but they haven't closed it yet." She was down on her knees tugging the door open. "Come on, we haven't much time."

"Why can't you just jump us out of here?"

She slid herself into the narrow opening and dropped from sight. Suddenly her head appeared and she lifted her wrist.

"These bands block my powers," she explained. "I can't."

Powers...

"Hold on!" I ran back in search of the Braid box. It would be my only chance to save Callon.

"Cheyenne, no!" Nakari hissed, but it was too late.

I fumbled in the main cabin. Colt had had it last. Where had he left it?

From out of nowhere, a large hand snaked around my waist. I screeched and was lifted from the ground. Conall's steely arm clamped down across my chest, thrusting me into his body. Soon Jahlem and Darrien rushed past in search of Nakari.

My heart raced, and Conall's hold tightened, making it hard to breathe.

"Let her go!" Colt growled. "She's turning blue, you fool!"

Conall snarled and turned. "She's not your concern anymore, Colt!"

Jahlem and Darrien returned. "Nakari's gone."

The veins in Colt's neck bulged, and his biceps flexed. Darrien pushed Colt back while Jahlem eyed me closely.

"Put her down, Conall," Jahlem said calmly. "She's not going anywhere."

A door slammed, and the jet began to move. Finally Marcus appeared. His eyes focused on Conall while his jaw grew rigid.

"Let her go, now!" he snapped.

I fell to the floor, gasping for air.

Jahlem helped me to my feet, but Marcus grasped my arm and whisked me away towards the back of the jet. He opened a door and shoved me in. I tripped and fell onto a bed. A pair of jeans and a shirt were neatly folded there.

"Change," he commanded.

I eyed the clothes and then looked up into intense gray eyes. His incensed expression looked even fiercer with the scar running across his brow.

"Will you leave so I can change?" My voice trembled.

"No. It's obvious I can't leave you alone." His tone was clipped.

I stared at the clothing again and then sat up, pulling the jeans from the bed and wiggling them up under my dress. I turned away and untied the tulle halter and slipped the shirt on over the dress. My fingers fumbled with the buttons on the back of the dress when suddenly they were ripped away. The soft patter of them hitting the floor sent a chill over me, and I took a deep breath. He'd done it to get a reaction. I pushed the remnants of the dress to the floor and waited.

His fingers once again found their way around my arm and I was led back into the main cabin. He pushed me into a seat, and I stared out the window as the plane taxied down the runway. A flash of red caught my eye, and I saw Nakari standing near a dimly lit hangar, alone. I pressed my eyes closed and said a quick prayer of thanks. At least I knew she was safe and alive.

Marcus's hand slipped over mine and he began caressing my rings. He stopped on my index finger, his thumb circling Callon's ring; the gift he'd given me two years ago at Christmas.

"Why do you wear this?" he asked. "It's not a clan ring."

"It was a gift," I said. "It has meaning to me."

"Meaning?"

I didn't reply. He didn't need to know what it meant to me. I tried to pull my hand back, but his fingers locked around my wrist.

"It shows your lives are intertwined together, each connected to one another," he stated calmly.

I still didn't reply, regardless of the fact that he'd guessed it right.

He fingered it again then said, "You don't need it anymore."

He quickly pulled it from my finger and I lunged for it. A wicked smile grew on his lips and panic rose inside me. My heart pounded against my ribs as I watched his eyes move to my engagement ring. I balled my hand into a fist.

"No!" I hissed and fought to bring my hand to my chest, my body thrashing in my seat. "No!"

A dark shadow came from above and pinned me to my seat. Conall's smirk said it all as Marcus opened my hand and ripped my engagement ring from my finger.

I couldn't control myself as the tears spilled down my cheeks.

"Please," I begged. "Please, stop it!"

Marcus eyed the ring closely and then snapped his fingers. Darrien appeared and Marcus tossed the rings at him. Conall released me, and I tried to recoil from Marcus, but he wouldn't let me. He kept a firm hold on my hand while I stared out into the night sky, wishing I could fly away or leap from the jet and die...anything but be here with him.

Not enough time passed for me to wallow in my sorrows before we were landing once again. The sun's morning rays were just beginning to rise when the jet came to a stop and we exited. The concrete was cold on my bare feet. Marcus and Conall dragged me along, one on each side firmly grasping my arms. I was sure the arm Conall was holding onto would be bruised later.

I squinted into the light. Wherever we were, large mountains loomed in the distance.

Cheyenne! Maes's voice came to life in my head. I struggled to turn around. They were here!

"Go!" Marcus said between his teeth. Conall dropped my arm, but not before Colt took a firm grasp around my waist.

He hoisted me up off the ground, and Marcus let go. A helicopter stood waiting five hundred feet ahead. I pinched, pushed, and squirmed against Colt, to no avail. Even if I could have broken free, Marcus was a mere arm's length away. I couldn't run far...but I only needed Daniel to touch me!

Marcus stopped.

He waved Colt on, but I could see why he'd paused. Maes, Koda, Brogan, Callon and Daniel emerged from behind a hangar. Conall stood with his legs apart, ready for battle just a few feet away. Would they battle it out in plain sight? Callon had come to rescue me, but he had no powers, just like me. Fear, deep, dark and almost overwhelming pushed at the seams of my mind. With the flick of his wrist, Marcus could kill Callon! Darrien and Jahlem flanked Colt and we continued to move toward the helicopter.

"Colt, no!" I cried as they pinned me to the seat and buckled me in. "This isn't right! You need to let me go!" I struggled to unfasten the belt when Colt captured my hands in his. I stilled, not hiding my pain. His icy blue eyes that once held softness were nothing but sharp edges and harsh lines. I lowered my head in defeat. I heard a scuffle outside, and then a roar that sounded like a Tresez. Moments later, Marcus and Conall boarded and we left the ground. Conall was holding his thigh.

We'll find you, Cheyenne, Maes said. We won't lose you, mon espoir.

Colt didn't release my wrists, but his hold somehow had changed. I stared at the black mat beneath my bare toes, my heart filling with the same vile colored liquid of hatred. I pulled my legs to my chest and lay my head down, burying it in the denim.

How had it all come to this?

The helicopter churned, but I ignored the sounds and pulled myself inward. It was my only safe haven, but for how long? How long would I last in Marcus's hold? How long till I gave in like the rest? I'd escaped once, but somehow this was different. It was as if I could feel the noose tightening around my neck and my feet slipping...everywhere I turned, bars rose, caging me in. Pushing me back towards the crimson-eyed beast.

At some point, Colt released my hands, and I drew them around my legs, enclosing me in my own space. The only space that I might survive in—maybe.

"Cheyenne," Marcus's voice had softened.

I didn't move.

"Cheyenne," he said again but firmer and grasped my ankle. "Come with me."

I refused to move. I didn't want this—ever.

His cool fingers slid up my pant leg, wrapping around my calf and he tugged gently. My heel slipped from the seat, and he moved quickly to unbuckle my belt. I kept my head down till he pulled my chin up and wiped away the remnants of tears from my cheeks.

"Betrayal hurts," he said quietly, "especially when it's from one you loved."

I clenched my jaw. How dare he talk of betrayal! I opened my mouth to speak, but he pressed his finger to my lips.

"Don't say something you'll regret. You're angry right now. I stole you from your wedding and Colt's betrayal stings." He cupped my cheek, and I pushed myself back into the seat. "You ran from me. You caused yourself this misery, not me. However, I will do what I can to help ease it." He pulled me forward and out of the copter. "In time, you'll see that I was right."

My foot struck a gravel path leading to what looked like a medieval fortress with gloomy stone walls. A large wooden gate stood guard at the castle's entrance, just like in fairytales. The compound lay between two vast mountain ranges, with what looked like a glacier lake nearby. I stared up at the sun for a few moments, determining our location. We weren't in Idaho or Montana anymore. It had to be Canada; that had been where he'd tried to take me before.

I winced as my bare foot caught a sharp rock. Marcus looked down, and in the next moment scooped me up and carried me inside the gate. I didn't bother to fight. It was pointless at the moment. I had nowhere to run, and no powers to protect me.

This was more than a compound; this was a fortress. Small outbuildings and stables dotted the lower level while the main house loomed up on the small hill.

He stopped at the lower terrace just below the manor and set me on my feet. A shiver escaped me as the cold from the stones traveled up my legs. Trackers and Tresezes roamed about the lower level while Darrien, Jahlem and Colt waited nearby. Raina had yet to make an appearance. If she wasn't here now, I was sure she'd be arriving soon.

Marcus led me up the remaining terrace levels till we paused just before the manor. I stared out over the stone wall; the manor was nestled up alongside the lake. The sunlight reflected like glass on the smooth surface.

"It's beautiful, isn't it?" Marcus said.

I didn't reply, but moved my gaze towards the large French doors. We entered what appeared to be a bright and sunny entry. To our left lay an arched doorway. He tugged me towards it. It took a few moments for my eyes to adjust to the dreary room.

"It's my sitting room." Marcus felt the need to describe it for me.

While the sheer size of it should've impressed any woman, all I saw were windowless walls, deep colors darkening the room and oil paintings of men and women who looked miserable. The room itself was neatly arranged, but the only light came from the French doors in the hall where we'd entered and a row of windows at the rear viewing the mountainous landscape. Even the enormous stone fireplace seemed sad and lonely. It was as if the life had been drained from the very walls.

He pointed me towards the entry again and took me up the winding marble staircase. We turned right and headed down a long, dark hallway. My feet padded on the gray runners. Just as we rounded a corner, he stopped and opened a door. A symbol was painted on the door, a symbol that resembled the design of my Servak ring.

"This is your room. I chose it because I knew you'd appreciate the view. It's quite stunning to watch the sunrise over the landscape."

It was a room like any other bedroom. A canopy bed took center stage and a small sitting area was nestled near a window. There appeared to be another doorway leading to a bathroom. I chose to move towards what looked like terrace doors and stepped out onto a small balcony. Although my room was set back in what looked like an alcove of the manor, a garden lay below, and I had a perfect view of the valley, mountains and lake.

He stood behind me, his shoulder touching mine.

"I had the garden made for you," he said thoughtfully. "I even had them plant wildflowers so you could care for them." He lowered his head and breathed near my ear. "I want to make you happy here. This is your garden, your safe place to go, anytime you want to. I'll have Darrien and Jahlem show you how to get there later."

I didn't answer, but attempted to scoot further away. His fingers caught my elbow, preventing me from moving. The pulse in my neck throbbed. I hated it when he touched me.

"Your closet is filled with clothes for you. I suggest you rest and get cleaned up before you come down for the evening. Darrien will be back later to fetch you."

Fetch me? Like I was some possession?

He released me and turned to go, but then paused. I turned to meet his eyes.

"You can't walk around alone here. Darrien and Jahlem are your guards. Where you go, they go. Understand?"

It didn't surprise me. I didn't expect to have any freedoms here.

"It's for your own safety, Cheyenne," he felt the need to add. "You no longer have your powers, and you won't be able to defend yourself if you're attacked."

I blinked. "Who'd attack me here?"

"There are plenty who are not fond of you because of your mother, and would take the opportunity, if presented, to cause you harm...even death."

Why did so many people hate my mother? And why would they take it out on me?

"Do you understand?" he questioned.

"I understand."

"Then I shall see you later." He headed towards the door, but not before he glanced back.

I stared out over the terrace rails again, my fingers running over the empty spot where my rings once lay. I glanced at my wrist; even Nakari's charm bracelet was missing. Their absence reminded me that they had been stolen from me. I wasn't sure how much longer I could hang on and not lose myself to the crimson-eyed beast that was just waiting for the opportunity to lurch to the forefront once again.

If I let it out again, allowed it to have control, I'd be unstoppable, but without my powers, I would pay for it with my very life.

CHAPTER 25

Fetch me...

The words grated on me. It wasn't like I was some prize. I was *the* prize. Marcus had waited long and hard to capture me and now that I was here, I was supposed to do what he wanted. It was obvious he could switch moods faster than a light switch, but the question was, could I handle the mood swings and the repercussions from it?

I rubbed my temples. A dull ache had begun to form, and regardless of the fact that I'd rested on the plane, exhaustion was hitting me hard. It was a familiar type of exhaustion, like when I had first gotten my powers. Apparently having your powers removed was taxing on a Timeless as well.

I crawled up on the dark blue silk-covered bedding, grabbed the blanket at the base of the bed, and curled up under it. I didn't want to rest. I didn't want my mind to stop whirling about how I was going to deal with this, but my body had other ideas.

I stared at the open terrace doors and longed for my freedom again. How had it all come to this? We'd worked so hard to prevent this outcome and yet...and Callon, what was he going through right now? He had to be frantic, or was he overwrought with failure? The last image of his panicked face tugged at my heart. After all we'd been through, everything we had to overcome...it had ended like this. I fought off the exhaustion, but before long my lids grew weary, and my body heavy. I drifted off as a dreary darkness fell over me.

"Cheyenne," somebody called my name and fingers tenderly brushed my brow. "Cheyenne, can you hear me?"

I couldn't open my lids. They were too heavy, and my mind was foggy, but the voice was familiar.

"Colt?" I whispered. Was it really him, or was I dreaming?

"Cheyenne, can you wake up for me?"

A heavy breath left me, and my head rolled to the side. Why did I have to wake up?

"I'm tired." I pushed him away. "Let me sleep."

"You've already slept a long time. You need to wake up."

"No," I moaned.

"Come on, sweetheart. They're waiting."

Who was waiting? Daniel and Callon? Had I been sleeping too much again? I'd had a bad dream that felt so real. My heavy lashes fluttered. Colt was sitting on the edge of my bed. A small grin appeared when I looked at him.

"Come on, sleepyhead. You need to get up."

I sat up and quickly and threw myself into his chest, hugging him tightly.

"I had the most horrible dream ever, Colt!" I pressed in closer, staring down at the comforter and inhaling his musky scent. "I dreamed you died and..." I blinked. He smelled different, like spices and wood. I drew back, taking in my surroundings.

Where was I? This wasn't the cabin. My gaze traveled to the man whose hand still held my arm. Marcus...

I scrabble back, trying to break his hold, but instead he held me steady.

"You're disoriented, my angel," his voice was low and even. "You've been through a lot in a short amount of time. I'm sorry. I should have realized this would happen."

"What? Why?" I whispered, still not sure what was transpiring.

"You almost bound your powers with another. It can be draining, make you feel tired and unsettled. Give yourself a few days, and it'll clear itself up."

I glanced towards the terrace doors. The sun was just rising, and the early morning rays were dancing across the marble floor. I lay down before the sun had set...

"How long have I been sleeping?"

"Three days."

I'd been away from Callon for five days now. Was he feeling the same way? Was he recovering or so fixated on a plan to rescue me that he'd pushed everything aside, risking his health in the process? Had they tried to pull me out while I slept, and I didn't know? Had an opportunity presented itself, and I missed it?

Marcus slid off the bed, taking me with him. I lost my balance, but quickly regained my footing.

"I want you to clean up and rest until this evening. Darrien and Jahlem will be here soon."

He walked me to the bathroom door and then hesitated for a moment, staring out towards the terrace doors. Was Callon out there now? He lifted his hand to brush back my hair, but I took a step back. Irritation flashed in his gray eyes.

"We'll have plenty of time to get to know each other before we wed, my angel. You're not going anywhere."

He turned on his heels and stormed out of the room. The heavy wooden door banged against the frame, and I jumped. I didn't want to get to know him. I knew enough right now to know I didn't want to be with him.

I closed the bathroom door and leaned against it, staring down at my wrists. The gauze had been removed, and Raina's burn was healed. A red ring resembling a chain still remained. I sighed. It would serve as a reminder that I was chained to this destiny with no hope of escape.

I stepped further into the bathroom. It had the same gray marble flooring as the bedroom, but the bathroom itself was twice the size of my bedroom in Idaho, and I hadn't even entered the closet yet.

A large jetted tub was in the corner with a frosted glass window blocking the view, but allowing plenty of sunshine in. How odd to have such a modern tub in what looked like a castle from the outside. There were also double sinks with a vanity large enough to lie across. Just to the left was an enormous walk-in shower, one that made Lilly's French-styled bathroom pale in comparison.

For as much as I didn't want to enjoy it, the sprayer heads on the shower helped ease my aches and allowed my mind to wander. There was so much I didn't understand, mainly how I'd failed so badly. I'd worked so hard to remain out of Marcus's grasp, trained, studied, endured misery and agony and still ended up right here, right now, and I couldn't change a thing.

I'd truly lost everything...my parents, my adoptive parents, Dex and Lilly and the rest of my adoptive family, Daniel, Colt and Callon.

Chances were I'd never see them again, regardless of the fact that Colt was here. The only reminder he'd bring would be the pain and misery of betrayal.

I dried off and headed for the closet. I shouldn't have been surprised; it was enormous, stacked with hanging clothes from shirts and pants to formal attire and shoes galore. I should have been impressed, but instead, it just caused more depression. I no longer had the freedom of choice. I had to wear what was here, what Marcus wanted to see me in.

I dug through some drawers and found panties and bras. How the man knew my size should have shocked me, but he had been watching me for a long time. That, and Colt must've had a hand in this, too.

I yanked down a pair of cotton pants and a blue blouse. Not a pair of jeans or T-shirt could be found. I dug through the shoes and found a pair of flats. I grabbed a sweater on my way out and quickly brushed through the tangled mess of hair. I didn't bother to look in the mirror. It didn't matter what I looked like anymore. I didn't have anyone to impress.

I found Darrien and Jahlem waiting. They stood near the bed and eyed me carefully, like they were unsure. Marcus had made it clear; they were my bodyguards. Where I went, they went. I headed towards the terrace door and stepped out. The terrace was small, but a bistro table with two small chairs had been placed where I could sit and enjoy the view....and search for signs of my family.

I sat and stared at the stone walls caging me in. A prison potentially for the rest of my life, unless Callon could find a way to remove me, but the chances were slim. Marcus had brought me here for a reason; he knew he was untouchable here.

I trembled as a cool morning breeze drifted past. I should have dried my hair, but I was actually hoping it would chill me, numb my feelings. The sunlight hit the lake and cast its reflection onto the stone walls and inched its way up. Flickering iridescent lights scattered out before me and caused me to squint. It seemed to be coming from the sunlight's reflection off the water. I lifted my hand to shade my eyes. It was strangely familiar somehow. Like fireflies dancing...

An enchantment!

My heart sank. Marcus had an enchantment just like Callon had at the estate. The others would never be able to get to me! But if Marcus had broken through the enchantment by using Colt, couldn't Callon break through the enchantment by using Maes?

"It can't be broken," Jahlem said quietly.

He stood behind me. I'd heard them both follow, but ignored them till now.

"What can't be broken?" I chose to play dumb.

"The enchantment," Darrien replied. "Maes can't break it."

I turned on them, my eyes narrowing. How did they know what I was thinking?

"We can't read your mind," Jahlem said, "but we can sense what you're thinking."

"How?"

"We're Servak, like you. And you are your mother's daughter."

"You're Servak?"

Darrien nodded.

"But you sided with Marcus?"

"It's not that simple," Jahlem answered. "When Sahara refused to marry Marcus and ran away, she didn't inherit her father's power. That left the Servak weak and vulnerable. Marcus exploited this, and has now taken control of our powers as we've been without a leader for so long. He uses this to make the Sarac stronger, but it comes at a cost to us," Jahlem answered. "We have nothing to resist him with."

"So you're powerless against him, too," I observed.

They didn't answer, but knew I hit the nail on the head. Even my bodyguards were as stuck as me.

"One day, it will not be so," Darrien said. "One day the Servak will be free again. That was the last thing Sahara promised us."

"You knew my mother?"

"Yes," Jahlem replied.

I fiddled with my Servak ring, twisting it on my finger. I had so many questions.

"Why did everyone hate her?" I asked. "Was she an awful person?"

"The hatred spills over because she fled," Darrien said. "She allowed her father to die, and many blame her for the loss of Jorell as well. They see her running away as what led to the undoing of the Servak."

"Because without a strong leader the clan weakens," I said and then hesitated. "Did you hate her?"

There was a long pause before Jahlem responded. "Your mother did what she thought was right, and I can't fault her for that, but deserting her clan in the process wasn't a well-thought-out plan."

"So you blame her for Jorell's death," I stated.

"No," Darrien said. "We blame her for your condition."

Why did it all come back to Sahara? The Servak, Consilador, Laundess, and Coltooro clans...they all blamed my mother's actions for putting me in the position I was in now. Surely she would have known that her actions one day would affect me, or any child she had. If I'd been born male, I'd probably already be dead, but because I was female, it made me more valuable. I was marriageable material, able to bind clans together and create stronger alliances—strengthen their powers through their rings.

I stood abruptly, the metal chair scraping on the stones. I needed to leave this room. Marcus said I had a garden I could freely roam, I needed to breathe.

I headed straight for the bedroom door, Darrien and Jahlem directly behind me. If they could sense what I was thinking, then I didn't need to tell them where to take me. They'd know.

I stepped out into the lifeless dark hallway, and Jahlem moved ahead of me, leading the way. We turned to our left. I wouldn't have thought the hall could get any bleaker, but it did. We stopped before a metal door, and I waited for Jahlem to unlock it. The stone staircase was dark, damp and smelled of musty rocks.

A long, narrow winding staircase led us to another metal door. Jahlem once again unlocked it, and the bright light from the sun caused me to shield my eyes. I blinked a few times as gravel crunched under my shoes.

I glanced around. Stone planter boxes lined the pathway, which had many different rows. Some of the planters contained trees that were just now blooming soft delicate flowers. A bench rested against the gray stone wall, and a patch of grass was spread out before it.

It wasn't a large garden, but it was laid out nicely. One large solitary wood and metal door sat in the far corner of the garden. It looked like a narrow pathway leading to the front of the manor. There was a keyhole for what appeared to fit an old skeleton key, but no knob to twist it open, only a lone circular handle.

"It's locked," Jahlem said. "Very few have access to the key."

I nodded and headed towards the grass. I removed my shoes and picked a sunny spot to lie down. I closed my eyes.

"You're safe here," Darrien said. "We'll leave, but will remain close by."

I didn't reply, but heard their footsteps departing.

I listened to the wind blow against the stone wall. The wall itself blocked it from my sanctuary. I was grateful it didn't take away the sunshine, at least not yet.

A shadow drifted above me and I looked up. Icy blue eyes stared down at me...Colt. I looked away and stood, brushing myself off. I had nothing to say to him and looking at him made me angry. I slipped my shoes on.

He didn't say anything at first. It was as if he was contemplating something. I looked up. His face was hard, rigid, but his eyes said something else. He looked torn, his emotions getting the better of him. An internal battle was taking place.

Was he finally coming to his senses? I couldn't stop myself as I reached out to touch his hand.

"What a predictable little girl you are," Colt said with an iciness that trickled over me like a cold freeze. "Makes me wonder what I ever saw in such a simpleton."

My chest tightened. I drew my hand back and gritted my teeth. Apparently I was wrong, but no matter what he said, I wouldn't let him get to me.

"Wait, I know what it was." Colt began to circle me. "It was what my brother wanted, that's what drew me to you. A game of sorts, a game to see who could make you fall the hardest and fastest." He paused, waiting for the words to sink in. "Callon was in on it, too, although he'd deny it."

I bent my head, balling my hands into fists to stop them from shaking. They were words, nothing more than words...but they were coming from Colt, and it caused the wound to fester. Gone were any conflicting emotions that he might have had.

"I won, of course. You easily fell victim to my charms, like the little schoolgirl you are. A well placed wink and grin was all it took, really, and you spilled your heart out willingly."

He stopped in front of me and grasped my chin, forcing it up. A glint was in his eyes, and a smirk rose on his lips. Why was he saying this? Why was he trying to goad me?

"I even got you to forsake your betrothed and tell me I was the one." He laughed. "Even now your tears betray you, *sweetheart.*"

I shoved him away and ran towards the door we had entered the garden through. I yanked on the handle, but it was locked, and Colt was right behind me. He spun me around, lowering his head and grasping my face again.

"There's no more running for you, Cheyenne."

I clenched my fingers and swung hard, hitting him on the cheek. He blinked and stepped back, rubbing it. The sting of it rippled through his eyes before he pushed it back and smirked.

"I never loved you, Cheyenne." The words dripped from his tongue, feeding the crimson-eyed beast within.

"Leave me alone!" I said between my teeth. I ran towards the far corner of the garden. Why was he being so mean and hurtful? Was he trying to get me angry? Did he know of the crimson-eyed monster? Was Marcus having Colt act like this to draw it out? No! I wouldn't let the beast take control! I wouldn't give Marcus access to it!

"Aww, is that all you can do, *child?*" He drew the word out. "You meant nothing more to me than a simple fling, like all the rest. I had hoped you'd be a challenge, but you fell like all the rest—easily and willingly. *Pathetically...*"

He towered over me again, snaring me in the corner like a frightened rabbit. I backed up against the wall, searching for a way out. Where were Darrien and Jahlem? Weren't they supposed to be protecting me? Marcus had said that as a Consilador, Colt's powers would be diminished, but he was still three times my size and stronger than an ox with or without his powers.

I lunged to the right and he met me, blocking my exit. I jumped to the left and again he stopped me. He was toying with me! Anger bubbled up inside, and the crimson-eyed beast clawed its way free. I ran towards him, shoving my shoulder into his chest, using all my weight. I then bent and swung my foot out, hitting his ankle hard. A move Skylar had taught me. He tilted, then tumbled to the dirt in shock. In one smooth movement I yanked the pitchfork from the wooden planter and lifted it over my head ready to plunge it into his chest.

"You dare call *me* pathetic?!" I hissed, my eyes flaring. "When you betrayed your own flesh and blood? When you turned your back on us...on *me*?" My hands shook. "You're nothing but a weak coward, Colt O'Shea, and I'll never let you rip my heart apart again!"

My arms braced, ready to thrust the pitchfork down, when I caught Colt's eyes. The cold glare had vanished, replaced with...remorse?

Tears streamed down my cheeks, my heart pounded and pulse raced. What was I doing?

He didn't break his gaze from me, nor raise a hand to defend himself. Shaking, I dropped the pitchfork and ran towards the side gate that was locked. I leapt up the stone wall, my feet making contact on a small ledge, and thrust myself up, grasping the top of the gate in the process, and swung myself over. I tumbled to the ground on the other side and quickly scrabbled to my feet. I ran down the narrow pathway between the manor and wall and heard heavy feet hitting the path behind me. I didn't stop once I reached the edge of the manor; instead, I flew down the same gravel path Marcus had brought me up, searching for a hiding place.

My feet left the ground, and I screeched as an arm snaked around my waist. I was pulled into a large chest and lost my breath. Another arm came around me. I lost the will to fight and slumped forward. I shook with raw emotions and sucked in a ragged breath.

"Don't run," Marcus whispered near my ear. His head pressed against my neck. "Shh, calm down, my angel."

How was I supposed to calm down when I'd almost killed Colt? How was I supposed to calm down when Marcus was holding me like a trapped animal? When all everyone wanted was to set this monster free!

Ever so slowly, his arms loosened, and he turned me towards him. He stroked my damp hair and rested his head on mine while he held me close.

"You can come with me," he said softly. "If you want someplace quiet where no one else can bother you, I'll take you there."

I nodded, knowing I really didn't have a choice. He'd probably sent Colt to torment me...to get me to this emotional state. I just wanted to be alone.

We walked, side by side, entering the manor and passing the stairs. He took me down a long stone corridor that wasn't as dark and dreary as the others. We stopped before double wooden doors and he pulled out a key. Unlocking it, he opened it and escorted me into a library.

The smell of leather and old papers hit my nostrils. Mahogany shelves lined the ten-foot-tall walls. Ladders on rollers allowed access to each section. Smaller, lower shelves were stocked with easily accessible materials, and comfortable seating areas with leather chairs sat in groups. A lone dark cherry table was placed nearby. Pens, paper and other writing supplies were lined up ready to be used.

"There's just about every book imaginable here, Cheyenne. There's even a card file to tell you where the books are." He pointed to a wooden box just behind the desk.

He gestured me towards to a leather chair to sit. I complied and looked out the large picturesque window. A small valley sat in the distance just outside of the wall. A small stream ran through it, and deer lingered nearby, drinking. Marcus handed me a book and sat across from me, a book of his own resting in his lap.

"You can read or stare out the window. The choice is yours, but I'd like to stay here with you if you'll allow it."

I knew I really didn't have a choice. I lay the book in my lap and stared out the window, thinking about what just took place.

Colt had purposely sought me out to torment me, to goad me, but it felt forced. I'd seen something in his eyes before he spoke. I saw the remorse after his hurtful words, but when I thought to comfort him, he turned on me. What frightened me the most was the way I reacted. As I held the pitchfork over him, the crimson-eyes beast was ready to kill him...what if I'd had my powers? What if I'd just reacted and threw him into the wall or over it. What if I'd picked up the pitchfork with my powers and plunged it into his heart?

A cold chill ran over me at the thought of harming someone I once loved. What was I becoming? Would I turn into the monster that sat across from me? Would I kill because those I loved had been killed? Would the vicious circle ever end?

I didn't need to look up to know gray eyes were watching me. He was studying me, watching my every move, trying to figure me out. He'd been fairly kind to me; unlike the last time we were together. He was trying to show me Matt again, the one who befriended me, and the one who deceived me.

Everyday was becoming a battle as Marcus tried something new to get me to open up. They were simple things really, taking me on walks around the compound, reading with me in the library and sitting in my private garden. He hadn't been harsh, had only spoken kind words.

I forced myself inward, following a routine of sorts, fighting back my emotions for everyone...Callon, Colt and Marcus. I'd been able to avoid Colt with Darrien and Jahlem's help, but I knew my time was running short with him. He was waiting for his next opportunity to corner me, and this time I didn't know if I'd be able to stop the crimson-eyed beast.

I hadn't seen or heard from Callon since my arrival, nor had Maes spoken to me in my thoughts. My hopes of ever leaving this compound were dwindling. Not to mention resisting Marcus was draining. I was a zombie, merely going through the motions to keep myself alive, but for what purpose?

I paced across the opulent rug in my bedroom. The sun's rays were just now rising over the stone wall, my cage. I was antsy today. It was my birthday, my twenty-first birthday to be exact. I should have been celebrating with Callon and my family. I should have been happy and content, but instead I was trapped in this dark and dreary manor, and the walls were closing in around me. I knew my time was running short, but I had no plan, no means of escape, and I didn't see any in the near future.

I pressed my shaking hand to my forehead. Why did my life have to turn out this way? Why couldn't I have been born to anyone else but Sahara and Qaysean? Why was destiny so cruelly taking out her punishment on me? Everything that I'd ever loved had been stolen, crushed into the cold hard ground without regards to my feelings and needs. And now I was being pushed into a position that never should have existed. Why hadn't my mother followed through on her betrothal? And why was I being forced into it?

I headed for my bedroom door, regardless of the fact that Jahlem and Darrien hadn't arrived. It was too early yet. They didn't expect me to rise for a few more hours, but I needed out of these four stone walls barricading me inside.

The door creaked open, and I peered around the corner. Nothing but shadows lurked there, and I quietly stepped out. I hesitated for a moment, not sure which direction to head...the garden or the library. I sighed, neither would do today. I needed a change of scenery.

I turned towards the front of the manor. With luck, I could possibly sneak out the entry and down the gravel path to the stables. I knew it would be dangerous. Marcus had warned me, and I'd avoided them, but seeing the horses and petting them would remind me of Mandi...and I needed a happy memory today. I had received her on my birthday after all, a special gift that I'd never stop loving. The only one who'd always loved me for just being me.

Footsteps sounded behind me, and I twirled around. A dark shadow was nearing quickly, a shadow I didn't recognize. I pressed up against the wall, as he walked with purpose. I was unsure if he was a threat or not. I should have waited for Darrien and Jahlem...

He glanced back behind him, as if he were checking to see if he were being followed. The hall may have been dark, but I saw intent in his mismatched blue and brown eyes. The closer he came, the larger his frame grew. I swallowed. Black hair fell over his shoulders as he looked down, checking for something in his pocket. His head whipped back up, and he snarled at me as he rounded the corner. Apparently I wasn't on his list. I inhaled. I'd stopped breathing again.

I peeked around the corner, following his movements. Colt was just leaving his room and suddenly stopped when he saw the other man. I recoiled back around the corner, then listened to the voices.

"Get out of my sight, Michael," Colt growled. "Marcus may have you here for a reason, but the first chance I get, I'll kill you."

"Such mighty words from a man who's betrayed his own family," Michael snipped.

"I may have betrayed them, but I haven't murdered in cold blood."

Michael snorted. "Your father was a weakling, just as you and your brothers are. He didn't deserve to be in the position he was in."

"You were his closest friend and ally..." Colt accused him.

"And you weren't the same for your brothers?" Michael said calmly.

The sound of a body hitting a wall caused me to jump.

"Stay clear," Colt growled through his teeth.

It grew silent. I peeked around the corner again and lost my

340

breath. Colt saw me.

His chest heaved, and his blue eyes fixated on me. My pulsed sounded in my ears, and my heart raced. I turned and ran back down the hall, his heavy footsteps following close behind me.

I hadn't even made it halfway down the hall when he was over me. He pushed me against the wall, his arms slamming into the plaster, creating a cage. He pressed in closer and lowered his head. I turned away as his hot breath brushed my cheek.

He remained still for a few moments, as if he were contemplating his next move, then moved in closer, his mouth dangerously close to my lips. He closed his eyes as if he were going to kiss me, and the muscles in his neck flexed. It was as if he were fighting against his own will to give in, a will that had been controlled by Marcus.

"Colt," I whispered and lifted my hand to his arm. He suddenly tensed and drew back, his jaw firming into solid granite.

"Where do you think you're going, *child?*"

I clenched my teeth. I hated it when he called me that. I didn't reply.

He pressed closer, trying to intimidate me. I pushed my hands to his chest, maintaining the distance. Why was it every time I reached out to him he'd switch modes? Like he was afraid to show his emotions...or he was being watched.

"Were you expecting Callon to swoop in and rescue you today of all days?" His voice was low and dangerous. "On your birthday?"

I inhaled a shaky breath. He was goading me on purpose again. Trying to get me angry, but why?

"You meant nothing to him, Cheyenne. You were merely a means to an end, just as you are with Marcus. Callon never loved you. It's always been Nakari."

"Stop," I pleaded, my voice shook. "You're lying." His words rolled over in my mind.

"I'm telling you the truth, and the truth hurts."

"No." I lowered my head further, fighting the crimson-eyed beast that wanted to protect me.

"You don't know what love is. You've never been loved." He pulled my chin up, forcing me to look at him, into his cold, cruel, hatred-filled eyes.

He'd switched emotions faster than I could imagine. I couldn't figure out which personality was really him.

"If your mother truly loved you, she'd have never put you in this position. If Gene and Alexis had loved you, they'd have taken you to Ireland when Callon told them to. If Callon had loved you, he wouldn't have used you as a weapon." His gaze hardened even more. "You're a worthless piece of nothing, and why Marcus thinks you're valuable is beyond me."

Something snapped inside, and I began clawing at his arms and face, kicking and punching, trying to free myself and run away. He quickly clamped my hands together and opened a door, shoving me in. I landed on my back, my breaths heavy as he towered over me.

"You need to learn to control your temper, *sweetheart*." His jaw firmed, but then his right eye began to twitch. He made to bend down, but it was like an invisible force pulled him back. He hurriedly turned and slammed the door shut. The sound of a click told me he'd locked me in.

I rushed to my feet and pounded on the door, cursing his name until my hands hurt, and I succumbed to the tears. I collapsed to the floor and pressed my legs to my chest. I wrapped my arms around them tightly and soon found myself rocking back and forth.

A numbness I'd never felt before began to fall over me. A hardening of my heart to any love I'd ever felt towards him. This wasn't my Colt—this was the monster Marcus had created. My Colt was forever gone. He was constantly fighting what few glimpses I might have seen, and they would eventually be pushed down. I'd known it, but denied it till now. He'd broken my heart for the last time, but I couldn't help but think he was hiding something.

I had no idea how long I sat curled in a ball, before I noticed sunlight breaking through a crack in what looked like curtains. I wiped my eyes and moved towards the small strip of light. Maybe it was a way out.

I pulled the material apart, revealing what at one time would have been a bedroom. Dust particles floated in the air, and I coughed as they drifted by. The broken frame of a bed was pushed in the far corner. A dresser was overturned, and the drawer's contents were spilled out across the dusty carpet. The remnants of a chair lay crumpled in a pile, and a nightstand with papers spilling out was near what appeared to be a doorway.

I moved cautiously in the room, being careful not to disturb the contents. I studied the clothes lying near the dresser. They were women's attire, along with perfume bottles on top.

I stepped over them and moved towards the nightstand. Yellowed papers spilled from the drawer, papers that looked like they'd been ripped from a journal, as their edges were ragged. I gently pushed them around; I was sure it was a woman's handwriting. I picked up a few pieces, lifting them up into the light. There were dates at the top, and some had hearts and flowers or other doodles drawn on them. I skimmed over the words...

July 21

He was watching me again today. His gaze following me wherever I went in the room. My father says it's because he likes me, but I don't feel warmth from his stare. His eyes are cold and calculating, like he's plotting something below the surface, and it scares me. I don't like it when my father leaves me alone with him, he makes me feel uncomfortable.

September 8

Father says he's leaving for a while and that I'm to stay here. He's been fiddling with his spells again. He thinks I don't know, but it's affecting his mind. He says things, odd things that make no sense, and I'm becoming worried for his safety, for mine as well. I also heard him talking, planning...my future. He wants an alliance with them, but I don't think he realizes what he's getting into.

I grabbed more sheets from the floor, now more curious than ever about who the author was.

June 15

So much has changed, so much that I don't have words to express. Two years have nearly passed since my betrothal was announced, and I grow more frightened every day. My heart is heavy. The burden is great, but I don't know how to bring this plan into play without passing it down to my children, if I should ever have any. I'm not strong enough. My powers are too weak to bring this monster down, but I know one day, it will come to pass...it will be my children that end this misery that has ruled with an iron fist over the Timeless race.

I wish I could have borne this burden alone, but I know that I cannot. I know whom I must turn to, and I know the fate that will become my burden to bear. I know the anger that it will stir, and many will suffer beyond repair.

I am heavy hearted as I write this, knowing what I shall pass along. But they will be strong, and they will know what needs to be done when the time comes. They will see, like I did, that there is only one way to defeat...they will be stronger than I ever was.

I pressed my hand to my lips, catching an initial at the bottom. S. I knew who the remnants of this journal belonged to...Sahara.

The lock on the door clicked and I shoved the papers into my pocket.

"Cheyenne?" Darrien's brown head peeked around the corner.

I stood, brushing the dust from my legs.

Both he and Jahlem hurried to my side. They eyed the mess around me and then stared at me, before they helped me step over the debris. They didn't say a word, but they knew, just like me, whose room this had been.

They escorted me back to my room.

"Marcus wants you downstairs when you are dressed," Jahlem said cautiously. "We'll wait till you're ready."

I nodded and headed for the bathroom. I knew they'd seen the tearstains on my cheeks and the crumpled papers in my pocket. I opened the vanity drawer and shoved the journal pages inside. My mom had left me a message, whether she intended to or not, and I needed time to study it.

I washed my face and pulled my hair back. I stared at myself in the mirror for a few moments. Dark circles etched my eyes, and my cheeks looked sunken. I could have put some makeup on, but I just didn't care anymore. Grabbing a jacket from the closet door, I pulled it on and entered my bedroom.

Jahlem's caramel eyes softened as I neared.

"Happy Birthday, Cheyenne," he said.

Darrien reached out and squeezed my hand. "Happy Birthday."

"Thank you," I whispered. It'd been the kindest thing they'd done for me so far, because it came from their heart with no strings attached. I may not have had long conversations with them, but since my arrival they'd done everything they could to make me comfortable. They hadn't been cruel and calculating. They'd been kind and concerned about my safety. Willing to step in when needed. They were holding onto me by a thread, afraid it would snap and they'd lose me.

I held up my hand asking for a minute while I went to stand on the terrace. I stared out into the valley, searching for anything, any sign that I wasn't alone. I studied the outline of the trees far away, wanting, hoping to see a shadow.

Jahlem stepped beside me.

"They're out there, Cheyenne," he said softly. "They're trying."

I looked down at my hands. I knew Jahlem was trying to give me a speck of hope, but if he knew, Marcus knew, and if Marcus knew...he was preventing them from being seen or making contact. Marcus was working hard to drain away any and all hope I had of a rescue—ever.

I followed them to the sitting room, my dark mood deepening as the gloominess of it tugged at my sleeves. Marcus was standing near the windows, staring out at the lake. He turned and smiled while I remained near the fireplace, waiting to find out what he wanted now.

He closed the distance quickly and grasped my hands. I didn't flinch or pull away like I had in the past, and a pleased smile rose on his face. His gray eyes softened.

"I'd like to take you for a walk outside the compound this morning," he said.

I didn't reply immediately, unsure if he truly meant what he'd said. Since the moment I'd arrived here, the main gate had been closed, and guards roamed the stone walls watching for signs of my rescuers. I'd barely caught sight of Conall. It seemed Marcus had him busy protecting his compound. Why was he offering to take me outside the compound now, unless he was doing it to prove a point, but what was his point? Was it that he wanted to flaunt his powers in front of Callon or was it that he'd succeeded in killing off his opposition?

"If you'd rather not," he said, releasing his hold.

"I want to go," I replied.

His smile returned.

"Shall we?" He held out his hand for me to take.

I hesitated for just a moment, before extending my hand. He grasped it, and we left the manor promptly. A tall figure stood in the shadows near the lower terrace. I didn't need to see clearly to know it was Colt. Darrien and Jahlem closed the distance behind me, and we stopped at the main gates while they were opened for us.

My hands grew sweaty as we exited the medieval gates, and then my heart sank when I saw the pack of Tresez waiting. Gold-rimmed eyes met mine and then looked towards Marcus. A moment later, we were surrounded. This was what it was all about. It was a show of power for Callon. Marcus wanted Callon to see that no matter what he tried, Marcus's army always surrounded me. He wanted Callon to know that he was always in control.

We walked in silence down the narrow path, with only the pad of the Tresezes' paws hitting the ground. Even the birds had grown silent. I pulled my hand free and touched the tall grasses and wildflowers, causing the scent to rise in the air. I inhaled, thinking of all the times my mom picked them and had the scent floating through the house. How she always loved flowers, particularly poppies.

I stared out at the large valley below his compound, hoping for a sign...any sign that Callon was here. Grasses swayed in the breeze, and a lone deer tracked through the opening before the forest. I picked a dandelion and blew the white wispy seeds in the air, scattering them. A few drifted out towards the vast valley and then trickled to the ground as the iridescent glitter from the enchantment prevented them from passing through. Marcus had pushed the enchantment out further than just the stone walls. He'd created a pathway of sorts to the mountain lake.

We stopped before the lake. The sun danced off the surface, and the mountains' reflection was perfectly etched on the smooth shell. The rugged mountains shot straight up from the base of the water, and the dense forest ran to the rocky shore before pouring out at the edge of the valley.

Steam poured from my mouth with each breath I took. It was cool, but not cold. Soon the sun would rise further and warm the field and rocks. Soon the birds would emerge and chirp their merry songs. Soon, I'd be forced to make a choice, although I'd have rather drowned myself in the cold glacier lake before betraying those I loved.

I closed my eyes and tried to think of happier days. Days that I'd spend with Callon and Daniel, days I laughed and smiled. Days where I felt love.

A silky caress ran across my neck. From under my lashes I watched as Marcus placed a single red poppy below my nose. I inhaled, the sweet scent tickling my senses. He pulled it away and broke the stem off. Stepping closer, he brushed my hair behind my ear and put the flower in my hair. He leaned in and placed a kiss on my cheek.

"Happy Birthday, Cheyenne."

CHAPTER 26

I sat in the sunshine, in the middle of my private garden. My fingers traced the handwritten words over the yellowed paper. They were my mother's words, her journaling, pouring out her soul, and I'd found them. She'd seen the progression, the long slow journey into madness her father made, before she had come to the conclusion that there was no other way out.

But what puzzled me the most was that she knew she'd leave this burden to her children...to me. Why did she say she wasn't strong enough? What did she mean by those words? Her last sentences kept running through my mind.

"They will be strong, and they will know what needs to be done when the time comes. They will see, like I did, that there is only one way to defeat...they will be stronger than I ever was."

What would I see? I just wanted to know, wanted it spelled out so I'd make no mistake...the one way to defeat him. It had been a week, and I still wasn't any closer to deciphering her hidden message.

"Cheyenne?"

I jumped and quickly crumpled the thick papers in my lap. I hadn't heard Colt approach. I glanced over my shoulder. He stood behind me. My jaw tensed, and I curled my legs into my chest. I could run, but he'd catch me and torment me even more. I was tired of running and hiding from him. It was time for him to see he had no effect on me any longer.

He sat beside me, but I refused to make eye contact. If I saw his hatred or his mixed emotions one more time...

"You should hate me," his voice was low and full of emotions. "I deserve every ounce of bitterness you feel in your heart towards me."

Oh no, he wasn't going to try and play me for the fool again. I stood and walked towards the gate, knowing it was locked. He followed.

"I don't blame you for turning your back on me, for running away. But you have to know, everything I've done, it was for you."

"So the hatred, the condemning, vile spewing words, were all for me?" I said through clenched teeth. "You're too kind, Colt. How can I ever thank you?"

I stopped in front of the gate, focusing my attention on the corner, trying to block him out.

"That day, the day you thought I died...I did. Marcus may have brought me back to life, but I died on the inside, knowing what I'd have to put you through."

"It would have been better if he'd never brought you back!" I hissed.

He stilled. "I deserve that," he murmured. "What I've done, what I've said, I'm sorry."

I lowered my head, staring at the black rusty hinges. They were old, just like this conversation was getting old. I was tired of having my heart ripped to shreds and then glued back together. The old Cheyenne was gone. I tried to slip past him when I saw what he was holding in his hands. My throat tightened and I pressed back up against the gate. Why did he have the other half of his bracelet?

His fingers uncurled, revealing a crumpled piece of paper. Carefully he smoothed it out. It was my note...the note I'd left him at the cabin.

You're my one and only true light, Colt. You're my sunshine, my hope and my love. A part of me died with you upon that hillside, and I shall never be whole again.

You stole my heart from the very first moment, and it'll always be yours to have.

I love you, Colt O'Shea. I choose you. I wish with all my heart that you'd come back to me.

~C

"I've never been without this, Cheyenne. I've kept it on me from the moment I found it," he whispered.

Words played in my mind, the words he'd spoken when he'd given me the bracelets.

If they were together, it would always light my way—if we were together, he'd always light my way.

He made to slide the bracelet on my wrist, but I pushed him away.

"No," I muttered. "You don't get to ask for my forgiveness. You don't get any more second chances, Colt. I don't even know who you are any more."

"You know who I am, Cheyenne. I've just had to hide it from everyone, especially for your sake."

"What do you mean by that?"

He gave no reply.

I pushed past, but his fingers laced around my arm. His hold was gentle but firm. I looked up into remorse-filled eyes. "This is not how I wanted you to find me, not how I wanted to see you again. But I had to do something, something so I wouldn't have to see you suffer so much."

"Your words, Colt," I tried to explain the hurt he made me feel. "You can't ever take them back."

"I never meant a word I said."

I shook my head, my mind whirling around all that he'd just said. I had no idea what was true...was this another lie?

His fingers cupped my cheek, his thumb stroking it.

"I'm sorry."

I pushed him away, and he released me. I stood still for a moment staring at him, searching for the truth.

"I almost killed you," I whispered. "And you wouldn't have stopped me."

I turned and hurried toward the metal entry door. Jahlem stood beside it. He didn't bother to hide his concern as he opened it and pulled me inside. He stopped me from running up the stairs and drew me into a hug. I wanted to run away screaming, but instead I allowed his comfort.

Why was Colt telling me this? Why was he playing with my heartstrings again? And why was I susceptible to it? I didn't know whether to be angry or overjoyed at the possibility the real Colt had returned. But my thoughts turned dark. He'd tried to harm me. He helped bring me here...who was the man in the garden?

Jahlem didn't say a word as he held me. Eventually I drew back. I followed him up the dark, winding, narrow staircase and went straight to my room. Darrien opened my door, but not before he and Jahlem exchanged glances.

I headed for my terrace and then halted as I saw Colt standing in the garden, staring up at me. Darrien pulled me inside and closed the terrace doors. He then pointed towards my sitting area, and I took a seat in the black velvet chair. I curled my legs under me and stared at the gray marble flooring. When was this nightmare ever going to end? My thoughts were becoming so jumbled.

I had no idea how much time had passed while I sat there thinking about what just transpired when Darrien slipped what looked like crumpled journal papers on the arm of the chair.

I looked up.

His hazel eyes softened. "I found them recently and thought they might be helpful for you." He hesitated. "I know you've been carrying the others with you since you found them."

I should have been upset that I'd been so careless with the other papers, but Jahlem and Darrien were here for me, no one else. If they hadn't seen them, they might not have known what they meant to me.

"Thank you."

I shuffled the few pages, glancing over them when Jahlem cleared his throat.

"We'll leave you alone, Cheyenne," he said, "but we won't leave you vulnerable. We'll be just outside the door. All you need do is call our names, and we'll come."

I nodded and watched them leave my room. I headed towards the bed and spread the papers out, focusing my attention on the dates to get them in some sort of order.

The papers weren't as yellowed as the first ones I'd found, but it appeared they'd been ripped from a journal as well. Some of the writing was crisp and clean, while others seemed to be scribbled, wearily written.

October 22

It's been a long time since I've last made an entry. So much has transpired, both good and bad. It's been a long journey to get where I am today. A long, lonely, tiresome and heartbreaking journey that has taken years.

I've not written my thoughts for the fear of exposing myself, my

351

heart and all the sorrows I've had to endure. All the failures I've made and the failures yet to come. But if I don't come to terms with them, then I'll never be able to move on, and I must move on.

My father is gone. He was murdered at the hands of Makhi and Marcus in revenge for my departure. But I know in my heart, he was long gone before Makhi and Marcus ever finalized it with death.

My father dabbled with the magic too much. He was too eager to please Makhi, to find his favor, and he succumbed to the powers within the rings. I'd begged him to stop, begged him to come with me, but it was too late.

I blamed myself for his death, but in the end it was never in my hands to control. He made the choice and lost himself in the process.

February 14

Again it has been too long since I've poured out my heart. But today is different, because I have hope, which has been nonexistent for such a long time I thought I'd never feel it again.

I've met him. The man I've been searching for, for so long.

He rejected me at first. Knew my power of persuasion and thought I'd use it on him. It's taken months, many long months to finally win over his trust and the trust of other clan members. But where I had thought I might fail again, a surprising twist occurred. Along with his trust, he's given me his heart as well.

June 21

Today's the day and I've never felt like this before, happiness, fulfillment...love. It's like my heart might explode and crumple to the floor in pieces if anything were to happen to him. The alliance that we're creating is so much more than I thought it could ever be...because in return I gained the one thing I never thought I'd have, true love.

December 25

Again it's been too long, too many long years of fighting and I'm exhausted.

We're alone, in hiding, as we have been for the last seven months. We're hiding because of you. Our hearts are already breaking at what we know we have to do—what your future will be. And the risk I'm taking writing down these words for you to see.

You need to live. You need to live and fight for us, for the Timeless race.

I was never strong enough to do what needed to be done, but you, my child, you will have your father's powers. You will be stronger than those before you. You will understand what needs to be done when the time comes.

It's your strength, your love and your determination in the end that will defeat him. You will be hurt. You will be judged by those around you. You will face obstacles that break my heart, knowing the burden you will bear alone. It's only you—it's only your powers—that will bring down what magic has raised.

Keep your allies close, and your enemies closer.

This is your destiny, my child, your destiny alone.

Tears poured down my cheeks. I'd been with them while she wrote this. It would have been my first and last Christmas with them. Their first and last words to me—ever. I pressed the papers to my chest, desperately trying to draw strength from her words, but they only brought me sorrow.

It was *my* strength, *my* love and determination that would defeat Marcus. But how? I knew there'd be obstacles; I'd tripped over every single one of them. The burden I bore weighed heavily on my shoulders regardless of the fact that I'd tried to share it with Callon...*my powers*.

I dropped the papers to the bed again and scrambled to find the last entry.

This was my destiny, my destiny alone. The words jumped from the page.

I couldn't share this burden with Callon by marrying him. I couldn't share it with Colt either. It was by my powers...by keeping my enemy closer.

My hand flew to my mouth, and I couldn't catch my breath. I knew what she was asking, what she wanted me to do!

"No!" I hissed. "No!"

I leapt from the bed, the papers flew to the floor, and I dashed for the bedroom door, swinging it open.

"Cheyenne?" Darrien tensed and tried to grab me as I ran down the hall. "Cheyenne!"

Thundering footsteps followed behind me as I leapt down the stairs, taking two at a time. Marcus ran out of the sitting room and tried to stop me but I slipped through his arms and dashed out the entry doors onto the terrace. I stopped for a moment, my chest heaving. I looked back. Marcus was nearing, his arms stretched out to show he wouldn't hurt me.

Darrien and Jahlem were panicked as they slowly made an approach.

I sprinted off the terrace, knowing they were directly behind me. My feet slipped on the gravel as I tore down the path. The front gate was open, and I bolted past the Trackers and Tresezes, but they didn't try and stop me. I found the narrow path leading to the lake and followed it. I slowed as I came to the water's edge.

I fell to my knees and stared out across the water. The calm and seemingly serine landscape angered me. How could this lake remain tranquil when I was faced with such turmoil?

My mother had just told me why she had me...to destroy the one who destroyed her. She wasn't strong enough, but I would be. I'd bear her burden, the entire Timeless race's burden...I had to keep my enemy closer—I had to marry Marcus.

It was the only way. I had to form an alliance, an alliance that no one would understand. They'd judge me, say I betrayed them—and I'd lose them in the end. Anything I'd ever fought for would be destroyed, burned, and I'd be the one holding the matches. They'd never be able to look at me again with love and understanding. I'd be hated as much as Marcus was—I'd become like Marcus—I'd take his place once I'd destroyed him. It was just another vicious circle...

"Cheyenne?" Marcus said softly. He moved beside me and kneeled. "You're upset?"

I sat on my legs and turned to him. I didn't bother to hide the tears or sorrow.

"What's wrong?" He wiped a falling tear away. "Tell me what makes you so sad."

I opened my mouth to speak, but closed it. What could I say to him? He sat beside me, genuinely concerned about my well-being. How could I tell him that by marrying me, it would destroy him in the end? That his marrying me would destroy me in the end too.

He carefully drew me into a hug, but I didn't fight it. This would be one of the few tender moments he'd ever get from me before I ruined his life. He rubbed my back gently and cradled my head in his hand. I didn't have the strength to tell him I'd marry willingly—I didn't want to have the strength.

A commotion sounded behind us, and Marcus's hold tightened.

He helped me to my feet. When I looked up, Daniel was only a few feet away. My breath caught, and I rushed to his side, only to have Marcus hold onto my wrist, preventing me from reaching him.

I raised my hand as the iridescent lights flickered, and Daniel raised his to match mine. It was my hope, but it had come to late. His deep blue eyes held such sadness. I felt the electricity tingle my skin as I pressed my palm forward and the pained looked on his face as he did the same. The enchantment wouldn't allow us to touch, but just knowing he was reaching out like I was made me feel loved. The last love I'd probably ever feel again.

"I'm sorry," I mouthed. "I've failed you."

I closed my eyes, not wanting to see his despair. It was bad enough what I was feeling inside. Marcus drew me back, and we walked towards the gate. This would be the last time I'd ever see Daniel again, and I wanted to remember him and the love he so freely gave.

I remained secluded in my room, trying to find another solution other than marrying Marcus, but there was none. I pored over my mom's writings, and every time I read it, I came to the same conclusion. It was the only way.

A guitar sat in the corner near the terrace doors. I knew Colt had brought it in while I slept. He was still trying to convince me that he was sorry for all he'd done, for what he'd put me through, but it was pointless. The only thing he'd done was send me further into despair. He'd been the one to lock me in the room where I found my mother's papers...he'd been the one to seal my fate.

The last of the evening's light began to fade from sight, and I picked up the guitar and walked onto my terrace. I sat, my fingers hovering over the strings, willing myself to let go. I closed my eyes as I began to strum, releasing all the pent-up emotions that had been swirling in my head. All the anger and regret that washed over me threatened to drown me in sorrows. All the words of betrayal I knew were to come...all the love I was about to lose for the sake of saving them.

Faces floated in my mind: Callon's last panicked expression, the hurt and pain of failure. Daniel's lost blue eyes, unsure what was to become of us...and Colt's seeming betrayal of my heart. I'd never see them again, never know their touch or words of love. They soon would only be a memory, fading into the mist.

I wrapped the notes around me, tightening their hold and keeping what remnants remained inside me. Salvaging what I could before it all changed again—for the worse.

I played long and hard. I played until my fingers ached and I had nothing more inside me to give. Until every last ounce of me had poured itself out and exposed me for who I was...a weapon to destroy another.

I stilled and rested the guitar across my lap. The moon was now shedding its light across the garden, and I looked up, surprised at what I saw.

My small garden and the stone walls in front of me were filled with Trackers and Tresezes. They'd been drawn here by my music, entranced as they stared up at me. The entire time I'd been here, they'd kept to themselves, avoided me. I was sure Marcus had threatened them, but now they had seen for themselves. It was just like when I played around the fire in Marcus's camp. They were spellbound.

Blond hair moved in the crowd. Colt inched his way to the front, but his face was hidden in the shadows. I rose and entered my bedroom, setting the guitar back where I'd found it.

I lurked in the shadows, watching the crowd dissipate from my garden. I wanted to walk around in it. I wanted to lie in the grass and stare up at the moonlit sky. I wanted to be alone.

Darrien and Jahlem met me outside my door and followed me to the locked metal door. Darrien opened it, and I followed them down the passage stairs and out into the garden. I stopped them before they followed.

"I want to be alone tonight," I said putting up my hand.

They nodded and stayed behind. I knew they wouldn't be far, but I wanted to be as alone as I could before I would come to grips with telling Marcus I'd marry him.

My shoes crunched over the gravel path, and I stopped to pick a lone pink daisy before lying down on the grass. I twirled the stem in my fingers as I stared up at the starlit sky. The scent of the freshly cut grass brought back memories of my mom and me. During the summer months we'd lie out on the freshly mowed field and stare up at the stars, counting, laughing and dreaming about what lie ahead for us. Neither of us would have ever dreamed this up, neither of us thought we'd be apart.

A shadow moved across the stone wall, and then the thud of feet landing on the grass neared. I knew who it was, knew he wouldn't leave me alone till he got his sorrow off his chest and begged for forgiveness.

I didn't acknowledge him at first. I kept my gaze elsewhere. Eventually he sat beside me.

He remained silent for a long time, staring out into the darkness. When he finally spoke, he couldn't keep the raw emotions from pouring out.

"I wanted to take the burden of fighting Marcus away from you, Cheyenne." He paused. "I didn't mean for it to be like this. I thought I could defeat him from the inside. Even if I had to hurt you in the process, it would be nothing compared to the pain he would put you through. So I tried to push you back, to keep your emotions away from me. To stop you from loving me again." He looked down at me. "But I made a mistake, and have paid the price." He sighed. "I don't deserve forgiveness. Yet no matter what you think of me, I love you, and I'll do whatever it takes for us to beat him. Together."

I sat up. The shadows hid his eyes from me, but I knew who was speaking to me...*my* Colt. Why now? Why did he decide to reveal this to me now rather than earlier when he could have swayed my decision? Why did he have to be so cruel and drive me to the point of breaking?

"Why? Why'd you act so mean and heartless? You didn't have to..." I trailed off, my mind wandering to the past encounters.

"I didn't have a choice once I made the decision."

"What do you mean you didn't have a choice? There's always a choice, Colt," I snapped.

He shook his head. "No, there was no choice when I decided I'd rather die protecting you than see you suffer more. I just didn't know the consequences to my decision."

I stared up at him, waiting for more.

"When Marcus brought me back, I could either fight him and die, or make him believe I'd conformed to his will. I made the decision to try and end this from the inside before he ever got to you again."

"But you played a part in my capture. You're the one who brought me here!" I hissed.

He sighed, his head sinking lower.

"It was never supposed to come to this."

"But it did," I said.

"And I'll regret it for the rest of my life."

We remained silent for a few moments before he spoke again. This time his head rose and his hand wrapped over mine, like he'd just made a sudden discovery.

"I know how we can get out of here."

"How?"

"The enchantment, Marcus expanded it over the lake." A sly smile rose. "It can't go under the water." He squeezed my hand tighter. "I can't believe I just now realized this..."

I pinched my brows tighter. "What do you mean?"

"The enchantment can go around, or even over water, but never through."

I still didn't understand and shook my head.

"We can leave through the water, by going under the enchantment."

I blinked. Our escape had been before us and I didn't even know it.

He jumped to his feet, taking me with him. Hope lit in his eyes, where I knew I had none.

"I'm going to make this up to you, Cheyenne." He leaned down and pressed a firm kiss to my lips before disappearing up and over the stone wall.

I paced the gray marble floor in front of the terrace in my bedroom. I hadn't seen or heard from Colt since he'd made his confession to me a week ago. Regardless, I knew I couldn't go with him. My fate had been sealed. I had no choice but to stand tall and accept destiny. It was just that my heart was breaking in the meantime.

A knock at the door drew my attention.

Darrien entered, holding a scrap of paper in his hands. He handed it to me.

I carefully unfolded it. It was a note from Colt. He wanted to see me in the garden. I looked up at Darrien.

"Did you read it?"

"Yes," he replied.

My heart began to race.

"Are you going to tell Marcus?"

"No. We're here for you, Cheyenne, no one else."

I pressed my eyes closed for a moment. For all of Colt's stupidity, thinking he could defeat Marcus, I couldn't have him die on me now. I headed for the garden.

Colt was waiting, hiding in the shadows of a tree. He immediately pulled me beside him, hiding us from sight.

His fingers began to stroke my cheek.

"We can leave right now, Cheyenne. I've got it all worked out."

I didn't reply, unsure how to tell him the decision I'd come to. His icy blue eyes searched mine in the dimming light. The sun was setting. He'd planned our escape, waiting for nightfall.

"What?" he questioned. "I know where Callon and the others are. We'll be able to escape before Marcus knows what's going on."

I shook my head and saw his eyes narrow.

"No," I whispered, knowing what I was admitting. "It's not your battle. It's not your burden. It was always mine—mine alone."

He pressed closer placing a kiss on my lips. My lower lip trembled. I had to push him away.

"It's not yours to bear alone," he protested. "Come with me. I can get us out of here right now." He pulled me closer, and I pushed back.

"No, Colt. I'm not going anywhere."

The moonlight hit his face, and I saw the confusion wash over him.

"You don't know what you're saying, Cheyenne. I can get you out of here. We can leave together..."

"And run again? Marcus won't stop, Colt, ever. You're fighting a losing battle. It's time I stepped up and did what my mother should have."

His fingers balled into fist at his side, then suddenly he reached out to grab me, but I stepped back.

"No," I repeated. "I won't leave Callon powerless. I won't leave the Consilador clan weakened. I will fix this mess." *I'll marry Marcus.*

"If you want to fix this mess, then you need to finish your vows to

Callon!" He lunged for me again, but I was faster.

"With what, Colt? Marcus has the Braid. It contains my powers and Callon's." I knew that if I married Marcus, Callon's powers would be restored, and I could give the clans the freedoms I'd never had. They'd have freedoms, and I'd forever live in a cage...but I couldn't tell him that now. He wouldn't understand, and he'd still try to drag me out of here. I had to stay.

"You don't know what you're saying!"

Gravel crunched, and Colt's glare hardened. We weren't alone anymore. He made one last attempt to snare me.

"Just go!" I barked.

Colt's face twisted. He backed away, as I felt Marcus step up behind me. They exchanged hard glares.

"I'm coming back for you, Cheyenne," he warned. "I promise!" He turned and ran towards the side gate, disappearing from sight.

I remained still, listening to Marcus's breathing behind me. He came forward, and his gray eyes caught mine in the moonlight. I was sure he'd heard the whole conversation. Yet he said nothing. He just stood there, silently taking me in.

My heart should have been racing. I should have been frightened at what he would do to me, but I wasn't. Fear had disappeared just as the rest of me had.

"You didn't go?" Marcus asked quietly.

"No, I didn't," I whispered. I didn't need to explain myself. We both knew why.

"I think this is the first time in my life I'm speechless, Cheyenne." He turned on his heels, facing a group of Trackers and Conall. "Find him and kill him." He waved the Trackers off, but Conall didn't leave. He only stepped back.

"You've made a wise choice," Marcus said.

More footsteps neared, but I didn't look over my shoulder. I knew who was there, who was always there with me, watching me every moment of every hour of every day...Jahlem and Darrien.

Marcus began circling me slowly, deliberately—like he were stalking his prey.

"You continue to surprise and amaze me."

"If I am to marry you, I have three things to ask of you," I asked boldly.

He waited, wearing a faint smirk.

There was no more anxiety, no more worry. I would ask and he would give. Simple.

He extended his hand and nodded wordlessly, giving me his attention.

"First, I ask that you let Colt live. I stayed, he left. The threat is gone. Along with letting Colt live, you leave my family alone. You have what you came for, and I want reconciliation. You'll live with me peacefully. No more hunting down Timeless, no more senseless deaths, no more war."

He ran his fingers over his stubbled chin and stared at the ground for a few moments. I straightened my back. He would give or he wouldn't receive.

"Secondly?" He tilted his head and eyed me carefully.

"Secondly," I continued, not sure where all the demands were suddenly coming from. It wasn't like I'd thought them out. "I won't live with you here in this dreary, life draining, gray stoned compound." I paused for a moment as hardness set into his stone cold eyes. "You'll provide a home for us in the French countryside. I want gardens, graveled paths, manicured lawns, trees, a lake, pond or stream. I want acres for me to wander, horses to ride and a stone wall surrounding it so I know where my boundaries are..." so I'd be reminded of the cage that I'd built for myself. The cage I'd have to endure to end this war.

"No home on this estate?"

"A home that is bright and cheery, a library and a music room."

He nodded thoughtfully.

"And the third?"

"To marry at the mountain lake just outside the compound."

He studied me for a few moments before he spoke.

"Then I have requests as well," he said.

My jaw tightened. I should have known he'd have his own agenda.

"First?" I asked and tilted my head.

"First," he said and began to circle me again. "You'll allow me to romance you. You'll willingly dine with me. You'll willingly spend time with me, and you'll give me the opportunity to show you who I am and what I am capable of."

I squared my shoulders, but didn't answer. How much worse could it be?

"Secondly," he continued. "You'll wear what I lay out for you."

I opened my mouth to protest, but he held up his hand.

"You are a beautiful woman, Cheyenne, and I want to see you as such. I've provided you with a closet full of striking outfits, and you won't wear them. You are to be my wife, and my wife will look the part."

My jaw clenched. It was a control thing and we both knew it.

"Third?" I said between my teeth.

"Third." A glint formed in his eyes. "I'll give you the third when I think you're ready for it."

I'd gotten cocky, and he took advantage of it. I made for my bedroom when he grabbed my arm.

"I'll take you to your room. We're having dinner tonight, and I want to see you in an evening gown." His crooked smile grew, and I lowered my head. I'd do what I had to do to keep my family safe. I'd bear this burden alone and always be the betrayer.

Conall's gold-rimmed eyes stared at me in curiosity. Apparently I'd surprised him too.

Marcus took me to my room and I changed into what he wanted for the evening. A silky black gown with a scooped neck and back. Darrien and Jahlem waited while I prepared both mentally and physically for Marcus's onslaught. I hadn't had a choice in the path I had to follow. I just had to survive.

They escorted me to a rear terrace, one I hadn't been to in the past, one I didn't know existed. A small bistro table was dressed with a bright white tablecloth and covered silver serving trays sat at each chair. Candlelight illuminated the terrace and soft music played in the background. The hidden terrace overlooked my garden...he'd watched me from here when I thought I was alone. How had I not seen this before?

A warm hand touched my back, and I startled. Marcus was beside me, dressed in a black tuxedo. Apparently he was taking this dinner seriously.

"I can watch you from here without you seeing me," he confirmed, speaking low in my ear.

"Why? I thought the garden was supposed to be my private space." I turned to face him.

His soft finger slid across my cheek and stopped at my neck. "Because I like watching you. You're completely different than anyone I've ever met. There's a complexity to you that I want to

362

understand. You shouldn't intrigue me, but you do."

I fought the urge to push him away. I was the one who agreed to this, and I'd have to deal with this after the wedding. My jaw firmed. If he could touch me, then I could touch him. I lifted my hand as he tilted his head in curiosity. I traced the scar on his forehead. I had a good idea where it'd come from.

"I did this to you?"

His gray gaze remained focused on me. "Yes."

"I was angry." He'd just electrocuted Colt.

"You were."

"Don't make me angry."

"I'll try not to," he said with a smirk.

He pointed towards the table. "Shall we?"

We dined in silence, but I felt his gaze upon me. Was this what it was going to be like for the rest of my life? There'd be no conversation, only plotting when I could do what I was born to do? In haste I'd made demands. I'd given him the idea that we could live together far away from everyone...and maybe I was right. I'd take this burden and not have to destroy him. He'd agreed to live in peace with me, or at least I thought he had.

"Will you dance with me?" He stood beside me. I hadn't even seen him move.

I took his hand and moved around the terrace with him, my mind still wandering, contemplating my next move.

His hand moved lower across my back, and he gently tugged me closer. I knew he felt my body quiver because a satisfied grin emerged.

"I think you're ready for my third request," he said. His warm breath passed over my cheek as he leaned in closer. "We'll marry tomorrow at sunset, at the lake like you requested."

I stiffened, and we paused in the dance.

I calculated the date.

"It's not the fall solstice." I looked at him blankly.

He shook his head and laughed. "You believed everything they told you, did you?" He leaned in and abruptly kissed me.

I gaped at him wide-eyed.

"What do you mean, Marcus?"

"They've been feeding you a pack of lies from the start, all of them. They didn't bother to tell you that I could marry you at anytime, or Callon for that matter."

"No," I pushed him back. "No, Dex said that we had to have the counterbalance of the sun and the moon on the solstice so I wouldn't kill Callon."

He shook his head again. "Callon would have been fine. He was strong enough to handle it. It was their mistake in being overly cautious."

"What about you then?" I spoke the words already knowing his answer.

"Because I've got more powers than all of them combined, I don't need anything to counterbalance me, or you for that matter. You could've been married six months ago, but Callon's predictable. I knew he'd plan the ceremony for the summer solstice."

I couldn't move. I could only stare in disbelief.

"That's why you want to marry tomorrow, to prove a point," I murmured.

He pulled me in closer, his voice dangerously low. "It's more than to prove a point, my angel. I've waited a long time for you, and I won't wait any longer."

His thumb brushed my lower lip and a shiver escaped me. I'd been avoiding him, and he hadn't pushed me, but now, everything was different. The gray in his eyes darkened to reveal the predator he was, his hunger clear, and I was the prey snared in his trap...with no means of escape.

His lids lowered, and I had nowhere to go as his mouth touched mine. It was soft, gentle, and not what I expected.

"I'll make you happy," he murmured over my lips. "Just give me a chance. That's all I ask. You promised to give me a chance."

His kiss suddenly deepened and caught me off guard. It took sheer willpower to not fight back. His hold tightened, crushing me to his chest, when his thumb pressed on my lower lip, forcing my mouth open.

He surged forward, pushing for a response out of me. He tilted my head back, reaching deeper. And a duel began as each breath I took, he stole from me. He suddenly drew back, and I gasped for air. In the next moment, my back was up against the cold stones, and he'd twisted my right hand in front of me as he locked our rings together.

Instantly my arm began to tingle. A power built beneath the surface that spread through my limbs so fast I could hardly breathe.

He wasn't gentle this time as he crushed his lips to mine again. He was using the rings to have power over me, to force me to submit like Callon had.

I began shaking, losing myself in the sensation reeling throughout my body. The power, raw and untamed, wanted to push me over the edge, and I couldn't fight his kiss anymore.

I gave back what he'd been seeking; I fought back with my mouth, dueling to regain control. He wasn't going to win this battle; he'd only brought my task back to the forefront. He'd wielded his powers over me for the last time.

His hold over my ring loosened, and his kiss slowed. He drew back, releasing my hand, leaving me breathless. A wicked smile gleamed in his eyes. He thought he'd won.

"Tomorrow, Cheyenne, tomorrow you're mine."

I sat on my bed, waiting for Darrien and Jahlem to come and take me to Marcus. In just under an hour, I was going to walk down the aisle, for the second time.

Marcus had laid out a dress, a surprisingly simple white silk gown that hugged my shape well. The neckline and plunge in the back were lower than I'd have liked, but I wasn't doing this for me. I was doing this for every single Timeless that existed, both now and in the future. I was doing it to ensure they lived.

My hand curled over the note from Colt one last time. Darrien had delivered it this morning. I was to expect Skylar at the lake. He was going to pull me to safety before the vows were said. I crumpled it and threw it in the trash. It didn't matter if Marcus found it. I'd be marrying him anyway.

A soft knock at the door drew my attention.

"Come in," I said.

The door opened, but where I expected to see Jahlem and Darrien, Marcus stood, wearing a black tux again. He eyed me carefully as he neared and motioned for me to turn around. With great care, he gently placed a necklace around my neck. I glanced down. It was my mother's necklace, the one he'd taken from me.

"It's only fitting," he said, "that you wear this, as it was destiny that brought you to me." He placed a soft kiss on my shoulder.

He looped his arm in mine, and we headed for what I knew would be the end of my life. There was no more hoping for a rescue, no more plotting our battle tactics...this was me showing my betrayal and marrying the man they'd all fought to keep me from.

There'd be no understanding, no mercy shown. Only hatred at what I'd done...with them never knowing the sacrifice made that could never be undone.

We stopped at the main gate, but though I'd thought Marcus would bring his Trackers and Tresezes, there were none. Only Darrien, Jahlem, Conall and another man was there...*Michael!* The man Colt had threatened, the one who'd betrayed his father.

Michael watched me closely as I stared back. His leathery skin was showing his age. He'd been around for a long time. His blue and brown mismatched eyes were probing, questioning my allegiance...and they should have been. We passed him, and I looked up one last time. There was nothing trustworthy about him. He'd betray just about anybody in a heartbeat. His cold calculating stare told me all I needed to know.

We stopped at the lake. The sun sat lower in the sky. It glistened off the water despite the ripples the breeze created. Michael moved in front of us. He carried the silver etched box, still glowing with my and Callon's powers, and a small leather journal. He motioned for Conall to hold the silver box as he tucked the journal beneath his arm.

Marcus turned me to face him and captured my wrist so the Braid could be wrapped around us. The blue hue remained as Michael wrapped the Braid around our wrists. My power pulsed in the leather, waiting for its return.

There was no delay, no chance for me to be fearful, no opportunity to contemplate what Colt's note said. I had to complete this. I had no other choice, and Marcus was watching too closely. I sighed and listened to Michael as he began the vows. There was no special message like Dex had given. It was short and to the point. Michael read them, and then Marcus repeated.

"I, Marcus Guerry, of the Sarac clan, pledge my love and my life to you. To forever be your partner in life and your one love. I will cherish each moment I have with you more each day than the day before. I will trust you and rule with you, I will laugh and cry with you. I will love you faithfully no matter the outcome, regardless of the trials we shall face. I give you my heart and my soul from this day forward as long as we both shall live and until in death we should break our bond."

Love...what did Marcus know of love? I'd say the words, but I knew in my heart I'd never mean them. I could never love the man who'd murdered so many I'd loved. And yet I felt sorry for him. He wouldn't know until it was too late that by marrying me it would be the end for him.

"Your vows, Cheyenne," Michael said.

I nodded. I looked down at the Braid, watching it glow even brighter than before. Marcus's powers had transferred. Now it was up to me to seal his fate.

"I, Cheyenne Alexis Wilson, of the Servak and Kvech clans, pledge my love and life to you. I will forever be your partner in life, your one love." I hesitated, guilt rising. "I will cherish each moment more each day than the day before. I will trust you and rule with you. I will laugh and cry with you. I will love you no matter the outcome, regardless of trials. I give you my heart..." My throat tightened as I said the final words, knowing I'd never give him my heart. "And my soul from this day forward as long as we both shall live and until in death we should break our bond."

It started with a tingling sensation. Marcus's hand clamped tighter on my wrist as mine clamped tighter on his. I began to shake, just as he did. His jaw firmed, and his eyes narrowed. My legs grew weak, and then suddenly it was like a bolt of lightning hit me. I jerked back, the Braid falling to the ground, and I screamed as my arms flayed out. A burst of light blinded me, and I fell to the rocky surface, the cold lake water splashing my cheek and saturating my hair and dress.

Marcus lay a few feet away. He blinked a few times; obviously he'd never been through something like this before. We lay there, staring at each other, stunned at the impact, the force of power wielded through the Braid. Was this what it would have been like for Callon and me? Was this why Dex had said we needed the solstice to counterbalance our powers? Fear struck me. If it had been Callon, it could have killed him.

More anguish rolled over me. I was in the water. Skylar was going to come and grab me! If I left now, Marcus would hunt me down again...we'd be back to the same place. Me running, him chasing.

Nausea rose in the pit of my stomach at the thought of what I'd have to endure staying here...but it would keep my family safe. I'd requested that we lived in France. I'd done it for a purpose, to keep Marcus as far away from my family as possible. I'd rather sacrifice myself, knowing they were safe. Chances were that when I fought Marcus, I'd die right along with him. They didn't need to see all their hard work end this way, and I didn't need the reminder of what I'd never have again—my family.

Marcus inched closer, waving Jahlem and Darrien off. Apparently it had knocked everyone to the ground. Michael was just now rising out of the water.

"You're going to be fine," Marcus said leaning down and kissing my forehead. "You'll be disoriented for a few days, but it'll clear up."

I nodded, the ache in my head already coming to life. I lay there perfectly still. I knew I wouldn't be able to move yet, regardless of the risk I was taking with Skylar. Marcus stood and bent to help me up when something latched onto my wrist. I yelped, but it was too late as I was yanked under the cold surface.

"No!" Marcus's bellow vibrated the water.

I struggled under the water to see what was taking place, but we were moving so fast I could barely open my eyes. It only took a moment for me to realize Skylar had a hold on me. His legs kicked furiously by my side. He'd come, just as planned!

My arm began to hurt, waves of pain rippling from my wrist to my shoulder. He'd jerked me hard to get me into the water, and now I was sure he'd dislocated my shoulder. My chest began to burn. I may have had my powers restored, but they weren't available for use. Just when I thought water would fill my lungs, we burst from the water, and I gasped for air.

Skylar quickly caught me, and I sucked in a deep breath. My chest heaved as he set me on the ground, and I blinked to take in my surroundings. We were in cave of sorts. Voices echoed in the small space and soon a crowd gathered around—my family. Stares of disbelief and pain stabbed at me.

What had they done?

CHAPTER 27

Colt pushed his way to the front and kneeled down, his eyes avoiding mine. He lifted me to my feet while Callon approached to help. I braced myself for what I knew was about to happen. With a quick jerk, Callon slammed my shoulder back into place.

I gasped, my knees growing weak, but I didn't even have time to catch my breath before I was swept away to a dark section of the cave. Layla and Nakari quickly took over, helping me change into dry clothes.

No one said a word till Maes's dark shadow loomed over me.

"We need to leave now!" he barked and then turned on his heels.

Koda's head appeared behind me. He was wearing his cloak...how had he gotten a new one? His jaw tensed as he opened the fabric and swallowed me up inside. I was completely covered when I felt him mount what I was sure was Midnight, his monstrous horse.

The pain in my arm was growing worse than the ache in my head. I was sure Koda wasn't trying to find every branch and stump to cross over, but the continual banging against his chest was about to push me over the edge. But this would be nothing compared to the berating I was sure was waiting for me when we'd stop.

His arms tensed as he tried to lift me higher in the saddle. He was trying to absorb the motion of the horse through his body, trying to help ease my pain, but it was too much to bear. I felt my eyes roll back without my consent and my head roll to the side.

Fingers were stroking my cheek, and the breeze was cooling my heated face. I opened my eyes to find more darkness, but it wasn't from being inside Koda's cloak...and Koda wouldn't be stroking my cheek like this. I stiffened.

"It's me, Cheyenne. It's Colt," he whispered.

My head began to swim through the fog of recent events. I'd married Marcus, and my family had stolen me away. The chain of events was already in play again. Marcus would be coming after me once his powers were restored...but I'd have powers restored as well too. Powers that could destroy Marcus as well as myself.

"Why did you come for me?" I whispered. They were supposed to have left me.

"Why did you do it?" he countered.

I pressed my eyes closed for a moment, knowing no matter what I said, he—they'd never understand.

"I had to."

"No, I gave you an out. You didn't have to do the one thing we've been trying to prevent all along."

"It was my destiny, Colt. It was my destiny all along."

His hold tightened.

"No, this was never your destiny!" he growled. "You've made a mistake..."

"Like your mistake, Colt?" I shot back. "Like you handing me over to Marcus himself? Like you hunting me down and hurting me like you did?"

He sighed heavily as he thought out his reply. "I can't change what I did, but I could have changed the outcome. I told you I'd come back for you."

"I could never change the outcome, Colt, regardless of how hard I fought. I found pieces of my mother's journal, even she knew what my role in this whole mess would be. She saw it and then I saw it, and as much as I tried to deny it, it was *my* destiny—always."

He gave no reply, but instead he rested his head on mine. I glanced around. It was clear that we'd broken away from our group. I was sure they were trying to deter any Trackers or Tresez, confuse them with tracks leading in different directions.

Dawn began to break through the dense forest trees. Streams of light flickered to the forest floor, and the fresh smell of pine hung heavy in the air. Steam rose from my lips, but I wasn't cold. The familiar ache remained behind my eyes, and I knew it would only be a matter of time before it grew worse. Losing my powers to the Braid had an effect on me, and I knew now that my powers were united with Marcus's...the impact would be bigger. I just had to hold on till I knew we were safe, although in the back of my mind I knew we'd never be safe till Marcus was gone.

My arms tingled. I knew what it was...Marcus's powers were now beginning to bind to me. I knew I'd still be powerless till they'd reach full capacity, but when they did, there'd be hell to pay.

Horses whinnied nearby and I straightened. Just ahead my family waited. Waiting, I was sure, to have me explain how I'd once again failed them all. We came to a stop and Colt dismounted, taking me with him.

A small fire had been built. Clayton, Skylar, Nakari, Bree, and Andre stood around it. The clanking of metal caught my attention. Nakari still had her bracelets on. She was still powerless. I caught her eyes, and the others followed me in a stunned silence. I knew, as much as I'd try to explain, they wouldn't understand.

Brogan and Maes were nearby, arms crossed, glares clear. I knew they hadn't forgiven Colt yet, but worse than that, I knew those glares laced with flaming arrows of dismay, anger and betrayal were aimed at me.

Daniel pushed his way forward and pulled me into a hug. I didn't feel the peace that he could usually produce for me, but I felt something ten times better—his love.

"I was so scared for you, Chey," he murmured still holding on. "I never thought I'd see you again. I thought we'd lost you forever."

And I thought I'd lost them forever too...and still might.

He drew back. Koda, Brogan, Maes and the others moving in closer. Callon stood back behind them, his eyes emotionless, but his stance rigid.

"Why?" Daniel said. "Why didn't you come with Colt?"

I looked away, unable to tell him while looking into his eyes. I didn't want to see his anger or disapproval—not from Daniel.

"I'm sorry," I whispered.

"Sorry?" Maes growled. "Sorry is all you have to say?!" He pushed closer till Koda held him back.

"We were waiting, Cheyenne!" Brogan snapped. "We were waiting for you, and you never came! Our whole purpose was to prevent you from marrying Marcus, and you did it willingly! How could you?" His hands flew in the air, and he turned his back to me.

"It was my destiny. I had to marry Marcus," I said quietly and waited for the explosion.

"Your destiny?!" Maes began swearing in French and pacing before me. "Where the hell did you get that idea?!"

"My mother's journals."

Maes stopped his pacing and abruptly stopped in front of me, too close for comfort. He pulled my chin up, jade-rimmed eyes bore into me.

"You found your mother's journals?" he asked.

"I found bits and pieces."

"So you based your decision off bits and pieces?" Brogan bellowed.

"Calm down!" Koda snapped. "We need to hear Cheyenne out first." He nodded to me.

I looked beyond him. Callon still said nothing.

"I had enough information to know why she fled. She knew she wasn't strong enough. She sought out my father with the intention of making an alliance and creating something strong enough to destroy Marcus—me."

My jaw firmed, as they remained silent. I knew I was confirming what I'd known all along.

"I was the weapon needed to defeat Marcus. She knew by uniting her powers with Qaysean that they then stood a chance...but there was a catch to it. I had to marry him."

"No." Andre shook her head. "You didn't have to marry him. Marrying Callon would have made you strong enough, you know that."

"No, Andre," I said sadly. "I had to marry Marcus. Only Marcus's powers are strong enough to defeat him...the powers that are now surging through my veins."

Brogan shook his head and turned away.

"You were supposed to leave me with him. I was removing the threat from you, but now—now you've changed it all. Now he's going to come after me, and he won't stop till all of you are dead." I clenched my fingers together tightly. "I was sacrificing one for the lives of many."

Callon shook his head, but still didn't speak.

"I believe in you, Chey," Daniel said. "I know you can still defeat him." Daniel reached out and grasped my hand. "I haven't lost faith in you. You were right about Colt being alive. You've been right about a lot of things. I'll fight with you."

"Daniel's right," Koda spoke up. "Cheyenne's been right in the past when we had reason to doubt her. We need to trust her regardless of our feelings."

"And what has she based all of her decisions on, Koda? Emotions, feelings!" Brogan sneered.

"And they've been right," Colt said, his shoulders squaring. He moved closer beside me, his hand coming to rest on my shoulder. "She knew I was alive, knew she couldn't give up till she found me. We can't give up on her now."

"And this coming from the man who willingly helped hand her over to Marcus?!" Brogan bellowed.

"I made a mistake, one that cost us dearly, but I'm here now, and I'm not deserting Cheyenne when she needs us the most. And neither should you."

Callon moved forward with purpose. His eyes were dark and hooded, his cheeks unshaven. His fingers curled together tightly forming a fist. He opened his mouth to speak, but then closed it. Daniel neared and placed his hand on his shoulder, but Callon brushed it off. His jaw tightened.

"I—I can't believe you, Cheyenne," Callon said between his teeth. "Colt tried to bring you out and you refused! We were ready to take you to safety. We were ready to risk it all...but instead you gave it all to Marcus!"

He stepped towards me, and I jerked back, running into Colt's chest. Daniel pulled him back.

My lower lip shook from his anger. I knew they'd never understand. I'd been warned they'd see me as the traitor...all they'd given me here was false hope.

"Not only did you betray my heart, Cheyenne, but you gave my powers to the one who would destroy us all."

"No..." I whispered. "That can't be. Marcus said you'd get them back!"

Callon turned his back on me.

He lied to you, Cheyenne, Maes said, He lied and you believed him.

I stared hopelessly at my family. No one would make eye contact. After all the running away they said I'd done...when I finally didn't run from my responsibility but met my destiny head-on—they scorned me!

All those words of me never being alone—I never felt more alone than I did now.

Callon gave one last glance before he walked away. I watched in stunned silence as he disappeared into the thick forest.

Callon was leaving me...he was abandoning me just like my mother had said.

His words hit me hard...

I betrayed his heart.

"Give him time," Colt said, stroking my shoulder. "I'm still not even sure what you're planning, Cheyenne, but I meant what I said. I'll stand by you no matter what."

"I will, too," Daniel chimed. "We're your family, and family don't give up on each other."

Andre sighed. She stepped past Brogan, a hand on her hips.

"I'll never understand you," she said. "But your aura tells me you didn't take this decision lightly." She took my hand. "Part of me wants to believe that you've done the right thing, but..." She shook her head. "I don't know."

My head lowered. Footsteps crunched, but I didn't need to look up to know it was Nakari. I didn't dare meet her gaze.

"I made you swear to me that you wouldn't break Callon's heart," she said, her voice cold. "Why, Cheyenne? He gave everything for you, and this is how you repay him?!"

I kept silent. No matter what I said, what excuses I gave, I knew she wouldn't listen.

"Maybe Marcus is what you deserve." She spun on her heel and stormed off, seeking Callon.

"I did it for you," I whispered. "I did it for everyone."

Colt drew me closer, as finally the tears started to fall. I'd known they'd react like this. My mother had warned me, but it didn't make it hurt any less. They'd given me everything; a loving family, a welcome home. I hadn't wanted to throw it away like this. But I couldn't run anymore. Destiny had finally captured me, and I'd have to endure her final heartache.

Alone.

TIMELESS CLANS GLOSSARY

Timeless – a form of immortality, aging one year for every one hundred years.

Kvech Clan

Adalmund – former leader of the Kvech clan – Cheyenne's grandfather - deceased.

Jasalyn – spouse to Adalmund – Cheyenne's grandmother - deceased.

Qaysean – former leader of the Kvech clan – Cheyenne's father – deceased.

Cheyenne Wilson – leader of the Kvech clan – betrothed to Callon and Marcus.

Consilador Clan

Callon O'Shea – leader of the Consilador clan – betrothed to Cheyenne.

Colt O'Shea – brother to Callon, second in line for clan leadership.

Daniel O'Shea – brother to Callon and Colt, third in line for clan leadership.

Bree – clan member.

Sarac Clan

Makhi Guerry– father of Marcus – deceased.

Marcus Guerry – leader of the Sarac clan – betrothed to Cheyenne.

Servak Clan

Jorell – former leader of the Servak clan – Cheyenne's grandfather – deceased.

Sahara – daughter of Jorell – Cheyenne's mother – deceased.

Cheyenne Wilson– leader of the Servak clan – betrothed to Callon and Marcus.

Darrien – guardian of the Servak clan leader. Skilled warrior, twin brother of Jahlem.

Jahlem – guardian of the Servak clan leader. Skilled warrior, twin brother of Darrien.

Raina – Former clan member, loyal to Marcus and now a Cloaker.

Coltooro Clan

Dex – leader of the Coltooro clan.

Lilly – spouse to Dex.

Gene Wilson – clan member, Cheyenne's adoptive father – deceased.

Alexis Wilson – clan member, Cheyenne's adoptive mother – deceased.

Silloquize Clan

Koda – leader of the Silloquize clan.

Nakari – member of the Silloquize clan.

Clayton – member of the Silloquize clan.

Skylar – member of the Silloquize clan.

Andre – member of the Silloquize clan.

Laundess Clan

Brogan- leader of the Laundess clan.

Layla – spouse of Brogan.

Tre & Jayna – clan members, twins.

Quinn – clan member.

Quaysaar – the forgotten/forbidden clan

Maes – leader of the Quaysaar clan, a Tresez.

Conall – A Tresez, and loyal follower of Marcus.

TIMELESS SERIES NOVELS
DATA SHEET

See what lies ahead for Cheyenne in Awakening, the final installment. Coming Spring 2014.

For more information on the Timeless Series Novels visit:
http://www.lisawiedmeier.com/ or timelessseriesnovels.com /
www.facebook.com/TimelessSeriesNovels /
http://lisawiedmeier.blogspot.com/

A Timeless Series Novel – Available on Amazon

#1 Cheyenne – July 15, 2011
#2 Promises – May 25, 2012
#3 Daylight – May 20, 2013
#4 Awakening – Spring 2014
*Fated – A Novella – December 2012, Part I
**Fated – A Novella – Fall 2013, Part II
***Fated – A Novella – Spring 2014, Part III
****Fated – A Novella – Fall 2014, Part IV

* Part I of this novella is intended to be read after reading Cheyenne, A Timeless Series Novel, as it is a companion to the story from Callon, Colt and Daniel's point of view. **Part II can be read after Promises, as it will contain point of views from characters in the story. ***Part III can be read after Daylight, as it will contain point of views from characters in the story. ****Part IV can be read after Awakening, as it will contain point of views from characters in the story.

**Cheyenne's story will end with Awakening,
but the Timeless Story will continue on with:**

#5 Deceptions - under editing
#6 Revelations - under editing
#7 Resolutions - under editing

Side stories:

#8 Bailee - under editing
#9 Sahara – draft

22120405R00227

Made in the USA
Charleston, SC
11 September 2013